INNOCENCE AND SEDUCTION

Amaryllis had the delicately disheveled look of a woman who had just been thoroughly kissed. Moreover, a delightful blush now stained her cheeks . . . delightful, because he'd never seen a similar show of modesty in any woman offering herself in such a fashion.

"Let me get this straight," he demanded. "Are you saying that *you* had plans to seduce *me?*"

"I had contemplated the notion, yes," came her tart reply, though her blush deepened.

He managed a laugh that ended on a groan. "Then since it seems we both had much the same idea, let's make a pact. You seduce me, and I'll seduce you. Is that an agreement, Miss Godwin?"

"It is, Lord Blackstock."

At her words, he waited no longer but gathered her in his arms and kissed her. This time the very taste of her lips sent a shudder of pure need through him. Almost without thinking, he grasped her by the waist and lifted her onto the edge of the table beside him.

"W-what are you doing?" she asked.

"Why, seducing you, of course." His hand roamed up her thigh. "Unless you've changed your mind about what we're about to do—"

A gasp was her only reply.

ROSES AT MIDNIGHT

Alexa Smart

Pinnacle Books
Kensington Publishing Corp.

http://www.pinnaclebooks.com

PINNACLE BOOKS are published by

Kensington Publishing Corp.
850 Third Avenue
New York, NY 10022

First Printing: September, 1997
10 9 8 7 6 5 4 3 2 1

Printed in the United States of America

For my mother-in-law, Mary,
who has always been supportive,
and in memory of my father-in-law, Tom.

Special thanks to
my friends and fellow writers,
Holly, Yvonne, and Gail,
who offer ongoing encouragement
and know what it's like out
there in the trenches,

and to my agent, Ethan Ellenberg,
who always tells it like it is.

One

I fear, dear friend, that my life has grown Exceedingly Dull since you and your Dashing Young Poet left the city in search of adventure abroad. I have not yet found the Grand Commission as an artist for which I have hoped. Alas, teaching small children to sketch and mending lace are hardly the proper sort of careers for a Modern Woman. Lest I sink into Perpetual Boredom, I shall write often and share even the smallest fragments of news . . .

—letter from Miss Amaryllis Meeks to
Miss Mary Godwin

London . . . May, 1816

"Now then, gentlemen, I believe you will find this next demonstration most edifying."

A murmur of anticipation rose from his fellow physicians as the speaker—a thin, intense man barely into his third decade—stepped aside from the wooden table. He stood in a circle of yellow light, illuminated by the dozen lamps strategically placed about the makeshift platform. Those lamps emitted heat enough so that, even though the drafty, high-ceilinged stone chamber lacked any sort of furnace, he could feel the sweat beading upon his forehead. He began removing his black frock coat.

As always, Talbot Meeks drew out this moment deliberately, aware that a sense of the theater was not amiss here. Indeed, standing before the score or so men of medicine who had paid a crown each to watch, he wryly realized that he bore an unfortunate resemblance to some Drury Lane actor.

The only difference was that his fellow player upon this particular stage was a naked corpse.

Having shed his jacket, he caught up a pair of porcelain-handled copper probes from which trailed lengths of thin wire. Those wires were, in turn, connected to a boxlike device the approximate size of a linen chest. The assembly of wire, metal rods, glass discs, and liquid-filled jars appeared innocuous enough to the untrained eye; a few cranks of its handle, however, produced a charge that could knock a man off his feet.

Coolly Talbot once more faced his audience. They were seated in the carved wooden pews that were a legacy of the building's previous function—namely, a chapel. Though they were cloaked in shadows so that he could not make out their faces, he could hear their impatient rustling and catch the occasional murmured word being exchanged. The air was thick with challenge and skepticism, as it was every time he offered his anatomy lessons.

He felt a muscle in his cheek twitch as he struggled to contain his irritation. His demonstrations were conducted in the strictest of scientific fashion, with his intent to dispel the superstition and ignorance that still pervaded his profession. Far too many of his fellow physicians cared little about their patients and even less about plumbing the workings of the human body. Rather, they prescribed noxious concoctions and let copious amounts of blood by way of treating every condition from gout to childbed fever . . . and then afterward extracted an exorbitant fee for their services. For most of the physicians here this night, then, attendance had been motivated more from idle curiosity than any true urge to learn.

Here now, gents. I'll give you your crown's worth and more, he thought with an inner grimace. He did not betray his emotions by so much as a lifted brow, however, but instead took a step forward.

"The apparatus you see behind me is an electrical generator based upon designs first developed by Messieurs Ramsden and Ingenhousz before the turn of the century. With these probes"—he paused to raise them like a priest offering up the Host—"I shall demonstrate how a current of electricity applied to the appropriate nerve centers of our subject can simulate living movement."

So saying, he inserted one rod into the grounding plate installed on the table, then momentarily pressed the tip of the other rod to the cold, white flesh of the dead man's lower torso.

The withered leg promptly kicked heavenward.

Talbot waited for the muffled exclamations to die before continuing. "We see similar results with other nerve centers," he explained and applied the probe to the corpse's upper chest. This time the dead man's waxen right arm shot out, as if he were a pugilist blocking a swift jab.

To the accompaniment of growing murmurs, Talbot moved the probe across that dead flesh until his subject fairly twitched like a man with the ague. The demonstration lasted no more than half a minute, but by then the pungent scent of discharged electricity filled the converted sacristy. Eyes burning, Talbot set aside the probes and let his unprotesting partner subside into his previous graven stillness.

"Quite fascinating, Dr. Meeks," spoke up a reedy Edinburgh burr, "but hardly more than parlor tricks. I dinna ken what medical purpose that generator of yours serves."

Talbot glanced toward the darkened arena before him, recognizing the speaker by his voice though his face was hidden in shadow.

"Dr. McArdle, your presence honors me," he smoothly answered. "As to your objection, might I remind you that numerous of our esteemed colleagues here in London and elsewhere have begun experimentation using electrical current. I presume you are familiar with the work of Doctors Malham, Fursey, and Kent, to name but a few. Though the results of their work are inconclusive, future applications will surely prove to be many. For example, restoring function to lame limbs . . . the relief of melancholia . . . perhaps even stimulating the regrowth of hair."

That last suggestion drew a ripple of laughter from the audience, for the balding McArdle's attempts to disguise his deficiency of locks had long been a source of amusement to his fellow physicians.

"Aye, jest all ye wish," the Scot countered, "but ye canna change me mind. Ye're dabbling wit' heathen powers, an' no good will come of it."

"I must disagree," spoke up another voice from the darkness. "Every major advance in human history came only when men of vision were willing to stride past their prescribed boundaries of knowledge into strange and wondrous new territories of learning."

"Aye, Dr. Cramer," McArdle sourly addressed that man, "an' if that be the case, then the Barkshire Demon does the Lord's work, ridding the city of fallen women."

That acerbic mention of the unknown killer who had been stalking London's backstreets these past months promptly quelled further comment. Talbot took advantage of the silence to regain control of the conversation.

"And now, gentlemen, we will continue with a study of the internal organs," he said with a cool smile and reached for the leather case containing his surgical instruments.

From her perch in a curtained alcove directly above the makeshift stage, Amaryllis Meeks set down her charcoal stick and allowed herself a sigh of relief. She had feared that, goaded by the Scot, her brother might have given way to the cold anger that of late seemed ever to bubble just beneath the surface of his usual gentlemanly mildness. Instead Talbot had handled the situation with an aplomb that made her proud.

While her brother arranged scalpels and surgical knives along the examining table, Amaryllis took a moment to flip back through her sketchbook. Her presence here, hidden within a dusty, velvet-curtained alcove once reserved for titled personages to observe Sunday services, had been Talbot's doing. For the converted chapel was his, housing this tiny amphitheater, an examining room, and private chambers in which he had lived since his wife first had taken ill.

She turned yet another page, squinting in the half-light. Even had the sun been brightly shining without, the hall would have been dark. For the stained glass windows—save for the circular one in the ceiling above them—had all been boarded over to keep prying eyes from seeing within. Talbot had allowed her but a single candle lest someone note her presence, and that faint glow had made her work difficult. Still, she gave a satisfied nod as she looked over the studies of legs and torsos that she'd thus far managed.

Her subject was the corpse upon Talbot's examining table. Unlike most young women, she was not discomposed by the sight of a dead man. Such was commonplace to her, since her father was the sexton of St. Pancras Church, and she had grown up practically within the churchyard. Indeed she had already succumbed to whimsy and mentally dubbed the deceased fellow George, given his passing resemblance to the current monarch.

For this cadaver was no Adonis-like model with a smoothly muscled physique but a wizened old man with scrawny chest and limbs, his only feature of note a full head of silvery hair. He would have to do, however, as this would be the closest that she would ever come to a life school. As a woman, she could hardly be admitted to such a gathering, where a nude model posed for the benefit of the assembled artists. Thus she deemed herself deficient in several crucial areas of anatomy . . . so much so that she even once had stripped down to her chemise before a mirror and used herself as a model.

Talbot, however, respected her work as a painter and watercolorist. Unlike their father, he never laughed at her declarations that she would one day earn her keep with her artwork, perhaps because he considered himself something of an artist in his own field. Whatever the case, he understood her need to study the human form. It had been he, in fact, who suggested she attend his next anatomy lesson. The only restriction was that no one—most particularly, their father—must know she was there.

Now the sound of Talbot's voice pulled her attention back to the makeshift stage. Impatiently she brushed aside an auburn curl that had come loose from its pins to hang rakishly over one eye. Then she twitched aside the curtain again.

Lamplight glinted from the scalpel her brother held in one hand, and she bit her lip in consternation. Earlier he had warned her that the greatest portion of his lesson involved the dissection of a human subject. At the time, she had been too excited by the opportunity he was affording her to consider just what that meant. Now, however, as she watched him make the first incision into George's sunken chest, she felt her stomach lurch.

By the time he had split open the dead man like a Christmas goose primed for stuffing, she felt distinctly faint. Swiftly she pulled on her cloak and gathered up her drawing materials. Seeing a dead man was one thing. Watching his innards being removed and cataloged was quite another. But as she prepared to pinch out the candle and grope her way to the curtained exit, she recalled Talbot's final admonition as he had settled her in the alcove.

Wait here for me until after the lesson, and I will escort

*you home. After all, it's far too dangerous these nights for
a young woman to wander the streets alone.*

He was right, of course. Over the past six months, the
Barkshire Demon already had claimed four victims. All had
been impoverished females of various occupations—from
prostitute to shopgirl—with the oldest, Amaryllis's same age
of two-and-twenty. That last, combined with her gender and
humble station in life, left her uncomfortably close to being
the sort of woman that attracted the Demon's attentions.
Anyone would say she was a fool to consider making her
way home alone and on foot.

Or was she? Amaryllis bit her lip again, considering. The
tabloids all had made note of the fact that the Demon struck
only on foggy nights. This evening was clear, and her way
home marked by modern streetlights, so that she would be
safe enough. Moreover it made no sense for her brother to
make the long walk to St. Pancras and back simply to ease
her fears. For she was a modern woman, after all, adhering
to Mary Wollstonecraft's dictums regarding women's rights.
Surely she possessed the sternness of mind not to be frightened by phantoms.

For, while wandering the fog-shrouded streets was unnerving, the thought of returning inside and witnessing poor
George being served up like Sunday dinner was equally distressing. Even if she shut her eyes, she would still be able
to hear everything. And poor George, through no fault of
his own, had already developed the ripe odor of a corpse
left unburied too long. She would still be able to smell him,
as well. And while she might be stern of mind, she most
definitely was weak of stomach.

The distinctive sound of a saw ripping through brittle
bone that now rose from the stage below goaded her to action. Swallowing back her queasiness, she tore a page from
her sketchbook and dashed off a note of explanation to Talbot. Then, posting the paper on a convenient splinter just

outside the alcove, she tiptoed her way down a narrow flight of steep stone steps and slipped out the back way.

Once outside, however, she halted in dismay. In the intervening hour since the anatomy lesson had commenced, a serpentine fog had slid its way off the Thames to wrap chill white coils about the city streets. Now it was the sort of night when a person could hardly see his hand before his face. Indeed it now was the sort of night when the Barkshire Demon walked the city.

Sternness of mind, she reminded herself. For she was well away from that unsavory area near the river where the Demon prowled. And, should she become unnerved once she had walked too far to turn back, the solution was simple. She would simply flag down a passing hack and spend a few precious coins.

The matter decided, then, Amaryllis plunged into the fog.

Glimmers of the gaslamps' yellow light had escaped the fog's sinuous coils, so that fitful illumination was sufficient for her to negotiate the walkway with moderate ease. Even so, by the time she had covered a block, she could scarce make out any detail of her surroundings. Only the fact that she made this walk on a regular basis kept her from stumbling hopelessly lost through the anonymous streets. A few minutes later, however, the fog lifted long enough for her to glimpse a millinery shop where she occasionally stopped.

Halfway home, she determined with a faint smile as she let out a breath she had not realized she was holding. And then footsteps echoed in the distance behind her.

Reflexively she halted. By chance or design, the other set of footfalls fell silent, so that she wondered for a moment if she simply had imagined them. They had sounded nothing like ordinary footsteps. Muffled by the night and the burgeoning fog, they had been reminiscent of tree limbs being slowly dragged across the damp cobbles. Steeling herself, she turned for a look at whoever was behind her.

No one was there.

After a moment, she resumed her pace, though her heart was thrumming at a quicker rate than before. Surely it had been but her imagination that had conjured phantom sounds. She and her friend, Mary, often made a game of frightening each other with fearsome tales, so that perhaps she was predisposed to hearing ghostly noises.

But now the only sound was the soft click of her own sensible boots against the walk. The dull rhythm was unnerving in its own way, announcing her presence more loudly than she would have wished, but it was a far preferable sound to the unearthly gait that she'd imagined had echoed her steps.

A few moments later, however, she almost wished for the company—unearthly or not. The fog had thickened again, leaving her to strain her eyes against the swirl of white in hopes of spotting some landmark—a signpost, perhaps, or else another familiar shop front. This time, though, none rose out of the fog.

"Blast," came her unladylike mutter that now held a small note of desperation. Even had she wished now to flag down a hack, none was to be found. She would have to keep on going.

Hesitantly she extended one arm. The tight sleeve of her bottle-green gown stretched the limits of its seams as she groped before her. When her gloved fingers closed over nothing more substantial than mist, she cautiously swung her arm to one side, only to connect with brick.

A wall. She edged closer to it, relieved she had not managed to wander into the middle of the lane. Now should she remain where she stood and hope that the fog might lift a bit, or else guide herself along by means of following the building's edge? Yet even as she inwardly debated the question, she heard a faint, familiar shuffling somewhere behind her.

Her flesh prickled at the furtive sound. *It was the same person . . . and he was still following her.*

Frantically she shrank back against the wall and strove for calm. She had no proof, after all, that this unseen person was in pursuit of her. And if he were hidden from her by the night and the fog, then it stood to reason that he also could not see her. Unless, of course, he were the Demon.

For the tabloids had attributed almost supernatural powers to the fiend who seemingly wandered the foggy nighttime with the same aplomb a regular man strolled about on a sunny day. The fact that no one had ever witnessed his crimes, nor had he yet left any sort of clue behind as to his identity, only added to the mystery.

Even as a thrill of horror swept her, she determinedly embraced common sense. Again she reminded herself that the Demon had never struck this far north of the river. His fanciful sobriquet had come from the fact that each of the murdered women had been found in an alley off a narrow little twist of a dockside street called Barkshire.

But what if the Demon had decided, this night, to venture farther afield in his fearsome hunt?

Then she simply would outwit him, she told herself with a stoutness she did not entirely feel. Using the wall as a guide, she began moving away from the source of those shambling footsteps with as much speed and silence as her sensible boots and limited visibility allowed.

Rough stone bit through the worn kid of her gloves, and she stumbled half a dozen times on a protruding doorstep or a section of wrought-iron handrail. To her despair, none of the barred doorways or shuttered windows spilled forth any welcome light from beneath stoop or sill. No one was within . . . that, or the inhabitants were simply quailing within the dark, shuttered safety of shop and home.

And still the unseen walker followed after her, neither gaining on her nor falling behind. Yet even while she moved with frantic haste, her ears straining to track his menacing progress, her thoughts were fixed on the lurid newspaper accounts she had read of the bloody crimes.

Another Horrid Murder.

Demon's Rampage Continues Unchecked.

Police Officials at a Loss.

Though the tabloids vied with one another to uncover ever more outlandish details of the case, a few facts had remained constant. Each murdered woman had been found in an alley several days after her disappearance, naked and with her clothes neatly bundled beside her. The cause of death in all four cases had been deemed strangulation, for each victim's neck bore marks of brutish hands.

But that was not the worst of it.

Amaryllis shivered again, wishing she had heeded her brother's opinion that proper women did not read newspapers. Had she been less diligent in keeping up with such stories, she might have been spared the knowledge that now taunted her. For, if those accounts were to be believed, the killer had not contented himself with merely killing the women.

Afterward the fiend had cut them open with almost surgical precision and neatly plucked out their hearts.

The shuffling sound behind her rang closer now. She stifled a moan of pure terror . . . and then the wall she had been using as a guide abruptly fell away beneath her hand.

A street corner, she realized after an instant of fear. Thankfully she rounded it. Perhaps she could lose her pursuer now. Even better she might find an occupied building in which to take refuge. But a dozen paces down that side street, a second brick wall loomed out of the fog before her.

Too late she realized her mistake. She had turned down what must be a blind alley. The rank smell of rotting garbage

around her confirmed her suspicions. Frantic, she groped
her way down the length of this second wall until, but a few
feet farther, she reached the corner where it butted up
against a section of wooden fencing.

Trapped.

She choked back a panicked cry, sagging against the
damp planks as she debated whether to take refuge here or
retrace her steps. This shallow passageway could prove the
ideal hiding place, for her pursuer might well pass by its
narrow entry and continue on into the night.

But what if he didn't? What if he stumbled across her
instead? She would have no place to flee to, no chance at
escape. Hers would be the next name to appear in the tabloids as the Barkshire Demon's latest victim.

Better to keep running than risk being cornered, she decided, and started back in the direction of the main road.
For did she not have an advantage over the Demon's previous victims? Doubtless none of them had been modern
women such as she, capable of rational thought and—unen-
cumbered by impractical footwear—swift flight.

She paused once again at the alley's narrow mouth . . .
and that was when a hellish face appeared from out of the
fog.

*That face! Skin a waxy, grayish shade . . . black eyes dull
and yet ablaze with brimstone. And the smell that clung to
him, the sweet sickening scent of decay that could never be
mistaken for anything else. Dear God, it was the face of a
corpse—the face of some creature that had been disgorged
from the ranks of the dead!*

What swept through her mind was less coherent thought
than it was reflexive impression, and so fleeting that she
barely had time to register its meaning. She took a step back
and opened her mouth to scream.

And then the creature extended a corpselike hand at her.

The scream died on her lips. *Run!* a frantic inner voice
shrieked, but her feet remained planted on the uneven cob-

bles. She could merely watch while, like some fumbling swain, the being made an ungainly swipe at the hood of her cloak.

The woolen covering slipped from her head, while her tangle of waist-length auburn hair, loosened from its pins by her earlier exertions, spilled past her shoulders in a fiery blaze. At the sight, a flicker of emotion—triumph, perhaps?—passed over the slack gray face. Then, with a guttural sound of satisfaction, he reached out both pallid hands toward her.

Inwardly she screamed, a piercing wave of unadulterated terror. Outwardly, however, she remained unmoving, as if the fog had wrapped her in innumerable misty threads that held her firmly as chains. No sound escaped her, not even when the cold, dead fingers wrapped themselves around her throat.

Was this how the Demon's other victims had faced their end? Had they, too, been paralyzed with fear and unable to make even a token attempt at resistance?

She should struggle, should claw at his hands . . . yet the thought of touching that corpselike flesh was more than she could bear. Even as she gasped for breath, even as red sparks exploded before her eyes, all she could manage was a frantic wish that it would be over, and quickly.

She heard it then—the clatter of wheels against stone that was an approaching carriage. At the sound, the brutal grip on her throat abruptly loosened. She felt herself drifting toward the chill ground like a laundry bundle carelessly tossed aside.

Talbot, she faintly thought. *He realized I was gone and came after me.* But hardly had the words formed in her mind than the cobbles rushed up and darkness enveloped her.

Two

Victor Saville, third earl of Blackstock, coolly surveyed the half-naked young blonde before him.

Quite deliberately, his dark gaze took in the heavy globes of her white breasts, their pale nipples rouged a startling shade of red that matched the silk of her dressing gown, left artfully loosened all the way to her slim waist. He let his gaze drop lower still to her lush hips, their outline clearly visible beneath the sheer fabric. The sight, he knew, was designed to arouse any man not yet in the grave.

The problem was, he just wasn't interested anymore.

And, just as problematical, he suspected that Miss Penelope Worthington knew as much . . . and that she was not prepared to give up her titled lover.

"Oh, pish-posh."

With that pouting plaint, Penelope tossed her blond curls and rolled her kohled blue eyes, even as she sidled toward him. Toying with his starched white neckcloth, she pressed her ample breasts to the superfine of his black waistcoat.

"Really, Vic, you can be quite tiresome at times," she went on and began to unfasten that well-tailored garment. "Any other gentleman being greeted like this would have fallen to his knees and told me I was as beautiful as Aphrodite herself."

"Indeed I find you quite as beautiful as Aphrodite herself. I would kneel," he added with a wry lift of one dark brow, "but my valet Moresdale insists upon dressing me in pantaloons that are far too tight for such acrobatics."

His dry answer set the ersatz goddess's artificially reddened lips drooping into another studied pout.

"It's hardly a compliment, when I practically have to drag the words from you," she retorted as she finished unfastening the last of his waistcoat's gold buttons. "Besides which, it's been two weeks since last you visited me. I was beginning to wonder if there is someone else."

On the surface, her comment was nothing more than the casual query of a professional businesswoman. Still, Victor heard the faintest note of desperation in her voice that told him what he had begun to suspect . . . that Penelope had broken the *demimondaine's* cardinal rule and allowed herself to become emotionally involved with one of her patrons.

"There's no one else," he truthfully told her, then inwardly winced at her expression of triumphant relief. Bloody hell, putting her aside was going to prove harder than he had expected. Still, terminating their connection had to be done.

As if determined not to give him a free moment to consider that action, Penelope commenced with her usual bright chatter as she led him toward her bedchamber. He made no protest but followed, using that interval to collect his thoughts.

It wasn't that she had not kept up her end of their bargain. Indeed she had proved quite a satisfactory mistress—beautiful and articulate, if not exceedingly cultured. That last was not to be expected, however, given the gambling hell where he had first encountered her.

Save for a few rare occasions during his military career, he had never been one for consorting with prostitutes. In fact, he had approached his relationship with Penelope as sort of an experiment, something along the lines of creating a flamboyant hybrid bloom by the skillful crossing of two lackluster parent roses. And her proficiency in the sensual arts more than made up for her lack in the parlor. But as a man could not serve two masters, neither could he serve two mistresses . . . and given his current obsession with the horticultural manuscript he was in the process of preparing, the redoubtable Miss Worthington would have to be the one to go.

"Really, Vic, you haven't listened to a word I've said."

Penelope's mock-chiding words as they halted at the bedchamber door brought him back to the matter at hand. He was doing her no kindness by putting this off any longer, he told himself as he gazed down into her pretty, painted face. Firmly he caught hold of her slim fingers that had begun wandering down the front of his black breeches with tantalizing familiarity, then stepped back out of temptation's range.

"My apologies for not being attentive," he said as he released her hand. "I fear that I have something to discuss with you that you might find . . . distressing."

"Pish-posh, you know that you can tell me anything," came her playful reply, though he saw the sudden uncertainty in her expression that was at odds with her light tone. "If you are dissatisfied with my—"

"It has nothing to do with you," he cut her short. "It has to do with me."

He paused at the pained uncertainty in her eyes, then bluntly went on, "I fear, Penelope, that I have no wish to see you any longer."

"You—You mean, you are casting me off?"

Her voice trembled, but her pointed chin lifted in pride as she met his gaze. "So what brings this on, my lord?" she demanded with an icy formality he'd never seen in her before. "Have I offended you in some way, acted less than eager in bed?"

"Hardly, Penelope. It merely happens that—"

He broke off, debating just how forthright he should be. *It merely happens that I find your company unutterably tedious compared to the challenges of crossing* Alba Maxima *with* Celsiana? Though firmness in such a matter was necessary, cruelty was not. He had never considered himself callous in his dealings with others, merely efficient. His defection from his own family a dozen years earlier was a case in point. If someone took offense, it was his—or her—own bloody fault.

"It merely happens that I have little free time these days," he finished. "But do not worry, I will not leave you in financial straits. In fact, I have deposited a substantial sum in your account and paid up your lodgings for six more months."

He paused to catch up his walking stick and hat from a nearby chair. Then, efficient as always, he plucked a folded, waxed-sealed sheet of foolscap from his coat pocket.

"I have also taken the liberty of jotting down the names of three gentlemen of my acquaintance who might be looking for a discreet arrangement," he explained as he proffered the paper. "If one of them meets your fancy, I would be happy to arrange a formal introduction—"

"I can find me own bloody connections, thank you," she cut him short, a trace of her East End origins momentarily coloring her words.

Snatching the page from his grasp, she ripped it in two, then unceremoniously flung the pieces heavenward. With the same abruptness, she stalked to the front door and, heedless of her half-dressed state, jerked it open.

"You're a coldhearted bastard, Lord Blackstock," she said with feeling. "My only consolation is that perhaps one day you will meet the right woman and fall in love, yourself . . . and end up being quite as cruelly used by her as I have been by you."

"Believe me, cruelty was never my intent," he said as he stepped past the threshold into the foggy night. Pulling on his gloves, he turned one last time to face her. "You might do well to reconsider those names I gave you, Penelope. Indeed, you can count yourself lucky—"

"I count myself bloody lucky you cast me off before I was murdered by you and one of your fancy friends, my lord," she hissed out and slammed the door in his face.

The sound reverberated like a thunderclap down the silent avenue. Victor barely heard it, however, over her mocking words that still echoed in his mind.

Murdered by you and one of your fancy friends.

A shaft of white-hot anger pierced his gut, so that his first impulse was to rip the gleaming brass doorknocker in the shape of a Cupid's leering face from its moorings. Christ, even she believed the stories, and here he'd been sharing her bed a dozen times a fortnight over the past few months.

His grip tightened on his stick as he fought to regain control. He'd heard the same accusation—sometimes spoken aloud, more often whispered behind his back—time and again since the events of last winter. By now he should be immune to its sting.

Obviously he was not.

His anger now in check, he turned from Penelope's door a final time and headed for his carriage. It was a sleek black conveyance pulled by a matched pair of spirited bays. Emblazoned on either side was the Saville family crest, which featured a reclining stallion upon a quartered field of stylized roses.

Derek, his driver, jumped down from his perch atop the vehicle. "Short evenin', milord," came the younger man's murmured observation as he tugged open the door for him.

Though Derek's pale, pockmarked features were devoid of expression, his tone held a suppressed note of sympathy that assured Victor his employee had witnessed that final scene with Penelope. Oddly touched by his words, Victor gave the man a reassuring nod. For Derek was one of three people whose loyalty to him had never wavered; his valet, Moresdale, and his sister were the others.

"I suspect it could have gone much worse," he replied as he stepped up into the conveyance. Once the door had closed behind him, he leaned out the open window to address his man. "I believe I would just as soon call it a night and return home."

"As ye wish, milord. The fog's lifted eno' that we should not 'ave any trouble makin' it back safe an' sound."

A moment later and to the accompaniment of jingling harnesses and clomping hooves, the carriage started down the cobbled lane. The lamps at either side of the vehicle directed a respectable glow onto the street despite the lingering fog. Satisfied that Derek had the situation well in hand, Victor pulled up the window and settled back against the black leather bench for the short journey to his fashionable Mayfair home.

By now the echo of Penelope's accusation had faded, but he found himself reluctantly remembering another, far more painful parting. A dozen years earlier, at the age of eighteen, he had determined that he was not cut out for his role as heir to the Blackstock title. Whether it was a deficiency in his upbringing that had brought him to this pass, or simply a clearer vision than granted his fellow lords-in-waiting, he was not certain. All he did know was that, to his mind, the English peerage as it existed was a farce and a fraud . . . and that he wanted no part of it.

Abolish the class system? his sire, Timothy Saville, had roared in disbelief when Victor had informed him of his revised personal philosophy. *Bloody hell, lad, next you'll be offering for women to stand up in Parliament.*

With that unfair sally—for, as Victor heatedly had reminded the older man, he'd merely broadened his political views, not gone mad—a breach between them opened. Lady Blackstock had taken her husband's part, chiding her son for his liberal views and his disdain for familial responsibility. The gap soon became a chasm until, a few months later, Victor put an end to the conflict by purchasing a commission in the king's army.

The experience had proved enlightening, though not quite

in the ways he had anticipated. He spent time with Wellington and escaped India unscathed. By then, however, he had found himself facing the same class distinctions in the army as he had left behind at home. He endured it all a few years longer and then finally sold his commission. Left to his own devices, he commenced upon a successful career in the unlordly realm of trade. Not long afterward, word reached him that an epidemic of influenza had claimed both his father and mother.

Idly he twisted the heavy gold ring with its engraving of the Saville family crest that he wore on the third finger of his right hand. That ostentatious piece of jewelry had been passed down from father to son for four generations. Now it was his.

He had felt the loss of his parents more keenly than he had expected, with a decade's worth of estrangement between them. He'd been even less overjoyed by the Saville family titles and estates falling prematurely to him. Given that he was the last of his immediate line, he might well have relinquished the whole lot to the crown, save for the fact that he'd also become sole guardian of his younger sister, Monique.

She had been but a child when he had left, but now Lady Monique was a pert young woman soon to make her debut. Upon their renewing their sibling relationship, he had come to the conclusion that his parents had spoiled the girl mercilessly. Taking a firm hand with her, however, proved a more daunting task even than facing Bonaparte's men.

Among her bad habits were a lamentable tendency to listen at closed doors and a propensity for voicing her opinion when it was not asked. But her greatest flaw, to his mind, was the fact that Monique was—in her own brightly frivolous way—quite as stubborn as he.

That thankless parental role aside, he soon learned there was not a hell of a lot for a new earl to do beyond drinking to excess, wagering outlandish sums at the card table, and evading marriage-minded debutantes. Finally wearied of being the sole voice of sanity among his fellows, he conceded defeat. For the first year and a half in his role of Lord Blackstock, he gamely set out to prove himself in all three areas.

He shook his head now at the memory. Six days out of seven had found him and a handful of friends well in their cups and at the faro tables at Brooks's or White's. Other times, he and his cronies would seek diversion at less fashionable spots, gambling hells such as the Golden Wolf. Most often he won at his game of choice—a fortunate state of affairs, considering he rarely could recall the next morning just what had happened the night before.

And always those prolonged sessions of drinking and gambling were preceded by obligatory appearances at any number of social events. Those gatherings he had found painful in the extreme after the life he'd been living. Having never taken to the role of beau or blade, it was only his sense of duty that forced him to grit his teeth and endure the calculated social rituals involved. After a handful of dances with giggling young women who never failed to sigh over his unfortunate resemblance to a minor poet named Byron, he would slip away to the next such function. The question of marriage and begetting heirs of his own he had managed to avoid thus far, confining his romantic dalliances to women of Penelope's ilk.

But the events of last winter had curtailed those excesses. His withdrawal from Society had been forced upon him as much as it had been his choice, and that knowledge was all the more bitter for the fact of his innocence.

Within days of that tragedy, he had found himself unwelcome in the same clubs and salons that, a week before, had greeted him and his purse with open arms. As for the invitations, they ceased like a coal mine that was played out. He'd been on the verge of taking himself and Monique off to their country estate for the remainder of the Season when, impulsively, he had decided to explore the boarded-up hothouse that had been the pride of his father and grandfather before him.

And it was there, in that dank overgrown jungle, that he'd found a new purpose for himself.

The carriage jolted to an unexpected halt. The suddenness of the stop put an abrupt end to Victor's musings even as it sent him half-tumbling onto the opposite bench. He regained his seat and pounded on the ceiling.

Derek's pockmarked face, paler even than usual, appeared at the trap door. "Sorry, milord," came his breathless apology. "I didn't mean t'—"

"What in the bloody hell is going on here? If you cannot manage the team in this bit of fog, I'll take the reins for you."

" 'Tain't the fog, milord," Derek returned in a queer, choked voice. " 'Tis what I seen in it. Ye'd best come look."

Abruptly the trap slammed shut. Victor jerked open the carriage door and climbed out, his jaw set. He had hired Derek for, among other things, his common sense. If the man was going to start seeing ghosts and phantoms in the night, then he could find himself another post. But even as he strode past Derek and the nickering team, impatient to take his look and be done with it, a flash of intuition sent a chill through him.

Though he rarely perused the scandal sheets, he had heard recounted innumerable times the gruesome exploits of the killer known as the Barkshire Demon. Given that the Demon preyed only upon females of the lower class, he had reasoned that neither he nor his sister was in any danger of becoming the killer's next victim. Thus he had paid scant attention to the details. The one tidbit that *had* stuck in his mind, however, was the fact that this killer struck only on foggy nights.

Nights such as this.

Resignation swept him even before he glimpsed the supine figure of a woman at the mouth of the alleyway. She was wrapped in a dull brown cloak that had parted to reveal the dark green of her modest gown. In turn, the dress had twisted high above her slim ankles to reveal a flash of white petticoat and a pair of sensible black boots.

No duke's daughter, this. He shook his head, his gaze sharpening to take in another, far more telling detail. For the carriage lamps' bright gleam washed over her with light enough that he could see the upper half of her body was surrounded by a puddle of scarlet.

Blood, was his first thought. She had met the same end as the Demon's other victims, her body savaged by a knife. It was a hellish way for anyone to meet his end . . . the more so for a woman.

He started to strip off his jacket to cover her, wanting to allow her this one last dignity. But as he moved closer, he saw that what he had taken for blood was instead the spill of her unbound red tresses about her. As for knife wounds, there was none to be seen from his vantage point.

"Looks like the Demon's work, all right," came Derek's mournful voice directly behind him that nearly sent him jumping out of his skin. " 'Tis said 'ow the fiend only kills young an' pretty strumpets."

"Young and pretty strumpets, eh?" Victor softly echoed, turning his attention back to the unfortunate victim sprawled at his feet.

He had always been partial to blondes, like Penelope. With this woman, however, he might have been tempted to make a change. Even in the dim glow of the carriage light, he could see that she was far more lovely than the soiled doves one normally found walking the streets. Even now her face had an innocent look about it, as if she were but sleeping.

Sleeping. With a frown, he studied the still figure more closely. Had not the scandal sheets made specific reference to the fact that all the Demon's victims had been mutilated? Yet he'd already determined that the only outward sign of injury to her were the livid bruises he could now see on her throat.

Then his frown deepened. It had to be a trick of the light . . . that, or else a product of his imagination. Still, he might almost swear now that he could see the faint rise and fall of her chest as she lay there.

" 'Ere now, milord," came Derek's frantic protest as Victor abruptly knelt beside her, stripping the kid glove from one hand to wrap his fingers around her slim wrist. " 'Tain't no call for ye to be worrying o'er the poor girl, now that she's past hope. Let me whistle up a Charlie to take care o' this nasty bit o' business, an' we'll be off."

"I rather doubt you will find a constable nearby on a night like this," Victor muttered, his attention focused on the task before him.

He thought he detected the faintest thread of a pulse beneath his fingers . . . but then it might just as easily be the racing of blood through his own veins that he felt. The fact that her flesh still held a hint of warmth meant little, as well. Perhaps the chit had been killed only moments before, and the sound of Victor's approaching carriage had warned off the murderer. That would explain why she, unlike the others, had not been mutilated. If only he had a shaving mirror, some cold shiny surface to hold at her lips to assure himself whether or not she still breathed.

"Quick, Derek, give me the knife you carry in your boot!"

" 'Ere ye go, milord," the man uncertainly replied and handed over the weapon.

It was sharp if short-bladed, an efficient sort of tool that a cutpurse might carry about in practice of his trade. Victor had first become acquainted with that knife almost two years earlier as a victim of a particularly inept member of that underworld fraternity. He'd collared the would-be thief and offered the youth the choice of accepting gainful employment or being turned over to the watch. Derek had opted for work and, these days, used his knife strictly for paring his nails.

Now propping the woman's head in the crook of his elbow, Victor positioned the borrowed knife so that the blade's flat edge was but an inch from her pale, parted lips. The cold metal misted over with a faint sheen of moisture.

Derek, meanwhile, had forgotten his previous squeamishness to peer over his master's shoulder for a better look. " 'Ere now, looks like the Demon didn't get this one, after all," came his awed exclamation as he leaned still closer.

Even as Victor allowed himself a triumphant grin— *bloody hell, the chit was alive!*—she chose that moment in which to open her eyes.

They were the clear verdant color of spring leaves, framed by thick fringes of black lashes that were a sharp contrast to her fiery hair. Blinking, she gazed up at him, her expression one of pain and confusion. Then, slowly, she focused on the glint of silver that was the knife blade he still held unthinkingly before her.

Before he could reassure her, the emerald eyes darkened in utter horror. Her pale lips parted in what surely would have been a scream of terror, save that no sound issued from her bruised throat beyond a muffled little croak.

And then the black-fringed eyelids fluttered shut as she lost consciousness.

Three

"Bloody hell, she's fainted again."

Victor bit back a second, more pungent oath at his own stupidity as he returned the offending knife to its owner. No doubt the chit, upon seeing that weapon brandished before her, had believed him about to slit her throat. Farcical as the idea was, all he needed was for her to regain her senses and accuse *him* of being the Barkshire Demon. His reputation had suffered enough so that he was not prepared to risk a similar sort of scandal again.

Abruptly he scooped her up in his arms and swung about to face Derek.

"We're taking her back to the house. Gather her belongings"—he nodded in the direction of a reticule and a book of sorts that lay scattered nearby—"and we'll be off. A warm bed and a nip of brandy should bring her around again. We'll find out exactly what happened to her . . and make certain she realizes who her benefactor this night was."

"But, milord, ye can't just be takin' 'er 'ome wit' ye," Derek protested, trotting ahead of him to pull open the carriage door yet again.

Victor halted. "And what would you have me do, leave her in the street and hope she survives the night? Or I suppose we could drop her on the steps of the nearest charity hospital and let some quacksalver have his way with her."

" 'Tain't wot I meant, milord. Wot I should o' been sayin'

was"—he paused and swallowed hard—"wot if the Demon decides 'e still wants 'er an' follows after us?"

"I hardly think that likely. Now lend a hand."

It took but a moment for them to wrap the unconscious woman in a lap robe and settle her across one leather bench. That accomplished, Victor climbed back inside, and Derek once more whipped up the team in the direction of Mayfair.

While the carriage clattered through the silent streets, Victor settled back against his own seat to take stock of the situation. Already he was regretting the impulse that had made him assume responsibility for the chit. So what if she *did* think him the killer? Considering that she'd had only a glimpse of him before she fainted, surely she would never be able to pick him out of a crowd again . . . let alone march up to the nearest watch station and announce it had been the Earl of Blackstock who had attempted to kill her! Hell, he could have done his duty by dropping her at the nearest church and then washed his hands of the situation. There'd been no real need to cart her back home just to convince her of his innocence in the matter.

Moreover he could picture quite clearly the reception he would receive from his household when he arrived at his doorstep with this red-haired doxy in tow.

Quite noble of you, brother mine, he could almost hear Monique's light, mocking voice. *How selfless of you to offer aid to one of the lower class. But I venture that if she had been hatch-faced and a dozen years older, you would have gladly left the chit to the watch.*

As perhaps he would have.

Dispassionately he let his gaze travel over her limp form. Settling her inside the coach, he'd had opportunity to take stock of her feminine attributes—an ample if not voluptuous bosom; trim waist; sleekly generous hips. As best he could tell, her striking features were not enhanced by paint, nor was she drenched in cheap scent designed to disguise a lack of regular bathing. She was a cut above the usual, so that he almost wondered if he might be mistaken in dubbing her a member of that fallen sorority.

But then what sort of woman other than a prostitute would be wandering the streets alone at night and with a known killer stalking the streets?

Just then the coach hit a particularly rutted section of street. Only Victor's instinctive intervention kept the unconscious woman from tumbling to the carriage floor.

With a muttered curse, he caught her up in his arms yet again. Struggling against the coach's low ceiling, he attempted to resettle her upon the seat. The lap robe had slid off her, however, tangling between his legs so that he found it nearly impossible to manage his insensible burden in the swaying vehicle. Conceding defeat, he half-fell onto his own seat, the chit now sprawled in an unseemly manner across his lap.

"Bloody hell," he muttered as he attempted to regain both his balance and his dignity.

The former, if not the latter, he swiftly accomplished. The question remained as to what to do for the duration of the journey with his still-unconscious companion.

For she had not awakened despite this rough treatment. Doubtless the twin shocks she had received this night—the first, at the Demon's hands and the second, unintentionally, from him—had sent her into some form of hysteria.

Victor grudgingly shook his head. Hell, he'd probably be in similar shape had he believed he'd come face-to-face with death twice in a single night. He only hoped that when she finally regained her senses, she also was capable of reason. But even as those thoughts crossed his mind, he realized that, for some reason, he still cradled the woman in his arms.

And, oddly enough, he found himself in no great hurry to set her down.

In the bright glow of the coach's interior lamp, he could see that her face now held a bit of healthy color. Too, her chilled flesh had regained its proper warmth, so that he could feel the heat of her body through the thin wool of her cloak and the finer spun fabric of her dark green gown. A good sign, he told himself, an indication that perhaps she had suffered no serious harm. Yet even as he made this dispassionate analysis, other more frivolous observations demanded to be given voice.

Somehow a goodly portion of her red-gold tresses had become entangled in one of his hands. Reflexively he curled his fingers more tightly about the soft strands. Though the lamplight seemed to imbue her hair with fiery life of its own, so that he might imagine a single lock would burn whatever it touched, its feel was the comforting coolness of expensive silk.

Or rose petals.

He allowed himself a wry smile at this unexpected lapse into poetry. Taking the comparison further, he determined that the pale skin above the damnably modest neckline of her gown resembled the white petals of an *R. alba semiplena.* Given the color of her hair, he might have expected to see a sprinkling of bright freckles on her skin that would have brought to mind a *Rosa damascena versicolor,* a white-petaled bloom flecked with pink. Save for the darkening splotches that were the imprint of her attacker's splayed fingers, however, nothing marred the creamy paleness of her smooth flesh.

An unexpected jolt of desire raced through him at the thought. The reaction intensified as, almost without thinking, he subtly shifted his position so that the rounded curve of her buttocks pressed against his groin. Now, with every jolt and jostle of the carriage, her body moved in a loverlike rhythm against him.

The sensation swiftly brought him to a state of full arousal, so that his erection now strained painfully against the taut fabric of his breeches. He leaned back in his seat and bit back a frustrated groan. Given the fact that it had been some time since he'd last had a woman, he should have slaked that particular need with Penelope before he put her aside. Now he was paying the price for his precipitous behavior.

Yet, even knowing the folly of what he was doing, he let his thoughts wander to still more interesting possibilities. Had his hands been free, he might have given way to temptation and run his fingers across that soft skin. Perhaps he would even slide a hand up under her skirts to see if the flesh of her thighs was equally as warm and satiny. Hell, with no one to stop him, he might just—

"Bloody hell."

This time guilt added a sharper edge to the muttered words as it occurred to him that he had just been contemplating something akin to rape. He'd never taken a woman without her consent before, and he damn sure wasn't about to start now. The fact that the chit was a prostitute made no difference.

His desire now quenched, he abruptly slid her off his lap and propped her upright on the seat. He resettled the blanket over her, then took the opposite bench again, a litany of recrimination playing in his mind.

What in the hell was wrong with him, lusting over an unconscious woman who had narrowly escaped a murderer's grasp but minutes before? He'd always had nothing but contempt for men who forced themselves upon their partners, spouses or not. Preying upon a woman who had already been victimized was nothing short of barbaric—even conceding that nothing actually had happened, except in his mind.

He was spared further inner debate on the matter when, a moment later, the coach halted outside his elegant town home. Victor had the carriage door open, himself, even before Derek had clambered down from his post. By now bright light spilled forth from the town house's entrance and framed a short, balding man of middle years and unctuous expression.

"Ah, Peters, you're still up and about," Victor observed in mingled dismay and relief as he caught sight of his butler.

He shook his head. He would have preferred the assistance of his valet, Moresdale, instead. A blunt, wiry man Victor's own age, Moresdale combined shrewd good sense with the closed-mouth discretion of a confessional priest. Unfortunately, Victor reminded himself, he had given the man the evening off. Peters would have to do.

Climbing from the conveyance, he gestured at the bundled figure he had left propped upon the seat. "Lend Derek a hand. We have an ill guest whom we need to get inside . . . and quickly."

"Certainly, my lord."

With Prinny's own stiff dignity, Peters descended the few steps to the street where the coach waited. His shiny face betrayed no sign of surprise at this turn of events, even when Derek scooped up the unconscious woman from the seat and unceremoniously deposited her in the butler's arms.

" 'Ere now, Petey lad, ye 'eard 'is lordship," Derek spoke up with the hint of a smirk. "Let's get 'er inside, an' be smart about it."

The driver's careless words reflected the barely checked rivalry between him and the older man that had existed since the day Derek first joined the Saville household. Peters had long since dismissed the younger man as an uncouth rogue, unfit to be part of a peer's household. For his part, Derek took every opportunity to air his belief that a fireplace poker had, at some point in Peters's career, found its way up a certain portion of that man's anatomy.

Refusing to be goaded by Derek—at least not before the master—Peters merely turned a blandly questioning look in Victor's direction.

"Shall I put this, er, person in the guest chambers, my lord, or would you prefer her to stay in the garret with the other servants?"

"Put her in the Blue Room," he shortly ordered and

turned away, but not before he glimpsed the look of well-bred shock on the other man's face.

He could hardly blame the man for being nonplused, Victor told himself. The butler had just been instructed to install a woman in the bedchamber that adjoined Victor's own—the room that, had he been wed, would rightfully have been occupied by Lady Blackstock. What else could the man think but that the earl had taken leave of his senses and decided to flout convention by installing his latest mistress in his own house?

"Oh, and Peters," he added in deliberate afterthought, "I want to keep any knowledge of our guest's presence from the other servants until tomorrow. And I would expressly ask that you try to avoid running into Lady Monique until after you have settled the young woman in her quarters. I would prefer to explain the situation to her myself."

"As you wish, my lord."

The man's tone was slightly strangled, as if he'd gulped down an entire pot of lemon tea the wrong way. His round face, meanwhile, had darkened several shades of pink with the effort of managing his unconscious burden.

He swallowed, then went on. "You need not worry about Lady Monique, my lord. She already has retired to her rooms for the night."

"Excellent. Derek and I shall see about bringing around a physician, then, while you settle our guest upstairs."

While Peters struggled toward the staircase, Victor turned back to his driver. "I want you to drive out to the home of my personal physician. Give him no particulars of what has happened tonight, but simply tell him that I have a guest in need of his ministrations . . . and then bring him as quickly as possible."

"But milord, wot about the Demon?" the man ventured in a stage whisper, nervously glancing back over his shoulder lest that killer be within earshot. "Shouldn't I summon the watch so you can let them know what happened?"

"What we *think* happened," Victor corrected in a chill tone. "For all we know, she was fleeing an abusive husband or perhaps even escaping the authorities herself. But until I've had a chance to question the chit, you'll mention nothing of our suspicions. Should anyone ask, all you know is that the young woman is an acquaintance of mine. Is that clear?"

"Quite clear, milord," came his doubtful reply as he gave a quick nod and skittered back out to the coach. The clatter of hooves a moment later signaled his departure.

Victor listened until the sound of the carriage had faded; then, frowning, he slowly started for the staircase. He'd been lucky, at least, in that his sister was otherwise occupied. Monique would not be fobbed off with anything less than the sort of explanation he was not yet prepared to give. As for the good doctor, a doubling of his usual fee would likely buy his silence on the matter. It had once before.

He reached the room two floors up where Peters had settled their guest, just as the butler stepped out and was closing the bedchamber door behind him.

"Everything is under control, my lord," he said in a low voice, indicating with a meaningful nod the door beyond which Monique's tiny suite of rooms lay. "I took the liberty of removing the young woman's cloak and shoes and tucking her beneath the blankets. I also lit the fire, since the room held a bit of a chill, and had one of the maids fetch a pitcher and washbasin. And now, my lord, might I bring you anything—perhaps a spot of brandy—while we await the doctor's arrival?"

"Brandy would be fine," Victor absently agreed as he reached for the latch. "I will be locking the door after me, just as a precaution, so knock first when you return."

He paused, hand on the knob, for a final glance down the hall. Given her almost uncanny affinity for intrigue in any guise, he half-expected to see his sister's curly brunette head poking out from behind her door. Satisfied that her intuitive abilities had failed her tonight, Victor slipped past the door.

Halting on the threshold, he closed the door behind him and latched it . . . and then he winced, just as he did every time he entered the chamber.

For the Blue Room had been aptly named. Every possible variation on that color theme, from the palest of robin egg blues to a hue so dark it was almost purple, was represented here. From bed hangings to rugs, the monochromatic decor had been chosen with the utmost deliberation, not by some eccentric ancestress of Victor's, but by his own mother.

Helene Saville, Lady Blackstock, had occupied the room for the years prior to her and her husband's death. Blue had been her favorite color to the exclusion of any other. In a rare bout of sentimentality, Victor had decreed that the excruciating color scheme would remain intact until such time that he brought home a bride.

Not that he had anything to fear on that account tonight, he now thought with a grim smile. The woman currently occupying the bed hardly qualified for the role of earl's wife.

Inside the chamber, the blaze of a just-lit fire provided the only light. Beyond its yellow glow lay the bed. Shadows from its curtains were so deep that he could only just make out her slim form beneath the pale blue coverlet tucked almost to her chin. In welcome contrast to the abundant blue, her mane of red-gold hair spread about her and rippled over the pillow. The brilliant color beckoned him like a flame.

Mothlike, he started toward her. His booted footsteps were muffled by the cobalt blue rug beneath his feet; still, he took care to move with silence lest he disturb her rest. Reaching the foot of the bed, he paused.

He'd erred once already this night in his treatment of her. He realized now that there was something rather voyeuristic about what he was doing. Still, he could not shake himself of the compulsion, watching her as she slept.

And sleep, he now judged it to be, rather than the deathly

stillness that earlier had held her. But with it came an odd sort of connection between them that went beyond simply being alone there together.

Almost without realizing it, he matched his own breathing to every soft inhalation she took. His chest rose and fell in the same shallow rhythm as hers, while faint rasps of breath passed his parted lips in regular issue. In the silence, he could hear a steady throbbing that was the echo of her heart pounding . . . or was it simply the rush of blood that was the sound of his own heartbeat instead?

For an instant, he wondered what it would be to find her here like this every night of his life . . . sleeping, perhaps, yet ready to awaken at his touch. Just as swiftly, he shook his head at the unlikely thought. When or if he ever married, it would be to a woman of his own class, certainly not a waif he had plucked from the streets.

How long he stood there, simply watching her, he did not know for certain. He only roused himself from this revere when a faint knock sounded. Suppressing an unwarranted frisson of irritation at the interruption, expected as it was, he lightly treaded back to the door and opened it a fraction.

Peters stood there in the hallway. A half-filled decanter and a pair of snifters was balanced on a silver tray he held, and an unctuous expression had settled upon his round face. Derek peered from around the man's narrow shoulder, looking more than a little dismayed.

"I have brought the brandy, my lord," the butler announced in a dignified whisper, "but I am afraid that Derek has returned empty-handed."

" 'Ere now, 'twasn't my fault," the other man protested in a low tone, then turned his worried glance on Victor. "I went to the doctor's place right off, milord, but no one was to home. Do ye want 'ow as I should keep tryin' to find 'im?"

"I don't think that will be necessary, since our guest seems to be resting quite comfortably now. But I would have you return there to leave a message that the doctor stop by first thing upon the morrow."

"Very good, milord." Sparing the briefest look of triumph for Peters, the driver hurried to do just that.

The butler waited until the skittering footsteps died away, then softly cleared his throat. "And what will we do about the, er, young woman, my lord? Shall I rouse one of the maids to look out for her tonight?"

"I believe that I shall keep an eye on her for a while, myself," Victor casually declared, as if the idea had just occurred to him. In truth, he had decided the moment he stepped into the room that he did not want any of the servants taking a turn with her.

Peters, meanwhile, had gone pale. Then, sputtering, he managed, "Are you c-certain, m-my lord?"

"Quite certain," he clipped out. Taking the tray from the dumbfounded Peters, he set it down on the azure blue marble pillar just inside the doorway, then addressed the man again. "I doubt that she will waken before morning, anyhow . . . but just in case, I'll leave the connecting door between the chambers open when I retire, so I can hear her if she moves about."

"As you wish, my lord. It's just that—"

He paused, and Victor frowned. "It's just that . . . what?" he prompted in a chill tone.

The butler's round cheeks reddened as candor and prudence seemingly warred within his breast. Finally he blurted in a stage whisper, "It's just that it isn't proper, my lord, not with your sister but a few steps down the hall."

Victor's first reaction was a mild flicker of irritation. Blast it all, this was *his* house. If he wanted to play sentry-cum-nursemaid to a dozen unconscious women, then he bloody well would!

Then the import of the man's words hit, and a wave of cold anger swept him. Bloody hell, his own butler—a man who had been with the family for a score of years—believed he was capable of forcing himself upon an injured woman.

"You can set your mind at ease, Peters," he said in a deathly soft voice. "I have no plans to compromise this or any other young woman while she is under my roof. After the doctor has paid his call tomorrow morning, I will make her presence known to the rest of the household. Until then I expect your cooperation in keeping that knowledge from everyone, especially my sister. Do I make myself clear?"

"Quite clear, my lord," came Peters's subdued reply as, with a swift bow, he turned and started back down the hall.

A muscle twitched in Victor's jaw as he deliberately closed the door again and shot home the bolt. He shed his coat and cravat, then caught up the decanter and poured himself a generous glassful. Setting aside the carafe, he claimed the overstuffed blue chair in the far corner beyond the fireplace.

He propped his booted feet on the hassock before him and downed a fortifying sip of the brandy. Even as the cheery blaze worked upon his outer chill, the smooth if potent liquid sent a satisfying warmth through him that dispelled a fraction of his cold anger. Another substantial sip washed away a portion of the tension that now gripped him.

In its wake came a sudden weariness that seemed to seep into his very bones. It was, he realized, the same sort of soul-draining exhaustion as had settled over him in the wake of the scandal. Time and new interests had rousted that emotion, or so he had thought.

Grimly he fought the feeling. He would stay here awhile longer, he vowed. When he'd assured himself that she would sleep through the night—and that Peters had not defied orders and spread the word of her presence—he would retire to his own chamber. Until then he would enjoy his brandy and the murmured crackling of the fire, along with the odd sort of companionship that she unknowingly had brought him.

A third swallow emptied his glass. He roused himself long enough to refill it. He was prepared to resume his chair, until his gaze lit upon the dressing table. What appeared to be a broad, slender book lay beside the woman's reticule that Derrick had rescued from the alley.

An odd item for a chit of her sort to be carrying about, he thought with a frown. Giving in to idle curiosity, he caught up the volume and settled back in his chair. He flipped open the cover to discover that it was neither text nor novel, as he had first assumed, but instead an artist's sketchbook.

As for its contents, they were decidedly gruesome.

The first drawing to catch his eye was almost a caricature. The subject was a thin man dressed in sober garb bent over a table, upon which lay a naked corpse. A shadowy audience of men—their expressions ranging from bored to angry to absorbed—watched the unlikely pair. The scene had been caught in but a few quick strokes of charcoal, yet it exuded undeniable vitality. Another drawing showed a back view of that same gentleman, his arms raised in benediction over the dead man. Still a third sketch had captured the corpse's face, eyes closed and cheeks sunken.

The remainder of the drawings were more disturbing . . . disembodied arms, legs, and torsos rendered from various angles. They reminded Victor of Leonardo's sketches, even though this artist's abilities fell far short of that master. Still, she showed unmistakable talent, along with a tendency toward whimsy. For though most of the torso drawings depicted the male genitalia in full detail, one featured an ermine-trimmed robe coyly draped over those nether regions. Another sketch showed a gnarled hand clutching an equally withered rose.

Thoughtfully Victor shut the book and glanced over at the unconscious woman. How such a collection of drawings might have come into her possession, he could not guess, save that she might have accepted them as payment for some service rendered. He could hardly picture any woman of his acquaintance coveting such pictures; still, one could never account for taste.

With a shake of his head, he put aside the book. The fire had died now to coals that gleamed like dozens of tiny red roses lit behind by the sun, so that now the entire room was bathed in shadow. Somehow he preferred it that way.

Raising the brandy snifter to his lips, Victor took another sip and commenced his vigil.

Four

I can hardly commit this to paper, so Outlandish does it sound . . . but you must Believe that what I tell you is the literal truth. Last evening, while walking home, I was Set Upon—nay, quite nearly Murdered!— by some Fiendish Monster disgorged from the very bowels of Hell!

—letter from Miss Amaryllis Meeks to Miss Mary Godwin

Heaven was blue?

The irreverent question was Amaryllis's first thought as she blearily opened her eyes to find she was lying upon a sumptuous bed draped with yards of turquoise silk. The coverlet was of the same bright hue, as were the half-dozen fringed pillows propped around her. Bright light streamed through the parted drapes of pale blue velvet whose hue was echoed in the wallpaper. Stenciled with a dozen gardens' worth of tiny blue roses, the pattern appeared to march like an army of petaled soldiers in quite a disconcerting fashion across that paler blue field.

She blinked a few times, and the roses subsided into their proper design. Satisfied, she snuggled deeper into the covers and smiled.

Was it not common knowledge that heaven would be nothing like one expected? This cheerful if gaudy chamber was certainly a far cry from the touted Pearly Gates, not that she had any intention of complaining to Him about the decor. It did strike her as odd, however, that the room held a distinct chill. Moreover she was thirsty—terribly so. And, embarrassingly, she felt in sudden need of a chamberpot. But no one should have no such bodily concerns in heaven.

Unless, of course, she was not yet dead.

Yet she had to be. The final image that lingered in her mind was that of a man . . . a dark angel with pale skin and eyes the color of the night who had brandished a wicked-looking knife before her. She had seen her terrorized face reflected in that gleaming blade, had seen her own end approaching.

At the memory, she bit back a moan that was little more than a croak. Equally frightening was the hellish memory of the creature that first had attacked her. Try though she might to forget, she could not help but remember the sensation of its cold dead hands wrapped around her throat, its fingers squeezing the life from her. And its eyes had been dead, too . . . flat orbs like slivers of black mirror that revealed nothing, but merely reflected what lay beyond it.

Had the two beings—the dark angel and the demon— been one and the same? Could it be that Death had two faces, and she had been privileged to see them both? Maybe that was why she had been spared.

The possibility, though farfetched, made as much sense as anything that thus far had happened. Another memory niggled at her, but she could not seem to capture it long enough to give it voice. Instead, determined to know her true fate, she cautiously raised herself up a few inches against the pillows.

She promptly decided she must be alive. For surely those who had passed to the Beyond were not subject to such pain as she was now feeling. Her entire body ached, as if she'd been bounced about on the cobbled street. As for her throat—

She put an uncertain hand to that bruised flesh, puffed

and tender beneath her fingers. Even breathing was an agony
and swallowing nigh impossible. She steeled herself and
tried to utter an experimental "hello," but the sound she
managed was little better than a painful croak.

With the same careful gestures, she ran both hands down
her arms and along her torso. She seemed to be in one piece,
she decided in relief. No knife wounds rent the bodice of
her bottle-green gown, though grimy streaks from where she
must have lain upon the street gave her the look of a street
urchin. As for her hair, it streamed in an untidy wave around
her shoulders. That, if nothing else, decided her. For surely
in heaven, one did not go about with one's hairpins scattered
to the four winds.

So she was alive, then. Her relief at the realization was
quickly tempered by a surge of doubt. Alive, yes, but where
was she? And, just as importantly, how had she gotten here?

She pushed the coverlet to one side and eased her legs
over the edge of the bed. Then, sweeping back the tangle of
hair from her face, she glanced about her again . . . and
froze.

For she was not alone in this room.

In an overstuffed blue chair in the corner opposite the
elaborately carved door sprawled an unknown man, apparently asleep. That latter fact stilled the worst of her panic,
so that she could take the measure of him with a small
degree of calm.

The most she could discern from her vantage point was
that he was dark of hair and long of limb. With his chin
sunk onto his chest in sleep, his face was all but hidden by
the points of his collar and the dramatic sweep of black hair
across his brow.

His garb, she noted, was far more stylish than his surroundings. He must have dressed originally for an elegant
evening out, for she noted the black jacket and snowy neckcloth carelessly tossed over the chair back. Now, however,
he was wearing only black trousers and waistcoat, along

with a white linen shirt, the top few buttons of which were scandalously unfastened. His feet, encased in gleaming black Hessians, were propped on the ottoman before him. One arm dangled over the chair's edge, the limp fingers pointing to an empty brandy snifter on the blue rug.

That last detail gave her pause.

For he was no manservant put to watch over her, she felt certain. Even in repose, this man had a decisively patrician air about him . . . if not the master of this particular household, then someone of similar import. The sumptuous furnishings, the lush fabrics, the exquisite furbelows, all bespoke deep if less than tasteful pockets, so that she guessed herself to be in the household of someone of distinction—a baron, perhaps, or even an earl.

But did not explain what this man was doing in her bedchamber and, from the looks of him, quite the worse for strong drink.

Swiftly she cast about for some manner of explanation. Perhaps he had stumbled across her in that ill-fated alley and, not knowing her name or direction, offered her sanctuary in his own home. As for his presence in her room, maybe he'd feared that the madman would somehow come after her. Then, growing bored with his duties as guard, maybe he had indulged in a single brandy before falling into innocent sleep.

She frowned. The scenario was not past believing, even though experience had taught her that the gentry were more likely to pass by than deign to assist a commoner in need. Still, he might indeed be her gallant.

But what if his motives had been more base? What if he had found her lying unconscious in the alleyway and carried her off for nefarious purposes of his own? Or what if *he* were the man who had attacked her?

A shiver raced down her spine at the possibility. She could, of course, take a closer look at him and learn the truth. Conversely she could take the coward's way out and flee now, never to know if the man were a murderous fiend or guilty only of gallantry.

Reminding herself that she already had taken one foolhardy risk this past four-and-twenty hours, she took a deep breath and opted for the coward's way.

A glance about the room showed that her boots were neatly placed beside the dressing table in the opposite corner, atop which her reticule lay. Her cloak had been draped across a chair near the fireplace, where the remains of the previous night's blaze gave off the barest hint of warmth. Of her sketchbook, however, she saw no sign. Doubtless her hard-won collection of anatomical drawings had been left behind in that anonymous alley.

Disappointment welled in her breast at their loss. The emotion was greater for the fact she could not be certain when the next such opportunity as last night's exhibition would again be available to her. She consoled herself with the knowledge that she was lucky, after all, to be alive. Little good a library's worth of anatomical sketches would do her tucked away for all eternity in St. Pancras's churchyard!

Her bottle-green skirts whispered against the silken coverlet as Amaryllis eased her way off the bed. She made her way on tiptoe toward the dressing table, passing as she did so the closed door with its large brass key left in the lock. Beside the door, she noted, was a marble pillar upon which sat an empty brandy decanter and a second snifter.

Had he presumed that, upon awakening, she might require a fortifying sip? she wondered with a frown. Or had he been expecting yet another visitor to join them?

Shaking off the question, she continued toward the dressing table. The carpet beneath her stockinged feet muffled her steps; still, she kept a wary eye on her unwitting guard, lest he stir.

It was the glimpse of her own reflection in the dressing table mirror that almost was her undoing. Choking back a gasp, she stared in shock at the livid pattern of bruises on her throat. Distinctly she saw each imprint, larger than a crown piece, where brutish fingers had tried to crush the life from her. No wonder she had lost her voice, she thought with a horrified shiver.

Spurred to haste by the sight, she took but a moment to reclaim her boots and pull them on again, then grab up her reticule. Then she shot an uncertain glance at her cloak. The chair over which it was draped sat before the fireplace, half-way across the room . . . and an arm's length away from the man who might or might not be her last night's attacker.

Leave it, the coward's voice spoke up. Why risk awakening him, when she could simply slip into the outer hall and flee the house, with him none the wiser? After all, it was but a length of drab brown wool.

But how will you explain its loss to Father? her practical voice wanted to know. *Besides which, the walk home will likely be chilly and you hardly have cloaks to spare.*

This time, sternness of mind won out. Hardly daring to breathe, she started toward the fireplace and the garment that dangled there like the trampled banner of a conquered army.

It was a journey of perhaps a dozen paces, though each seemed the distance of a paddock. By the time she reached the mantelpiece, a fine beading of sweat pearled her forehead despite the room's chill. Yet the man had not stirred, though to her ears every step she'd taken had echoed like an empty church. Bolstered by this tiny triumph, she stretched out a hesitant hand, her fingers closing on the worn wool. Then, deftly, she eased the garment from the chair.

It wasn't until after she had slipped on the cloak and spared a final glance in the sleeping man's direction that she noticed it . . . her precious sketchbook, propped upon his lap.

On his lap!

Her relief that her work had not been lost, after all, was promptly supplanted by a surge of outrage. Even Talbot had never been allowed to see her works in progress, yet this complete stranger apparently had passed a portion of his evening thumbing through her sketches!

But barely had she acknowledged her heated anger than it dwindled into chill despair. Leaving behind the drawings was unthinkable, yet however could she retrieve the volume without disturbing him?

A corner of her mind chided herself for turning the task into a veritable Drury Lane melodrama. How much simpler it would be to awaken her host, kindly ask him to return her property and then, with a word of thanks, be on her way. But the risks if she judged wrongly, if the man turned out to be the demon she had met in the fog . . .

Sternness of mind, she silently reminded herself. The choice made, she drew the cloak more tightly about her to prevent the errant fabric from brushing against him. Then, brow furrowed and lower lip caught between her teeth in concentration, she reached out an unsteady hand.

One edge of the book's spine had slid off the man's knee, so that it would be an easy enough matter to grasp the wide volume. More difficult would prove the task of removing it from his lap. Should she ease it from him in careful stages, she wondered, or retrieve it in a single swift move?

The latter, she boldly decided as her fingers closed over its edge.

To her immense astonishment, the man never stirred, not even when the edge of her cloak brushed his Hessians despite her caution. She straightened and shut her eyes in a brief gesture of relief. Then, tucking the slim volume beneath her arm, she turned on silent feet to leave.

Barely had she taken a step, however, than she heard a low, strangled gasp from behind her.

"Bloody hell, not again," rasped a man's hoarse voice an instant later, those few words laced with anger and despair.

Choking back her own gasp, she spun about to see that her ersatz host had straightened in his chair. A second groan issued from him as he scrubbed both palms across his face in an attempt to banish the last vestiges of sleep. Then, seemingly reconciled to wakefulness, he lowered his hands and abruptly met her gaze. Eyes wide in disbelief, Amaryllis stared back.

Dear God, it's he.

Swiftly she took in the man's familiar features. Black hair, black eyes, pale skin. It was not the face of the corpselike demon but, rather, the sinfully handsome visage of the dark angel. And he was here alone with her!

Her attempt at a scream tore forth from her bruised throat in a croak of horror, and she started toward the door at a dead run. A heartbeat later, she heard the muffled thud of booted feet that was the dark angel abandoning his chair and giving chase.

Terror lent her a gazelle's fleetness. Brushing past the marble column stationed there, she reached the door before her pursuer. She gave a sob of relief and twisted the knob only to discover that the room's sole exit had been barred.

Frantic, she wrenched at the key left protruding from the lock, scarce noticing when her notebook slipped from her grasp and skittered to the floor. She heard the welcome click of well-oiled metal as the tumblers fell into place. She caught the knob again and gave it another turn. This time the door sprang obediently open.

And then two well-manicured hands, one splayed on either side of her, slammed against that carved wood panel to shut it once more.

She stood where she was, fingers still clutching the knob as she struggled to understand that her only means of escape was cut off. It took a moment longer for her to realize that, worse, the fiend had trapped her in his embrace.

She choked back a horrified moan. His chest was all but pressed to her back, while on either side of her, a long arm encased in tailored white linen barred her way. She could feel the heat of his body, warmth emanating from him like a well-stoked furnace. She could breathe in his very scent that was equal parts expensive brandy and fine-milled soap mingled with the faint if unmistakably male scent of his flesh.

It occurred to her then that the man would likely now finish the job that he had started the night before. Perhaps that was why the Demon's victims had been found well after their disappearances. Perhaps he had captured all of them alive and then killed them elsewhere.

Even as that terrifying thought formed, she felt the dark angel's warm breath upon her neck. In a steel-edged voice, he demanded, "And just where in the bloody hell did you think you were going?"

Five

The prosaic question restored Amaryllis to a bit of sanity. She pressed a hand to her breast in a reflexive attempt to slow her wildly thrumming heart. Taking a steadying breath, she turned around.

Her fearful gaze collided with the man's collar, scandalously undone. He was taller than she had realized, the top of her head just reaching his shoulder. As for his pose, it eerily mirrored that of a lover, the way he hovered over her with a familiarity that she'd never allowed any other man. He stood so close that she could make out the dark stubble roughening his chin and the amber blot on his snowy shirt-front where he must have splashed brandy the night before.

"I suppose that I will have to do all the talking," she heard him say, "since I suspect from those nasty bruises on your lovely throat that you'd have trouble carrying on a conversation. I will presume, however, that your hearing is unaffected."

I am just fine, she tried to retort with cool dignity, but the words came out in a pitiful croak. Frustrated, she managed instead a curt nod by way of reply and raised her gaze higher.

She lingered a moment on his firm yet sensual lips, so different from the cruel, slack mouth of last night's demon creature. His were the lips of a rake, a roué . . . the sort of lips from which would spill sweet lies designed to ensnare an unwitting female, the sort of lips that had kissed and conquered any number of women.

And what would it be like to kiss such a man, the idle question flashed through her mind, *heaven or hell?*

Shocked by the wanton thought, she jerked her gaze up to meet his eyes. No soulless orbs, these eyes were instead alive with cool intelligence, seeming to probe her thoughts and fears as casually as she might page through the latest novel. Far more unnerving, however, was the flicker of sensual interest she saw beneath the pose of chill indifference.

Then an emotion she could not identify flashed through those dark eyes. He reached a hand toward her, and she glimpsed a heavy gold ring adorning it just before he brushed his fingers along her bruised flesh.

Recalling the cold, dead hands of the demon creature wrapping around her throat, she tried to pull away. The door at her back blocked her retreat, however, leaving her no choice but to endure his touch.

Yet it was not so much a touch as it was a caress. Unlike the Demon's hand, his was warm with life. And despite the elegant ring he wore, his was not the soft, smooth flesh of an aristocrat, but the workworn hand of a laborer. As he drew his fingers back, she could see those digits were crisscrossed with several scratches, as if he habitually toyed with some small, clawed beast.

"What a shame to mar such a work of beauty," he murmured, and it took her an instant to realize he referred to the bruises on her throat. "I wish I might have spared you this."

Spared her, indeed! A frisson of anger swept her, dispelling her momentary confusion. No doubt his plans were to dispatch her, here and now. But she would not make things easy for him, she vowed. Defiantly she raised her chin and then sent her open palm careening toward his stubbled cheek.

He must have read something of her intent in her expression. In a single deft move, he caught her wrist in his free hand just before she contacted his face. She winced at the sudden, cruel pressure of his fingers, regretting the impulse that had spurred her puny attack against him. No doubt she had sealed her fate with that mutinous act.

And then his grip on her eased, while cool amusement lightened his dark gaze. In a deliberate gesture, he lowered her hand to her side, his fingers still encircling her wrist as he favored her with a wry look.

"Quite the red-haired vixen, are we not? I rather suspect I am lucky that you are speechless, as well, for the moment."

Then the humor died from his eyes. "And now I think we need to sort through what happened last night . . . that is, if you will grant me a moment to speak without your trying to run away or pummel me again."

Sort through? She stared up at him in disbelief. She knew quite well what had happened, remembered all too clearly the knife he had held at her throat. How he could hope to explain away such villainy, she could not guess, but neither did she care to listen to his lies.

Then her practical inner voice spoke up. *Indulge him. Let him believe that you've given up, and perhaps he will lower his guard.*

Cautiously she nodded her agreement, schooling her expression to blandness as she cast about for some sort of weapon. All she need do was find some way to distract him, disable him, and then she could be out the door.

She was rewarded when, releasing his hold on her, the man lowered his other arm and took a few steps back.

"There, much better," he said, raising both hands in mock surrender. "So now let me begin by telling you that, contrary to what you obviously believe, I have no dishonorable intentions toward you. Neither did I try to murder you last night, although someone else apparently did make such an attempt. I merely had the misfortune to find you lying in an alleyway. At first glance, I presumed you dead—hence, the knife."

When she raised her eyebrows in silent alarm, he gave her the barest hint of a smile.

"I believe that the standard test to ascertain whether or not an unconscious person is breathing is to put a mirror to his lips," he explained. "As I had no such convenient item upon my person, the blade had to suffice. And since I knew neither your identity or direction, I thought it best to bring you home with me so you might recover from your attack in some degree of comfort. If you care to know, you are in Hanover Square, some distance from where I found you."

Hanover Square.

A fashionable address in an area given over to the peerage, and quite the proper place. As for his explanation, it, too, was reasonable enough. Indeed his was far more conceivable a scenario than that of two separate persons—him and the Demon creature—each attacking her upon the very same night. Yet his story seemed a trifle too neat, too glib. Moreover she sensed beneath his bland exterior some darker emotion, something that sent a superstitious shiver running through her.

All at once, she was certain that he was lying or, at the very least, omitting some important portion of the truth.

"I do hope that explanation satisfies you," he added. Then, a knife-edge of steel hardening his matter-of-fact tone, he finished, "And I trust that, once you regain your powers of speech, you'll not go about the city trying to convince people that the respectable Earl of Blackstock is in truth the notorious Barkshire Demon."

The Earl of Blackstock, was he?

She gave a quick nod of agreement to his last words, even as she edged closer to the marble column stationed at the door. Just because he was Quality did not preclude his being a cold-blooded murderer . . . nor did his attempt to fob off this innocuous tale on her mean that he did not plan, after all, to kill her.

But even as she came to this conclusion, satisfaction flickered in his dark eyes. "I knew I could count on you to be a sensible sort," he said, his tone wry though the words were approving. Then, with a host's polite aplomb, he gestured toward the chair that he had just vacated.

"Do take a seat," he offered and turned in that direction. "I'll stir up the fire a bit, then ring for a bite of breakfast. And you should know that I left word last night for my personal physician to stop by and attend you as soon as possible this morning. In the meantime, however, perhaps we should—"

What he intended them to do, Amaryllis was not to find out. The moment he turned from her, she snatched up the decanter from the marble column. Not stopping to consider the consequences, she smashed that vessel against the back of Blackstock's head.

He dropped to his knees amid a gentle rain of crystal shards and fine brandy. Then, with a groan, his lordship collapsed onto the bright blue carpet and lay still.

Amaryllis stared down at his supine form, the broken neck of the decanter still clutched in her hand. From this vantage point, the man looked far less threatening, almost defenseless. Had she killed him, she wildly wondered, or merely rendered him unconscious? Her intent, after all, had been but to gain her freedom, not commit murder.

Frantic, she tossed aside the remains of the decanter and dropped to her own knees beside him. She ignored both the broken glass and the inner voice that asked why she worried over a man who might well be a killer. A quick look assured her that he was breathing; still, blood gleamed in a crimson patch against his dark hair, proof that she indeed had dealt him a serious injury.

But what else could you do? she sternly reminded herself. Certainly he would have shown her no mercy. Her concern should be fleeing the house before anyone else took note of her presence, not ministering to this villain. Besides which, had he not just mentioned that he'd already summoned his physician? Doubtless the good doctor would be as happy to prescribe for his lordship as for she.

Oddly reassured by the thought that Blackstock would be attended to, she scrambled to her feet again and pulled open the door a few inches. The hall beyond, she saw in relief, was blessedly deserted.

With the same care, she slipped through the doorway and into the corridor. She paused there long enough to reach back around the door's edge and grasp the oversized brass key. That accomplished, she pushed the door quietly shut again and locked it from without, then shoved the key into her reticule.

Let him see how he likes being held prisoner, she thought with a triumphant nod. Now, even should her host regain consciousness before she made her escape, he would be hard-pressed to follow after her.

The room in which she'd been ensconced lay at one corner of this floor. Other doors led to what she presumed were additional bedchambers. Opposite her lay a broad spiral staircase, the landing of which was rimmed by elaborately carved balustrades. Likely she was at least two floors up from ground level, which meant she had any number of steps with which to contend. Still, chances were that this town house, though larger than many she'd seen, was laid out in the usual simple lines. She need not fear losing herself in a warren of odd hallways and unexpected chambers common to country estates.

Mindful of squeaking boards that bedeviled even the finest of establishments, she reached the staircase without incident. There she crouched level with the balustrade and peered through the gracefully turned dowels. A series of white marble steps stretched below her. Halfway down lay a second landing, where the stairway split into a pair of swanlike curves that extended to the ground floor. From her vantage point, she could see no sign of any other household member moving about.

Sternness of mind, she faintly repeated the comforting litany. Conscious of the seconds ticking by, she opted now for speed, rather than for stealth. She caught up the hem of her gown lest she trip herself; then, with a final steadying breath, she started down the steps at a dead run.

The clatter of her sensible boots upon the marble rang like shod hooves upon cobble, loud enough to rouse even the dullest servants from their early morning tasks. She was dismayed but not surprised, then, when she heard the answering echo of someone else's hasty footsteps drifting up to her from the sumptuous foyer.

"Here now, young woman, what is going on here?" demanded a pinched, unfamiliar male voice some distance away.

Barely had Amaryllis reached the bottom of the stairway than she glimpsed the source of those disapproving words. He came trotting with undignified haste from one of the foyer's half-dozen doorways, a shiny-faced man of middle years dressed in a butler's sober garb. Heart pounding, she paused an instant to catch her breath and take the measure of him.

Was the man but an innocent servant, she frantically wondered, or was he instead a willing minion bound to do his master's evil bidding?

In the next moment, the butler spotted her and halted. Wittingly or not, he stood between her and the broad pair of carved doors that she knew must lead to the street beyond—and to freedom.

His look of distrustful recognition warned her that he was not surprised by her presence there; however, he did not appear unduly alarmed at the fact that she was still counted among the living. At the very least, then, he must know of the earl's penchant for bringing home unknown women.

Whether he was privy to his master's darker proclivities, she could not guess but certainly she dared not trust him.

"Here now, young woman," the man repeated in the same reproving tones, "you cannot go bounding about his lordship's town house like this. I suggest that you return to your chamber at once to await the physician's arrival."

Physician.

Amaryllis frowned. The earl, she recalled, also had mentioned summoning a doctor, but to what end? This unknown person might as easily drug her into submission as act the role of rescuer. Chances were that the good doctor was situated comfortably if figuratively in the earl's waistcoat pocket. Even if she could convince the man that her life was in danger, he likely would turn a blind eye to her plight.

She had but one choice, then . . . to flee this house.

Even as she prepared to evade the butler, a faint if unmistakably enraged thudding drifted down to them from two floors up. Blackstock must have regained his senses and was trying to summon aid, she realized.

The angry pounding served to distract the butler. Well-bred distress was plain upon his face as he debated which was the wiser course—checking out the disturbance above or detaining her as doubtless were his orders.

Amaryllis gave him no time to make up his mind but rushed toward the entry door. By the time the butler realized what she was about, she had grasped the shiny brass knob and twisted it.

"Stop . . . what will his lordship say?" came the man's agitated cry as, cloak aswirl, she darted out into the crisp morning and slammed the door after her.

She paused on the stoop just long enough to take in the scene before her—an elegant, well-tended square, blessedly bustling with liveried servants and carriages, lined on all four sides with elegant town houses. In the midst of that splendor sat a hired hackney parked but a few yards from her down the cobbled street, as if waiting her instructions.

She started toward that vehicle at an undignified run, though she did pause once to glance behind her. Doubtless she would be directing a constable to this very spot in the near future, so that she should be quite certain as to just where it was that Blackstock lived.

His town house was a tasteful, three-story residence similar to, if larger than, its neighbors. Like the rest, only a few steps separated it from the broad lane that it overlooked. Painted a discreet shade of cream trimmed in brown, its only distinguishing characteristic was the brass number affixed to one side of its front door.

Thirteen.

A grimly appropriate address for such a man, she thought with a shiver as she reached the coach. With an effort, she summoned voice enough to croak out her direction to the bemused driver. "And do hurry," she finished with a final frantic look behind her. No one was in pursuit as yet, she saw in relief.

The hackney driver's doubtful expression vanished with the coins that she plucked from her reticule. She had just settled inside before he whipped up his team and they began clattering down the road. It was only when Amaryllis was in sight of St. Pancras's Church and home that she realized she had not quite made a clean escape.

Her sketchbook, with its pages of precious drawings, had been left behind . . . hostage to the dark angel.

Six

How I escaped the Fiend's lair is another tale in itself, but suffice it to say, my dear Friend, that I am safe . . . at least, for the moment. Now my task must be to learn what I can of this man and his doings, so that I might determine whether it is he or that soulless creature that is the Scourge of our city.

—letter from Miss Amaryllis Meeks to
Miss Mary Godwin

"She coshed you with a brandy decanter?"

Her tone incredulous, Lady Monique gazed up with wide, dark eyes at her older brother. Then, sidestepping the sprinkling of broken crystal that had yet to be cleared up, she unceremoniously shoved aside his valet. Moresdale, who was holding a damp compress to the back of his master's head, relinquished his post with only a modicum of poor grace.

Still unsteady on his feet, Victor was in no position to protest as Monique raised up on tiptoe and took a look at his injury for herself. Inwardly, though, he cringed at the indignity of it all. Here he had rescued the red-haired chit from likely death, and she repaid him by turning on him like the proverbial serpent.

Thankfully it had been Moresdale who had first responded to his heated calls for assistance. Every bedchamber on the third floor could be opened by the same key, so it had proved an easy matter for the man to gain entrance. Upon unlocking the Blue Room, the valet had been greeted by the sight of Victor clutching the doorjamb to steady himself, while blood dripped with a rather ghastly rhythm down the back of his fine linen shirt.

The former boxer had promptly struck an offensive posture as he glanced about the chamber for whatever villains had overcome his master. Remembering that the valet had not been privy to last night's events, Victor had gritted his teeth and assured the man that no gang of thugs had broken into the town house. Then, alternating between hot outrage and keen embarrassment, he had gone on to explain about the mysterious woman he'd rescued.

Moresdale had listened with interest, agreeing with Victor that it would likely do no good to pursue the chit. "She's long gone by now, milord, and ye're well rid o' 'er, any 'ow," the man had opined as he splashed a bit of water into the washbasin and caught up a clean towel.

A muffled shriek from a passing maid in the hallway had cut short the valet's comments and set Victor's head to throbbing even worse. With a few curt words, Moresdale had sent the frightened girl off in search of Peters and Derek. That accomplished, the valet had set to mopping the blood from the back of Victor's skull.

"A flush hit to the nob, milord," he had diagnosed in pugilist's cant, "but 'tain't a fatal blow. E'en so, 'tis a nasty scalp wound, which is why ye're bleedin' like a butchered goose at Christmastide."

By that time, the commotion had drawn a yawning Monique to the Blue Room door. Neither man had been able to shoo her off. Her threats to call in a constable finally had compelled Victor to give her an account of what had passed last night and this morning . . . up to and including his unfortunate encounter with the business end of the brandy decanter.

Now he heard his sister's faint gasp as she took in his

bloodied appearance. Her rare show of sisterly concern almost made worthwhile his pain . . . almost. For that gratifying response was followed by a gurgle of musical laughter as she pranced by him to settle herself in the same blue armchair where he'd spent the past night.

"Why, she truly did do you a bit of damage," the girl exclaimed as she smoothed the bright yellow silk of her dressing gown. "Indeed I've been tempted to try the same with you any number of times the past two years, but I fear I am far too civilized to carry through with my plans."

She tossed her dark curls and laughed again. An echoing peal of humor uncannily similar to hers issued from the plump, red-and-gray-feathered parrot jauntily perched upon her slim shoulder.

Victor shot both the bird—Wilhelm, by name—and his owner a baleful look. He'd long since quit expecting even a pretense of respect from his sibling, but he'd be damned if he'd let a talking feather-duster play him for the fool.

"It's hardly a joking matter," he hotly countered, then winced as his emphatic tone sent another wave of pain through his skull. Biting back a curse, he snatched the compress from the hovering Moresdale and dismissed the man with a gesture. He waited until the valet was out of earshot before he addressed Monique again.

"I'll have you know, I was unconscious for several minutes. Hell, the wench bloody well could have killed me, and where would that have left you?"

"Free to do as I please, brother mine," came her saucy reply . . . far too pert for a chit of sixteen years. "But given that hard head of yours, I am certain that you were in no danger of dying, though it would have served you quite right. Whatever possessed you, bringing a fallen woman off the streets and into our home?"

"Whatever possessed you?" Wilhelm primly echoed, with a tsking sound reminiscent of Peters in a disapproving mood.

Victor clenched his jaw. One day soon, he would bribe

Cook into making a small substitution the next time she served up her famous squab pie.

"I don't know that she was a 'fallen woman.' " This was in answer to Monique's question, rather than her pet's, though both regarded him with identical bright interest. "Hell, I don't even know her name. All I know is that I could hardly leave her lying in the street, not after she survived an attack by the Barkshire Demon."

"The Barkshire Demon?" Monique straightened in her seat, the amusement draining from her expression. "That is who tried to kill her, then?"

"I'm only guessing, but it seems a logical deduction. She is an attractive young woman; she was out on the streets alone; it was a foggy night."

"No wonder the poor creature was half out of her mind!" the girl exclaimed and gave an exaggerated shiver. Then she frowned. "Why, your mystery woman might be the sole person in the city to know the killer's true identity. Did she not even hint as to who he is?"

"Unfortunately she was either too frightened or in too much pain to speak. Judging from the bruises on her throat where the fiend must have seized her, I would presume it was the latter, since she proved quite brave enough to make an escape from here. At any rate, we did not discuss a list of possible suspects."

Which was just as well, he sourly reflected, given that his own name likely would have topped her roster.

For her part, the garrulous Monique—who had never in her sixteen years suffered from any similar such loss of vocal power—looked properly appalled at the thought of the woman's injuries. "I cannot imagine such a thing. But just think, Vic, had she been able to talk, you might have been the one to solve these horrid crimes."

"I would rather doubt that. Assuming that she even saw who attacked her, chances were that she would not be able to put a name to his face."

"But surely she would recognize him should they ever meet again," the girl persisted. "Why, you could have driven her about the city each night searching for likely suspects. Of course, you would have had to wear disguises, and I could have come along to allay suspicion—"

"Begging pardon, my lord," Peters's subdued voice from the hallway interrupted, "but the doctor is belowstairs. Should I show him up, or do you prefer to go down?"

Victor favored the butler with a sour look. Peters had already made a previous appearance on the scene to dolefully admit how he had let the red-haired woman make good her escape. Only the fact that Victor himself had been outwitted by the chit had kept him from sacking the servant on the spot.

"Send him on up," Victor now decreed in answer to Peters's question, then turned to his sister. "I'll see my physician alone, if you don't mind. Go on, now, and take that feathered monstrosity with you."

"But I—"

"Go."

He stabbed a finger in the direction of the open door, the gesture sending another wave of pain through his skull. Manfully he ignored the sensation and watched while Monique flounced her indignant way out of the chamber. Wilhelm, still perched on her shoulder, cocked a bright eye in his direction.

"A joking matter," the bird solemnly opined and then gave another silvery laugh that echoed down the hallway.

Victor resisted the urge to slam the door after the pair. Instead he settled back in the blue armchair to await the doctor's appearance, recalling as he did so what had happened the previous night after he had set aside the sketchbook.

He'd not intended to fall asleep last night; rather he had planned to keep watch over his mysterious charge until she awakened the next morning. But the effect of the brandy combined with the cheerful crackling of the fire had proved a powerful soporific. Before he had realized what was happening, he had dozed off, the volume with its pages of unsettling images forgotten on his knee.

Unfortunately his few hours of sleep had proved anything but restful.

Even now Victor found himself fighting off a sense of unease as he recalled snatches of his fitful dreams. For the most part, they had consisted of kaleidoscopic images of human body parts—hands, feet, heads, torsos—all torn straight from the pages of the sketchbook he earlier had perused. Interspersed with these bloodless if gruesome figments had been the even more disquieting images of the red-haired woman whom he'd rescued.

Rather than bruised and unconscious, she had been vibrantly, tantalizingly awake. Her flame-and-gold hair spilled about her shoulders like a sunset as, laughing, she had beckoned to him. Yet every time he drew closer, she danced out of reach like a playful chestnut filly unwilling to be bridled. At last his dream self had proved swift enough to seize her, only to have her dissolve like mist in his arms.

Even as he had mourned his loss, another woman appeared in her place. The image was one he'd seen in his dreams time and again these past months, one he had striven to forget . . . that of a young, once-pretty female whose bloody, battered visage was the savage work of a man's fists. Her blood was on his hands, her death on his conscience, and even in his sleep he knew she did not rest easily.

It had been the dead woman's cries that had awakened him. And then his sleep-blurred gaze had met that of the red-haired woman, awake and standing before him, and he had forgotten everything but her. But barely had their gazes locked than he had seen the fear in her eyes. She had fled, he had pursued, and things promptly had gone from bad to worse.

"Good morning, my lord," came a man's voice from the corridor, the words returning Victor to the present.

He glanced up to see framed in the doorway the soberly garbed figure of Talbot Meeks, his personal physician. At the sight of him, Victor managed a faint smile and gestured him in.

"Ah, yes, Dr. Meeks. It would seem I have summoned you here under false pretenses," he said, as the man made his bows. "You see, I had another patient waiting for you earlier, but it appears I am now the one in need of your care."

"So I see, my lord."

With those smooth words of agreement, the man set down his leather satchel on the blue marble pillar and began removing his worn frock coat. As always he exuded an air of cool competence at odds with the swagger and bluster that was second nature to numerous of his colleagues.

Indeed he rather reminded Victor of a cleric, with his high forehead and sunken cheeks that bespoke late hours and forgotten meals. As for the rest of the man's features, they were pleasant enough if unremarkable . . . that was, save for a pair of cool, assessing gray eyes that could size up a man with a keen accuracy belied by his mild demeanor. It had been Meeks that Victor had summoned the night of Jane Belfleur's murder, confident that the man would prove closed mouthed as a Papist confessor in the handling of the matter. Victor's confidence—and his coin—had not been misplaced.

"Peters and Moresdale advised me of the general situation," the doctor now continued as he set aside his jacket. "If I understand correctly, last night you rescued an unfortunate young woman from the streets. You brought her home with you to recover, only to have her take a most unceremonious leave of you this morning. And now, my lord, if I might make a brief examination of your injury . . ."

A moment later, Meeks stepped back and gave Victor an

appraising look. "A distressing wound, milord. Still, since the bleeding has ceased and you do not appear to have suffered a concussion, I would predict a swift and uneventful recovery with no further efforts required on my part. Of course, if you wish, I can send over a surgeon to stitch you up."

"That won't be necessary," Victor hastened to assure him. In the course of his military career, he'd seen too much of the sort of butchery that such men performed for him to willingly fall under a surgeon's care. Though a handful of that profession were gifted healers, too many more were ill-trained and tended to hack away at a man at the slightest provocation.

Meeks nodded. The barest hint of a smile that played on his thin lips indicated he knew the direction of Victor's thoughts and concurred.

"Very good, my lord."

He returned to his satchel and plucked forth a small paper packet, which he set on the marble pillar beside the unused brandy snifter. "This powder will ease the worst of your discomfort. For the next two mornings and nights, add a spoonful or so to a glass of water and drink the mixture. If it brings no measurable relief, send me word and I will have an apothecary bring around something a bit more potent. I will, of course, inform Moresdale to keep a close watch on you for a time, just in case. And now, my lord, might I be of any further service?"

Victor started to shake his head, then paused. While awaiting rescue earlier, he had noticed a familiar slim volume lying forgotten on the carpet beside the door. Oddly unwilling to let anyone else in the household besides himself view the collection of gruesome images, he had secreted the sketchbook beneath the chair moments before Moresdale unlocked the door.

Now, however, it occurred to him that the good doctor might be the one to shed some light as to what those drawings meant.

Whether or not they had any connection to the woman, he could not say. If they could help him track down the chit, however, so much the better. His head still throbbing, he got to his feet and searched beneath the seat cushion.

"There is one favor I might ask of you," he replied and plucked forth the volume. "Our mysterious young woman had this in her possession. I wonder what you might make of it."

With an obliging nod, Meeks took the proffered sketchbook and flipped it open. Barely had he scanned the first page, however, than he shut the volume with a hasty little snap.

"This appears to be a collection of anatomical drawings, perhaps belonging to a student from the Royal Academy, or even a physician in training. Doubtless it was lost by someone else earlier and coincidentally turned up alongside this young woman of yours. Or perhaps the chit found the volume on the street, herself, and hoped to sell it to the rag man for a few cents. At any rate, I cannot see how these drawings have any but the most superficial connection to her."

By now Victor had come to much the same conclusion. Before he could point out as much, however, the doctor went on. "Would you mind telling me in greater detail, my lord, just how you happened upon this woman, and in what state you found her? The information does have a bearing upon the situation, I assure you," he hurried to add when Victor lifted a questioning brow at this bit of impertinence.

Succinctly Victor related events from the time that Derek first had halted the carriage until the girl's flight from the manor house an hour before. The doctor listened, his lean features taut and gray gaze intense.

"And her appearance, my lord. Would you mind giving me a description of her?"

A battered rose, was his first instinctive response, recalling her petal-soft skin, brutally bruised, and the glorious red of her hair. Putting aside poetry, he instead gave the doctor a dry recitation of her features.

"And you say that when you found her, my lord, she was unconscious?"

"She regained her senses only for a moment as I stood over her, and then fell back into a swoon." No need to mention that it had been the sight of his wielding a knife practically in her face that had provoked the chit's reaction.

"So she never gave you any description of her attacker," the doctor persisted, "not even this morning when she awakened?"

"There was no opportunity for such discussion—besides which, the nature of her injuries was such that she appeared unable to speak," he opined, going on to describe for the doctor the extent of her bruises.

Thoughtfully Meeks nodded. "And have you perhaps formed your own opinion as to who her assailant might have been?"

Victor started to shake his head, then paused. Something in the doctor's carefully worded questions had begun to send a ripple of unease down his spine. It was almost as if Meeks knew the attacker's identity, or else thought he did. And suddenly he realized in what direction the man's suspicions were headed.

"Bloody hell, you think *I* was the one who assaulted her," Victor choked out. Though Talbot Meeks was the one living person who had reason to believe him capable of such actions, he had paid dearly enough for the man's discretion not to be subjected to such accusations in his own home!

Something flickered in Meeks's gray eyes—not so much understanding as the cool sort of pity a physician reserved for his less tractable patients.

"To the contrary, my lord, I am quite convinced that you are but an innocent party to this madness," he smoothly countered. "Had you any evil intent, you certainly would not have gathered a host of witnesses who could connect you with the young woman in question. Rather my concern is for her."

"So you think she could identify her assailant, then?"

"It would seem likely." The doctor paused, his gray eyes narrowing. "You have heard mention, I suppose, of a brutal killer dubbed by the scandal sheets as the Barkshire Demon?"

At Victor's nod, he went on. "I have followed the accounts of these murders, purely from a scientific point of view, of course. If the stories are correct, the injuries suffered by the past victims all seem quite similar and by their nature would indicate that the women had found themselves face-to-face with their attacker. The description you gave of the injuries suffered by the young woman you rescued is consistent with those of the Demon's other victims . . . only this victim managed to escape him."

"And if she knows who the Demon is," Victor slowly finished for him, "then her life might yet be in danger."

"Which is why I intend to run the young woman to ground. It will be but a simple matter to make the rounds of the charity hospitals and gin mills—places in which you would not care to set foot, my lord—and see if I cannot discover someone of her description marked by such bruises as you have noted. If I learn anything of use, I will certainly inform both you and the proper authorities. And now, my lord," he finished, gathering up his satchel and tucking the sketchbook beneath one arm, "if I might take my leave . . ."

"One moment, Dr. Meeks. I believe that, by default, I am now the owner of those drawings."

The man's expression was impassive as he relinquished the volume. "Forgive me, my lord. I had thought to attempt to locate whoever it was who lost the sketchbook. Such a collection, while of little use to yourself, would prove a sad loss to its owner."

"Even so, I find myself fancying the book."

Victor gave an idle flip through pages, pausing at one or

another clever rendering of the anatomy lesson. The good doctor did have a point. He would be doing its legitimate owner no service by keeping the volume himself.

He paused, however, at one sketch . . . that of the worn hand clutching a faded rose. Perhaps it was just that particular flower that intrigued him, or maybe it was the sad symbolism he read into the drawing as a whole. Whatever the reason, he found himself impulsively tearing that page from the book. Then, with a wry shake of his head, he handed the volume back over.

"Ah, well, perhaps you are right," he conceded. "However, I trust you do not begrudge me a souvenir of my adventure."

"Certainly not, my lord," Meeks replied in an equally smooth tone. "And I am sure that some luckless young surgeon will indeed thank you for keeping the balance of the drawings safe. And now, my lord, good day."

Victor waited until the man, with a final bow, pulled the door shut behind him. Then, his battered skull forgotten for the moment, he settled once again in the blue chair.

Would Meeks find the red-haired woman? The odds of his stumbling across her in some dockside tavern seemed poor, at best. Chances were better that the chit simply would lead the authorities back to *him*. No doubt she would do just that, if she believed him responsible for the attack on her. Hell, he might as well resign himself to waiting for a constable to show up on his doorstep and accuse him of being the Barkshire Demon.

Unless, of course, he had *her* arrested first.

The idea was not without its appeal. He could accomplish two tasks at once—satisfy his curiosity as to her identity, and saddle her with an appropriate bit of punishment for the literal blow she had dealt him. For, intriguing female or not, she bloody well couldn't go around battering peers of the realm.

A moment later, however, he dismissed the notion. For

better or worse, the woman was now out of his life. Nothing would be served by pursuing her, save drawing an unwanted connection between him and the Barkshire Demon murders. That was the last thing he needed. Let Meeks find her, if he would. As for himself, his responsibility for the chit was at an end.

The decision made, Victor rose and made his slightly unsteady way over to the pillar. He caught up the packet the doctor had left behind and dumped a portion of its contents into the brandy snifter. The water promptly turned an alarming if appropriate shade of blue.

"Sweet Christ," he muttered and shook his head. With a mock toast to his like-colored surroundings, he tossed down the potion in a single swallow. Then, shuddering at its bitterness—foul as the draught tasted, it bloody well better cure his headache—he started back toward his own rooms.

It wasn't until he had closed his bedchamber door behind him that he realized he still clutched the drawing of the gnarled hand with its wilted rose. He stared at it a moment, wondering just what it was about the sketch that drew him. And then it occurred to him that perhaps this was a glimpse of what was to come. The unknown artist somehow had captured on paper Victor's own future—old and alone, save for his roses.

With a muttered curse, he crumpled the sketch in his fist and tossed it aside. Doubtless such morbid fancies were simply a result of the drug taking hold. Though the throbbing of his skull had begun to abate, he was feeling decidedly light-headed.

Not bothering to strip off yesterday's clothes, he climbed onto his bed and settled against the pillows. Sleep claimed him almost immediately . . . and when he finally dreamed, it was of red roses.

Seven

"Bloody Resurrection men struck last night, they did."

With that aggrieved announcement, Ezra Meeks clomped his way into the tiny parlor where his daughter awaited him. Amaryllis winced at the trail of fresh grave dirt he left behind on the threadbare carpet but held her tongue on that particular subject. Instead she tugged her shawl a bit higher around her bruised throat and assumed an expression of unfeigned concern.

"Again, Father?" she replied, her voice still twisted by an unmistakable croak. "Why, that is the third time in as many weeks. I thought you were to post a guard."

" 'Twouldn't have done much good," came his blunt reply. "Most o' them what would stand watch in a churchyard is the sort that can be bought off with a few coins or a nip o' daffy."

He paused and shot her a suspicious look from beneath beetled brows. " 'Ere, now, wot's wrong wit' yer voice, girl?"

"I'm afraid I've caught a bit of the croup," she replied with a silent prayer that he would not pursue the matter further.

Her answer seemed to satisfy him, for he grunted in acknowledgment. "Send word to that worthless brother o' yers, so 'e can make up one o' 'is nostrums for ye, then. 'Twouldn't do for ye to be serious ill and fall behind on yer work."

Knowing it was to her household duties rather than her painting that her father referred, she merely bit her lip and nodded. Neither did she reply to his slur on Talbot, having long since reconciled herself to the fact that the rift between the pair would likely never heal.

Ezra, meanwhile, had plucked off his worn black beaver to reveal an unkempt fringe of gray hair. He left on the threadbare black frock coat that was his sexton's trademark livery. His sunken cheeks, well lined from years of exposure to the elements, held a lingering hint of color from the brisk morning air. His bulbous nose was red as well, though that last was due less to the chill weather than to his habitual indulgence in gin. His spare frame still bent as if against the North wind, he caught up the chipped cup of tea Amaryllis offered him and took a swallow.

She settled back in her own chair and took up a cup. It had been but half an hour earlier and well past her usual time for rising when she had paid the hackney driver and slipped unseen into the tiny gray stone house behind the churchyard. A few embers had remained in the stove from last night, so that it had been but a few minutes' work to stir up a fire and put on the kettle for tea. Breakfast was the usual simple meal of bread, jam, and a crumb of cheese, at hand in the larder.

She had assembled everything in the parlor, as was her habit, just moments before her father returned from his daily stroll about the cemetery and surrounding church grounds. He would have no reason to suspect she'd been gone the entire night, save for the fact she still had on the same bottle-green gown she'd worn the day before. She could only pray that, like most men, he had no eye for feminine fashion and would not notice that trifle.

As she had hoped, the question never came. Instead Ezra settled heavily into the chair beside her, close enough so that she could smell last night's gin upon him. She frowned, forgetting her own transgressions. Doubtless he had again drunk himself into a stupor the evening before and would not have stirred had she returned home at the appointed hour.

"A bad business, that, diggin' up the dead," Ezra went on in a more complacent tone as the tea warmed him. "Still, I wager 'ow the old gent those scoundrels took off won't be missed, since none o' 'is kin bothered wit' the service yesterday. Fine-lookin' fellow 'e was, too, for 'is age. A shock o' gray 'air the Prince Regent 'isself would 'ave envied, an' every tooth in 'is 'ead still there."

Old gentleman. Gray hair. All his own teeth.

Uneasily Amaryllis recalled last night's anatomy lesson and the unfortunate George. In addition to his mane of silver hair, the old man had sported a fine set of teeth she had assumed were made of ivory. Dear Lord, what if he had been the one whose body had been snatched from St. Pancras's churchyard?

"A bad business, to be sure," she echoed. "But perhaps the man would be pleased to know that he performed a final useful service, even in death. That is," she finished with a guilty flush, "if he ended up being sold to an anatomist."

" 'Ere now, girl, wot would ye know about such things?"

His gray brows twisting in an ominous frown, Ezra set down his cup with a clatter. Not for the first time, she wondered if perhaps her own father had a hand in the recent spate of morbid thefts from the churchyard. It would be but a simple matter for some unscrupulous sort to mark the sexton's fondness for drink, then assure his temporary deafness and blindness with a bottle of gin and a few coins.

Determinedly she put that disloyal thought aside.

"All I know, Father, is what I've heard Talbot say—that we've not sufficient numbers of executed criminals in London to serve as anatomy specimens for all the city's physicians and surgeons. Until the laws are changed, there is no way to stop the body snatchers from continuing their grisly work, and no way to prevent good doctors from stooping to such criminal behavior."

Ezra merely grunted again—whether in agreement or dissent, she was not certain—and then took another swallow from his cup. Given it was still early in the day, he had not fortified the brew as he usually did with a generous portion from the bottle he always kept upon his person.

She took another sip of tea herself. Perhaps the hot liquid would soothe her sore throat. There was nothing to be done, however, for the livid pattern of bruises on her throat. All she could do was to cover the marks as best she could and pray that no one took any notice.

For, given her promise to Talbot, she could not confess to her father the frightening events of the previous night, lest he also learn where she had been beforehand. His anger over that, however, would be nothing compared to his outrage should he find out that his daughter had spent the night alone—no matter how innocently—with a man.

She bit her lip, envisioning the scandal should a drunken Ezra Meeks show up on the Earl of Blackstock's front stoop, demanding satisfaction. Her father would be appeased by nothing less than her marriage to the man—hardly a possibility. And as for notifying the authorities, what could she tell them? That she had been set upon by a nightmarish parody of a man?

For she had come to an amazing conclusion on her chilly carriage ride home this morning. She now believed Blackstock's contention that he had done her no harm.

Now, safely home and with all her wits recovered, she could scarcely say why she ever had come to the opposite conclusion. Of course, there had been that minor point about the knife, though Blackstock had explained away that detail quite logically. She could see now that it had only been her unsettled state of mind and her lamentable weakness for melodramatic novels that had caused her to cast him as villain.

That did not mean, however, that she had not been truly in danger last night, and that there was not some foul murderer still walking the London streets. But she did not know that man's name . . . nor could she go to the authorities with her tale, lest her father somehow learn of the affair.

A knock at the front door put a prompt halt to her musings. She put aside her tea and scrambled to her feet, aware that it was much too early in the day for visitors.

"I'll see who it is, Father," she offered. She did not expect a demur from him since, to her recollection, Ezra never had answered the door in his own house.

This time proved no exception to the rule. He gave her an absent nod of approval, his attention seemingly fixed upon the half-empty teacup. She hurried from the room, conscious that her heart had begun an uneasy pounding.

But what was there to be nervous about? *Sternness of mind,* she reminded herself. Chances were the caller was but a parishioner seeking a word with the sexton. Still, her palms were unaccountably moist as she tugged the concealing shawl more tightly about her throat and reached for the knob.

She pulled open the heavy wooden door, only to be met by a rush of yellow light that temporarily blinded her. The sun had risen high enough by now for its rays to split the neat row of poplars that surrounded the church grounds and shine directly on her eastward-facing doorstep.

For a moment, all she saw was the silhouette of a man, stark against the golden glare. There was something unyielding, almost sinister in his stance, and her first frantic thought was that the Earl of Blackstock somehow had tracked her down. Had he come to silence her, once and for all, or was his intent simply to have her arrested for her attack upon him?

A series of unpleasant images flashed through her mind. Her father, finding her strangled body on their doorstep . . . herself, locked away in a filthy, crowded Newgate cell for the rest of her days. But as those frightening scenarios played themselves out, the man stepped forward and she caught a clear look at his face.

"Talbot," she rasped out in relief. "Whatever are you doing here at such an early hour?"

"Might I come in, my dear?" he replied, neatly overlooking her question as he gave her a cool smile.

Seeing no help for it, she pulled the door open wider and stepped aside. But as she closed the door behind him again, she realized that their prosaic exchange had done little to relieve her nervousness. It wasn't that she did not trust Talbot, for she did. It simply was that her brother possessed a most disconcerting habit of seeing through a person and discerning the truth.

He plucked off his high-crowned beaver, then turned that keen gray gaze upon her. She clutched the shawl more securely about her throat, feeling the telltale warmth begin to creep into her cheeks. That was the problem with her fair coloring, she thought in dismay, allowing her every emotion to be read by the blood rising and falling in her face.

"Father is in the parlor, having his morning tea," she said by way of distraction. "Why don't you join him there, and I will bring another cup."

Not waiting for him to reply, she hurried down the hallway. She reentered the parlor a moment later to find Talbot, hat upon his knee, seated in the same chair her father had occupied a few minutes before. Ezra himself was gone, his half-empty cup a mute testament to a hasty departure.

Disappointed but not surprised, Amaryllis suppressed a sigh and took her own chair. The breach between father and son first had opened when, a dozen years earlier, Talbot had expressed his intention to become a physician. Rather than encouraging him, however, Ezra had flown into a rage.

Goin' above yer station, are ye? Mark me, fer all yer schoolin' an' fine airs, ye'll be no gentleman when ye're through, no matter 'ow many lords an' ladies ye think to cure. An' don't come whinin' back to me when ye fail.

But Talbot had not failed. Somehow his success seemed to have enraged the older man still further, the more so when Talbot had been accepted into the Royal Academy. In the intervening years, the pair shared not even a pleasantry. And Ezra had not been present two years earlier when Talbot had married a fragile young beauty named Cordelia, the daughter of a minor baronet. Neither had he offered a word of condolence the following year, when a distraught Talbot had been forced to settle his new wife in a sanitarium after diagnosing her with a terminal weakness of the heart.

Pushing aside those sad memories, Amaryllis poured the tea, then handed over the cup to her brother.

"It appears that we have missed Father. Doubtless he did not realize it was you come to call and went off to take care of his usual duties," she hurried to excuse her parent's absence.

As usual, Talbot obligingly took up her polite fiction. "I know that a man in his position has responsibilities; however, my dear sister, it happens you are the one I have come to see."

"Me?" she asked, an unsettling presentiment gripping her as her cheeks grew warm again.

In turn, a hint of genteel anger darkened his face. "As you might guess, I was surprised last night to discover you had ignored my orders and hurried off quite on your own. Surely you must have realized that a note was not sufficient, that I might be worried about you."

He paused, and Amaryllis steeled herself to hold her tongue. For this was a tactic that he had used on her to his advantage many times in the past, making her so uneasy that she always blurted out what was uppermost in her mind.

This time, however, he did not wait for her reply but went on. "Unfortunately it was almost an hour after you left that I discovered you had set out alone. All those gentlemen who had paid to attend my lecture were still milling about the place, and I practically threw them out into the street in my haste."

"McArdle, in particular, was difficult to dislodge. Then the fog was so thick that no carriages were to be had, so my only choice was to go on foot. It was nigh on midnight by the time I reached here, and you can imagine my terror when I discovered you had not yet returned home."

Amaryllis's eyes widened. "Oh, my, surely you did not tell Father—"

"I took the precaution of peering inside the window first," he said with an ironic lift of his brow. "Father was peacefully snoring away—too much gin, as usual—so that he had no notion that his only daughter was not sleeping peacefully in her own bed, as well. I rather suspect I would never have learned of your adventure, save that it happens I am personal physician to one Victor Saville, Earl of Blackstock."

"Earl of Blackstock?" she faintly echoed, feeling the blood flee her face.

He nodded. "Indeed. When I returned home sometime just past dawn, after spending the entire night frantically combing the streets for my missing sister, I discovered a note posted on my door. It seemed that his lordship had a young female guest who required prompt medical attention."

He paused and sternly eyed her. "To be sure, my concern for you was uppermost in my mind, but I could not neglect my patients. I made my way to Blackstock's town home as quickly as I could, only to discover my would-be patient gone and his lordship the one requiring medical attention. And imagine my amazement when I discovered that Blackstock had this in his possession."

So saying, he plucked forth a slim volume that looked like—no, it actually was!—her lost sketchbook.

A collage of disjointed possibilities gathered in her mind as, for the second time that morning, she found herself speechless. Finally she reached out an unsteady hand and took the drawings from him.

"It was quite the most extraordinary thing," Talbot went on, as if she were not gaping at him like a half-wit. "His lordship's entire household was in quite an uproar. You see, it seems the young woman in question had been brutally assaulted in some dark alleyway last night, presumably by the so-called Barkshire Demon."

His expression grew still sterner. "By his account, Blackstock found this woman in the street, unconscious, and brought her home with him. This morning she awoke recovered from her injuries, attempted but failed to murder the earl, then fled the premises before anyone could stop her. Blackstock was only superficially injured, however, and thus able to give a detailed description of his assailant. Moreover the young woman also left behind one of her possessions as a clue to her identity."

"Then I need not tell you where I spent last night," Amaryllis managed in a despairing voice. "I suppose you told Blackstock that the sketchbook was mine . . . and that I was your sister?"

"Certainly not. I would not have it known that a sibling of mine was so foolish as to get herself into such a situation. Besides which, Blackstock had somehow formed the impression that you were, shall we say, a woman of a certain profession. I merely recovered your drawings, told his lordship I would find their proper owner, and assured him I also would scour the backstreets for the red-haired wench who had assaulted him. And now, my dear sister, would you care to relate *your* version of last night's events?"

She told him everything then, beginning with the shambling footsteps she had heard in the fog. By the time she recounted the way she had managed to overcome the earl and flee the manor, her brother's usual air of professional calm had given way to an uncharacteristic expression of unease. But her next words sent his eyebrows lifting in disbelief.

"I fear I was precipitous in blaming his lordship for what happened . . . and, most especially, in bashing him over the head so I could make my escape. For, you see, I have given the matter much thought ever since I left his company. I have concluded that the earl was innocent of any intent to harm me, and that he did me a service by carrying me home with him for the night."

"Indeed," came Talbot's cool reply. "Who, then, do you believe is the responsible party?"

"Why, the creature, of course."

Even as the words left her mouth, she realized how incredible the claim sounded. To his credit, however, Talbot merely nodded.

"Quite fascinating, my dear, but I must confess that your tale sounds like something from one of those novels by Mrs. Radcliffe that you and your friend, Mary, always were sharing. So now tell me again about this creature you claim attacked you."

"It . . . he was quite tall and well built, his features regular, his hair and eyes both black," she replied, tamping down a shiver of repugnance as she struggled to recreate his features in her mind. "He would have been handsome, I expect, save for the horrible grimace that twisted his face and the fact that his skin was deathly pale, like the corpse in the anatomy lesson. For all that, I had the impression that he was young. But then, when he t-touched me—"

Her voice, already halting, faltered a moment along with her courage. She took a shuddering breath, then finished, "When he touched me, I swear that I could smell the scent of the grave upon him."

"Fascinating," he murmured again, leaning forward, "but hardly probable. And now, my dear, let me examine the bruises on your throat."

With shaking fingers, she unwound the shawl and raised her chin. He studied the livid pattern of bruises for a long moment, his features hardening.

"A wormwood poultice will help with the bruising. Should I assume that you suffered no other sort of assault," he asked, "either from this creature of yours, or else Blackstock?"

"No, only the marks on my neck," she hurried to assure him, blushing as she understood the meaning behind that delicately phrased question.

At her reply, he sat back again and resumed his usual cool air of professionalism.

"Given the extent of your injuries, I can only say that chances are you narrowly escaped death last night. But what troubles me is your insistence that you saw two separate men—this so-called creature and the Earl of Blackstock."

"But it is true!" came her croaking protest. "It was the first man—the creature—who almost choked the life from me, and the earl who carried me home with him."

Her brother met her anxious words with a wry lift of his brow. "Indeed. And now, my dear, perhaps you might humor me by describing his lordship's appearance."

"In general terms, he is of above medium height, with a strong build," she obediently began, ticking off each item on her fingers. "He dresses rather conservatively for a man of his station, but still within fashion. He has dark hair—a bit longer than the mode—and dark eyes, a rather stern jaw, a pale complexion with no scars that I noted. I am certain that most women would judge him more than passably handsome . . . that is, if they fancied that sort of dramatic good looks."

"Indeed." Talbot settled back in his chair, a humorless smile flickering over his lips. "Do realize, my dear, that you have just given me a description almost identical to that you earlier made of your so-called creature?"

"Really, Talbot, I cannot see how—"

"And you have already admitted that the fog was quite thick, and your sensibilities distraught. It seems far more likely to me that this is but a typical case of female hysterics brought on by an abundance of emotion. There was but one man last night—the Earl of Blackstock."

"But the vile creature that attacked me . . . I—I saw its face quite distinctly, and it did not belong to Blackstock," she protested, suppressing a shiver at the memory.

Talbot shook his head and held up a restraining hand. "My dear Amaryllis, let me explain this to you in layman's terms. Your first glimpse of his lordship was colored by an acute if quite understandable fear. That fear distorted your very image of the man, so that he appeared to you as some nightmarish creature. But one's senses can be deceived in such a manner for only a brief time. When you awoke from your swoon to find him bending over you, you saw him as he actually appears."

"But you do not understand—"

"No, my dear, it is you who do not understand."

Talbot sprang to his feet and paced about the tiny parlor, his gray eyes aglitter. Amaryllis let the shawl slip to her shoulders as she stared up at him in alarm. But when she would have risen to lay a restraining hand upon his arm, he abruptly stopped and faced her once more.

His tone harsher than she'd ever heard it, he went on. "I would have spared you this, if I could, but I see now that I must be direct. The truth is that I have good reason to believe it was the Earl of Blackstock who tried last night to kill you. You see, a mere six months ago, he and a second gentleman together brutally murdered another young woman."

Eight

"Murdered?"

Amaryllis stared up at her brother in disbelief. By dint of rational thought, she had concluded that Blackstock was not the man who had tried to strangle her. Now, however, Talbot could point to an earlier incident that proved the earl was indeed a vile killer.

A reflexive shiver of denial flashed through her. She did not doubt her brother's words; still, she needed more to convince her that the accusation was true. Some proof, something irrefutable.

"Tell me what happened . . . please. I—I must know," she hoarsely demanded.

Talbot stood silent a moment, so that she thought he might ignore her plea. Then, as if coming to a decision, he resumed his seat.

"Perhaps I spoke out of turn. What I should have said is that he was suspected of the crime. Whether or not he committed it, I cannot say with certainty. The circumstantial evidence did weigh heavily against him, though he never was convicted of any wrongdoing."

"Go on."

He frowned. "Some of what I know, I witnessed myself, for I was the physician called in that night. More of the story, I heard from the servants . . . and a few odd fragments of it, from Blackstock himself.

"At that time, the earl was keeping company with one Sir

Harry Shaw," he continued in a blunt tone. "Shaw was a personable young gentleman known for his spendthrift ways and reckless manner. He and Blackstock had spent the better part of the evening in question at the theater. And it was there that a pretty young actress who called herself Jane Belfleur caught Sir Harry's fancy.

"As was his habit with such women, Sir Harry asked Miss Belfleur to join him and Blackstock at their club for a late supper. Witnesses later testified that all three were well into their cups by the time the pair persuaded the young woman to accompany them back to Sir Harry's town home. By all accounts, she did so quite willingly."

Talbot paused, a flicker of unreadable emotion passing over his mild features. For herself, Amaryllis suppressed a craven impulse to cover her eyes and ears against what was to come.

"My role in all this came just before dawn of the following day," he went on. "I was awakened by an urgent summons brought by Blackstock's driver. He claimed that there had been an accident of sorts, and a woman had been grievously injured."

"And was it . . . an accident?"

Talbot gave her a brief and quite humorless smile. "If you would call a woman being raped and then bludgeoned to death an accident, then perhaps it was."

Amaryllis bit her lip. "Tell me more."

"The rest is not pleasant, I must warn you. When I arrived at the manor, the driver led me upstairs to a bedchamber well removed from the rest of the household's living quarters. The sole illumination came from the fireplace that was blazing quite merrily. It gave off light enough for me to see a young woman sprawled in the room's far corner."

He frowned again at the memory. "In my profession, I have seen many unsettling sights, but this scene sent a chill through me. The woman was naked, save for a single blood-soaked white stocking. Toothmarks and bruises covered her entire body, as if she had been savaged by some wild beast, while her face was so swollen as to be unrecognizable. She had not been dead long when I found her, for her flesh still held a hint of warmth."

He paused, his gray eyes narrowing as if calculating the effect he was having upon her. Then, apparently satisfied with her expression of horrified disbelief, he proceeded.

"Once I had determined there was nothing to be done for her, I discovered Sir Harry lying atop the bed, clad only in his breeches. My first thought was that he had been murdered, too, for my attempts to rouse him brought no success. Then I noted the smell of strong spirits upon him and determined he simply was the worse for drink."

"And what of Blackstock?" Amaryllis choked out in a voice little more than a whisper.

"I looked up from Sir Harry's unconscious form to see him standing in the shadows, looking like the very devil himself. He was quite cool about the whole business, I must say. In contrast to his companion, he was still dressed in full evening attire. He had a snifter of brandy in one hand, and as he raised the glass to drink I could see the fresh blood that streaked his shirtcuff. His white shirtfront bore crimson stains, as well. I started toward him, ready to question him as to what had happened . . . and that was when I noted the trail of dried blood leading from that poor woman's body to where he stood."

"Then he admitted his guilt?"

Talbot grimly shook his head. "To the contrary, he denied everything. He claimed it was his friend who did the deed, and that he had been in the library and only come upon the scene afterward. The blood on his shirt was hers, he freely admitted, but he'd gotten it on himself while checking to see whether or not she still lived. The servants could neither confirm nor deny his story, for they had all slept through the killing and Blackstock's driver had remained with the carriage."

"And Sir Harry?" she prompted when he paused for breath. "Once he regained his senses, did he then turn around and accuse his lordship?"

"It was not quite that simple," her brother conceded. "By the time the effects of the liquor began to wear off, the constable I had summoned finally arrived. The two of us then questioned Sir Harry at length as to what had taken place.

"He was, as you might expect, quite horrified by the crime but steadfastly claimed to know nothing about what happened. He insisted he had fallen asleep soon after the three of them had returned to the town house, but that Miss Belfleur was still alive at that time. And he was stunned to learn that the earl had accused *him* of being the murderer."

It was Amaryllis's turn to frown. "So you believed Sir Harry's account, rather than that of his lordship."

"Again, I cannot say with certainty," came his chill reply. "In the absence of any witnesses, it came down to which of the two men's stories was the more credible. Sir Harry swore that he had never laid a hand upon the woman, save in the friendliest of fashions. He did, however, express keen regret at her passing and feared that he might have been the indirect cause of her death simply by insisting she come home with the pair of them."

"And the earl?"

"Blackstock appeared entirely unmoved by what had happened."

The chill statement sent another shiver through her; still, she countered, "But I never read anything of this in the scandal sheets. Was his lordship not imprisoned, then?"

"He managed a brief stay at Newgate, but he never stood trial. You see, two nights after the murder, Sir Harry was himself found dead alongside the Thames. Witnesses later recalled seeing him walking along the riverbank earlier that same evening, his manner that of a man who had been indulging quite heavily in strong spirits. It was a frigid night, but he wore neither greatcoat nor hat and scarf against the elements."

Talbot's words took on a bitter tone. "The official report was that the young man had quite simply died of the cold. The circumstances were such, however, that some people asked if perhaps he and not his lordship had actually killed Miss Belfleur. They suggested that Sir Harry had succumbed to an uneasy conscience and intended to throw himself into the river in repentance, but froze to death before he could take that dramatic action."

He shook his head. "At any rate, the incident served to cast doubt on Blackstock's guilt, so that all charges were dropped. The matter was hushed up, of course, though it was common knowledge in Society that he'd been a suspect. He managed to avert the worst of the scandal by paying a substantial sum to . . . certain people for their silence."

He broke off, and Amaryllis shut her eyes against the mental images that swept her. The entire story was more horrific than any fictional tale of dread that she and Mary had ever composed. Had she known earlier what she did now, she likely would have been too frightened to make her escape from Blackstock's town house. As it was, it would be days before she would ever again sleep with any degree of soundness.

As that last thought crossed her mind, Talbot broke the leaden stillness between them. "Believe me, my dear, I did not mean to distress you unduly, after all you've been through. I simply wanted you to understand the sort of man that Blackstock is . . . or rather, might well be. And surely you can see now why I doubted your story of an undead creature roaming the city."

"I suppose that I do," she conceded. Then, as another thought occurred to her, she glanced up in sudden alarm. "Talbot, surely you don't intend to accuse his lordship of being the Demon?"

"With no proof, I cannot, though that doesn't mean I will forget the matter."

He fingered the brim of his hat, his expression grim. "I have already determined that Blackstock does not know your name, so you should be safe from any further harm so long as you keep out of his way. Given he is something of a recluse, that should not prove too difficult a task. For myself, I will continue to watch him from a distance and pray that he makes a misstep, so we might put a halt to his heinous behavior, once and for all."

So saying, he rose from his chair and caught up his stick. "Do get a bit of rest now, and try to put this unpleasantness from your mind. I will visit you on the morrow to make sure that you are experiencing no further ill effects from your ordeal."

He allowed her to accompany him to the door; then, with a final kiss for her, he clamped on his hat and turned on his heel. But barely had he taken his leave, than she called him back.

"Wait, Talbot, there is something more I must know." She hesitated as he waited, then asked in a rush, "If you suspected Lord Blackstock of being a murderer, why did you continue on as his personal physician?"

"Because, my dear sister, I was one of the people he paid for their silence."

With those bitter words, he turned again down the graveled path. She watched, sketchbook still tightly clutched in her hands, until he made his way past cemetery and church to the main road, where his gig awaited him.

She sank onto the cold stone step, her gaze fixed on the distance. As always, her artist's eye reflexively noted the intricate play of shadow against light in the scene. For it was a glorious spring day, the sort of day where one's thoughts turned to rebirth, not death.

The sun had risen well above the treetops now, its welcome warmth dispelling the remnants of last night's chill.

Separated from the main grounds by a black wrought-iron fence, the familiar cemetery with its numerous shrubs and trees just coming into bloom appeared as a cheerful little park. The irregular rows of stone monuments—some, mere humble slabs; others, elaborate sculptures—more resembled museum pieces than markers of various men's and women's final repose.

Even at night, death and its trappings did not frighten her, nor had they ever. *A part of the natural order,* she had taken pains to emphasize to her friend, Mary, whom she had first encountered melodramatically swooning over her long-dead mother's grave. This situation, however, was different. Something *unnatural* was afoot in London—though whether man or phantom, she was not yet certain.

But she intended to find out.

Knowing that her father must soon return, she rose and made her purposeful way toward her bedchamber. It was a modest room, nowhere near as grand as the blue chamber in which she had spent last night. Still, it boasted the elaborate lace counterpane, its once-snowy white fabric now turned ivory with age, that had been passed down to her from her mother.

Anne Fleming Meeks had learned the art of lace-making from her Belgian mother and had, in turn, passed on the skill to her own daughter. Amaryllis had proved equally adept at the tedious work. Thus she supplemented her meager earnings from teaching young girls to sketch by mending old-fashioned pieces of linen finery brought to her by various of St. Pancras's parishioners.

But painting had always been her first love. Legs crossed beneath her in Turkish fashion, Amaryllis settled upon the bed. Flipping open her sketchbook to a blank page, she snatched up a stick of charcoal from her bedside table and shut her eyes.

Deliberately she cleared her mind of everything save her memories of the creature. A nightmarish figure promptly sprang to life, so clear in her thoughts that she could almost smell the lingering odor of decay about him. She suppressed a sick feeling at the memory of his dead fingers upon her throat. Instead she let her artist's eye begin a methodical dissection of its features.

Dispassionately she noted planes . . . curves . . . shadows. She concentrated harder, seeing past the flesh to the squares and circles and rectangles that made up his nose, his jaw, his cheekbones. At last satisfied that she had broken down that monstrous face into its most basic components, she opened her own eyes again and began to sketch.

The mental image began to take life in a series of bold, dark slashes that covered the page. Once or twice, she paused to smudge out a line and redraw it. For the most part, however, the drawing came together with an uncanny swiftness that left her marveling. Barely had she started than she was setting down her pencil to stare at what she had created.

A fiend from hell glared back at her.

She paused but a moment to study its face, just long enough to satisfy herself that she had captured on paper the image that clung to her mind. Then, hands shaking, she tore that page from the book and grabbed up her charcoal again to begin a second sketch. This one evolved with equal swiftness until, moments later, two drawings lay side by side on the coverlet before her.

Two sketches . . . and two distinctly different men.

She picked up the first drawing again and studied it more closely. This was the creature that had attacked her, the being whose foul image haunted her. Now, however, she noted a few more telling details about him.

He was—had been?—a young man and doubtless acknowledged as handsome. Distorted as they were, his features still held a shadow of masculine beauty that only deepened the horror of his appearance. Who he was or where he'd come from, she could not guess . . . but she knew with certainty that she had not simply conjured him from the depths of an overwrought imagination.

Slowly she set down that drawing and reached for the second portrait. This man, she most definitely knew.

Victor Saville, Earl of Blackstock, stared back at her. An air of challenge emanated from the charcoal image, evident in the cool gleam of his dark eyes and the arrogant set of his chin. With her free hand, she lightly traced the penciled line of his temple, as if it were warm flesh that she was touching. Then, realizing just what it was she was doing, she snatched back her fingers as if the very paper might singe her.

Dear Lord, what was she thinking?

True, she had always possessed a keen interest in masculine beauty, though simply as an artist admiring nature's handiwork. Save in that detached way, never before had she been obsessed with any one particular male. And never before had she experienced this sort of heady, physical reaction . . . a reaction that manifested itself as an odd sort of flutter somewhere in the vicinity of her stomach and sudden tingling warmth deep between her thighs.

She squirmed against the coverlet, only to find that the movement merely intensified the unsettling sensation. She subdued that wayward weakness and set to studying the drawing instead. Earlier Talbot had pointed out that her description of both the creature and Blackstock were uncannily similar. With that in mind, she reached again for the first sketch and held them both together, comparing.

Her brother had been correct, to a point. A vague resemblance did exist between the creature and Blackstock, though only to the extent that one could claim a spotted bull resembled a dappled stallion. Having seen the former, one could not mistake it for the latter. Both sets of features—eyes, noses, chins—were noticeably different from each other. In this she could not be mistaken, for years of observing life with an artist's eye had left her with a keen memory.

Two sketches. Two men.

Talbot, of course, had already made his diagnosis of the situation, and she knew from past experience that no amount of argument would now sway him from it. Let him handle it, he had insisted. And Talbot meant to prove that Blackstock was the Barkshire Demon, thus solving the brutal murders of four women.

The problem was, he might well be pursuing the wrong man.

She thought back to the account Talbot had given of the young woman who had been murdered. The fact that the other man involved had, in all probability, taken his own life went far in proving the earl's innocence. Besides, she reminded herself, he'd had ample opportunity last night to kill *her,* and he had not.

Then another thought struck her. If Talbot suspected Blackstock of being the Demon, it stood to reason other people might come to that same conclusion. Thus the earl had better cause than anyone for wanting to uncover the Demon's true identity. She, on the other hand, was likely the only one in the city who knew that killer's face.

Why not persuade Blackstock to join forces with her, and the two of them track down the Barkshire Demon themselves?

Slowly the possibility began crystallizing in her mind, until a plan took shape. To be sure, its chances of success would be small; still, she could do little worse than had the authorities, to this point.

A shiver of reckless anticipation swept her. Of late, she had accounted her life decidedly dull. Indeed, for a self-proclaimed modern woman, she was living quite the circumspect life. This was her chance to prove herself the equal of a man in coping with adversity, for if her brother could pursue the Demon on his own, then so could she. If nothing else, she would share her idea with Blackstock and make her apology for bashing him over the head.

And, at the very least, she would have the opportunity to see him one more time.

But what would the earl think when he learned she was the sister of his own personal physician? She grappled momentarily with the question, recalling her earlier conversation with Talbot. He had warned her away from the man; moreover he had admitted that he had accepted money from Blackstock in return for his silence in the matter of that young actress's murder. Never would her brother condone what she was about to do . . . and, just as likely, chances were that the earl would never agree to help her should he discover her connection to Talbot.

Then she would not use her true name, she decided. With any luck, their connection would be but a temporary one, so that her identity would be of no consequence to him anyhow.

That last issue settled, she tucked the pair of drawings back into her sketchbook and slipped it beneath her bed, then got to her feet. She would go about the rest of her day as usual. Tomorrow, however, she would find some excuse to spend a portion of the afternoon away from the house and make her visit to the Saville town house.

Perhaps by then, the earl would be recovered from his injury and be in a more willing state of mind to hear her out. It would be a quick matter to speak her piece before him and learn if he dared to join her in this dangerous game. If he did not, then she would let the matter drop.

But if he did, the next foggy night would see her wandering the London streets again . . . this time the pursuer instead of the prey.

Nine

> *I had fancied my plan quite the Clever One . . . but then, is that not often the Folly of Youth? No matter, I was determined to confront the Earl of Blackstock and demand his help . . . for by that time, I was Practically Convinced that he was not the Foul Fiend whom I sought.*
>
> —letter from Miss Amaryllis Meeks to
> Miss Mary Godwin

"Vic, you'll never guess," came Monique's excited cry as she peeked her head around the library door.

Victor bit back an oath and glanced up from his desk, where he sat painstakingly translating pertinent passages from one of his grandfather's French texts on the history of roses. For once, his sister did not wait for his permission to enter, nor did she seem to notice his irritation at the interruption. Instead she fairly burst into the one room in the town house that he considered his personal domain.

Its furnishings were few—a broad cherrywood desk, cluttered with books and notes; a worn, oversized brown leather armchair behind it; a pair of gold-brocaded wingbacks flanking a waist-high, carved cherrywood table. All had been chosen more for function than for style. A small fireplace tucked almost as an afterthought behind him was topped by a plain mantelpiece, above which hung several framed prints of roses. Opposite, a pair of lace-curtained

French doors opened onto marble steps leading down to the gardens and various outbuildings beyond.

The remainder of the room was consumed by books.

They lined the walls, were stacked in corners . . . row after row of gilded leather and ink-printed rag. A goodly number of the volumes, he had accumulated himself. The rest he had inherited from his sire and his grandfather. Horticultural tomes, in general, and volumes dedicated to roses, in particular, filled a dozen shelves.

The balance of the bookcases held histories, biographies, and texts on any number of subjects, all three generations having possessed tastes in their reading matter that could most charitably be termed eclectic. Along with the thick Persian carpet that spread about his feet, the books served as an inner wall to dull the mundane sounds of the everyday world without.

Within its walls, he did not so much shut out the world as withdraw into another place where he could keep his memories safely at bay. Just as his hothouse was his sanctuary during daylight hours, so was his library a place of refuge whenever the shadows began to lengthen.

Now Monique ignored his unspoken rule as, soft slippers whispering against the woolen rug, she scampered over to where he sat. Wilhelm was, as usual, perched with regal splendor upon her shoulder, his glossy gray and red feathers a jaunty counterpoint to her buttercup-yellow gown. Victor gave the pair of them a baleful glance—had he not given strict instructions he was to be left undisturbed until dinnertime?—and then shoved his chair back from the desk.

"This bloody well better be important," he began, "since I happen to be in the midst of—"

"She's here," Monique cut him short, leaning over his desk to turn up the lamp. A bright yellow glow dispelled the blanket of late afternoon shadow that he'd not realized until this moment lay over the room. "You know," she persisted when Victor stared at her with impatience, "the woman who coshed you over the head yesterday morning."

"She's here?" he echoed in a harsh voice and dropped his pen. He barely noted the gobbets of black ink that spattered across the sheet of foolscap, but fixed her with a disbelieving look. "Are you quite certain of that?"

"Of course. Well, almost certain," the girl amended, her dark eyes alight with excitement. "I just happened to be downstairs in the parlor when I heard the front knocker sound. I peered out into the foyer in time to see Peters open the door and begin sputtering just as he always does when he is upset."

She paused for breath, while Wilhelm gave an obliging imitation of the sputtering butler that drew another giggle from his mistress.

"Needless to say, I rushed to the window for a proper look," she went on once the bird's melodramatic gasps died. "She was hardly dressed in the mode, so I was not surprised that Peters hesitated to let her in the front way. She hadn't a bonnet on, just an ugly brown shawl wrapped about her hair and shoulders. I couldn't see her face, but I caught just enough of a glimpse to be certain that her hair was red. And that was when I realized that she must be your mystery woman."

"Chances are just as good that the chit is some unfortunate in search of a post and who lacks sense enough to use the servants' entry," he returned in a cool tone, as a knock sounded from the hallway.

"Begging your pardon, my lord," came Peters's murmur as he poked his head around the open door, "but there is a certain, er, person here to see you. I believe, my lord, that you have already, shall we say, made her acquaintance. Shall I lock her in the parlor and call the constable?"

Victor ignored the triumphant smile his sister shot his way and clipped out, "If it's that red-haired chit you let get away yesterday, then just bloody well bring her to me."

Before Peters had made his bow and hurried off, Victor shoved back from his desk with such haste that his chair tipped. He hurried to right it . . . hurried, too, to conceal his eagerness from his younger sister, who had turned a speculative look upon him.

Though he had always been circumspect about his affairs, Monique was well aware that he'd had his share of mistresses over the past two years. Indeed, with no female relative to quash her unmaidenly curiosity, she had taken to quizzing him of late about those casual connections. He suspected that her fond hope was for him to marry, if only to afford her a bit of female company.

Seeing it as a brotherly duty, he'd finally thrust one of Hannah More's officious tracts into her hands one evening and bade her educate herself on the subject. When he had returned home the following daybreak, he had initially been gratified to find her wide-awake in his library, still reading. The volume in her lap, however, proved not to be Mrs. More's moral twaddle.

Rather it had been a collection of pornographic etchings and lascivious commentary innocently entitled *Essays on Far Eastern Marriage Customs*. The book—normally ensconced on a high shelf beyond casual reach—had come from their late grandsire's collection of ribald literature. So had the other equally shocking works by such sexual luminaries as de Sade that were piled about her chair.

Victor shook his head at the memory. As a boy, he had managed a look at those same volumes and was well aware that they were not fit reading for his sister. Thus he had spent the rest of that morning threatening her within an inch of her life if she considered exercising her newfound knowledge outside the marriage bed. She meekly had agreed . . . and then gone on to suggest several techniques about which she had just read that she thought he might care to try. Given that, he'd be damned if he would allow her reason to suspect that his interest in this particular female was anything more than academic.

"I'll conduct this interview alone, if you don't mind," he told her as he reached up to straighten his neckcloth, only to recall he had stripped off both it and his jacket sometime earlier and tossed them onto one of the chairs. Not that it mattered, he told himself. No reason, after all, that he need make himself presentable for the chit.

"I suggest that you and Wilhelm take yourselves off to your room for the duration," he went on. "Now would be an excellent time for you to go."

"But it's not fair," she protested with a toss of her dark curls, the gesture drawing a startled squawk from the parrot. "I missed out on all the excitement the other night and morning. I don't see why I cannot stay—"

"Because I bloody well said you couldn't," he shot back, silencing any further protests with a quelling look. "This could turn into dangerous business, and I want you well out of it. Now be off with you."

Pouting, Monique turned on her heel and stomped out of the room as loudly as she could in her soft footwear. Wilhelm, as always, got in the last word.

"It's not fair," came his aggrieved retort as the door slammed shut behind the pair.

Victor ignored both literal and figurative displays of ruffled feathers as he resumed his seat and neatly stacked his notes, save for a single crumpled sheet—larger than the rest—that he left propped against an inkwell. That accomplished, he idly toyed with the ring upon his finger, needing something with which to occupy his restless hands. He had never thought to see the chit again—that much was certain. Her presence here now triggered an odd sense of anticipation in him, the source of which he was loath to examine too closely.

A moment later, Peters's deferential knock again sounded. At a word from Victor, the library door opened. The butler, looking exceedingly put out, stepped inside and gestured the shawl-wrapped figure behind him to follow.

"Beggin' your pardon, my lord, but a Miss, er, . . . that is, a young woman to see you, your lordship." Peters stumbled through the announcement, while the chit bobbed the briefest of curtsies Victor's way.

At his impatient gesture of dismissal, the butler bowed his own way out again. Only then did Victor turn his attention to his guest.

She had let the mud-hued shawl slide from her head so that the cheap wool merely skimmed her shoulders. Now he could see her red-gold tresses, modestly bundled into a knot but still gleaming like silken fire in the lamplight. He also got a clear look at the white flesh modestly exposed above the high-cut bodice of her gown.

A lurid pattern of purplish bruises—far more hideous than he had recalled—discolored the pale skin, so that it appeared almost as if someone had wrapped soot-blackened hands around her slim throat. Noting the direction of his gaze, she tugged the shawl higher beneath her chin until it concealed the discoloration.

Coolly he gestured her forward. In the time it took her to reach his desk, he had made a deliberate inventory of her charms, from her breasts—barely visible beneath the edge of her shawl—all the way down to her sensible black boots. By the time he returned his gaze to her face, she was blushing bright as her hair. The reaction surprised him, given her occupation . . . unless, of course, he had been wrong in that, as well.

"And have you come back to finish me off, then?" he wryly asked, breaking the silence. "I'm afraid I am fresh out of brandy decanters, but perhaps the fireplace poker might prove more efficient against a man's skull."

"I am quite sorry for that, my lord," she replied and blushed still brighter, if such a thing were possible. "That is one reason I have come back, to thank you for coming to my aid and to offer an apology. I fear I did not have all my wits about me yesterday morning, so that my only thought was of escape."

"And you managed that quite neatly, did you not?"

At least his curiosity now was satisfied as to her voice. It had a certain, not unpleasant huskiness to it—doubtless a temporary result of her injuries—but other than that her manner and accent were more *ton* than *cit.* If not gently born, then she did an admirable job in mimicking her betters. Or perhaps she was not, as he had thought, a common prostitute but simply a woman in the wrong place at the wrong time. A couple of important questions did remain . . . to wit, had the chit come back of her own accord?

And, if so, then what did she want of him?

A host of possibilities, most of them grim, mentally presented themselves. He ignored them for the moment and leaned back in his chair, surveying her.

"Very well, I am willing to chalk up your actions to the fright you suffered, and I am pleased to know you are recovered from that unfortunate incident. Still, I find myself at a disadvantage here. You know my name, but I don't know yours. So just who in the bloody hell are you?"

Amaryllis met his implacable gaze and momentarily hesitated. She had not forgotten a detail of Blackstock's face— the coldly piercing black eyes, the sensuous mouth, the strongly chiseled nose and chin. Neither had she forgotten the almost palpable air of dark arrogance that cloaked him, like that of an errant angel who did not care he'd been banished from heaven.

What she *had* managed to forget was her own reaction to him, a decidedly female flutter of nervous admiration hardly appropriate to a woman who prided herself on her independence.

Sternness of mind, she told herself and quashed that wayward emotion before she answered. "My name is Amaryllis

Godwin, my lord," she obliged, deliberately using her friend Mary's surname in place of her own, as she had planned.

Blackstock shot her a quizzical frown. "I am vaguely acquainted with a William Godwin . . . a self-styled philosopher, once drew the like of Wordsworth and Coleridge about him, always dipped too deep. And if I recall correctly, his wife was responsible for some foolish tract on female emancipation. Bloody Christ!" He broke off, his frown deepening into outright dismay before he went on. "Surely those two aren't your parents?"

"I can claim no relation," she stiffly retorted, "but I can also assure you that the late Mrs. Godwin's writings are not foolishness. Hers was a single sensible voice rising above a sea of masculine bluster."

She regretted her heated words, however, when Blackstock allowed himself a cool smile. "Quite the radical, are you not? Tell me, Miss Godwin, are you also a philosopher?"

"I have not come here to discuss philosophy, my lord," she replied, eager to cut short that line of conversation lest it lead to further personal revelations. "It happens I am here on other business."

The amusement in his expression vanished. "Ah, yes, you mentioned that your apology was but one reason you were here. Shall I hazard a guess at that other?"

His question held a note of blunt insinuation, so that she choked back an outraged gasp. Too late she recalled Talbot's comment that the earl had presumed she was a fallen woman. With that the case, she had a good idea just what sort of proposal he expected from her.

His next words, however, took her quite by surprise.

"Very well, Miss Godwin, since we've made our way past the preliminaries, take a seat and let us get down to business. But I must warn you that if your intention is to soak me on a regular basis, you will find yourself sadly out of luck. I buy a person's silence but a single time. So, tell me, how much do you require not to tell the authorities that I tried to murder you the other night?"

Buy her silence . . . not tell the authorities?

Amaryllis straightened in the chair she'd taken and regarded him with unfeigned dismay. Here she had spent the better part of two days gathering her courage to ask Blackstock for his help, and the fiend suspected her of plotting blackmail? It simply was not to be borne! She might almost prefer he think her a woman of loose virtue.

But as she opened her mouth to protest, her gaze lit on a crumpled sheet of paper propped against an inkwell on his desk. Forgetting her indignation, she exclaimed, "Why, that is mine!"

Too late she realized her mistake as Blackstock followed her gaze to a charcoal sketch of an overblown rose and a gnarled hand. It was one of the drawings she had made during the anatomy lesson. She'd not realized it was missing from the sketchbook, though how it came to be here, she could not guess. But what mattered now was that she had all but revealed to the earl her connection with Talbot.

As she cast about for some means to cover that blunder, he caught up the drawing and shot her a keen look. "Do you mean, Miss Godwin, you found the sketchbook that this drawing came from lying about somewhere . . . or do you mean that you drew this and the other sketches yourself?"

"What I mean, my lord—"

She broke off, prudence waging a battle against pride. An expression of polite disbelief had settled over Blackstock's features, so that she knew he did not think her capable of such work. It would surely complicate matters if he accepted her claim as artist and then asked an unsuspecting Talbot to return the sketchbook to her; still, it went against all she believed in to deny her talent.

She took a deep breath. "What I mean, my lord," she curtly finished, "is that I drew them."

Blackstock regarded her with unfeigned surprise, and she

could almost read his thoughts. Any woman professing to artistic talent should properly draw flowers or, more daringly, country landscapes. But human torsos and limbs!

"Tell me, Miss Godwin," he drawled, "where does a young woman such as you find the models for those sort of drawings? Surely not at the Royal Academy, I would venture."

"Indeed not. The Royal Academy is a narrow-minded male bastion, with neither the wit nor the vision to allow women into their ranks," she replied. "As for my models, I merely observe the people about me."

"And do you often have occasion to observe gentlemen without their clothing?"

She shot him a scathing look. Really, but the man was almost beyond bearing. He made it sound as if capturing the naked human form on paper was somehow indecent, worse than being a woman of the streets.

"I believe, my lord, that is none of your concern. And now would you care to hear my proposal, or should I take my leave?"

"Propose away. I give you my undivided attention."

The look he fixed on her with those piercing dark eyes assured her that such indeed was the case. Clearing her throat, she began. "Very well, my lord. You might have been justified in your suspicions of my intentions, wrong as they are. You see, I have it on good authority that certain . . . people do suspect you of being the Barkshire Demon. As you know, the public is clamoring for that fiend to be stopped. I fear it is but a matter of time before these people whom I told you of make their suspicions publicly known, and you are arrested for murder."

"Believe me, Miss Godwin, it won't be the first time."

His dangerously soft reply stopped her. He seemed unconcerned by the prospect of such an accusation. It was almost as if he hoped it would come to that—scarcely the attitude of an innocent man. Deliberately, she suppressed those doubts and resumed speaking.

"I, on the other hand, know that you have nothing to do with the matter. You see, I managed quite a good look at the man who attempted to murder me, and you were not he. Moreover, I could readily identify him should I ever see him again."

"Indeed." Blackstock leaned back in his own chair, the very picture of a patronizing male as he surveyed her with a cool smile. "So why come to me with this? Why not tell the authorities what you know?"

"That is a reasonable question, my lord. Let me just say that I have my reasons for keeping silent in this matter. Perhaps it would help you to know that there are certain . . . unusual circumstances about what I witnessed that the police would undoubtedly not believe. I did, however, post an unsigned note to the chief inspector this very morning regarding the circumstances of my attack, along with a sketch of the man who assaulted me."

It had proved the best compromise open to her. She dared not let her father learn of the incident; still, she could not live with herself should another woman die at the Demon's hands, and she had withheld pertinent information from the authorities. Unfortunately she rather suspected that those unimaginative men would dismiss her claims as the ravings of a hysterical female, despite her earnest explanations.

"Then you have done your duty as a citizen, Miss Godwin," the earl decreed, "though I am at a loss as to know what further use you might now have for me."

"Actually, my lord, I have come to enlist your help."

When Blackstock lifted a questioning brow, she went on. "You see, I am not so foolish as to think I can undertake the task alone. Even should I find the Barkshire Demon again, I could hardly overpower him by myself. And that is where you come in."

She paused for breath, enthusiasm creeping into her voice.

"Since we know the killer's pattern in choosing his victims, it would be a simple matter for me to wander the streets the next foggy night and hope he would see fit to attempt to murder me a second time. As for your role, my lord, I would think that you might follow me at a safe distance—on foot or perhaps in your carriage—and then apprehend the man when he attacks—"

"One moment, Miss Godwin," the earl cut her short, his tone politely incredulous. "Am I to understand that you propose to track down the Barkshire Demon, yourself, when the king's best men thus far have failed . . . and that you want me to assist you in carrying out this plan?"

"I—I had rather hoped you would see the brilliant simplicity of it all and agree to help."

"Brilliant simplicity? How about bloody stupidity?" The politeness was gone, the incredulity replaced now by outright disbelief. "What on earth made you think I would consent to wandering about on foggy nights searching for a madman?"

"Really, my lord, you need not resort to insults," she replied, stung. "It had occurred to me that, given the fact you could well be a prime suspect in the murders, you might wish to see the true killer caught."

"And supposing I did consent to this folly, you have forgotten something important. Though you might know what the Demon looks like, I do not."

"But that is easily remedied. I shall provide you with a sketch such as I gave the police."

He made no reply to that, so that she wondered if he might not be giving her proposal consideration after all. His answer, when it came, dispelled those hopes.

"Much as I admire your mettle, Miss Godwin, I fear I must decline your offer. As I implied, what you're proposing is folly, at best, and sheer madness, at worst . . . and on your account, not mine," he added when she opened her mouth to protest. "You've escaped the fiend once. Why don't you simply thank your lucky stars you are still alive and go about your business?"

Though not the answer for which she had hoped, it was the one Amaryllis had expected. Mixed with her disappointment, however, was a niggling sense of relief.

Now that she'd had more time to think over her plan, it occurred to her that she truly did not care to meet the Barkshire Demon again. Her hand crept toward her bruised throat. Perhaps she should do as Blackstock had suggested—let the proper authorities search out the killer, without her interference.

"Thank you for hearing me out, my lord," she said with formal dignity as she rose from the chair and bobbed a quick curtsy. "And again, I am grateful for your aid the other night, and I regret any injury I did you. Good day, my lord."

She had almost reached the library door, when Blackstock's careless drawl stopped her short.

"One moment, Miss Godwin. You may be finished with me, but I have not concluded my business with you."

She turned to face him, aware that her heartbeat had quickened, though whether in dread or anticipation, she was not certain. With an effort, she schooled her expression to one of polite inquiry. "My lord?"

"It would seem, Miss Godwin, that your enthusiasm for making proposals is contagious. Indeed I have conceived a proposal for you. Quite bluntly, I wish to offer you employment."

"Employment?" she echoed in a cautious voice, drawing her shawl more tightly about her throat.

Whatever could he mean? In the particular world that his lordship inhabited, unmarried women of her class traditionally were relegated to one of two roles—mistress or servant. He could hardly wish to make her the former, not on such short acquaintance. But chances were he did not want her to keep house for him, either.

"What I have in mind," he went on, "is a position eminently suited for a woman of your talents. I would require your services six days out of seven, and for several hours at a stretch. Even so, I believe you would not find the work onerous. You might well enjoy yourself once we get to know one another better. As for the compensation, I can assure you it would be more than generous."

She listened in growing dismay, scarce able to countenance what she was hearing. The man might not be a murderer, but he most definitely was a scoundrel. For surely what he was proposing was nothing short of scandalous.

"I am afraid I cannot consider such an offer, my lord," she managed in a haughty voice that shook but a little. "I am an artist, not a concubine. Now if I might take my leave—"

"Indeed, Miss Godwin, you disappoint me. I expected greater originality of thought from a modern woman such as yourself."

So saying, Blackstock rose from his chair and started toward her. She watched him uncertainly, half-wondering if she might be forced to the same sort of drastic measures she'd employed at their last meeting. He halted but an arm's length away, so that she was compelled to look up to meet his gaze.

She had forgotten just how imposing a male he was.

It was not just the height and breadth of him, though those features were impressive enough. Rather it was the dangerous air about him, the air of a man who took what he wanted from life . . . the rest of the world be damned.

"Before you refuse me," he continued in the same unperturbed tones, "I suggest that you hear me out. You see, though I am certain you would make quite the charming concubine, I don't want you in my bed. It is your talents as an artist that I require."

"Oh. I—I see."

She blushed a fiery red, wondering if it were possible to expire from shame. If so, then her father would be preparing her grave right now, so foolish did she feel. How could she have supposed that a sophisticated man like Blackstock— and he an earl, no less!—would have any carnal interest in her?

As if he read her thoughts, the barest hint of a smile twisted his sensuous lips.

"You are right, of course. I could not expect you to accept a post without your first knowing a bit more about what it entails. So, if you dare accompany me elsewhere, I will show you in greater detail just exactly what I wish you to do."

Ten

The cool challenge in Blackstock's words was more than she could bear . . . as surely he must have intended it to be. Forgetting any doubts as to his motives, Amaryllis raised her chin and met his gaze with an equally chill look of her own.

"I *do* dare, my lord, so please lead on."

By way of answer, he walked over to the French doors and pulled them open. Immediately beyond, she saw, lay a narrow terrace of white marble that ran the width of the house. It was edged by a waist-high stone balustrade, unbroken save for an arm's breadth wide gap at its centermost point, where she glimpsed steps leading to the grounds below. Making her the slightest of mocking bows, Blackstock gestured her outside. Head high, she marched past him out onto that terrace . . . and then promptly halted in surprise.

For below her lay an unkempt section of blooming greenery, nigh impassable save for where vestiges of graveled paths divided the plot into quarters. At the juncture of these walkways sat a marble pool overrun with vines. From that tangle rose a naked stone maiden attempting to fill that dry basin from her empty vase. Four other statues, set equidistant from each other and lichen-scabbed almost beyond recognition, peered blindly about them. Bluish afternoon shadows spread like a pox and thickened the air of neglect that hung over the plot.

This had once been a charming formal garden, Amaryllis

guessed, drawing her shawl against the breeze that swept it. Now, however, it would require an army of gardeners to restore the plot to its original beauty.

Not waiting for any comment, Blackstock made his way down the cracked marble steps and plunged into the chaos. She had no choice but to follow after him.

Vines tugged at her skirt, while broken bits of crockery among the gravel bruised her slippered feet. Thankfully their destination proved no farther than the large outbuilding beside the stables. The single-story structure was of the same dark stone as the town house, but there the similarity ended.

Broad windows ran the length of either side and stretched almost from ground to roof. In place of the usual slate tiles above, framed panels of glass served instead, while an elaborate series of gutters ran its perimeter. At either end of that peculiar roof, a stone chimney breathed lazy wisps of smoke.

"Here we are, Miss Godwin," the earl's words cut short her inspection. He opened a pair of uncurtained French doors—their glass panes gleaming in sharp contrast to the unkempt garden—and once more gestured her to proceed him. Hesitantly Amaryllis stepped inside.

Her first impression was that of a single large room, its contents blunted by shadows despite the late afternoon sun gleaming through the glass roof above. The air within was damp and warm, heavy with the unmistakable scent of freshly turned earth that put her in uncomfortable mind of a new grave. Another scent was an equally identifiable—the faint, unmistakable odor of manure.

Her uncertainty grew as, soft footwear whispering against the damp flagstone beneath her feet, she started forward. Immense dark shapes loomed on either side of her while, before her, she made out a series of waist-high rectangular shapes. She hesitated, hearing the distinctive clink of metal against glass as Blackstock proceeded to light a lantern. A moment later, yellow light spilled around her to reveal the building's secret.

What she had expected to see, she was not certain. Surely not this veritable jungle that now confronted her. Along either row of windows, immense espaliered shrubs sprang from oversized wooden tubs. A few had been pruned back to a semblance of formal shape. The rest sprawled with unruly vigor, their tall canes and twisting vines—some sporting delicate new buds of pink or red—threatening to overwhelm their heavy lattice supports.

The building was a hothouse, she realized, well-lit and artificially heated so that plants could grow and blossom out of season. She noted in either of its nearer two corners what appeared to be rain barrels, with waterspouts cleverly set through the outer walls. Doubtless, they were meant to conveniently channel inside the water collected from the gutters she'd noted without.

She saw now that the wide aisle between those living walls of greenery was taken up by a series of sturdy wooden tables. The one immediately before her held all manner of gardening implements—spades, tuning forks, pruning knives—and a collection of odd-sized containers. Upon the other tables sat neat rows of clay pots, each containing small, green-leafed shrubs—some with but a hint of new buds, others in full flower.

By now Blackstock had lit another lamp, so she could see that from each pot hung a tiny wooden placard. Upon each placard was inked a name—some in French, a few in English, a goodly number of others in Latin. She straightened and shot his lordship a look of surprise.

"Why, all of these are roses."

Victor heard the note of cautious interest in her tone, and he nodded in satisfaction. "I believe that is a *Rosa damascena bifera* directly before you. You'll find other Damasks alongside it—the Tuscany, the Celsiana, and one of my late father's creations that he named the Maiden Helene, after my mother. The next table over, you'll find various species of Gallicas . . . and the tables after that, Albas and Chinas. Do take a closer look, if you wish."

She seemed not to notice his scrutiny as she wandered the row of the mature specimens that lined one windowed wall. She halted before one and reached a questioning hand toward a single burst of pink blossoms. He heard her quick gasp of dismay as she drew back abruptly and stripped off one glove. As he watched, a crimson drop welled from her forefinger.

"Did you know, Miss Godwin," he remarked, "that the ancient Romans believed the first rose sprang from the blood of the goddess Venus? And there are several other charming legends surrounding the rose. My favorite is the tale of how the red rose got its color. Would you care to hear it?"

"Certainly, my lord," she replied, then daintily sucked upon that abused finger.

He hesitated, distracted at the sight. There was something highly erotic about the gesture, the more so because he sensed her complete innocence of any seductive intent. A sudden heat flared in his groin as he imagined her kneeling on the flagstone before him while that soft pink mouth performed a similar service upon his person. They'd not be disturbed here, since he'd given Monique and the staff strict orders never to enter without an invitation from him. Hell, they could spend the rest of the afternoon—

Brutally Victor suppressed the remainder of that most intriguing scenario from his thoughts. Clearing a sudden huskiness from his throat, he began. "It seems the first rose blossomed with petals of so pure a white that it fairly gleamed. A nightingale was enraptured by its beauty and, passing too closely, became impaled upon its thorns. As he lay dying, his heart's blood spilled upon those snowy petals . . . and ever after the rose bloomed a brilliant shade of crimson in tribute to his love."

She gave him a faint smile. "Blood and roses . . . odd how they seem so closely tied together in legend. It is a charming story, Lord Blackstock. Still, it escapes me how this could be connected with offering me employment. If it is a gardener you seek, I fear I have no talent with growing plants."

"Ah, but you see, Miss Godwin, I do."

He spared a look of pride at the neat rows of flourishing cuttings and seedlings, then slanted her a darkly questioning look. "Of course, there are some that might consider such an avocation to be, shall we say, an unmasculine sort of pursuit."

"Not at all, my lord," she warmly protested, much to his relief. "It would seem to me that growing any sort of living creature, plant or animal, requires equal parts science and art . . . and surely much hard work."

"Then you are more perceptive than most. As it happens, growing roses has been a tradition with my family for the past several generations," he explained. "My great-grandmother was a rosarian of some note in her native France before she married an English man and made her home here. She passed on her love of roses to her son—my grandsire—who later built this hothouse. My father kept up the tradition, propagating various new species until his death two years ago."

"And you elected to carry on his legacy," she interposed and bent to sniff at a just-bursting red bud.

Victor let his gaze linger upon her rounded buttocks, neatly emphasized by the seductive drape of her gown's thin muslin. Then, realizing he'd been distracted again from his purpose, he gave himself a mental shake before making his wry reply.

"To be quite truthful, Miss Godwin, the legacy took over me. You see, I had long since rejected my father's obsession with cultivating his shrubs and creating new varieties by crossing various stocks. I saw all this"—he paused and gestured at the profusion of greenery—"as the idle indulgence of a man with too much time and money on his hands. I fear that, when I returned home after my parents' deaths, I simply allowed the place to run riot . . . much as that square of garden through which we just passed. One of the footmen kept the shrubs watered, but that was the extent of it."

"One would scarce believe that, for everything is so tidy and flourishing now," she said with a puzzled frown. "I always thought that roses did not bloom until the summer months, yet many of these already are in full flower."

"There are techniques used to make roses bloom at other times of the year . . . forcing, it is called. As you can see, I have had some success in that area, though I have far to go yet to become the expert that my father and his father were."

"But you seem to have made a magnificent start, my lord, for all you once claimed to scorn the work. Tell me, what happened to change your mind?"

He'd anticipated the question; still, he hesitated, wondering what sort of reply to make. That, in the days following Jane Belfleur's murder, he'd needed a refuge from the memories of her blood and her screams? That he'd been dogged by vicious rumors and banned from every elite club and polite household in London? That anger and resentment had consumed him, so he'd not been fit company for civilized people, anyhow?

He finally settled upon evasiveness.

"Let us just say, Miss Godwin, that I felt in need of solace one day and impulsively made my way out here. For a lack of anything better to occupy myself, I began pruning the dead canes from one of the overgrown shrubs. It was a mindless sort of task, but oddly satisfying once I'd finished. I came back the next day and the day after that. By the end of the week, I'd become just as obsessed with it all as my father had ever been."

"I see. But I still do not know what any of this has to do with me."

"It is quite simple," he said with a faint shrug. "In addition to restoring my father's hothouse, I have embarked upon a project of my own. I intend to publish a volume entitled *On the Care and Propagation of Roses,* with the text a comparative study of traditional sources and four generations' worth of my family's own observations."

He paused, watching her closely to judge her reaction as he continued. "It suddenly has occurred to me that such a book would be greatly enhanced by a comprehensive series of illustrative prints. I've already seen several samples of your work, and I am impressed with your skill. I would presume, as well, that you are equally adept at watercolors. Thus, Miss Godwin, I want to commission you to do the original paintings from which the etchings for my book would be made."

"You are saying, my lord, that you wish me to paint roses?"

"Exactly."

Amaryllis stared at him in silence a moment, excitement and dismay battling within her. This was what she had been dreaming of, a chance to actually earn a livelihood from her artwork. Moreover, should Blackstock give her credit as the book's illustrator, that professional exposure could well lead to similar such commissions. It was an opportunity that she could ill afford to refuse.

But she must.

She stifled an inner groan. From the earl's brief description of the project, she could see that it could well take weeks, or even months, to complete her work. How could she possibly keep her brother from learning what she was about for that length of time? His reaction should he discover the truth did not bear thinking upon. Moreover it would be nearly as difficult enough to keep up her fictional identity before Blackstock. What if he asked her about her family, wanted to know where she lived? And what of her name, when it came time to credit her for her work?

But those problems all paled before the matter of greatest concern, that she hardly knew the man well enough to say whether or not he could be trusted.

"You appear uncertain, Miss Godwin," his voice broke in on her thoughts. "Perhaps if I tell you the wages I intend to offer."

The figure he named made her gasp outright. Indeed, if the commission lasted but a single month, she would have garnered more money than she could make in a year of teaching young girls to sketch . . . and certainly more money than she could expect from mending a linen chest's worth of torn lace.

Almost without realizing what she was doing, she nodded. "Very well, Lord Blackstock," came her breathless reply, "I accept the job."

"I am pleased to hear it. I will, of course, supply you with whatever canvases and paints you might require. And I would like you to begin tomorrow. Nine o'clock, shall we say, since I don't keep Society's hours."

"Tomorrow will be just fine, my lord."

Her mind awhirl, Amaryllis waited while he turned down the lamps again and, gesturing her outside, shut the French doors behind them. Then, still marveling over the enormity of what she'd agreed to, she followed as Blackstock retraced their earlier path through the overgrown garden back to the library.

It wasn't until they were back inside that cozy room that he spoke again. "I'll have Derek drive you home," he said and gave the bell pull a tug.

She stared back at him in alarm. If this Derek learned where she lived, he could easily pass on that information to the earl who, in turn, might manage to learn her true name and her connection to Talbot. If so, her position might well be terminated before it ever began.

"Indeed that is not necessary. I can easily walk—"

"It is near dark, Miss Godwin, and I'll not have a female

in my employ wandering the streets alone. Or was not one encounter with the Barkshire Demon enough for you?" he asked with a lift of one brow.

She suppressed a shiver. In truth she did not relish the long walk home again, and she'd not coin enough to spare for another hired hack. She could simply have the man set her off a street away from her true destination.

"Put that way, Lord Blackstock," she replied, "I accept this offer as well."

His summons was promptly answered by Peters, whom he gave swift instruction. Though his surprise at the news of Amaryllis's employment was evident, the butler prudently made no comment.

"Oh, and Miss Godwin," the earl's voice stopped her as she prepared to follow the butler out, "one last thing. If you wish to retrieve your sketchbook, you might call on Dr. Talbot Meeks. I believe that he makes his lodgings at an old church somewhere on Whitten Street."

"I shall make a point of it," she answered, grateful that he had inadvertently solved one of her problems at least. She need only tell him on the morrow that she had located said doctor and recovered her property, and that matter would be settled. As for juggling the rest of her secrets, she would be on her own.

Bobbing Blackstock a quick curtsy, she let a dour Peters escort her out to the front step, where she waited for the carriage to be brought around. It proved to be an elegant black affair with the Saville family coat of arms prominently emblazoned upon either side. That crest, appropriately enough, prominently featured stylized roses on one of its quartered fields . . . the same design as engraved upon the heavy gold ring that the earl wore.

Not until after Derek, with a cheeky, "glad t'see yer recovered, miss," helped her inside, and they were rumbling down the street, did she realize that her hands were trembling. At the same time, she saw that she had left behind the single glove she'd pulled off when she pricked her finger.

"Blast," she murmured with a shake of her head, and then allowed herself a broad smile. It seemed she could not take her leave of Blackstock without leaving one or another of her possessions behind. Little matter. With the salary the earl was paying her, she could well afford a dozen new pairs of gloves, if she so chose.

Immediately she sobered. Given the extraordinary wages he would be paying, he would certainly expect nothing less than her best efforts. That she would give him. But what if he wanted something more from her than her skills as an artist?

She leaned back against the tufted seat and shut her eyes, unwillingly summoning his image to her mind. For, deny it as she might to Talbot, she did fancy Blackstock's dramatic good looks. Moreover she already knew what it was like to feel his strong arms around her. Then his had been the iron-hard embrace of a captor restraining his quarry. What would it be like, she wondered, to have him hold her that close but for entirely different reasons?

A sudden heat suffused her, and she shifted restlessly against the sumptuous bench. Was it her imagination, or did the butter-soft leather hold a hint of his scent? If she took a deep breath, she could almost breathe that now-familiar mixture of fine-milled soap mingled with the faint male scent of his flesh.

Just in time, she stopped herself from running caressing fingers against the leather and instead managed a shaky laugh. To think she had been concerned that Blackstock might force his attentions on her. Indeed it might well be the earl who was in danger of such unwanted attentions. For the romantic within her could not deny that there was something quite exciting about desiring a man whom one was not quite sure one entirely liked or trusted.

Sternness of mind, the practical voice within her, as always, spoke up. The earl had hired her to do a job, and she should do it . . . nothing more, nothing less. Let her friend, Mary, be the one to flit about with unsuitable men who could only bring her grief.

She would remain an independent woman and quite happily so.

Victor leaned back in his well-worn leather chair and contemplated the pale yellow glove on the desk before him. He had spotted it left behind on one of the tables on his way out of the greenhouse. Busy with turning down the lamps, he'd merely tucked the glove in his waistcoat, intending to return it to its owner once they'd reached the house. But she'd not asked, and he had forgotten until after the carriage pulled away. Now the glove—slim fingers slightly curled—lay in quirky counterpoint alongside its owner's drawing of the hand and rose.

He briefly shut his eyes, certain there was some profound symbolism to be found there but unable to interpret it. More pressing a problem now was what to do about a certain Miss Amaryllis Godwin.

He had been oddly pleased to discover that she was no soiled dove. The fact she believed him innocent of intending to harm her had been an equally welcome revelation. Still, her mad scheme to track down the real Barkshire Demon had proved her as impractical a female as his sister or any other woman. That was why his impulsive offer of employment had surprised him as much as it had her.

To be sure, his notion of adding illustrations to his book had been an excellent one. Doubtless that very idea would have occurred to him, sooner or later, and he would have been forced to seek out an artist anyway. But a female painter . . . and her in particular? Victor managed a wry smile. The chit must have dealt him a more serious injury to his brain than he had imagined.

But what other excuse could you have made for wanting to see her again?

The question arose unbidden in his mind, and he frowned. True she was attractive . . . not his usual type, perhaps, but the sort to stir a certain masculine interest wherever she went. And the air of innocent sensuality that clung to her like an attar of roses had drawn him from the first.

Drawn him? Victor shook his head in disgust. Hell, he'd pawed her like a lusty schoolboy that night in the carriage. Only the intervention of an inconvenient conscience had stopped him from taking her then, swooning or not. The series of rose illustrations he needed would require her working alongside him in the hothouse for hours at a time. With such proximity, how long would it be before he found himself in the same sort of situation again?

He'd always had contempt for the nobles who took advantage of their station, tumbling the governess or under-parlor maid whenever they took the fancy. They did so safe in the knowledge that the women would dare not complain lest they lose their post and be tossed onto the streets without a reference. And while he had no illusions as to Miss Godwin's innocence—for had she not proclaimed herself a modern woman?—he would consider her under his protection while in his employ and thus out of bounds for his attentions.

Deliberately he reached out to touch the glove's kid forefinger. As he did so, he recalled the way she'd sucked on that same injured digit as they had toured the hothouse. While Penelope would have turned the simple gesture into a provocative display—complete with coy glances and an excess of sound—Amaryllis Godwin had appeared totally unaware of the effect she was having on him.

Innocent, yes . . . but damned seductive all the same. The very memory was enough to send a hot, hard surge of desire racing through him. For a moment, he was tempted to snatch up that tiny glove and use it upon himself in a most creative manner to gain a bit of relief. Then maybe he'd be able to think with his brain instead of with his balls.

He stifled a groan and snatched back his hand, then waited for the burgeoning sensation in the region of his crotch to subside on its own. The entire situation was nothing sort of ludicrous, and any sensible man would put a stop to it at once. Still, he *had* made the offer, and she *had* accepted it. He could hardly renege now without looking the fool.

"The solution is quite simple," he muttered aloud. "You let the chit paint roses, and you keep your bloody hands off her while she's doing it."

He groaned again and raked an impatient hand through his dark hair. A simple solution, yes.

The question was, could he actually manage it?

Eleven

"My idea, Miss Godwin, is to furnish two plates for each variety of rose covered in the text," the Earl of Blackstock coolly said. "One will show the specimen in the early stages of budding, with emphasis on the leaves and stem. The second should depict the flower itself in full glory, with careful attention to color and petal shape."

He paused and pulled from his coat pocket a sheet of foolscap, which he handed to Amaryllis. Shading her eyes against the bright morning light spilling through the glass roof of the hothouse, she scanned the list. More than a score of varieties had been inked there in a firm, masculine hand.

"As you can see, some of these plants are still in the budding stage, while others are in full flower," he went on. "The latter are the ones you will want to concentrate upon first, since their display lasts but a short while. As for the rest of them, it will be anywhere from a week to a fortnight from now before they actually begin to bloom . . . though, again, their flowers will swiftly die off. Thus you will have your work cut out for you these next weeks."

"I am certain you are right, my lord," she said with a wry smile as she calculated the number of paintings required against the time allowed. "I believe that today I will begin by plotting the location of each species here on my list. Afterward, I will commence with a few preliminary sketches of those varieties already flowering."

"How you manage is quite up to you, Miss Godwin. I

simply expect results. If you need any of the larger specimens moved about for any reason, Derek"—he nodded in the direction of the coachman, who was lounging against one of the far tables—"will lend a hand. And now, if you will excuse me, I must be about my own work."

His tone was curt; indeed he'd been quite as aloof from the moment she rang the bell almost an hour earlier. Was he regretting the offer he had made her, she wondered, or was this simply Blackstock's usual way of dealing with people?

Probably a little of both, she decided now as she matched his formal manner. "I shall endeavor not to interrupt you, my lord. I would ask one favor, however." She hesitated, feeling suddenly quite the fool, then plunged on. "If you would, my lord, I would ask you simply to address me as Amaryllis."

Blackstock shot her a look of well-bred surprise, so that she felt herself blush. "Indeed, Miss Godwin, I have always discouraged this sort of informality with my female employees," he coolly returned. "It tends to lead to certain, shall we say, presumptions on both parts."

"I—I quite understand, my lord. I would ask, however, that you indulge me in this."

She met his gaze, even as she felt her blush deepen. It *was* a presumption, she knew, and he might well interpret her request as an invitation for a more personal relationship between them. Her motives, however, were much more basic. The simple fact was, her innate sense of honesty rebelled at keeping up a pseudonymous identity.

Not that she'd lied about her name for any more nefarious reason save than concealing her connection to Talbot, she reminded herself. Still, she would feel less guilty about the whole matter should she not be forced to answer to a name that was not hers. Besides, it would be embarrassing in the extreme should she momentarily forget the surname with which she had saddled herself.

To her relief, Blackstock merely shrugged. "As you wish,

Amaryllis," he replied, then allowed himself a faint smile. "Rather amusing, is it not . . a single exotic bloom among all these common roses?"

With that extraordinary comment, Blackstock turned on his heel and started toward the far end of the hothouse. There he disappeared into the small room that he'd previously informed her contained a modern watercloset and a separate dressing area. A moment later, he stepped back out, minus his black jacket, snowy neckcloth, and gray waistcoat. More shocking, his shirt collar was undone, and his shirtsleeves were rolled to his elbows. Having seemingly forgotten her presence, he gestured Derek over.

Amaryllis stared outright as the pair caught up a section of new wooden latticework, nearly as long as the hothouse itself, that lay along one row of windows. As she watched, they lifted that heavy framework head-high; then, amid much discussion, they began positioning it between a series of wooden pegs that had already been installed at intervals along that wall.

The process took several moments, long enough for her to marvel over the fact that the refined Earl of Blackstock was not averse to laboring like a commoner. It also gave her ample time to determine that his lordship possessed a physique that would be the envy of any Royal Academy model. Though she was too far away to make out the individual play of muscles beneath his fine lawn shirt and tight black breeches, her distant perspective allowed her to admire the magnificent way those various muscle groups worked together as a whole.

Aware all at once that she was gaping like a smitten schoolgirl, she turned her attention back to her list. Here she had been in Blackstock's employ a mere hour, and already she was finding it difficult to keep her mind on her work. Unless she practiced sternness of mind, she would never accomplish anything.

She gave herself a mental shake, even as she blotted her

suddenly damp palms against the cotton smock she wore over her simple gray muslin gown. Then, taking up a pencil and notebook, she began moving up and down the wood tables. Her first task was plotting a straightforward diagram of the various roses. Once she had worked with the plants for a while, she doubtless would be able to pick out the individual species on sight. For now, though, she would use the list to jog her memory.

As the earl had said the day before, the plants were grouped about the tables by class—Albas, Gallicas, Damasks, and Centifolias. Upon her arrival this morning, he had given her a brief explanation as to the breakdown of their scientific names. He quoted her Linnaeus's *Species Plantarum* with the same fervor that another man of his rank might spout Byron or Shelley.

But there *was* poetry to be found among these thorny brambles, and not only in their graceful lines. Their common names, she now saw, were listed upon their placards along with the Latin nomenclature. Amaryllis swiftly decided she much preferred those designations. How much more romantic it would be to hand one's beloved a *Cuisse de nymphe*—a "Maiden's Blush"—or a "Rose of a Hundred Leaves," rather than the scientific equivalent.

As she listed each variety by location, she decided to take preliminary notes on each rose's characteristics. Having never been much taken with botanicals before—men always expected women to paint flowers; therefore she rarely did— she found to her surprise just how different each species was from the others.

The Gallicas, she dubbed the gentlewomen of the group, slender and upright, their regal bearing enhanced by their small bristling thorns. Taller and more sprawling than their prim sisters were the Damasks, their large thorns and long leaves of gray-green leaves giving them a more blowsy air. The Albas were the hoydens of the group—taller still, yet oddly delicate, with only a handful of thorns. Most unusual were the moss roses, small and thorny creatures, the velvety capes of brown or dark green fuzz along a portion of their stems giving them their name.

The process of organizing the plants upon paper took her most of the morning. So engrossed was she in the task that she had no trouble ignoring the unsettling presence of Blackstock. Even the sound of the men's labor fast faded to the back of her thoughts. It wasn't until her stomach began an urgent grumbling that she finally halted. A glance at the sun through the glass panes above confirmed her stomach's contention that the noon hour was upon them.

She set down her notebook and pencil on the potting table, then brushed back a damp strand of red hair that had worked free of its pins. More than once, she had considered shearing her long tresses in the convenient short style that was the mode. Vanity, however, had always stopped her. Perhaps she should reconsider in the name of comfort, given that she would be spending the next several weeks here.

Indeed it was far warmer in the hothouse than she was used to, for her father was notoriously clutch-fisted with coal. She untied her long smock and slipped out of it; then, with a sigh of relief, she pulled out one of the tall stools that were shoved beneath the table and settled upon its teetering height. Little wonder that Blackstock elected to work here in his shirtsleeves.

Blackstock.

Frowning, she looked about only to discover that both the earl and Derek were gone. She had been so caught up in making her notes that the pair had slipped past her and out the door without her even noticing.

So what was she to do now? Presumably she was allowed a meal and a few minutes in which to eat it. The question was, did she go tapping at the kitchen door like a street waif, or did she join the rest of the staff? While she'd not mind breaking bread with Derek, the thought of Peters's sour face presiding over the table was enough to give one indigestion. Yet even as she was debating the issue, one of the French doors opened a few inches, and a pair of merry dark eyes peered around its edge.

"Good. He's not here," observed a tinkling voice.

As Amaryllis watched in surprise, the door opened all the way to admit a pretty, dark-haired girl in a white gown carrying a napkin-covered silver tray. Still more amazing was the fact that, perched upon the tray's edge, was a gray-and-red parrot. The girl slipped inside and started in Amaryllis's direction.

"You mustn't say a word to Victor about my being here," she urged with a conspiratorial smile. "Cook only let me carry this out to you because I threatened to put a toad in her bed if she didn't. And I would have, too. I simply was dying to meet you."

So saying, she set down the tray on the potting table. The parrot gave an aggrieved squawk and promptly flapped over to the nearest of the fledgling rosebushes, perching on the edge of its clay container. Then, with the grace of a rope dancer, the bird stretched out its neck and with its dark gray beak delicately snipped the plant in half.

"Oh, Wilhelm, whatever possessed you?" the girl gasped out and rushed to scoop up the wayward feathered creature.

The bird docilely hopped onto her outstretched hand. "Oh, Wilhelm," he echoed in a sad tone while the girl stared at what remained of the rose seedling.

"We mustn't tell Victor . . . promise me you won't," she exclaimed, turning a dismayed look on Amaryllis. "Why, he might wring poor Wilhelm's neck, and all for a silly old bush. You see, we're not even supposed to be in here, though it's not as if Wilhelm makes a habit of chewing upon plants . . . at least not too often."

"Not too often," the parrot agreed.

Amaryllis suppressed a smile at the unlikely pair's melodramatic manner. "I won't say a word," she promised as, catching up the mutilated vine, she tucked it into the pocket of her discarded smock. "There, I've hidden the evidence. When I go home tonight, I'll toss it into the gutter blocks from here, so that his lordship will never be the wiser."

The girl stared back at her a moment, then burst into tinkling laughter. "Oh, I knew I would like you from the moment I learned you were brave enough to cosh my brother over the head. Of course, Vic would never hurt a pet of mine . . . but he *would* carry on, so that you'd think Wilhelm's little lapse was the slaughter of the innocents or some such nonsense."

"The Earl of Blackstock . . . he is your brother?" Amaryllis asked in surprise, having heard nothing more of what the girl said beyond that extraordinary fact.

Somehow she'd assumed the earl had no family. Still, she could see a noticeable resemblance between brother and sister—their dramatic good looks, the arrogant way they held their heads, the sensual mouths. But taciturn as Blackstock was, his sibling was loquacious. And while his lips tended to twist with cool irony, the girl's quirked with suppressed humor.

She was smiling now. "Did you not know? I am Lady Monique. This, of course, is Wilhelm"—she paused to make kissing sounds against the bird's gray-feathered head—"and you must be Miss Godwin, are you not?"

At Amaryllis's nod, Monique gave her a considering look. "Surely you're not the same Miss Godwin whom the scandal sheets said ran off with that poet . . . what was his name?"

Amaryllis felt her cheeks redden. Blast it all, but she should have chosen a different alias, given her friend, Mary's, current notoriety. "I believe you mean Mr. Shelley, but I assure you it was not I. And do call me Amaryllis."

"So I shall. I suppose it's only fair then that I give you leave to call me Monique."

With that pert reply, the younger girl whipped the cloth from the tray to display an impressive array of dried fruits, cheeses, and a portion of baked chicken. A carafe of water and two fist-sized loaves of bread completed the meal.

"I'm sure you will find this all to your liking, Amaryllis. And I did have Cook send out a bit extra, in case you might like some company."

That last held a certain wistful note that belied the girl's forward manner. It occurred to Amaryllis that, given her brother's unsavory reputation, Lady Monique might have few female friends near her own age.

"I would be pleased to have you join me, Monique . . . but from what you said earlier, I had the impression his lordship did not want you associating with me."

"Oh, Vic can be so stuffy at times," the girl said with a dismissive wave. "I think it had something to do with the fact he had assumed you were a common woman of the streets."

With that blunt explanation, she deposited Wilhelm on the table edge, then pulled up another of the rickety stools to sit beside Amaryllis. Plucking a dried plum from the tray, she held it out to her pet. Wilhelm accepted the tidbit and proceeded to scatter bits of the purple fruit about as he made a feast of it.

"I used to come here all the time, when my father was alive," Monique confided as she reached for a plum of her own. "When I was young, I even helped him care for the bushes. I vow, it is quite a good deal of work. The roses must be watered and fertilized and fumigated on a regular basis. And the temperature must be kept just so—which means, depending on the season, one is always bringing in more coal or else adjusting the windows so that only a certain amount of fresh air and no more blows in."

"It does sound quite complicated," Amaryllis agreed as she helped herself to a wedge of fresh cheese and broke off a piece of the soft bread. "I must admit I never expected that caring for flowers could be so time-consuming. Your father must have appreciated all your assistance."

Monique nodded, even as she daintily wrinkled her nose. "I fear I was much less help to him once I grew older. You see, it became rather tiresome, spending all day stirring up dirt and pouring in cups of manure tea for so many plants, with Mama always complaining that I smelled like a stable boy. I finally decided that I much preferred my roses in a vase. But when Papa died, there were no roses at all . . . so that is why I am pleased Victor has decided to carry on the Saville tradition."

She paused for a bite of cold chicken, then fixed her bright gaze on Amaryllis again. "It was rather odd, my brother hiring you after what happened. He said you are helping him with the book he intends to publish."

"I will be doing the illustrations for the various plates," she explained, gesturing at the open notebook with its few preliminary penciled renditions of roses. "His lordship saw some of my sketches and decided to offer me the commission."

"You are a painter?" the girl eagerly asked. "Could you do my portrait then? My great-grandmother had the most beautiful painting done of her wearing a white gown and surrounded by an arbor of red roses. Someday I will show it to you."

She paused, her delicate features taking on a dreamy look. "Do you know, Amaryllis, that my great-grandmother always used to bathe in rose water? Every day she would take the petals of two dozen pink roses and scatter them in a marble tub filled with hot water. Then, after they had steeped a bit, she would climb right in with the flowers. That was why my great-grandfather fell in love with her, because she always smelled like roses. Perhaps if *I* bathed in rose water, *I* might have a suitor."

"But you must have dozens of young men dying for a kind word from you," Amaryllis protested in true surprise. "Surely at your coming out—"

"I have not yet been presented," the girl admitted, faint

color darkening her pale cheeks. "I was to have been, but Mama and Papa died. And then with Victor . . well, things just did not work out as one might have hoped."

Her words took on a world-weary, adult tone with that last observation, but Amaryllis heard the girlish pain that lay beneath. Doubtless Monique had been tarred by the same brush of scandal that colored her brother, so that she had been denied the opportunities that would ordinarily have been accorded a young woman of her rank.

Before she could offer any words of comfort, however, the girl resumed her cheerful tone. "At any rate, I would like *my* portrait to be just the same as Great-grandmama's, with me in a flowing white gown and surrounded by red roses . . . but with Wilhelm on my shoulder, of course."

"Of course," the parrot cheekily agreed.

"Of course," Amaryllis echoed them both with a smile. "If your brother proves satisfied with my work and wishes me to paint you as well, then I would be quite happy to do so."

Monique gave a nod, as if the matter were already settled, then changed the subject. "Did you know that Victor told me about your encounter with the Barkshire Demon? I vow, I would have died of fright, even if the fiend did not manage to kill me. Those bruises on your neck . . . they must be from where he tried to strangle you before Victor whisked you away to safety, are they not?"

Reflexively Amaryllis's hand went to her throat. She'd known she would never be able to work with her shawl wrapped about her throat like a mustard plaster. Thus this morning, she had applied a liberal dusting of rice powder to the purple splotches and tied a broad green ribband about her neck as camouflage. Though that stratagem concealed the worst of the discoloration, her mirror told her it would be several days more until she dared appear in public with her throat exposed.

"They are . . . and I am quite grateful to your brother for

his intervention," she replied, suppressing an involuntary shiver at the memory. "I most certainly would be dead now, had he not come along."

"But you saw the man who attacked you, did you not?" At Amaryllis's nod, the girl went on. "I told Vic that he should have pressed you for a description of the man. That way he could have pursued the Barkshire Demon himself and been a hero by catching him. Then perhaps people would not whisper such awful things about my brother."

Monique's voice quavered a bit on those last words, and again Amaryllis felt her heart go out to the younger girl. For herself, she had been duly shocked by Talbot's account of the Belfleur woman's brutal killing. How much more painful it must be for Monique to know Blackstock was suspected of such a heinous crime, and that there was nothing she could do to prove him innocent.

"I did tell his lordship that I could identify the man," she gently said, "and I even suggested that the two of us attempt to track him down. However, as your brother pointed out, that is a task better handled by the proper authorities."

"Oh, pooh," was the girl's dismissive response. "Why, you and I together could probably catch him."

Amaryllis half-feared that the girl would suggest as much. Instead Monique slanted a shrewd look in her direction and added, "You know, I never would have expected Vic to be interested in a woman like you . . . someone with no wealth and no title, I mean. Oh, don't try to tell me that all he cares about is your painting," she cut Amaryllis short when she would have protested. "He may think I am too young to know about such things, but I am not. I am quite certain that he finds you attractive. And I will not believe you one whit if you say you do not find him handsome in turn."

"Really, Monique," she finally managed, "this is hardly the sort of subject that—"

"I thought that, when he first came home after Mama and Papa died, he would take a bride that very year," the girl chattered on, blithely ignoring her interruption. "Why, half a dozen of the girls who'd had their coming out that Season swore he was prepared to offer for them, though he never did. Of course, he has had his share of *demimondaines,* but I do not think his heart was ever involved."

She paused long enough to nibble daintily on a crumb of cheese. "You are not stylish, nothing at all like the women of the *ton,* but you could be accounted an Original, nonetheless. And I know that Victor does not care for simpering females, so you are safe enough there. The only problem I could foresee is that, given his advanced age, he might prefer a woman with certain . . . experience."

She paused again, considering; then, favoring Amaryllis with a mischievous smile, she went on. "Victor has a copy of *Essays on Far Eastern Marriage Customs* in his library that quite explains everything one would ever need to know on the subject. I don't suppose you have ever read that particular volume before, have you, Amaryllis?"

"I would certainly hope that she has not," a grim masculine voice broke in.

Both women glanced up guiltily to see the Earl of Blackstock standing just inside the French doors. The look in his dark eyes was unreadable, though, had she to guess, Amaryllis would have said he was not amused. And, from his frosty tone, she also gathered that the book to which Monique had referred was not a work of high literature.

Though awash with mortification—*dear Lord, just how much of their conversation had he overheard?*—she climbed from her stool and made him a quick curtsy.

"Good afternoon, my lord. Lady Monique was kind enough to bring me refreshment, and I asked if she would join me. I trust you do not object."

Blackstock slanted her a dark look before turning an even more forbidding glance upon his younger sister. "Lady Monique knows full well that she is not to be wandering the hothouse, with or without her bird. Neither is she to disturb you at your work. As for you, Miss Godwin"—he turned his attention back to Amaryllis—"I must insist that you refrain from indulging my sister in her foolishness. She has an unfortunate tendency to prattle on about subjects that she has no business discussing—"

"Really, Vic," Monique broke in with a peevish sniff, "we were merely chatting, woman to woman. Why must you always treat me like such a child?"

"When you start acting like an adult, then I will accord you that courtesy. Until that time, I expect you to comply with my wishes . . . and that means keeping out of the hothouse and away from my employees. Do you understand?"

His sister shot him a mutinous look as she scrambled from her own chair. "I understand, all right," she replied with a haughty lift of her chin. "I understand that you are quite the perfect beast . . . and I hope that you and your silly roses are quite happy together."

So saying, she gathered up Wilhelm and then turned to Amaryllis. "I enjoyed talking with you, Miss Godwin, and I do hope you will still consent to paint my portrait one day. In the meantime, try not to let my brother bully you as he does me," she finished with an arrogant toss of her head and stomped out of the hothouse.

Uncertainly Amaryllis watched her go. On the one hand, she felt vague responsibility for what had just happened; on the other, this appeared to be an ongoing battle of wills between the Saville siblings. Perhaps a bit of calm-headed mediation was called for. After all, it was apparent that—all battles aside—Monique was devoted to her brother. Taking a steadying breath, she turned toward Blackstock.

"If you ask me, my lord, you were a bit hard on Lady Monique," she bluntly spoke up. "Contrary to what you might believe, she appears quite mature for her years. Indeed, from what I can see, she can be faulted only for a certain forwardness of manner . . . and that is far preferable to the usual simpering one sees in girls her age."

"But I do not recall asking you, Miss Godwin," came his dangerously soft reply, "nor do I intend to stand here and meekly listen while you lecture me. My sister's welfare is my business, and mine alone. Your business is painting roses. Do I make myself clear?"

"Quite clear," she answered, her sympathy for Monique growing. Truly the man was impossible. It was a wonder that more women had not given way to frustration and bashed him over the head.

Having made his point, the earl gave her a curt nod and strolled past her toward the rear of the hothouse. She sighed and took up her notebook and pencil once again. Then, goaded by a sudden mischievous impulsive, she started after him.

"One moment, Lord Blackstock," she said as she caught up with him. "Perhaps you might satisfy my curiosity. I must confess to being ignorant of this volume—I believe she called it *Essays on Far Eastern Marriage Customs*—of which Lady Monique spoke. Is it perhaps a reference work that I might wish to borrow?"

Apparently it was a more scandalous work than she had guessed, for she had the satisfaction of seeing the earl's face turn a dull red. His tone, however, was cold enough to threaten the more tender vines as he replied through clenched teeth, "You bloody well won't be borrowing it from me, Miss Godwin . . . and I suggest that you refrain from requesting a copy at the local bookstall. Now if you will excuse me."

He took his leave with more haste than dignity, and Amaryllis suppressed a triumphant smile. So the dark angel had a mortal side to him after all. She had almost begun to believe that he did not. Indeed there was some comfort in knowing that the aloof Earl of Blackstock was prey to the entire spectrum of human emotion . . . including embarrassment.

Then Amaryllis's smile faded. By accident or design,

Monique had stumbled across an uncomfortable truth. She *did* find Blackstock attractive—exceedingly so. But sensibly she'd held out no hope the earl might reciprocate her feelings . . . that was, until a few moments ago. Now she was free to wonder whether Monique's claim was but a girlish fancy or else an accurate assessment of her brother's point of view.

Neither answer boded well for her own uncertain heart.

Twelve

I now understand the need that compelled you to run off with your Dashing Poet. I have not seen Him since that first day, and I wonder if I am a fool to carry on so . . . yet I would not trade this Sweet Agony for the bland existence that I led before. It has banished all else of importance from my thoughts, even my memories of that Fiend who still walks the London streets.

—letter from Miss Amaryllis Meeks to
Miss Mary Godwin

The entire situation was fast growing intolerable.

With a snort of disgust, Victor set his pen back on the desk and shut the volume of Parkinson's *Paradisus Terrestris* that had been open to the same page for the past hour. Beside it lay a half page of translated notes . . . the sum total of work he'd managed over the course of the morning that he had spent here in his library.

The ink on the paper had long since dried. Not bothering with sprinkling a bit of sand over the document, he tucked it within the book's pages. Then, almost reluctantly, he turned to the collection of small sketches that had been demanding his attention over the task at hand.

She had submitted them for his approval the afternoon before, leaving them stacked upon his hothouse worktable for him to find later that night. A curt, unsigned note in an elegant female hand—*I trust this is the sort of depiction your lordship had in mind . . . please advise me as soon as is convenient*—had accompanied them.

The cool tone of her note had grated on him, so much so that he had set aside the drawings last night without so much as a glance at them. He would look them over when he damn well got around to it, not a moment sooner. But curiosity had clawed at him like an impatient cat, until he was ready now to concede that he'd not accomplish anything at all this day until he had complied with the chit's request.

With an air of silent challenge, he snatched up the top drawing in the stack and settled back in his chair. Then, abruptly straightening, he made his way through the rest of the almost two dozen different sketches.

They were but hurried depictions of every variety in his collection; still, with only a few pencil strokes, each drawing had captured the essence of that particular rose. From stamens and sepals, to calyxes and canes, they were set down with an attention to detail that he himself would have given. But it was not until he reached the last drawing in the stack that he found the true treasure . . . a single small watercolor of a *Rosa alba foliacea,* a white Alba rose.

Against a painted backdrop of yellow silk reminiscent of a woman's shawl, she had depicted the flower both as a bud and as a full-blown flower. The snowy petals of the former were softened by the slightest blush of pink, while the center ring of yellow stamens revealed in the mature rose glowed like a guinea. Even the roundish leaves and tiny thorns sprouting from a delicate stem were drawn in exquisite detail, so that he could almost reach out and pluck the rose from the page. But what caught his eye was a scattering of fallen petals and a single tiny brown feather in the drawing's lower corner, those objects half-hidden by a fold of the painted silk.

Blood had stained the once-white petals a brilliant crimson.

Victor stared at the painting for a long moment. She had remembered the legend he had told her of how the red rose got its color. Cleverly she had captured the tale of the nightingale and thorns in a few symbolic strokes, transforming a straightforward botanical study into something far more meaningful. Whether she had meant it as a jest or a warning, or simply as a display of her considerable skills, he was not certain. For the moment, however, none of that mattered.

He let out a breath he had not realized he'd been holding and allowed himself a cool, satisfied smile. If all her finished works proved as brilliant, then the first printing of *On the Care and Propagation of Roses* was bound to be a resounding success.

That brief moment of satisfaction faded, however, as his gaze drifted toward the French doors. Though they were closed against the afternoon sun, he managed through their delicate lace curtains to catch a tantalizing glimpse of the hothouse.

His hothouse.

With a disgusted snort, he set aside the watercolor and considered his current dilemma. These past several mornings, he had been rising with the servants to make his hurried rounds of his rose collection. In the gray light of dawn, he would stir the rose beds, water or fertilize each pot, snip off a dead bloom here and there . . . and then be gone. Just before nightfall, he would return to fumigate the plants with tobacco—that tactic designed to ward off leafhoppers—and finish up any other mundane task left undone. The hours in between, he spent cloistered in his library—this unlike the past months when every daylight hour had seen him taken up with his new avocation.

The excuse he'd put forth to Monique and the staff was that he needed more time with his manuscript. To himself, he would only concede that he wanted a bit of a break from the tedious work involved. The truth, however, was something much more simple. He was doing his damnedest to avoid a certain red-haired chit who had been given the run of the place.

Victor uttered a pungent curse and got to his feet. In the beginning, the hothouse had served him as a refuge. Later it had become the major focus of his waking hours. Now the place was forbidden territory, a Faustian sort of spot where he dare not set foot lest he risk losing—not his soul, perhaps, but maybe his heart.

For he had known from the start that hiring Amaryllis was a mistake, even as he had ignored that inner voice of reason and done so anyway. It had taken barely half a day to prove himself right. The moment had come when he had walked into *his* hothouse to overhear his sister discussing the more intimate details of his personal life.

He raked an impatient hand through his dark hair at the memory. His first reaction had been one of angry embarrassment. Christ, she'd been talking as if he were a stud being offered up for auction at Tattersall's . . . instead of her brother and thus due a modicum of respect. He had managed to control his temper, however, contenting himself with shunting her back off to the house where she belonged. The small satisfaction he had derived from that had blunted the worst of his outrage.

By day's end, however, his anger had been supplanted by an even more compelling emotion—that of avid curiosity. For it had occurred to him that he had not heard Amaryllis's reaction to Monique's careless chatter. He had no notion as to what she thought of him. For some reason, it was important that he know . . . while at the same time, he knew it wouldn't make the slightest difference in his future.

Victor wryly shook his head. It seemed that—the years spent denying his titles and responsibilities notwithstanding—a sense of familial responsibility had managed to sink ancient claws into him while he wasn't looking. Like it or not, he found himself finally ready to assume his proper role as earl and guardian of the Saville family name. The only thing he lacked now to carry out that obligation was a woman who could serve equally as a companion and a bed partner.

What he needed, it seemed, was a wife.

He had come to that conclusion over the past few days, and the notion still had an unsettling sort of newness about it. *Like tugging on a brand new pair of Hessians the first time,* he told himself with a faint smile. He knew without being told that he would have to be careful lest, caught up in that newness, he settled on the first female to whom he took a fancy. The problem now was that there *was* a woman whom he fancied . . . and she was entirely unsuitable for the purpose, no matter that she had the most enchanting mouth.

Then discharge her, that same inner voice of reason spoke up again. *Hell, you can always find someone else to take on that commission.*

But in doing so, he would be conceding that she had some sort of hold over him, which certainly was not the case. Would he let Cook run him out of his own kitchen, or Moresdale ban him from his own dressing room? No, he bloody well wouldn't.

His mind made up, Victor turned toward the French doors. He did not pause, lest he think the better of what he was about to do, but marched out into the tangle of garden down the path that led to the outbuildings. His determination lasted that brief walk and even took him past the doors of the hothouse.

His booted steps rang softly against the damp flagstone as he approached Amaryllis. She had set up her easel along the far wall to take advantage of the late morning light, so that her back was now to him. So engrossed was she in her work that he wondered if she had even noted his presence. Deciding that she had not, he took advantage of her absorbed air to study her.

As on previous days, she wore a paint-smudged and exceedingly ugly gray smock over her sensible morning dress—this one a becoming shade of pale blue. Her riot of red-gold curls had been bundled up under an unflattering mobcap, the only advantage being that the style emphasized the elegant line of her slim neck. All in all, though, it was an undeniably prim image that she presented . . . yet barely had he halted a few steps behind her than he felt the familiar sensation settle over him.

He wanted her.

God, how he wanted her.

He stood close enough to her now to see the few rebellious curls that had escaped her spinsterish cap to trail down the back of her neck. Indeed, had he wished it, he could have reached out to twine his fingers through those silken wisps. If she made no protest, it would be easy enough to slide his hand along her slim shoulders and beneath that frightful smock. From there he could slide his fingers beneath the neckline of her bodice and cup her soft breast in his hand.

He felt the familiar stirring in his groin as he unreined his imagination. He would pluck off her unsightly cap just for the satisfaction of seeing her hair spill in a blaze of fiery silk down her shoulders. By that time, she would be in his arms and eager to follow his lead. If he shoved aside a few rose bushes, the worktable behind them would be just the right height for her to sit along its edge and hike her skirts to her waist. It would take but a moment for him to unfasten his breeches and position himself between her thighs, a few seconds longer for her to wrap her legs around his waist and guide him into her warm, welcoming softness.

Their coupling would be over with just as quickly as it began . . . but, with luck, that physical release would be enough to sate his need. She could get back to her painting, and he could turn his attention to searching out a more suitable woman to fill the role he had created. All he had to do was reach out his hand.

Not bloody likely, he thought, his lips twisting into a grim smile. Hell, she would probably crack him over the head with her palette for daring to take such liberties. At the very least, she'd resign her post on the spot, leaving him minus one talented illustrator.

That in mind, he contented himself simply with watching her work. Her subject—an overblown pink *Centifolia*—sprawled from its pot on the table beside her, nodding like a dozing, turbanned dowager. It was one of his favorite varieties, warm in color and possessed of a heady fragrance. Numerous curling petals gave that bloom its look of blowsy elegance, as well as its common name, the cabbage rose.

While Victor silently looked on, Amaryllis captured each one of those crinkled petals in careful detail. Palette in one hand and brush in the other, she deftly applied transparent layers of color to the heavy paper pinned to her easel, building from the palest wash of pink to streaks of crimson. He knew it was a painstaking process, the more so because—unlike working with oils—that technique did not allow her the luxury of painting over mistakes.

He noted, too, that pinned beside the work in progress was a finished drawing of that same rose just barely budding. From its substantial brown thorns to its broadly toothed, bright green leaves to its graceful stems, the *Centifolia* was depicted in detail enough to satisfy the most particular horticulturist.

He waited to make any comment, however, until she paused to exchange the slim brush she was using for a broader version. Then deliberately he cleared his throat.

At the unexpected sound, Amaryllis gave a start and swung about. Her surprise was even greater when she found herself nearly toe-to-toe with the Earl of Blackstock. She managed to stifle a second gasp, though her thoughts were whirling.

To be sure, he was the only person who might be wandering the hothouse. Had he not, after all, banned every member of his household—his own sister, included—from setting foot there without him. Still, she had not seen the earl even once since that first day, so that she had begun to wonder if she ever would again. She had not even the excuse of her missing glove with which to approach him, for the article had mysteriously reappeared on the worktable only yesterday.

"Good morning, my lord," she managed. "Do forgive my rudeness in not acknowledging you sooner. I fear I was caught up in my work, so that you took me somewhat by surprise."

"You have nothing for which to apologize," he coolly returned. "Indeed I must confess that I rather enjoyed watching you paint."

"Then you are in the minority, my lord. Most people find the act of creation quite tedious when they are spectators and not participants."

Blackstock raised a wry brow. "The loss is theirs, I am afraid. For myself, I have always taken a vicarious interest in other people's pleasures."

Though his tone was dispassionate enough, his dark gaze was alight with an unexpected heat that added subtle nuances to his words. She stared back at him, all too aware that he stood but an arm's length away. He was so close that he could easily reach out and pull her to him. And if he did—

Abruptly it occurred to her how vulnerable she was here, alone and far from the main house. If Blackstock assaulted her, no one would know. If she screamed, no one would hear.

Though perhaps she would not scream.

A sudden heat suffused her entire body at the thought. Had she not already admitted to herself that she found the man quite attractive? And she could not deny the fact that his unexplained absence these past days had left her with

an unsettled feeling, like an itch she couldn't scratch . . .
but perhaps he could.

As if reading her mind, Blackstock reached out a strong,
well-manicured hand toward her. *Dear God, he was going
to touch her . . . and she had no intention of stopping him.*
She caught her breath, every nerve in her body singing in
agonized anticipation as his warm fingers brushed her
cheek.

Instinctively her eyelids fluttered shut as she wondered
what would happen next. Would he draw her to him, perhaps
even kiss her? Beyond that possibility, her mind faltered.
Still, she knew enough about the dealings between men and
women to realize there was much more that he could demand of her . . . and much more that she could give.

A heartbeat later, he withdrew his hand. "I hope you don't
mind," she heard his cool words through the pulse thudding
in her ears, "but you had a smudge of paint on your face."

Her eyes flew open again in time to see him display his
hand, so that she could see his forefinger bore a green smear
that matched the color she'd used to tint the rose stems.

"Oh . . . of course not, my lord."

She stumbled over the words, her inner heat transmuting
into full-blown mortification. Here she had thought him
about to seduce her, and all the while he was disapproving
her slovenly appearance. Whatever could have made her
think that he had any interest in her, save as a hireling? He
was an earl, after all, and she the daughter of a sexton.

To cover her confusion, she made a show of setting aside
her palette, checking the cups of color and arranging her
brushes. Even so, she could still feel embarrassment burning
hot on her face as she said, "Perhaps, my lord, you would
care to discuss the set of drawings I left you yesterday?"

"Actually, that is the very reason I have come."

He moved closer to the easel, near enough to her that she
might have leaned her head against his shoulder. Ruthlessly
tearing her thoughts from such unprofitable flights of fancy—

had she not already acted the fool enough for one day?—she mustered her wayward dignity and remained where she was. She was, first and foremost, an artist. She would behave with the decorum demanded of that particular role, no matter her own inner misery.

Blackstock, however, seemed not to notice her discomfiture as he divided his scrutiny between the completed watercolor of the *Centifolia* in bud and the companion drawing upon which she had just been working. Nervous all at once, but now for different reasons, Amaryllis awaited his response.

"As I previously made known to you, Miss Godwin . . . or rather, Amaryllis," he corrected himself even as he kept his attention on the easel, "I have certain distinct expectations for the sort of illustrations I would have in my book. From what I have seen of your work thus far, it does not meet them."

"It—It does not?" she half-whispered, aghast. Instantly her feminine concerns were supplanted by professional pride. How could he deem them inferior, when she knew these drawings for some of the best that she ever had done?

Coolly Blackstock glanced her way. "No, not meet them," he repeated. "To the contrary, your artistry far exceeds anything that I could have wanted. To be sure, the painting of the *Rosa alba foliacea* does not exactly fit the tone of my text. Still, I am satisfied that I made the correct decision in hiring you."

The relief that swept her left her weak-kneed. Forgetting all else save his praise, she gave him a broad smile.

"Thank you, my lord," she exclaimed. "I had rather wondered if I had overstepped myself with that watercolor. It *was* unconventional, and I knew when I finished that it would not do at all as an illustration. Still, I felt it would serve as a representative sample of my abilities in that medium."

She paused, a momentary sense of regret intruding upon

her pleasure. Despite her protests, she had been quite taken with that particular drawing and its allegorical feel.

"So that it does not accidentally mix in with the other works," she went on, "return that particular drawing to me, and I will see that it is destroyed."

"I see no good reason to destroy the painting simply because it will not do as an illustration. To be quite honest, I rather fancied it myself."

"Then do keep the watercolor, my lord," she warmly urged, "and I shall paint a new version of that Alba to replace it."

"See that you do. Tomorrow would be quite soon enough."

"But tomorrow is Sunday, my lord," she reminded him. "I believe we agreed I would work only six days out of seven."

"Of course." The barest hint of a smile curved his lips. "My apologies, Amaryllis. I fear that we pagans are rather lax about such matters. Take your Sabbath, then, with my blessing, and I shall see you again the following morrow. In the meantime, I will make certain that Cook sends you out your meal, since it is almost noontide."

So saying, he turned on his heel and quit the hothouse.

Amaryllis waited until the French doors closed behind him again. Then, with a sigh, she pulled off her mobcap and shook her head to clear the figurative cobwebs from it. This had been the most extraordinary interview. She now knew, as an artist, where she stood with the man, for he had said in no uncertain terms that he approved of her work. On that account, at least, she need have no fears.

But where did she stand with him as a woman?

The question nagged at her for the rest of the day. She saw no more of Blackstock, though she found her gaze straying back toward the French doors so frequently that she feared she might develop a crick in her neck. Between glances, she tormented herself with fearing that she had made a total cake of herself and wondering if it were possible that the earl was attracted to her, if only a little.

By the time the afternoon sun reached the point where the light was no longer favorable, she was more than ready to call a halt to her work. Perhaps with a day of rest, she would gain a bit of perspective as to the truth of the situation. For, despite her physical attraction to the man, she could not deny that he made her uneasy. It was nothing she could point to, merely a dark, unknown quality that clung to him like a stolen cloak. Common sense told her that a kind and upright sort of gentleman would never have been suspected of murder. What then did it mean that Blackstock actually had been arrested for so heinous a crime?

By now a cheerful Derek had appeared to drive her home, and it was with a sense of relief that she climbed into the carriage. As had become Amaryllis's habit, she instructed the man to drop her a short distance from her actual destination of St. Pancras. The drive took a bit longer than usual, however, given an abundance of carts and carriages filling the streets. By the time they reached that familiar point, darkness had all but fallen. She bid Derek a swift good-bye and scrambled out for the short walk home.

Some of the boldness that had been hers before the night of the Demon's attack had returned, so it was with a fair show of confidence that she made her way along the shadowed avenue. Indeed she made a point of not glancing around even when she heard the quick brush of footsteps against cobbles behind her.

Sternness of mind, she told herself, keeping her gaze fixed before her.

But when a strong hand clamped over her arm, she reverted to full-blown terror and started to scream.

Thirteen

"Lay out my evening clothes, Moresdale," the Earl of Blackstock said without preamble as that man answered his abrupt summons. "Nothing ostentatious, mind you. The places I will be going, I'll not wish to draw any unnecessary attention. And send word to Cook that I will be dining out tonight."

"Very good, milord," Davy Moresdale replied, schooling his surprise behind a bland expression.

It had not been much above an hour earlier that his lordship had stated that he would remain at home this evening. Since it followed in such cases that his employer would dispense with his services until the next morning, Davy had made plans that included lifting a few pints with the lads at the Cock and Bull. Now, however, he'd be obliged to cancel those arrangements and instead wait up half the night for the earl to return home.

"Derek should be back any moment from deliverin' the young lady," he offered, manfully putting aside his disappointment to focus on the duty at hand. "When 'e does, I'll see 'ow as the carriage will waitin' at yer convenience. Will there be anythin' else, milord?"

"Nothing you can help with," he thought he heard Blackstock mutter before the earl shook his head and dismissed him with an absent gesture. Just as Davy reached the library door, however, the younger man called him back.

"One last thing, Moresdale. I rather imagine I'll be out

until dawn. I see no point in your waiting up for me. Once I'm dressed and on my way, why don't you take the rest of the evening for yourself."

"Very good, milord," Davy agreed. His battered boxer's features didn't break into a gap-toothed grin until after he was back out in the hallway and headed toward his lordship's rooms.

He'd always said that, for all his odd way, the Earl of Blackstock was a right good sort. Not many men of his wealth and station would have given a broken-down bruiser a place in his household as his personal valet, no matter that Davy was known to the sporting crowd as the pugilist with a dandy's wardrobe.

And fewer still, Davy judged, would have taken on the same bloke as had landed him a facer during a brawl in one of the dockside's seedier taverns two years earlier.

Davy's grin broadened at the memory. He'd been at the Cock and Bull that night, too, downing pint after pint in an attempt to blunt the knowledge that his career as fighter was in its twilight. What a gentleman like Blackstock had been doing in that same place, he'd never learned for certain. What he *had* found out, however, was that the earl was right good with his fives himself.

Not that it would have made a difference to Davy that night had he guessed up front that his opponent was a gentry cove. He'd been three sheets to the wind and probably would have taken on the Prince Regent, had that royal personage suddenly appeared there. As it was, it had been the earl's bad luck to bump into him that night . . . and his worse fortune to spill Davy's pint, in the bargain.

Most of what had transpired during the melee that followed still eluded his memory. He had, however, stumbled his way home later that night with the earl's calling card tucked into his bright turquoise waistcoat. The upshot had been that—one eye swollen shut and his head pounding like a drum—he had called upon Blackstock the following afternoon. He had found himself with a new post that same day.

Then the valet's grin faded.

Though he had been happy working for the Earl of Blackstock, things had taken an odd turn in the past six months, ever since that young actress's brutal murder. Davy had defended his employer against any accusation that reached his misshapen ear, certain in his own heart that his lordship was not guilty of such a horrible crime. Still, it was a fact that the earl had been a changed man since that night.

Davy shook his head. Where once Lord Blackstock paid a respectable amount of attention to Lady Monique, he now kept to himself and saw his sister perhaps but once a day when he broke his fast. Rarely did he smile, save in that cool way of his, and even less often did he laugh. When he went out of an evening, it was no longer to Almack's and Brooks's. Rather he favored gambling hells such as the Golden Wolf, where a man's deep pockets and not his personal reputation gained him entry.

The only thing of late that had rattled the man from his black mood was the reappearance of the red-haired miss that his lordship had rescued from the streets.

By now Davy had reached the earl's bedchamber. He went about gathering the requisite articles of clothing his employer would need to make a subdued if appropriate turnout. His thoughts, however, still lingered on the matter of the girl.

The entire household, from the kitchen to upstairs, was all agog at his lordship's hiring of the chit to paint his roses. *Scandalous,* Peters had pompously dubbed it. *Right romantic,* Cook had sighed. Privately Davy was inclined to dismiss the whole situation a bit of folly . . . though he knew bloody well better than to mention as much to his employer.

Davy gave critical examination to a handful of snowy white neckcloths and selected the crispest. That accomplished, he took a brush to his lordship's black coat and made a show of removing any lint that might have gathered since its last wearing. He'd keep his opinions to himself, all right, but that didn't mean he did not have them. Had someone asked outright, he would have said he thought the earl had a bit more interest in the chit than that of a mere employer. If he were to be more specific, Davy would have said that Lord Blackstock was afflicted by an acute case of calf love.

The signs were all quite evident. Davy had seen for himself the pilfered glove of hers that had sat on his lordship's desktop for several days. He'd also noted the way the earl had scrupulously avoided the hothouse whenever she was in there painting while he spent an inordinate amount of time gazing out the window in its direction. And hadn't his lordship, out of the blue, brought up the chit's name in conversation with Davy a time or two?

But even as he toyed with that idea, he dismissed it as doubtful. More likely the earl had his mind on a quick tumble, only to have realized that the girl was of respectable upbringing and thus not fair game for such a pursuit. That would explain his sudden wish for entertainment tonight. For the Golden Wolf was known as much for its tawdry brand of female companionship, available to its patrons for a fair bit of coin, as it was for its gambling. A night spent having the itch in his breeches scratched would set his lordship right again.

Cheered himself, Davy caught up a pair of the earl's Hessians and began applying a coat of blacking mixed per Mr. Brummel's own formula. Things would sort themselves out, they would, and surely for the better. In the meantime, he would concern himself with more important issues . . . such as making sure his lordship was suitably attired for tonight's outing.

"I presume you have an explanation for this," an anger-choked voice demanded from the shadows as the grip on

Amaryllis's arm tightened. Fright swept her in a chill wave, only to be supplanted by a warm rush of relief when belated recognition dawned. She spun about to face her assailant.

"Talbot," she squeaked out as her relief faded to guilt. Dear Lord, what if he had seen Blackstock's coach and recognized the coat of arms emblazoned on its sides?

The grim look on her brother's face confirmed that he had indeed made the connection. "I came by yesterday afternoon to examine your injuries again," he went on. "When I discovered you were not at home, I managed to pry the grudging explanation from our father that you had taken on a new teaching post."

That was the explanation she had given Ezra, that she had obtained a position instructing the young daughter of an earl the rudiments of watercolor painting. Since teaching was deemed a proper enough career for a woman of her station, her father had voiced no objections—*so long as ye don't neglect yer duties 'ere, girl.*

Now shadows hardened Talbot's pale features, matching his tone. "I decided to drive out here to St. Pancras again today," he went on, and she noted his gig with its placid roan stopped several paces behind them. "Imagine my shock when I saw but a stone's throw away from the church the Earl of Blackstock's own carriage . . . and you alighting from it. I might ask why the driver drops you here, rather than at the church gates, save that I would guess our father knows nothing of your so-called employer's true identity."

"I—I can explain," she managed, though in truth she could not see a way to satisfy Talbot's anger. From his tone, it was almost as if he suspected something immoral was afoot.

Outraged indignation sparked within her at the thought. Even if she told him everything, she doubted he would approve her decision. Indeed perhaps she would not bother trying!

By now he had steered her toward his gig and was helping

her up. Seeing no help for it, she quickly settled upon the seat—the humble two-wheeler a marked contrast to Blackstock's elegant coach—and waited to see if he pressed the issue. *She* was not about to do so.

Despite her best intentions, however, Talbot's usual tactic of letting the silence stretch between them until she felt obliged to fill it with chatter worked. As he halted the gig at the churchyard gates a few moments later, she burst out with explanation.

"You must believe that it all happened quite unexpectedly," she told him, still seated at his side. "You see, I felt obliged to apologize to the earl and thank him for rescuing me from the Barkshire Demon—which I did. I did not expect the man to offer me a post in return."

As Talbot continued to stare ahead, reins gripped in his gloved hands, she explained about the hothouse and Blackstock's intent to publish a popular horticultural volume, making clear that she admired his willingness to take on that challenge. She avoided, however, any hint of a personal interest in the man.

She finished her account with a weak, "And the earl does quite like my paintings, he has assured me," before settling back to await her brother's reply.

"This is folly of the worst sort," came his swift retort as he turned toward her again. "Here I told you in some detail about the man's sordid past, yet you went out of your way to demand an audience with him. And as for his hiring you, has it not occurred to you that he might have some ulterior motive in mind beyond commissioning a few watercolors?"

She blushed at the implication, her embarrassment all the greater because she had half-hoped and half-feared that very same thing. "He has acted quite the gentleman toward me," she insisted. "And it is not as if we were alone there. He has an entire staff of servants wandering about, in addition to his younger sister, Lady Monique."

"I have met the girl," Talbot said, "and she is hardly a

IF YOU LOVE READING MORE OF TODAY'S BESTSELLING HISTORICAL ROMANCES.... WE HAVE AN OFFER FOR YOU!

4 BESTSELLING HISTORICAL ROMANCES BY YOUR FAVORITE AUTHORS CAN BE YOURS, FREE!

Kensington Choice, our newest book club now brings you historical romances by your favorite bestselling authors including Janelle Taylor, Shannon Drake, Rosanne Bittner, Jo Beverley, and Georgina Gentry, just to name a few! Each book is filled with passion, adventure and the excitement of bygone times!

To introduce you to this great new club which is part of Zebra Home Subscription Service, we'd like to send you your first 4 bestselling historical romances, absolutely free!   And once you get these 4 free books to savor at home, we'll rush you the next 4 brand-new books at the lowest prices available, as soon as they are published.

The way the club works is that after your initial FREE shipment, you will get our 4 newest bestselling historical romances delivered to your doorstep each month at the preferred subscriber's rate of only $4.20 per book, a savings of up to $7.16 per month (since these titles sell in bookstores for $4.99-$5.99)! All books are sent on a 10-day free examination basis and there is no minimum number of books to buy. (A postage and handling charge of $1.50 is added to each shipment.) Plus as a regular subscriber, you'll receive our FREE monthly newsletter, *Zebra/Pinnacle Romance News*, which features author profiles, contests, subscriber benefits, book previews and more!

So start today by returning the FREE BOOK CERTIFICATE provided. We'll send you 4 FREE BOOKS with no further obligation: A FREE gift offering you hours of reading pleasure with no obligation...how can you lose?

*We have 4 FREE BOOKS for you
as your introduction to
KENSINGTON CHOICE!
To get your FREE BOOKS, worth
up to $23.96, mail the card below.*

FREE BOOK CERTIFICATE

Yes! Please send me 4 Kensington Choice (the best of Zebra and Pinnacle Books) Historical Romances without cost or obligation (worth up to $23.96). As a Kensington Choice subscriber, I will then receive 4 brand-new romances to preview each month for 10 days FREE. I can return any books I decide not to keep and owe nothing. The publisher's prices for Kensington Choice romances range from $4.99-$5.99, but as a preferred subscriber I will get these books for only $4.20 per book or $16.80 for all four titles. There is no minimum number of books to buy and I may cancel my subscription at any time. A $1.50 postage and handling charge is added to each shipment. No matter what I decide to do, my first 4 books are mine to keep, absolutely FREE!

KC0997

Name _____

Address _____ Apt. _____

City _____ State _____ Zip _____

Telephone ( ) _____

Signature _____

(If under 18, parent or guardian must sign)

Subscription subject to acceptance. Terms and prices subject to change.

4 FREE
Historical Romances
*are waiting
for you to
claim them!*

(worth up to
$23.96)

*See details
inside....*

KENSINGTON CHOICE
Zebra Home Subscription Service, Inc.
120 Brighton Road
P.O. Box 5214
Clifton, NJ 07015-5214

suitable chaperone. I judge her to have as little sense as your young friend, Miss Godwin . . . and see what sort of scandals *she* has stirred up. But tell me, didn't his lordship wonder at the fact that you are his personal physician's sister?"

"I—I did not give him my true surname, so Blackstock does not know that you and I are related."

Talbot quirked a brow. "I see."

And he did see, she was certain. For the both of them knew that, had he been privy to the fact that she and Talbot were siblings, Blackstock never would have hired her. He'd have considered such employment unsuitable, given her brother's respectable position. And Talbot knew, as well, that should Blackstock learn the truth, he might well discharge her.

The question now was, would Talbot expose her lie?

She did not wait long for an answer. "You can guess my feelings in this matter," came her brother's heated response, "and not only in regard to your being employed by an unmarried gentleman, which is unseemly enough. Beyond that, what do you think would happen should the earl learn of the deception that you played on him . . . and that I knew of it? My post, as well as yours, would be forfeit."

"But if you keep silent, he need not know," Amaryllis countered in an equally fierce tone. "What is the harm in what I have done? I am performing the job for which I was hired, which is all that should matter. Besides which, Father and I could use the coin, and the earl is more than generous in his pay."

"I am certain that he is."

Talbot's voice had taken on a bitter note, and she recalled his admission that Blackstock had paid him for his silence on the matter of the Belfleur woman's murder. It was apparent that he still resented the man, even while he remained in his employ. Doubtless that was why her brother was being so stubborn in this particular case.

With an effort, she assumed a more conciliatory tone.

"Do be sensible about the matter, Talbot. My tenure with the man should not last much above a few weeks. Surely you can keep my secret for so short a time."

"I fear I cannot. Blackstock must be told immediately. I will not carry your sin of omission on my conscience."

His words rang with a righteous air that was more than she could bear. Had she not always supported her brother in *his* time of need? That was why she blurted, "But that is not at all fair of you, Talbot, when I have kept a secret of yours."

Her words had an effect well beyond any reaction she might have expected. Talbot's pale face took on a chalkier hue, while his gray eyes glinted as if with a fever.

"A secret of mine, you say?"

In contrast to his fiery gaze, his tone held an iciness that she'd never before heard from him. Abruptly it occurred to her that, under the right circumstances, she could easily be afraid of her own brother. That feeling intensified as he asked, "Tell me, Amaryllis, what is this secret that you know?"

Her first impulse was to claim that she had made up the entire accusation out of spite. She knew, however, that he could read her far too easily for such a ploy to succeed. And he would not let her leave until she told him the truth.

"I—I put matters together quite by accident," she admitted. "It was the day after my escape from the Barkshire Demon, just before you came calling. Father mentioned that the Resurrection men had struck the churchyard the night before, and he described the dead man whose body they stole." She paused for a deep breath, then finished in a rush, "It was the very same corpse that I saw you use in your anatomy lesson."

"Let me get this straight . . . you are accusing me of obtaining my subjects from grave robbers?"

At her reluctant nod, Talbot's chill expression thawed into an indulgent smile.

"My dear Amaryllis, surely you must realize that every physician worth the name has resorted to such tactics on one occasion or another," her brother exclaimed with an amused shake of his head. "Given our Court's penchant for transporting criminals rather than executing them, there are simply not enough bodies to be had from legitimate sources. We cannot make medical advances without the sort of experiments as can only be performed upon the dead—and they are dead, after all, so what is the harm? Indeed, if this is the worst secret that you can lay at my doorstep, I will not hang my head in shame."

Amaryllis stared back at him in chagrin. Put that way, his actions appeared quite humanitarian in nature, while her own small deception smacked of selfishness. Not that she was prepared for her brother to reveal what he knew.

"Can you not reconsider?" she urged, though doubtful that her plea would carry much weight. "This commission means more to me than you can know, and I do not dare risk losing it."

He sat silent a moment longer.

"Very well, I won't tell Blackstock," he agreed; then, as she stared up at him in dawning hope, he finished, "you will."

It was all she could do to suppress a dismayed groan. She knew from past experience that this was the only concession she would wring from him. Certainly arguing while the shadows deepened around them would accomplish nothing more.

"Tomorrow is Sunday, so I will not see him again until the following day," she pointed out. "Surely you can allow me that space of time, at least."

"As it happens, I will be in the country for the next three days, so I will give you until my return to set matters straight. If you do not, then I will be forced to make the announcement in your stead. I will, however, do my best to keep Father from learning of this scandal."

Cheered by that last concession, she focused on her brother's earlier statement. "You mentioned the country. Does that mean you will be visiting Cordelia?"

"Yes."

The single word held a mixture of hope, anger, and defeat. Forgetting her own troubles, Amaryllis's heart went out to her brother. For almost a year now, his young wife had been confined to a sanitarium a day's ride outside London. His visits always left him emotionally drained, so that Amaryllis often feared for his health as much as she did that of her ill sister-in-law. And the worst of it was that Talbot's considerable healing skill had not been enough to stem the fragile young woman's decline.

"Tell me, Talbot, how is she faring? Have the doctors sent word of any improvement?"

He shook his head, and she sighed. "I do wish I might be allowed to see her," she went on. "Are you quite certain—"

"The strain would be too much for her." Then he tempered his curt words with the faintest of smiles. "As always, I will be sure to tell Cordelia that you send your love. And perhaps if this new treatment that I have been testing proves effective, you'll soon be able to tell her so yourself."

On that note of somber hope, he alighted from the gig and helped her down. Then, reaching out with his forefinger, he tilted her chin up and scrutinized her throat.

"The bruises are fading, and your hoarseness has vanished," he said, abandoning the role of brother for that of physician. "Are you experiencing any further pain, any difficulty in breathing or swallowing?"

When she shook her head, he nodded and climbed back into the vehicle. "I will call on you again at midweek. Until then, my dear sister." So saying, he maneuvered the single-horse vehicle about and clattered back down the cobbled street.

By now dusk had deepened into night. Exhausted all at

once, she made her way past the churchyard to the tiny gray stone house. Doubtless, Father would be wondering at the delay, if only to his supper.

An hour later, she was in her own room, pleading the headache as she left Ezra to a solitary meal of cold mutton, boiled potatoes, and dried apple slices. The excuse was not without foundation; indeed her encounter with her brother had left her quite out of sorts.

What right had Talbot to dictate to her how she led her life? she thought in some pique. She was of legal age, after all, and able to earn her own living. How or where she chose to do so was none of his concern.

But he has only your best interests at heart, her practical voice reminded her. And the fact that he had been witness to an unfortunate incident in the earl's life—no matter that no one could say for certain if he were guilty—surely had colored Talbot's attitude toward the man. What sort of brother would he be if he did not express some misgivings about the current situation.

By the time she had finished her evening's routine and was preparing for bed, she had reconciled herself to the fact that she must reveal her true identity to the Earl of Blackstock. It had occurred to her that her figurative unmasking was inevitable; after all, she had no desire to use an assumed identity when named as the illustrator of his lordship's book. The question now was how best to tell Blackstock the truth so that he would overlook her deception.

Chances were she would be without a post upon Talbot's return; still, her mortification would be redoubled should her brother speak to the earl for her. And maybe she could make Blackstock understand just why she had done what she did, so that he might retain her services after all.

Fourteen

A burst of raucous male laughter split the dimly lit, smoky main room of the Golden Wolf. The sound rose, phoenixlike, above the muted if ongoing clamor of scraping chairs, clinking glasses, and clattering coins. Victor looked up from his losing faro hand to a nearby table that was the laughter's source. There an inebriated gambler sprawled facedown over his cards, while his fellow players were losing no time in dividing what remained of the poor wretch's winnings.

Victor gave a disgusted snort and turned his attention back to his own table, where a game of faro was in process. The house dealer was a spare, efficient sort by the name of Wiggins. Unlike most of his ilk, the man played an honest game of it—that, or else he cheated far too cleverly for Victor to spot how he did so. As for his fellow players, they were the rougher sort of gamesters to which the place catered. Soldiers and workingmen, they were for the most part, though he earlier had spotted mixed in with the crowd a few minor nobles.

Some of the latter, he judged, were there for the sport of brushing shoulders with the lower classes; others, because they'd gambled away their welcome at the more respectable clubs. And doubtless one or two were like him, looking for a refuge from the swirl of polite Society with its endless whispers and innuendo. For the Golden Wolf was the sort of place where a man was asked no questions . . . where, if he wished, a man could retire to a darkened corner, drink in hand, and escape notice.

That round of play ended, Victor tossed in his cards and scraped up his meager winnings. Moving on to an unoccupied table, he signaled for another glass of watered port, the only tolerable beverage served in the place. Unlike the elite clubs such as White's or Brooks's, this establishment was not renowned for either its ambiance or its chef.

No gilded furniture or velvet drapes lent a luxurious note, and no elaborate cold buffet or free-flowing champagne was offered the Golden Wolf's patrons. Rather than liveried major domos and footmen, the establishment was presided over by men who, like Moresdale, appeared to have spent time in the ring.

For the Golden Wolf was, quite simply, a gambling hell. It was sort of place that, had Victor a younger brother, he would have warned the lad against setting foot there. The gaming all took place in a single large room crowded with battered tables that offered whist, faro, and other popular contests of chance. The sums that changed hands here were rather smaller than he was used to seeing won and lost; still, a man could as easily forfeit his livelihood here as at any establishment on St. James Street.

But gaming was not all that was offered at the Golden Wolf.

Sport of another kind took place upstairs, conducted within the series of narrow, thin-walled chambers just large enough to accommodate an equally narrow cot. The women employed here were a cut above the usual street trollop . . . meaning that they bathed on a regular basis. Beyond that, a man took his chances spending his coin with them.

By the time his drink arrived, Victor had begun to feel the effects of his earlier indulgence. It was already well past midnight, and the Golden Wolf had not been his first stop of the evening. He had made the rounds of two other similar such establishments, gambling until he'd lost more than he had won, and drinking enough each time to now leave him fuzzy-headed.

His intent, however, was to stop short of getting outright drunk. In this part of the city, not far from the docks, a man of the upper classes was well-advised to keep a few wits about him after dark. Even the simple expedient of covering the distance between a tavern door and carriage left a man open to attack by cutpurses and footpads. Those foolish enough to wander the unlit streets while the worse for drink risked being relieved, not only of their blunt, but of their very lives.

"Lookin' for a bit o' comfort, milord?"

The sound of a female voice roused him from his thoughts. Blearily Victor looked up from his glass to gaze at the woman who had paused at his table. She smiled down at him and slid her pink tongue across her artificially red-dened lips in a calculated gesture of seduction.

As best as he could tell, she was young and attractive beneath her heavy dusting of face powder and rouge. Her garish emerald-green gown was cut low enough so that he could glimpse a pink hint of her nipples, like rose petals against her white breasts. But what drew his interest was the fact that her mass of curly hair was a brilliant shade of red-gold.

"Sit down," he told her.

For he had come here with one specific intent in mind . . . namely, to quench the purely physical desire that had been assailing him these past days. Perhaps if he slaked his need with a willing woman who resembled Amaryllis, he might be freed of this obsession that had gripped him.

His words of invitation were rewarded by another seductive smile. In a practiced move, the red-haired woman straddled his thighs so that she faced him. He discovered with interest that she was wearing no petticoats beneath her flamboyant gown.

" 'Ere now, milord, this is much more friendly," she

purred as she wriggled on his lap like a restless cat. Toying with his neckcloth, which hung askew, she bent forward to whisper, "And if ye'd like to take a quick walk upstairs, we could be friendlier still."

"I'll consider it," he agreed, aware that the inferior port that he'd been drinking had somehow thickened his tongue. It had also heated his loins to the point that the mere action of her sitting on his lap had made him suddenly and painfully erect.

His condition must have been obvious to her, for her smile broadened. She reached for the drink he still clutched in his other hand. Plucking it from his fingers, she set it on the table behind her. Then she wrapped both her arms around his neck and spread her thighs wider still, so that he could feel her warmth against the hard swollen ridge of his shaft straining against his trousers.

He swallowed back a groan and clutched her hips to hold her in place. If she bounced about much more, he might well climax where he sat, with that embarrassingly display sure to earn him the jeers of everyone in the place. Public humiliation was the last thing he needed this night.

Striving for a bit of control, he asked in a husky voice, "What's your name, then?"

"I'm Betty, milord. I'll give you a good time o' it . . . an' for a right good price," came her saucy reply. She leaned closer to whisper her fee—reasonable enough for this sort of establishment—in his ear. "I even 'ave a special treat I save for fine gents like you," she added with a giggle.

Her plump breasts loomed only inches from his face now, bobbing like soft melons. With this increased proximity, he noted lurking beneath the liberal application of lavender water something he had missed earlier—the distinctive scent of spent lust that wrapped her like a length of cheap tulle. Doubtless she'd already serviced her share of men in one of those upstairs rooms, and would take on others after him.

Christ, the treat she had in mind was likely a good dose of the French pox.

The thought quenched his desire, and he realized that satisfying his urges with a prostitute was not going to solve his problem. There was but one particular woman that he desired, and bedding a score of other flame-haired women would not change that fact. All that was left to him was to discharge his enticing illustrator, so that he would no longer have to face temptation on a daily basis . . . that, or put aside his scruples and try to sway Amaryllis into sharing his bed. And at this juncture, he had a pretty good idea of which tack he would take.

In a none-too-gentle move, he caught the chit by the arms and deposited her back on her feet.

"Not tonight, I don't think," he told her and reached again for his glass. He'd drink away the need that burned in his loins until he could find another way to satisfy himself.

Betty, however, did not accept his decision with good grace.

" 'Ere, now, milord, I thought we 'ad a deal," she exclaimed, planting her hands on her hips. "I spent m'time gettin' ye good an' ready, an' 'ere ye're cryin' off."

" 'He's right good at that, his lordship is," another female voice spitefully broke in before Victor could reply.

Not quite believing his bad fortune, he looked up again to see a familiar blonde now standing beside the scorned Betty. Bloody hell, he'd forgotten—or else not bothered to remember—that it was here at the Golden Wolf he had first made Penelope Worthington's acquaintance several months earlier.

He studied her with a jaundiced eye. It had been less than a fortnight since he had last seen the chit, and the change in her was striking. She had abandoned the tasteful gowns he'd bought her for her previous garb of cheap red satin cut scandalously low and decked out with a trunk's worth of pink ribbons. She had also resumed the masklike face paint she had once worn, so that any flush of anger that might now tint her cheeks was hidden by her powder.

Summoning a vestige of courtesy to mask his irritation—bloody hell, whatever had he seen in her, in the first place?—he said in an aloof tone, "Good evening, Penelope. I trust you've been well."

" 'I trust you've been well,' " she echoed with false gaiety, her kohled eyes bright with malice. "Indeed, Lord Blackstock, I've not been well at all. That 'substantial sum' you promised when you left barely covered my dressmaker's bills, let alone all the new gloves and bonnets I'd ordered. I've been reduced to selling myself here again to pay it off, and all because of you."

"If you'll recall, I left you with the names of several potential protectors . . . and you tossed the list back in my face," Victor countered her brittle tone with one of dead calm.

He rose, more unsteady on his feet than he would have liked, and stared down at her. "As for the matter of your mantua-maker, I had already paid up your last quarter's account and warned you not to charge anything more without my approval."

"The hell with your bloody approval," she cried, drawing the attention of several nearby tables of patrons. Furious, she turned on Betty, whose own moment of anger had faded into bemused uncertainty. "If there's anyone to be making coin off his lordship tonight, it'll be me."

Before Victor could react, she reached out a quick hand and grasped his vital male parts in a grip that stopped just short of being painful.

He grunted in surprise and made an instinctive grab for her wrist. Obviously anticipating that move, Penelope tightened her fingers just a fraction until he prudently subsided. Meanwhile a wave of disbelief had swept him. Christ, had the chit gone mad? If he didn't watch his step, she'd make a eunuch of him before the night was far gone.

"Damn it all, what do you want from me?" he gritted out, aware now of a throbbing ache in his balls far different from the earlier painful pleasure he'd felt.

Penelope favored him with a cool smile, her grip never slacking. "It's quite simple, Vic," she purred, pausing to let her hot gaze flit about the room. "Just tell Betty that I know how to work that long, thick shaft of yours better than anyone else. Tell her I can have you spilling yourself in my hand with just a few strokes . . . and I don't even have to take off my gown to do it."

"Bloody hell, Penelope, I'll do no such thing!"

He felt a tide of angry embarrassment rise along the back of his neck, while he tried not to grimace when her fingers tightened yet again. Though the greatest portion of his attention was fixed on his hostage genitals, he was still aware of the drunken guffaws and ribald comments coming from the nearby tables. In another moment, the whole place would doubtless be placing odds on the final outcome of his manhood. He'd be damned, though, if he would make a spectacle of himself for their bloody entertainment.

"Let's be sensible about this, Penelope," he countered in as even a tone as he could muster under the circumstances. "I've already turned Betty down, so you have nothing to worry about on that score. And if you still harbor some resentment toward the way we parted, we can discuss the matter again. So just let me go, and I'll—"

"Would someone care to explain what is going on here?" interrupted a silken male voice underlaid with a hint of steel.

Abruptly the pressure on Victor's privates eased as Penelope's grip faltered. He allowed himself a groan of relief before he took advantage of her distraction to grasp both her wrists and pin them at her sides. She seemed not to notice this, however, her attention fixed at a point beyond his shoulder.

"M-Milord Wolf," she gasped out, a look of fright flashing across her pretty, painted features. "I—I didn't see you standing there."

"So I gathered," came the same speaker's ironic reply. "Now luv, how about that explanation . . . or should I let this gentleman here do the honors?"

By now the newcomer stood before them, so that Victor got his first look at the man. This, then, must be the gambling hell's owner, a man known to both employees and patrons only as the Wolf. Victor had heard about the man but never met him, a notorious underworld figure who, rumor had it, would kill just to settle a gambling debt. He looked nothing like the mental picture Victor might have concocted of him, however.

For the man known as the Wolf was younger than he . . . barely past his twentieth year, Victor judged. He was of a height with Victor, though perhaps a bit broader. His shaggy mane of golden hair, longer than the mode, and his casual fashion of dress—black breeches, blue waistcoat, and cravatless white shirt—made the roughest of his customers look the dandy by comparison. But the most striking feature about him was the fact the man was running about unshod.

No tulip of fashion himself, Victor shrugged off this last and returned his attention to the matter at hand. Penelope was literally quaking where she stood, no doubt frightened of what the Wolf might do to her for this altercation with a customer.

Victor heaved an inner sigh as he released his grip on her. Though he could strangle the chit for the stunt she'd just pulled, honesty compelled him to admit that he had, in a sense, led her to this particular pass. If he could patch over things for her with her employer, then he would.

"There's no harm done," he offered, the ache in his balls making that a lie. "Penelope and I are old friends, and we were just having a bit of conversation."

"An interesting way to chat, is it not?" the Wolf replied, his green eyes narrowing in chill amusement. "As the owner of this establishment, let me apologize for any . . . inconvenience that you might have suffered, Lord Blackstock. And perhaps I might offer you in recompense an entire night of the charming Penelope's services—on the house, of course."

Only a little surprised that the younger man was privy to his identity—doubtless a man like the Wolf made it his business to know just who his clientele was—Victor shook his head. "I appreciate the offer, but I was on my way out anyhow. Perhaps another time."

"Whenever you wish," the Wolf returned with cool civility. With the briefest of nods for Victor and a final chill look in Penelope's direction, he turned and with lupine grace melted back into the crowd again.

The other patrons had returned their attention to their gaming, while Betty had long since scampered off at the Wolf's first appearance. Victor found himself standing alone now save for Penelope, who now flung herself into his embrace.

"Oh, Vic, can you ever forgive me?" she wailed into his waistcoat. "Here, I was so horrid to you, and you didn't betray me. I vow I don't know what that beast would have done to me had you complained."

"He seemed like a fair enough sort," Victor dryly remarked as he disentangled her from his shirtfront. "And perhaps the next time, you'll think twice before you abuse the clientele in such a manner. Now if you'll excuse me—"

"Wait, Vic."

Penelope clutched his arm, favoring him with the seductive smile that once would have had him dragging her upstairs. Now, however, he favored her with a wry look of query.

Her smile faltered, but her tone was still light as she went on. "What the Wolf said about a night with me on the house . . . perhaps you will reconsider? I'll quite forgive the way you set me aside, if we could only spend a bit of time together. I—I've rather missed you."

He heard the plea in her voice and felt a measure of sympathy for the chit; after all, he now knew what it was like to want someone whom he could not have. But taking her up on that particular offer would be fair to neither of them. With a shake of his head, he replied, "I think it would be best if we said our good-byes instead."

He gathered up his stick and hat and, limping a bit, headed in the direction of the door. Only the timely shout of warning from another patron caused him to dodge the glass that came flying past his ear to crash at his feet.

"And good riddance to you, Lord Blackstock," came Penelope's peevish cry after it.

Half-anticipating further crockery to follow, Victor made his hasty exit to the street beyond. He drank in deep breaths of the chill early morning air, not caring that it carried with it the distinctive stench of the river. Even the sharp aroma of that muddy channel was better than the mingled scent of acrid smoke, cheap perfume, and spent lust that permeated the hell that was the Golden Wolf.

He gazed up at the spattering of stars visible above. This would not be one of those nights when whiteness lay in a thick blanket across the city. Not the sort of night, he judged, when the Barkshire Demon would strike. Still, uneasiness settled over him as he looked around him.

Here the clamor of the gambling hell was muted enough for him to hear the other night sounds—the clatter and clomp of passing carriages, the drunken shouts emanating from neighboring grog shops, the rustle of rats in the alleyway. The street before him was relatively empty, save for a pair of waiting hacks and a handful of raucous drunks making their way down the narrow, mud-choked lane.

As for Derek and his own coach, he saw no sign.

This, then, was the reason for his sense of disquietude. Wondering if maybe it was merely the port that had befuddled him, he glanced again in both directions. Once more neither driver nor equipage was to be seen. Victor frowned. Unless Derek had run into a patch of trouble, he'd never take it into his head to leave on his own.

Victor started in the direction of the nearest cross street. He'd stroll about for a few minutes; then, if Derek still remained elusive, he would flag down a hack and make a search of the area that way. A coach the size of his, marked with his distinctive coat of arms, would not remain lost for long.

Keeping to a straight line on the uneven cobbles proved harder than usual, however. He assured himself that his tendency to sway was a result of Penelope's not-so-tender mercies, not how much he'd drunk this night. The situation was not helped by the fact that gas streetlamps had not yet made their way to this part of the city. Thus, only a few steps from the door of the Golden Wolf, he was plunged into virtual darkness.

It occurred to him that he was drunker than he'd first thought when he realized he had been aware of a faint shuffling behind him for some moments before he knew it was footsteps. It took him a bit longer to comprehend the fact that he was being followed. Thus, by the time he turned around, it was too late.

He managed a glimpse of a tall, black-garbed figure whose lower face was hidden by a length of cloth wrapped about his nose and chin. Then something collided with a painful crack against the side of his head, and the muddy cobbles rushed up to meet him, just before his world went black.

Fifteen

His face loomed but inches from her, the soulless black orbs reflecting her own terrified countenance like a hellish mirror. This time, though, she recognized her attacker, and the knowledge was like a knife in her heart. But even as she tried to scream, his cold dead fingers wrapped around her throat. For a fleeting moment, she saw in his eyes now the twin images of herself struggling soundlessly.

Then the image changed, and the face reflected there was not hers, but Blackstock's. She realized then with a thrill of greater terror that she no longer knew which one of them was the killer . . . and which, the victim.

With a shuddering gasp, Amaryllis struggled awake only to find herself safe in her own bed. The room was still veiled in darkness, so that she judged she had been sleeping but a few hours. How late it was, she could not say, unless she climbed from her bed to take a look out her unshuttered window.

But dare she do so? Indeed it would take little imagination to picture the Demon's dead white face pressed to the wavery glass, staring back at her.

Willing that gruesome image away, she shut her eyes again and sagged against the pillow. She had thought that she'd banished the Barkshire Demon from her mind, but it seemed that he still lurked there after all. More disturbing, however, was the fact that her dreaming self had believed him to be Blackstock.

But only for a moment, she reminded herself with a shiver. Then *he* had become the victim, once more leaving the question as to who was truly the killer.

Unwilling all at once to surrender herself back to sleep, she sat up in bed once more and reached for her candle. The soft yellow glow when she lit it gave her a bit of comfort. She would rest easier if she shuttered her window against whatever demons—dream images, or not—might lurk beyond.

She climbed from beneath her lace coverlet. With rather more haste than she would have displayed if not alone, she hurried over to her window. Still, as she caught hold of the shutters to close them, she could not resist a glance out at the churchyard, which lay but a short distance from the house.

Usually it was but a commonplace sight for her . . . the drooping willows and broad poplars nothing but cheerful flora; the heavy wrought-iron fence, merely decorative twists of black metal; the gravestones, simply prosaic signposts to the next world. Tonight, however, her unsettled mental state made it a place of frightful images.

The trees slashed angry branches toward the sky, while the iron rails looked like rows of wicked swords thrust into the ground as a warning by some unseen army of demons. As for the gravestones, they tilted at odd angles, as if disturbed by the uneasy dead lying beneath them.

If I stare long enough, she told herself with a shiver, *I doubtless will start fancying that I can see them wending their ghostly way among the graves.*

Amaryllis pulled the shutters to with a bang and scurried back to her bed with what she conceded was more haste than was appropriate for a stern-minded woman. Once beneath the coverlet, she reached for her sketchbook tucked under her bed. She flipped through its pages until she found the charcoal drawing she'd done of the Earl of Blackstock. She brushed her fingers along the charcoal planes of his strong features. The gesture was enough to reassure herself that her dream of his being the Barkshire Demon had been simply that . . . a dream. Not that she needed a sketch of him, for already every line of his face was engraved upon her heart.

Amaryllis sighed. How things had come to this particular emotional pass, she was not certain. She had never been the impulsive sort when it came to matters of the heart, though she would admit she was something of a romantic. Except for a childhood crush on one of Talbot's fellow medical students and a quite brief flirtation with the brother of one of her art students, however, her heart had never been truly engaged.

That was, until now.

For, like it or not, she was fast becoming obsessed with this enigmatic earl. And, save for a brief lapse that morning in the hothouse, he seemed completely indifferent to her. Now here she sat, sighing over his picture and acting every bit as foolish as Mary had behaved with her dashing poet. The only saving grace was that, given their respective stations in life, there was no hope for her and Blackstock anyhow.

Or was there? Amaryllis frowned. Even before she and Mary Godwin had become fast friends, she had embraced the free-thinking philosophies of Mary's late mother. Being wed to any man would only rob her of the freedom she now had to pursue her painting career, so that she had not changed her mind about marriage. Given that, what was to stop her from indulging in another, more modern relationship with Blackstock?

The idea sent an excited shiver through her. Yet, what would Father and Talbot say should they learn of her intentions? Doubtless they would be shocked—but then, of course, they both were men.

All at once, she was acutely aware that she had no female companions with whom she could discuss the matter. Her mother had died ten years earlier, while her sister-in-law Cordelia lay on her sickbed. Her female friends were few, and not the sort in whom she could confide. The only one of them who would have understood was Mary, and she was abroad. True, she wrote to Mary on a regular basis, but with the foreign posts as they were, it was a one-sided correspondence more often than not.

Even without anyone's advice, however, she could guess some of the pitfalls that awaited her. Mary's father and stepmother had disowned the girl, while polite Society shunned her and her poet lover. But the difference was that the latter still had a living wife, while Blackstock did not. Moreover, Mary had dragged her young stepsister along with them, giving rise to more scandalous rumors of far more unnatural goings-on. She, on the other hand, merely intended to experience a few nights of passion with the earl.

And, if she were quite discreet about the whole affair, her family need never know.

She returned the drawing to her sketchbook and tucked it beneath her tick mattress. Sternness of mind would be of no help in this situation. Would she be bold enough, she wondered, to follow through with that particular role? One advantage would be that, if she *were* to become Blackstock's mistress, he would be less inclined to discharge her as his illustrator.

Conversely, it would be mortifying in the extreme if he simply laughed at the idea of taking her to his bed. Though she knew she was accounted attractive enough, perhaps he only cared for experienced women. And experience was one thing she lacked.

She bit her lip, considering. She had a vague idea that a man could somehow tell when a woman was a virgin— though how she was not sure. Moreover, she knew that a goodly number of gentlemen were averse to deflowering an innocent. Perhaps if she could keep Blackstock sufficiently interested during their lovemaking, he might not notice that inconvenient detail.

Victor has a copy of Essays on Far Eastern Marriage Customs *in his library that quite explains everything one would ever need to know on the subject.*

Monique's words from several days earlier echoed in Amaryllis's mind. She had gathered from both Savilles' reactions that the book to which the younger girl had referred contained certain references to copulation. Perhaps, on some pretext, she might gain access to Blackstock's library and manage a look at that volume herself. After a study of it, she doubtless would better know whether or not the role of mistress was one that she wished to take on.

Or would she?

Amaryllis shook her head. Being a modern woman was no easy task, she was learning. But she had long since determined that she was not one to act out the prescribed role of servitude that, even in this day and age, was a wife's lot. Better scandal or solitude than such an existence. For, just as Talbot had disapproved, surely no husband would have allowed her to accept a commission from the notorious Earl of Blackstock.

Save, perhaps, a man such as the earl himself.

She dismissed the thought with a wry little laugh. She had already seen the strict standards to which Blackstock held his young sister. Despite his reputation, she rather suspected that he would insist that any wife of his conduct herself in a similarly conventional mode. And doubtless he would expect his future bride to possess, if not wealth, then a title . . . both of which requirements she lacked.

"Ah, well, so much for becoming Lady Blackstock," she murmured as she pinched out her candle and snuggled back under the coverlet.

" 'Tis a right good thing yer lordship 'as a tough skull," Derek observed as he pressed a handkerchief to the back of

Victor's bleeding head. "Are ye sure ye don't want me to summon a constable? The footpad wot done this might still be about."

"I doubt that," Victor replied, then winced as the very act of speaking sent a renewed shaft of pain through him. "He'll be long gone, my watch with him."

He snatched the wadded square of linen from his driver's hand and pressed that makeshift bandage in place. Then, legs still unsteady, he rose from the stoop where he'd been sitting. Bloody hell, but it was getting to be almost a habit, this being rendered unconscious by some miscreant coshing him over the head.

He shot a disgusted look down at his filth-caked attire. He now exuded a noticeable stench that was equal parts mud, rotting garbage, and manure . . . not surprising, since Derek had discovered him lying senseless in an alleyway not far from the Golden Wolf. By their combined reckoning, almost half an hour had passed since Victor set out on foot from that gambling hell to find his driver and the missing coach.

Derek's own search for his employer had proved easier than had Victor's for him. For, as Victor suspected, the younger man had not left on a whim. Rather Derek had been duped into leaving his post by a street urchin bearing a message purportedly from Victor himself.

Mindful of his aching head, he turned back to his driver. The younger man's face in the yellow glow of the carriage lamps reflected both concern and shame. "Tell me again what the boy looked like, what he said," Victor demanded.

Derek's pockmarked features dutifully twisted as he rallied his powers of recollection.

" 'E was a ragged lad, not above ten years old, the sort wot ye find wanderin' on any street," the man began. " 'E told me the Earl o' Blackstock 'ad paid 'im a shilling to deliver a message. 'E said 'ow as yer lordship would stay longer than wot ye planned . . . an' I should come back again at dawn for ye."

"And you had no cause to think that the message was from anyone other than me?"

Derek gave his head a helpless shake. "Ye'd given me the same sort o' orders once or twice before, so it seemed likely eno'. I drove off, but I couldn't help thinkin' 'ow as somethin' weren't quite aboveboard. I came back just t'make sure, an' one o' the Wolf's lads said 'ow as ye had already left. That's when I went lookin' for ye."

He paused, his face paler than usual as he turned a pleading look on Victor. "I 'ad a right good fright, seein' ye lyin' there like that. 'Twas right relieved, I was, to find ye still breathin'. Believe me, milord, if I'd known anythin' were amiss, I never would 'ave left in the first place."

"I'm sure you would not have."

Indeed he'd never had cause to question the man's loyalty in the past. He was not prepared to do so now, though it occurred to him that he had only Derek's word there had been a street urchin bearing false intelligence. Beyond that was the fact his instincts told him that this attack had not been a random one. Someone had deliberately targeted him. The question was, who . . . and why?

As if reading his thoughts, Derek went on. " 'Tis a right odd bit o' business if ye ask me, milord. Why would a footpad go to the trouble o' sendin' me off, when 'e could 'ave 'is pick o' gents wanderin' about? 'Twas like 'e wanted ye, in particular."

"Or something of mine, in particular."

What the thief had made off with was his gold pocketwatch bearing the Saville family coat of arms. To be sure, it was an expensive enough piece. Still, the man had left behind Victor's wallet full of blunt, a gold-headed walking stick and—far more valuable than any of the other items— his gold ring with that same family crest engraved upon it.

Victor frowned. Given that his assailant had taken such

pains with this robbery, and that he'd had the privacy of a dark alley in which to conduct the crime, why had the man not absconded with *everything* of value?

Unless, perhaps, this had not been a simple robbery.

"Mayhap we should be off, milord," Derek now suggested with a nervous look around them. "If ye're not wantin' to report the crime, there's nothin' more we can do 'ere."

Victor followed his gaze. It would be dawn in another couple of hours. The greatest portion of the Golden Wolf's clientele had no doubt dispersed or else were passed out on its splintered wooden floors. The hired hacks he'd earlier noted had picked up their last fares and clattered off into the cool night, so that the streets were well-nigh deserted. Even if his suspicions were right, and something other than robbery had motivated his attacker, he'd find no clues or witnesses now.

"Home, it is," he agreed and gingerly climbed into the coach.

As Derek whipped up the team, Victor sank back against the soft leather and gritted his teeth. He did not look forward to the return journey. Well-sprung as his carriage was, the ride would still likely prove excruciating in his battered condition.

Indeed, by the time they reached home, his head pounded like an entire company of foot soldiers crossing a wooden bridge, while the odor that clung to him had ripened to an unbearable stench reminiscent of a stable that had not been mucked out in some years. He suppressed a groan as, not waiting on Derek, he clambered down from the coach and started up the steps to the front door of his town house.

"Milord," Derek ventured from his perch atop the carriage. "Shall I go for Dr. Meeks?"

"No point bothering the good doctor at this hour."

Besides which, he silently added as he shut the door behind him, he'd feel like a bloody fool having the man treat him for the same injury twice in less than a fortnight. Meeks would doubtless think him incapable of being let out on his own, given that he seemed prone to attack from behind.

Once inside his bedchamber, he tugged the bell pull that would summon his valet; then, with as much speed as his pounding head allowed, he began undressing. By the time Moresdale made his appearance, Victor was standing naked before a pile of muck-stained clothing and holding a fresh compress to his head.

"No questions," he decreed in a weary voice as the bemused valet opened his mouth to speak. "Just take those rags down to the hothouse and burn them in one of the fireplaces. I'm going to get a bit of rest."

"Very good, milord," came the man's obedient reply, though Victor suspected the valet would have the entire story from Derek by the time he made downstairs again.

Or would he need to?

Victor watched while the other man scooped up the offensive clothes. Despite the hour, the valet was fully dressed, save for his coat. *As if he had just come in from a night out himself.* It occurred to him then that the former pugilist might have been responsible for the attack on him . . . perhaps conspiring with Derek in attempted murder. Christ, maybe the whole bloody household, not excepting his sister, was in on the scheme.

"Anythin' else, milord?" Moresdale prompted, and Victor realized he'd been staring at the man.

Brusquely he shook his head, only to regret the gesture an instant later as the pounding in his skull redoubled. "See that no one disturbs me for the next few hours . . . and that particularly includes Lady Monique. And don't mention this"—he indicated the bloody compress he'd been holding against his head—"to her, either. The last thing I want is her fussing over me."

"Very good, milord," he agreed as, holding the odiferous garments at arm's length, the valet took his swift leave.

By the time Victor crawled into his bed, he had dismissed

his momentary suspicions as a product of his jostled brain. Neither Derek, Moresdale, nor any of his household had cause to attack him. As to the puzzle of everything the thief had left behind, perhaps a passerby had simply frightened the man off before he could finish the job. Hell, that made more sense than his being the victim of some domestic conspiracy.

By the time uneasy sleep finally claimed him, he had all but convinced himself that the night's incident had been but a random crime, nothing more.

Sixteen

*I have made some quite Fascinating Studies into the
realm of physical pleasures . . . but fear not, my experience thus far is limited to reading a Most Interesting tome. Indeed it seems incredible that Certain
Acts as described there are humanly possible. But perhaps I shall yet have the opportunity to learn for myself if they are . . .*

> —letter from Miss Amaryllis Meeks to
> Miss Mary Godwin

Amaryllis stared down at the book in her lap in disbelief,
wondering if she had, at long last, overstepped common
sense in carrying through with this particular plan. Upon
first arriving at the Saville town house this morning, she
boldly had informed the dour Peters that Blackstock had
given her leave to browse his library for certain horticultural
tomes. To her relief, the earl himself had been otherwise
occupied and thus not available for the butler to confirm
her story.

Still, mindful that the man might appear any moment, she
had made her search for the specific volume she wanted with
haste. Locating it on a high, dusty shelf that required the rolling ladder to reach, she prudently snatched up a couple of
generic books on flora—*Bofford's Guide to Elegant Landscape Plantings* and *A Treatise on Medicinal Herbs*—as

camouflage. Then, not daring to look back, she had fled to the hothouse with her prize, planning to peruse its pages later.

Now with the greatest part of the day's work behind her, she sat upon the tall wooden stool she used while painting, the book in question propped on her knees. She'd long since formed a general idea as to the particulars of human procreation. Her artwork, meanwhile, had familiarized her with the nude male and female forms. Nothing in her experience, however, had prepared her for the shocking depictions to be found within the staid covers of the primly titled volume, *Essays on Far Eastern Marriage Customs.*

The few passages purporting to be "essays" were nothing short of lascivious. The etchings themselves were even more shocking. Crudely rendered, save for the exaggerated attention given every male organ represented, each showed a man and woman indulging in a different variation of sexual intercourse. A few of the poses appeared ludicrous; others, downright impossible. Yet she could not deny the primitive vibrancy displayed by the artist . . . nor could she ignore the growing sensation of damp warmth between her thighs as she perused its contents.

Her gaze widened as she turned to yet another etching. Bright afternoon sun splashed through the glass ceiling above her, its golden glow highlighting every detail of that page. The drawing was that of a naked female seated upon a short column, her plump thighs spread wide to reveal the almost mouthlike opening between them. A nude male figure was posed before her, his erect and impossibly large phallus in the process of entering that exaggerated orifice. The woman's face was contorted in an expression that, to Amaryllis's mind, one could interpret either as ecstasy or extreme agony.

The blush that already heated her cheeks deepened, so that she was grateful that the line of windows behind her were cracked open to allow in a cooling breeze. Still, she could not help but picture herself and Blackstock engaged in a similar pose. It might prove an interesting experiment, though she rather doubted her reaction would match that of the woman in the drawing. But this variation on the act of intercourse appeared more achievable than any other she'd thus far noted.

The question was, could she possibly persuade the earl to try so unlikely a maneuver?

Frowning, she flipped her way through the rest of the volume. What she had not yet discovered within its pages was any sort of clue as to how one approached a potential partner regarding such an activity. Surely it was not good form to ask a man into one's bed outright . . . but then, how did one hint at such a thing? Yet as she pondered the question, she heard the sound of booted footsteps on flagstones behind her.

Blackstock.

With a guilty start, she slammed the volume shut and spun about on the stool to see him striding purposefully between the rows of potted rosebushes toward her. He wore his usual black trousers and white linen shirt, topped this time by a dove-gray waistcoat. As on other occasions, he had flouted proprieties and was sans both jacket and cravat, with his collar scandalously unbuttoned as well.

Though the sight sparked a certain feminine appreciation, she gave a fervent prayer that he was there to work and not converse with her. True she planned to speak with him this day, but she would have preferred to have prepared her speech in advance, given the nature of the intended discussion. And she had no intention of letting him discover her reading an illustrated text on the subject of lovemaking!

She cast frantically about for somewhere to hide the book, but it was too late. She slipped it beneath the two horticultural texts sitting on the table beside her, hoping he would not have cause to examine the stack. Then, untying her paint-spattered smock, she draped it on the table where she already tossed her mobcap. That accomplished, she smoothed the skirt of her lemon-yellow muslin gown and faced him with what she prayed was calm aplomb.

If he had noticed anything amiss, he gave no indication as he halted before her. His expression was purposeful, and his dark gaze unreadable. Yet the sight of him worked on her like water on a wilted rosebush, so that she composed her own features lest her eagerness show on her face. If her plan were to succeed, she must appear as a modern woman, not a chit just come from the schoolroom.

"Good afternoon, my lord," she said with a polite smile, willing her gaze not to stray to the pilfered books. "Are you here to check on my day's progress? The new painting of the white Alba rose is finished, as well as—"

"Later," he cut her short, his voice holding a note that she had never heard from him before. "I have something else of greater import to discuss with you first."

He paused to rub the back of his neck, as if his head somehow pained him. Her confusion increased, so that she temporarily forgot her own intentions. He had not come for mere social chitchat . . . that much, she realized. Beyond that she would not hazard a guess, unless it was that Peters had told him about her raid on his private library, and he was here to voice his displeasure.

"I must tell you, Miss Godwin—Amaryllis," he went on, "that I did not plan for matters to unfold as they have. It is not customary for a woman to take on such a commission as this. I gather that you were somewhat surprised when I first offered you the post, were you not?"

"I had not expected any such thing, my lord," she answered, even as she favored him with an uncertain look. Indeed this conversation was growing more muddled by the moment.

He nodded, as if satisfied by the admission. "Then perhaps you have an idea as to my true motive for hiring you?"

"I believe, my lord, that you indicated you found my skills

as an artist quite acceptable—and that you thought I would be of help to your project."

"Then you believe wrong, my dear Amaryllis," came his cool reply, while a sudden heat sparked in his dark gaze. "I had one reason, and one reason only for employing you. I wanted an opportunity to see you again, and I saw no other means to accomplish the task save by that means."

"I—I see."

A battle waged within her breast between professional pique and purely feminine satisfaction. On the one hand, it was insulting in the extreme for him to have given her work such short shrift. On the other, the fact that he was admitting a certain level of attraction for her would make her own task easier. Perhaps that was why he was here now, to make her the same offer that she had hoped to make him.

"So tell me, my lord, where does this now leave us?" she went on, not daring to let her own eagerness show . . . at least not yet.

He took a few steps closer, until he stood but an arm's length away. "Where it leaves us, Amaryllis, is that I have no choice now but to discharge you from my employ."

Discharge her?

The dispassionate words all but set her reeling, and she wildly wondered if she had heard him aright. Had he not said two days earlier that he was more than satisfied with her work? What could have happened in the interim to change his mind?

"I'm afraid I do not understand," she managed, wondering if she sounded as stricken as she felt. "Even if your original intent in hiring me was less than honest, it does not matter now."

"It bloody well *does* matter."

Abruptly he turned from her. As if seeking distraction, he caught up the top volume from the stack of books on the table beside her. She waited in an agony of mortified anticipation for him to set it down and seize the next, revealing the title of the third and most incriminating book at the bottom of the stack. To her relief, however, he merely flipped through the pages of Mr. Bofford's *Guide,* then tossed it atop the other again and turned back to face her.

"Let me be quite blunt about this. Surely a modern woman such as yourself"—he gave that last phrase a subtle chill emphasis—"is aware that a man might well find himself faced with certain . . . temptations when in the company of an attractive female. And if that female also happens to be in his employ, the man might stoop to using that fact as leverage to persuade her into his bed. And as it so happens, I do find you attractive, and you do just happen to work for me."

She took a deep breath, wondering if he could hear how hard her heart was pounding. Perhaps this was the opening she needed to approach him on that very subject.

"Are you saying, my lord, that you are unscrupulous enough to use your position as my employer to compromise me?"

"What I am saying, my dear Amaryllis, is that I know my limitations . . . and that I've just about reached them."

Without warning, he seized her shoulders and pulled her to him, his fingers biting into her flesh. She gave a soft cry, and that was when his mouth claimed hers.

His lips were hot and demanding, drawing the very breath from her so that she felt herself in danger of swooning. Yet the sensation swirling through her body was not fear, but an urgent sort of longing that she could not deny. Instinctively she pressed herself to him, molding her breasts to the unyielding hardness of his chest.

He was all heat and steel beneath the civilized layer of fine-spun linen. Then his hands roughly slid down the curve of her back, pulling her closer still so that she could feel another sort of hardness throbbing now against her lower body. She gave a soft sigh of surrender and clutched at his arms, responding with tentative eagerness to the insistent probing of his tongue. Her actions drew a harsh, answering groan from him just before he broke off their kiss and all but shoved her from him.

Her limbs still trembling from these new sensations, she clutched at the table to steady herself and stared at him in dismay. He looked as shaken as she felt, his dark gaze almost black now as he stared back at her. She could hear his ragged breathing, like that of a man who had just run a long distance, the rhythm seeming to match her own uneven heartbeat.

His tone, however, was cool as always as he said, "I trust I have just proved my point. Now do us both a favor, and pack up your things. I'll have Derek waiting up front with the carriage to take you home again. And don't worry, I shall pay you a full month's wages for what work you've already done here."

So saying, he turned on his heel and started back down the rows of rosebushes toward the French doors. She watched in silence for the space of a few heartbeats, not really believing he was walking out on her this way. Then a rush of anger swept her, banishing her uncertainty.

"One moment, Lord Blackstock."

Her voice rang with cool confidence, stopping the earl in his tracks. Slowly he turned back around to face her, his features once more composed.

"I have said all that I intend to say upon this subject, Miss Godwin."

"But I have not."

She snatched up the bottom book from the stack on the table beside her; then, closing the distance between them, she halted before him and thrust the volume into his hands.

"I cannot see how it is fair that I lose my post," she hotly continued, "simply because you cannot control your baser male instincts. And as for your concern over compromising me, had it ever occurred to you that, as a modern woman, I might not be offended by such an offer?"

Victor barely heard that last as he stared down at the book he now held, not quite believing his eyes. Bloody hell, the chit had been rummaging about his private library. As to her choice of reading material, he wasn't sure whether to be shocked, amused . . . or simply more aroused than he already was.

The volume had fallen open to a most interesting plate. A naked woman was seated upon a column while her partner stood between her parted thighs, thrusting into her with what appeared to be more enthusiasm than skill. The pose corresponded with uncanny accuracy to the fantasy he had conjured the last time he had seen Amaryllis here, in this very spot.

The heat that had been building in his loins these past minutes reached a sudden, painful peak. He shut the book again and set it aside, then turned his attention back to Amaryllis.

She had the delicately disheveled look of a woman who had just been thoroughly kissed. Moreover a delightful blush now stained her cheeks . . . delightful because he'd never seen a similar show of modesty in any woman offering herself in such a fashion.

Forgetting the pain in his skull from the previous night's attack, he demanded, "Let me get this straight. Are you saying that *you* had plans to seduce *me?*"

"I had contemplated the notion, yes," came her tart reply, though her blush deepened.

At that reluctant admission, he managed a laugh that ended on a groan. "Then since it seems we both had much the same idea, let's make a pact. You seduce me, and I'll seduce you. Is it an agreement, Miss Godwin?"

"It is, Lord Blackstock."

At her words, he waited no longer but gathered her in his arms and kissed her a second time. This time the very taste of her lips sent a shudder of pure need through him. Almost without thinking, he grasped her by the waist and lifted her onto the edge of the table beside him.

The action left her lemon-yellow skirt hiked now almost to her knees. In a single efficient move, he tugged up her gown almost to her hips, exposing a pair of shapely legs clad in silk stockings tied at the knees and—not surprising for a modern woman—a pair of lace-trimmed drawers.

"W-What are you doing?" Amaryllis gasped out, staring back at him in alarm.

He slanted her a wry look. "Why seducing you, of course."

"Oh. I see."

Indeed things were progressing with dizzying rapidity, so that she could scarce catch her breath. Here she was, seated rather amid a tangle of small rosebushes and well on her way to being compromised. Moreover, it had just occurred to her that they were conducting this mutual seduction in the middle of the day in a room full of uncurtained windows and in sight of a pair of French doors. Surely there were *some* proprieties to be maintained, even under such circumstances.

"But what if someone walks in?"

He favored her with a ragged grin that made him look quite boyish. "No one sets foot here without my permission; besides which, you're still quite decently clothed," he reminded her as his hand roamed up her thigh. "So unless you've changed your mind about what we're about to do—"

A gasp was her only reply, for his fingers had found the opening in her drawers and were toying with the soft curls that covered her woman's mound. She shivered, certain she should protest but unwilling to let him stop as yet. Then, before she realized what was happening, he began to do quite extraordinary things to the tiny nub of flesh between her thighs.

She caught back a gasp. "Is this your means of seduction, my lord?" she managed to ask.

He gave her another ragged grin by way of answer. "It's a start. And I think that, given the current circumstances, you should dispense with titles and simply call me Victor."

But speech was suddenly beyond her. Indeed every sensation was centered in that one spot, building with an almost painful urgency to an unknown peak. She was aware now of a damp, sticky warmth there, the same sort of warmth as had assailed her while she earlier had studied the etchings. Embarrassed color flooded her cheeks, and she wondered what Blackstock must think of her. He, however, had a look of purely male satisfaction about him.

"You're warm and willing, just as I imagined," he murmured as he stroked her with a rhythm that set her entire body afire. "Shall I continue my seduction, then?"

"Oh, yes, my lord—Victor," she gasped out and caught hold of his shoulders to brace herself.

She shut her eyes and spread her thighs wider still. No longer did she care what he thought, so long as he did not stop what he was doing to her.

His free hand, she realized, had moved up her waist to the bodice of her gown. The sensations now were different, but equally delightful. He lightly squeezed one breast, and then the other, brushing his thumb across her nipples until they puckered like rosebuds against the thin fabric.

Yet even as she concentrated on her body's newest responses, the fingers of his other hand abruptly slid into the moist, tight heat of her woman's sheath.

She bit back a scream of painful pleasure and shuddered, feeling her inner muscles clamp down on him as he slid his finger in and out of her. If what he had been doing to her before had been exquisite agony, this now was unbearable ecstasy. Vaguely she was aware that her head was lolling back, just like the woman in the etching, and she knew now the answer to her earlier question. But then, without warning, he pulled away.

She could not help a protesting cry as she opened her

eyes again. "A-Are you quite finished, then?" she managed to ask, trying to hide her disappointment. From her perusal of the book she had pilfered from his library, she had been certain there was more to the process than this.

Victor's dark gaze burnt blacker still as he reached down to fumble with the buttons of his trousers. "I'm not finished yet . . . not by a long shot," came his husky reply as he freed his erect shaft from the confining garment.

The sight of his swollen male organ sent a swift moment of alarm through her. She had dismissed as exaggerated the etchings' depiction of that portion of the male anatomy. If anything, those drawings had not done it justice . . . at least, not in Victor's case.

She had no further time to consider the matter, for he nudged her thighs wider apart and positioned himself between her legs, much like the man had stood before the woman in that one memorable etching. He had cupped his thick length in one hand so that the swollen tip of his organ now brushed her slick folds of woman's flesh. The sensation nearly sent her swooning, so that she barely heard his murmured words of encouragement before he grasped her hips and thrust himself deep within her.

She was aware of a tearing sensation and a single sharp instant of pain, so that she shut her eyes and cried aloud. The pain dulled to a bearable ache, that feeling coupled with an inescapable sensation of fullness that reached to her very core. Her next realization, however, was that Victor had gone still within her.

She opened her eyes once more to find his dark gaze burning into her. Intimately entwined as they were, she had no trouble reading the full play of emotions—comprehension, disbelief, frustration—that flashed across his face.

Neither did she miss the outrage in his voice as he choked out, "Bloody hell, you're a virgin."

Seventeen

"Was a virgin," Amaryllis meekly corrected, a blush suffusing her features even as she willed herself to hold Victor's angry gaze. "I was not quite certain you would notice."

"Not notice?"

His words ended on a sound very close to a growl. Then, as if regaining his composure, he demanded in a chill tone, "Tell me, Amaryllis, just how in the bloody hell did you think I could have avoided noticing?"

"I—I supposed I presumed that, in the heat of the moment, you might overlook that small detail."

"Your being a virgin is no small detail."

As he spoke, his fingers tightened on her hips, and she felt the unmistakable stirring of his shaft deep within her. The sensation sent a surge of feminine possessiveness through her. For the moment, he was not the aloof and unobtainable Earl of Blackstock, but simply a man . . . and she, the woman who held him enthralled.

Instinctively she wrapped her legs around his waist, so that his swollen length was buried deeper within her tight sheath. The action drew a strangled oath from him, though she noted with satisfaction he made no move to disentangle himself.

"What in the bloody hell do you think you're doing?" he gritted out, a sheen of perspiration now beading his forehead. "What we're in the midst of here can't just be stopped anytime you please . . . that is, not beyond a certain point.

And the way you keep moving about, I'm damn well about to reach it."

"But if you will recall, I have never asked you to stop."

She raised a tentative hand to the hard line of his jaw, caressing that feature just as she had run her fingers across the charcoaled lines of his portrait. His flesh was warm and taut beneath a prickling of whiskers. As her hand slid down the well-formed line of his throat, she could feel the rapid thrumming of his pulse that matched her own.

Something flickered in his dark gaze, and she realized that this small act of intimacy had taken him by surprise . . . something that she, in turn, found unexpected. She had longed to touch him in this way almost from the beginning. She could not imagine that his past lovers had not wanted that same thing.

When he made no move to stop her, she boldly let her hand travel down the muscled expanse of his chest, feeling the heat of his body through the superfine of his shirt. In the process, a small pang of regret swept her at the way their lovemaking had progressed. True there was something exciting about the way they both were still clothed yet so intimately entwined; still, she would have preferred to explore the various muscle groups of his body without the hindrance of wool and linen.

"The next time," she ventured, "I think I would like you to remove your clothes first . . . that is, if you would not much mind it."

"We'll do it any way you like the next time," he groaned out, and she felt a shudder wrack him, "but let's finish this time first."

He began thrusting in and out of her—slowly at first and then with greater urgency, grasping her hips as he urged her to move with him. With a soft, eager cry she tightened her legs about him and matched that sensual rhythm. His face was taut now with a desire that she knew must reflect her own need.

Shy, all at once, she clutched his shoulders and buried her face against his waistcoat lest he read her heated features and know just how much she wanted this. Still, she could not hide the way her body was reacting. After only a few swift strokes, she had reached that same, almost unbearable peak of tension she had known but moments before.

Quite breathless by now, she vaguely realized that Victor's breathing had taken on a harsh, ragged rhythm as well. This time, however, he did not stop but kept driving into her, until her every sensation was focused on the hot, heated bud of desire deep within her. Then, just as she thought she must surely swoon, that tiny bud exploded into a dazzling bloom of release that made her cry out in pure joy.

As she reached her own climax, she heard Victor's harsh groan of completion. He thrust one final time into her, then wrapped his arms around her and was still.

They remained in that pose for several moments, with her snuggled against his chest so that she could hear as his rapid heartbeat slowed to a more regular pulse. Finally he eased himself from her and refastened his trousers. He avoided her gaze all the while, however, so that her brief moment of contentment faded to uncertainty.

She tugged down her gown as best she could, though she dared not climb from the table as yet lest her trembling legs not hold her. Something was amiss, she knew . . . but just what troubled him, she could not say. She reached a tentative hand to him.

When her fingers brushed his jaw, he gazed back up at her, and she saw that the earlier heat that had darkened his eyes was gone. Anger, and another emotion that she could not read, had replaced it.

"Victor, what is wrong?" she softly asked. "Did you not enjoy what we did?"

His harsh sound of amusement grated on her soul. "Enjoyment doesn't have a thing to do with it . . . not that I didn't enjoy myself, because I did. As for what's wrong, it seems that I've sunk to despoiling innocents, and I'm not proud of it."

"Really, Victor," she exclaimed with a frown, "you make what we did sound so sordid, and it was not. It was a simply wonderful experience, and I refuse to be sorry."

Despoiling innocents, indeed. Did all men lapse into melodrama following lovemaking, she peevishly wondered as she smoothed her crumpled gown, or was he the exception?

Quite out of sorts now, she hopped down from the table, wincing just a little at the soreness in her thighs. It *had* been something wonderful that had happened between them, a joining of twin bodies and souls. And if he were not quite clever enough to realize that, then it was his loss.

She gasped as he caught her arm and, none too gently, swung her around to face him. "It's not that simple, Amaryllis," he gritted out. "You might be able to dismiss what we did as of no account, but I cannot."

"I did not say it was of no account, I said it was not sordid. Besides which, it was as much my idea as yours, so I don't see why—"

"Bloody hell, would you listen to me for a moment?"

Abruptly he released her again and raked a hand through his dark hair. "Don't you see, I never would have touched you in the first place if I had known you were a virgin. I assumed from the way that you kept terming yourself a modern woman that you'd had your share of experience in these matters. Now I've taken what, by rights, you should have given to a husband . . . or, at the very least, someone who was in the position to marry you."

"But I don't wish to wed," she protested, "and I cannot see why the simple loss of a maidenhead must lead to a ceremony."

"But what if you were to find yourself with child . . . or were you not aware that was a possible result of our simply wonderful experience?"

The cool irony in his tone made her blush, the more so because she *had* managed to ignore that possibility. Her dismay increased when he added in the same blunt tone, "It's not like I'm a stablehand and you're a parlormaid, and we've just had a friendly tumble in the hay. I'd not marry you, just to give the babe a name."

"Indeed, my lord, I had no such expectations," she replied in the same chill tones, though his words stung more than she cared to admit. "You must agree it would be ludicrous to saddle an earl with the responsibilities of a stableboy."

She glimpsed a flicker of embarrassment in his expression at her gibe, though anger promptly supplanted that emotion. "I never said I would sidestep my responsibilities, only that I wouldn't marry you. Don't worry, I'd see to it that any child of mine had everything he needed."

Except for a father.

True as it was, the brutality of his thought made Victor wince. Though how matters had gotten so far out of hand in the space of a few minutes was beyond him. He had come to the hothouse with the express intention of dismissing the chit. Instead, he'd managed to deflower her and then involve himself in a debate over a hypothetical child and unlikely parental obligations. He had never had to worry over such issues in the past, given that the females he bedded were ones well versed in the ways of preventing such situations, from the start.

So why was he suddenly concerned in this particular case?

Unbidden came the image of children—his children—playing in the garden beyond, that tangle of thorns and vines tamed to a bright formal garden. The girls would have reddish-gold hair like hers, while the boys would be dark, like him . . .

Abruptly he suppressed this oddly appealing fantasy. Still, he could not deny that, as he'd made love to Amaryllis, he'd felt something that went far beyond mere physical pleasure.

If he had to put a name to it, he would have said it was a sense of rightness . . . of completeness. Something he had never before felt with another woman.

He deliberately returned his thoughts to the matter at hand. He had to decide whether or not to send Amaryllis on her way—that was, if she did not make the decision for him. And if she stayed, it still remained then for them to settle just how far her duties would then extend.

She was staring at him, green eyes narrowed as she awaited some manner of response from him. With an effort, he resisted the impulse to reach out and brush a stray curl from her forehead. He was bloody well tempted simply to take her again, to see if he could turn her angry protests into cries of passion. For, despite her prickly air of anger, she still had an appealing softness about her that made him wish he *were* a stableboy after all. The situation would be a damned sight simpler, to be sure.

He suppressed a weary sigh, his own anger easing. The truth was that he wanted her to continue her painting almost as much as he wanted her in his bed. But both choices—stay or go . . . warm his bed or break his heart—he would leave up to her.

Wryly aware that he was now slipping dangerously close to melodrama, he managed a conciliatory smile. "I think we should start again. Why don't you ask me the same question that you did just a few moments ago?"

Her eyes widened. Then a faint smile touched her soft lips as well. "I believe, my lord, I asked if you enjoyed what we did."

"And my answer is, yes, I quite enjoyed it. So my question to you is, what do we do now?"

Amaryllis hesitated, her smile fading. The moment had come, it seemed, for her to tell him her true name, as well as her connection to Talbot. For, if they were to reach any point of understanding, they would first have to meet upon the plain of mutual trust.

"If the choice were mine, my lord, I would ask to continue on in your employ," she began. "And, if you were to desire it, I would not be averse to a more personal relationship as well. But I fear that, before we go any farther, I have another small deception to confess."

A flicker of suspicion lit his dark eyes. All he said, however, was, "Go on."

"You see, I—I rather misled you as to my true identity. My surname is not Godwin. It is Meeks." She paused and took a deep breath, then finished in a rush, "I believe that you are already acquainted with my brother, Talbot."

His dark eyes narrowed abruptly, while an expression of incredulity flashed across his features. "Do I understand you correctly? Your brother is my personal physician, Talbot Meeks?"

At her swift nod, his mouth tightened into a grim line. "Bloody hell," he softly swore. "So this is what it has all been leading up to, these past few days. You must remind me to congratulate the good doctor the next time I see him. He played his role that morning to the hilt."

"But Talbot had no notion—"

"I'd say he had a very good notion indeed," Victor cut her short in a dangerously soft tone. "All he had to do was offer up his virgin sister to the notorious Earl of Blackstock and then wait to see what sort of settlement I'd make to squelch the scandal. He would walk away with a tidy bit of blunt in his pocket, with you the only one standing to lose anything on the deal. Unless, of course, the good doctor simply managed some trick of surgery to give the impression that you'd never been with a man before."

That last accusation set twin patches of angry color burning in her cheeks. "My brother would never stoop to so unscrupulous an act," she choked out. "And if you would give me a moment to explain, you would know that he would never had known it was I whom you found that night, save that he saw my sketchbook. As for why he remained silent then as to our connection, he wished to spare all three of us embarrassment. He had no idea that you would offer me employment, or that I would accept it."

"So you would have me believe that Meeks knows nothing of our arrangement, then?"

She gave a stiff nod. "He learned of it only the other night . . . and then quite by accident. He even threatened to tell you the truth as to my true identity, if I did not."

A humorless smile twisted his lips. "I see. I take it, then, that your brother objected to your working for me?"

"As a matter of fact, my lord, he had already quite bluntly warned me away from you."

Even as she spoke the words, Amaryllis regretted them. He must know as surely as she what Talbot had said, and for an instant she felt a flicker of fear. What if she had misjudged the man, after all, and he was the brutal killer Talbot had implied he might well be? What steps might he take to silence her?

Yet as the thought crossed her mind, she rejected it. She could never have felt such fulfillment with a murderer, she was certain. Moreover any man who had such a disregard for another human being's life would never have bothered to debate the fate of a theoretical child.

Impulsively she reached out and caught his hand. "Talbot admitted that he is not sure whether or not you actually were guilty of that crime. As for myself, I cannot believe such a thing of you. So can we not put this all behind us and start over again?"

"No."

With that single blunt word, Victor pulled his fingers free of hers and took a step back. She glimpsed a fleeting emotion in those dark eyes—need or maybe regret?—before his features assumed a shuttered expression.

"What you believe or don't believe about me has no bearing on the situation. The fact happens to be that you are the sister of a respected physician. It will serve neither of our reputations for people to learn that you are in my employ, no matter how innocent the circumstances. As for any other sort of relationship between us, that is simply out of the question."

She recoiled from the words as if from a blow. Then, taking a shuddering breath, she protested, "Victor, I don't care what people think—"

"But I do."

He shook his head and gave a harsh, humorless laugh. "I suppose that must sound a bit odd, coming from someone of my reputation. Let's just say that I know what it means to walk into a crowded room knowing that every person there believes you guilty of some heinous crime . . . and that nothing you can say or do will ever convince them otherwise."

That chill moment of amusement faded as he went on. "Through no fault of her own, my sister must endure much the same sort of treatment every time she sets foot outside the house. I'll not subject her or myself—or anyone else I care about—to more of the same. Now I'll see about having the carriage brought around for you."

A moment later, the French doors had closed after him.

Feeling rather like a rosebush stripped of its blooms, Amaryllis numbly made her way to the back room. As always, a basin and pitcher of fresh water was set out. She caught up a small towel and washed away the lingering traces of their lovemaking, blanching only slightly at the crimson smears along the creamy flesh of her thighs.

Then a smile quivered upon her lips. Perhaps this was a more literal interpretation of the story Blackstock had told her that first day in the hothouse. She was the nightingale and he, the rose . . . and she had recklessly spilled her virgin's blood upon the thorns of his lovemaking. And though it had not cost her life, she suspected that it might have cost her a piece of her soul.

She tidied herself as best she could, then gathered up her paraphernalia and returned to the main house. Victor was not waiting for her, only an uncomfortable-looking Derek. He gave her a respectful nod and helped her into the coach, then reached into his jacket pocket.

"This 'ere's for ye, miss. Yer wages," he explained when she gave a puzzled look at the small bag that jingled with the unmistakable sound of coin. " 'Is lordship said 'ow ye'd been forced to give notice. 'Tis a right shame."

The bag that the young man dropped into her palm weighed far more heavily than it should have. She waited until he had whipped up the team, then untied its strings and spilled its contents into her other hand.

Despite herself, she gasped. She was holding a full year's salary—more money than she'd ever had at a single time. Then the import of what that glittering coin meant struck her, and her fingers clenched convulsively.

Victor was buying her silence . . . just as he had done with Talbot.

Her full lips thinning into a line of barely suppressed outrage, she dumped the money back into the bag and tied it shut again. She would mend lace until her fingers bled rather than take a single shilling from the man!

She waited, however, until Derek had dropped her at her usual spot. Bidding the driver a tremulous farewell—she had grown rather fond of the cheeky youth these past days—she marched straight to the doors of St. Pancras. Bolted to the wall just inside the darkened church was the poor box. Before she could change her mind, she dumped her entire year's wages into the slot cut in its top, the coins clinking like a metallic waterfall.

Her sole satisfaction lay in the fact that no one was there to see the tears spill down her cheeks with equal swiftness.

Eighteen

" 'Ere now, girl, wot' this about?" Ezra Meeks demanded, gazing up from that night's first gin-laced cup of tea to look at his daughter. "Ye've been mopin' about these past days like ye just planted yer best friend in yon churchyard. 'Tis it because ye was booted out from yer position wit' that fine 'ousehold?"

"I wasn't booted out, Father," came Amaryllis's stiff reply as she finished stacking up the last of the supper plates. "I explained to you at the beginning that this was but a temporary post. The family merely dispensed with my services a bit earlier than I had hoped."

" 'Twasn't that the lord o' the manor were eyein' ye, an' the mistress took it wrong?" Ezra guessed with a sly glint to his eye, hitting far closer to the truth than she would have liked. "Ye're a right good lookin' piece, just like yer mother was. Ye'd best be watchin' out, lest one o' those fine gents in those fancy 'ouses where ye work takes a likin' to ye an' starts pawin' at yer skirts."

"I—I shall keep that in mind."

She made a hasty retreat lest her father read in her face the angry pain and mortification that she had nurtured since that fateful afternoon in Victor's hothouse. In the five days that had followed, she had spent as much time as possible working about the house and church grounds when she was not mending lace. Her paints and brushes, however, had lain untouched as—for the first time in her life—her artwork brought her no joy.

Had it been in her power, she would have returned to Victor's town house and burned every rose painting she had done . . . as if such an action might somehow eradicate every vestige of emotion that had passed between them. She'd not even written to Mary about what had happened. The act of setting words to paper would have forced her to examine her feelings with more care than she was yet willing.

For, were she to stare squarely into her own heart, she would have to admit that her feelings for Victor had not changed in the least.

Quite simply, she still loved him.

But love, she was beginning to find, mattered very little in the scheme of things. Proclaiming that emotion aloud opened one to all manner of uncomfortable situations. At least she'd had the presence of mind to not declare her feelings before him, or her mortification would be complete. This way Victor saw her merely as foolhardy and not as hopelessly besotted.

Her thoughts on the subject were interrupted by a swift tapping at the front door. Frowning, she pulled the apron from her bottle-green gown and started in that direction. It was not the usual hour for callers. Neither would Talbot be stopping by either, she felt certain, for she already had sent him a note saying she had complied with his wishes in telling Victor her true name. Likely their visitor was but a parishioner in need of her father's services.

By now the tapping at the door had intensified into an unceasing series of thuds against the heavy wood. Wavering between concern and irritation, Amaryllis pulled the door open a crack and peered out at their impatient visitor.

Her first glimpse was of a shawl-wrapped figure, hand still raised as if to knock again. Stepping back a pace, the visitor pulled back the topmost length of wool to reveal a pair of familiar dark eyes.

Amaryllis gasped outright and threw the door wide open.

"Lady Monique, whatever brings you here?" she exclaimed, gesturing the younger girl inside.

The first thing she noticed was that, for once, the girl was without her constant parrot companion. The next was that the younger girl's eyes were reddened, as if she'd been crying.

Sudden dread swept her. Only one thing could have sent the girl out alone in search of her.

"What is it, Monique?" she urged. "Has something happened to his lordship?"

The question prompted a fresh outburst of tears from the girl, and Amaryllis felt an odd lurch in the vicinity of her heart. *Dear Lord, please don't let it be,* rose the swift fervent prayer within her as she clutched Monique's arm.

"Please, you must tell me. Is he . . . dead?"

When Monique tearfully shook her head, Amaryllis choked back her own sob of relief. "Is he injured, then?"

"N-No, nothing like that," Monique wailed, dabbing her nose with the hem of one shawl. "It's even worse. He—He's been accused of m-murder."

"Murder?"

She glanced into the parlor, where her father was sipping his gin and tea, oblivious to the commotion right outside his door. Then, grasping Monique by the arm, she dragged the girl in the direction of her bedchamber.

"Sit down and explain all this in a sensible manner," Amaryllis commanded and steered her toward the bed. "Surely there has been some mistake made."

"Well, of course there has been a mistake," Monique exclaimed, pausing in her weeping long enough to roll her tear-filled eyes in exasperation. "Victor did not kill that woman, nor any of the others. Just because they found his pocketwatch beside her body—"

"Wait."

Gesturing the girl to silence, Amaryllis sank onto the bed

beside her. "Now begin again, and slowly. Who was murdered, and when did it happen?"

"I only heard a part of what was said, since Victor and the police inspectors were closeted in his library most of the time. I never learned her name, only that she was some woman who worked in a gambling hell. And I'm not certain exactly when she was killed, only that they found her body this morning."

"But what is this about Vic—that is, his lordship's pocketwatch, and why do they think he committed the murder?"

If Monique had noted her reflexive lapse into familiarity, she gave no sign. "They found his watch—the one with the family crest on it—lying beneath her body," she began, looking faintly cheered by Amaryllis's interest. "He tried to explain that a footpad had coshed him over the head and robbed him of it several nights earlier, but no one would listen."

At her words, Amaryllis recalled that fateful afternoon in the hothouse. She had noticed him absently rubbing the back of his neck, as if it pained him. That would explain how he had been hurt . . . though why he had not cared to confide in her, she was not certain.

"Indeed you would not believe how frightfully they treated my poor brother," Monique went on, not noting her distraction. "One of the inspectors—a sly little man with red hair—said that witnesses had seen Victor with that woman in that very gambling hell earlier in the night. They also claimed that the two of them had had a fight of sorts."

That last bit of intelligence distressed Amaryllis almost as did this talk of murder. Whatever had Victor been doing in a gambling hell with a woman of easy virtue? Had he tried to slake his lust with a prostitute that night and then, unsatisfied, turned to her?

"—and now they've taken him away."

It took a moment for Monique's last words to filter through her mental cloud of anguished outrage. When their import struck her, she grasped her arm. "What do you mean, taken him away?"

"Th-they took Victor off to the magistrate at noontide, and I have not h-heard from him s-since. Perhaps he is in Newgate, even now . . ."

She trailed off on another wailing sob, which Amaryllis was hard-pressed not to echo. Surely it was the most circumstantial of evidence which had been brought against him. Yet given the gravity of the crimes, and the fact the police had been helpless as yet to solve them, it was not surprising they had seized him.

But would they let him go again, or would he be imprisoned and then brought to the dock?

She took a shaky breath and tried to compose her frantic thoughts. The fact that he had once been accused of a similar crime must surely weigh against him. Unless—

She glanced back at Monique, who had fixed her with a look of tearful yet eloquent appeal. She stood again, feeling suddenly put upon by the entire Saville family.

"So that is why you have come here," she said, as the girl's motive became apparent. "You want me to tell the magistrate that I also was attacked by the Barkshire Demon, and that he was not the same man as Victor. Is that not so?"

"You must!" Monique cried with a vigorous nod. "Perhaps they would believe you, even if they would not listen to him."

Her first impulse was to refuse outright. After all, why should she care what happened to Victor, when his lordship had so coldly used her? He deserved every bit of unpleasantness that came his way. Let him talk his way out of this predicament, just as he had talked his way out of their fledgling relationship.

That moment of rebellion was short-lived, however. Her romantic's heart would never allow her to leave Victor to his fate, no matter what he had done to her. The question was, how much help could she be to him?

"I doubt my word would carry much weight," she answered with a small shrug. "As it is, I supplied the police with a sketch that I made of my attacker. They know what the true killer looks like. I kept the original. Here, I shall show it to you."

So saying, she reached beneath her bed for her sketchbook. She rifled through it, then plucked out the drawing she had made of the Demon and handed it to Monique.

The girl let out an audible gasp at the sight.

"Th-this is the man who attacked you?" she demanded, tearing her gaze from the sketch to stare, wide-eyed, up at Amaryllis. "Why, he *does* look quite frightful."

"Believe me, Monique," came her wry reply, "he was a far more terrifying sight in the flesh."

Monique nodded, her features hardening as she stared down at the picture again. "I think that Victor should see this . . . and you should come back to our town house with me to await him."

"Certainly not. Take the drawing, if you wish, but I am staying right here."

"But you must come with me," the girl protested, her moment of strength waning as tears welled up in her dark eyes again. "I—I cannot bear to wait for him alone . . . especially not after I've seen this drawing."

"Monique, you are acting quite foolish. You can't believe the Demon would come after you in your own house?"

"He might," she said in a bleak tone, pale lips trembling. "Do keep me company, at least, for a time. Derek can take you home again later, if you truly wish it."

Amaryllis sighed, her mental debate finished almost before it began. For, in truth, she would never sleep a wink this night, worrying over Victor's fate. She would derive as much comfort from Monique's company as the younger girl would get from her.

"Very well," she agreed with a sigh. "Let me find my cloak and tell Father where I will be."

She thought she saw a flash of triumph in the girl's dark eyes before Monique nodded. Tucking the drawing beneath her shawl, the girl scrambled to her feet and followed as Amaryllis led the way toward the front door.

She paused at the parlor to find her father still sitting where she had left him. He was well into his third cup of tea now and more agreeable than usual as she gave him an edited account of the Saville family's travails.

"Be off wit' ye then," he said with a cheerful nod. "If they'll be puttin' ye up for the night, ye can stay wit' the young mistress until tomorrow . . . or e'en the day after, if ye wish it."

His sudden charitable impulse aroused her suspicions, until she decided it must be the gin that had spurred him to such largess. Bidding him good-bye, she joined Monique in the familiar black carriage.

They rode in silence for several minutes, Monique sneaking glances at the drawing she held, while Amaryllis sought to marshal her own troubled thoughts. It was a cool, clear night out. Even so, she was relieved that Monique had tied down the coach's heavy velvet curtains against the darkness and turned up the inside lamp. To be sure, she was being just as foolish as the younger girl, fearing some sort of attack from without. Still, one could not be too careful these days, though the Demon struck only on foggy nights.

Foggy nights.

A niggling sense of something amiss settled in a corner of her consciousness, kneading at her brain like a restless cat. She had no time to examine that uncertain feeling, however, as Monique spoke up again.

"I am certain you must feel that I have taken unfair advantage tonight," she began, her gaze not quite meeting that of Amaryllis. "Of course, I wanted you to help Victor, but that is not the only reason I came here. I—I rather thought that you had a bit of fondness for my brother, and that you would have wished to know what had happened."

"I *am* glad that you came—for your sake as well as his. But tell me, Monique, how did you know where to find me?"

"Why, it was quite simple."

She gave an airy wave of one slim hand and smiled, looking like a sly kitten in the lamplight. "Derek took me to the same spot where he had dropped you off each day. Then, since I knew you were truly Dr. Meeks's sister, and I recalled that he had once mentioned his father was a sexton, I had Derek drive us about until we came across a church."

"You knew that Talbot is my brother?"

She frowned as she met the girl's smug gaze. Victor could not have been so callous as to tell his entire household about her small deception . . . yet how else could the girl have known?

"Oh, don't worry," Monique assured her, noticing her dismay. "My gallant brother did not reveal a word of your secret. I just happened to be outside the hothouse the day you told him, and I overheard your confession."

"You were outside the hothouse that day!"

Amaryllis sagged against the butter-soft black leather, her dismay blossoming into outright alarm while a wave of mortified color flooded her cheeks. If she had been close enough to hear that, then what else had the girl seen and heard?

Apparently quite a bit, for Monique favored her with a look of knowing approval. "I did not plan to spy on you . . . at least not at first. I only wanted to make sure that Victor did not discharge you before you had a chance to paint my portrait. And then, when I saw what was happening, I decided it would be an educational experience for me."

"Educational?" Amaryllis echoed in a weak voice, her mortification complete as she recalled in vivid detail just what had happened between her and Blackstock there. "Monique, that was quite a wicked thing for you to do, watching us."

The girl gave her a sly grin in return. *"I* was not the

wicked one," she countered in a pointed tone. "Still, I was glad to see that *Essays on Far Eastern Marriage Customs* proved of use to you after all. I recognized that pose . . . though, of course, it would have been far more authentic if you both had taken off your clothes first."

"Monique!" she chided the girl, feeling her blush deepen still further. Surely her entire face must be glowing like a streetlamp. "This is not a proper topic of conversation for a young woman to be having."

By way of answer, Monique stuck out her tongue in an impudent gesture. "I vow, you are quite as stuffy as Victor. The two of you suit quite well."

She paused and tilted her dark head, considering. "The fact you are not just a sexton's daughter, but the sister of a physician, is a help. Of course, it would have been preferable if your father was a peer; still, Victor has title and wealth enough for you both."

Before Amaryllis could form any sort of reply to that last incredible statement, the carriage jerked to a halt. The town house, she saw, was lit by but a few lamps, presenting an unwelcome facade.

"I wonder if he has come home yet," Monique wistfully wondered as Derek climbed down to open the door. "Perhaps he is waiting for me in the library even now."

She rushed headlong inside, leaving Amaryllis to follow at a more decorous if no less anxious pace.

He was not there, nor anywhere else in the house. Indeed the place seemed deserted, so that the sound of footfalls as they returned downstairs to the main hall took them both by surprise.

"Lady Monique . . . miss," came Peters's dour greeting as that man halted near the main stair and made them both a nod. "I thought perhaps it was you."

"Have you had any word of his lordship?" the girl cried as she swept off her collection of shawls. "I thought surely he would be home by now."

"His lordship has not returned . . . nor, thankfully, have the police paid us a return visit."

"Then what is going on here?" she demanded of the butler, gesturing about the empty hall. "It is still early. I cannot believe everyone is abed yet."

"Ahem." Peters cleared his throat, looking ill at ease now, so that Amaryllis guessed the reason before he spoke. "It would seem, my lady, that all of the staff save myself, Moresdale, and Derek have given notice and left."

"Given notice?"

She glanced about her in bewilderment, as if expecting the missing servants to reappear. "But why have they gone? They were treated well here, were they not?"

"They had no complaints as to their treatment or wages, my lady," Peters replied, the color rising in his face. "It simply was that they objected to working for the Barkshire Demon."

"But that is ridiculous!" she exclaimed, her shawls swirling as she flung her arms open in a dramatic gesture. "Victor is no more the Demon than you or I. I have never seen such disloyalty. How can they think—"

"Monique, do not carry on so," Amaryllis broke in as the former's agitation continued to build. She grasped the younger girl's arm and gave her a firm shake. "I am sure they will all think the better of things and return on the morrow. As for disloyalty, I would think that they were frightened instead. You must know that they would be hard-pressed to obtain a new post without a letter of reference from his lordship."

"But it's not fair," she wailed. "Victor is *not* the Demon. I know he's not."

"As do I."

With those firm words, Amaryllis turned her attention back to the butler, who looked as if he'd rather be anywhere else at this moment.

"Peters, I believe that Lady Monique and I will wait in

his lordship's library for a time. Do you think it possible to arrange for a tea tray for us?"

"I will see what I can do, miss," the man agreed in obvious relief as he took his quick leave. The matter settled, Amaryllis ushered her young friend upstairs to the library.

That chamber proved cold, empty, and decidedly unwelcoming, even when Amaryllis had turned up all the lamps. A fire had been laid on the grate but not lit, so she turned her attention to that task. By the time Peters entered with the requested tea tray and set it on the edge of the desk, however, a merry blaze was dispelling the chill.

"Do pour," Monique ordered from the large leather chair behind Victor's desk, where she already had settled with a proprietary air.

Smothering a smile at the sight of the girl dwarfed by that massive piece of furniture, Amaryllis complied. She paused in the act of catching up the cream pot, however, and gave a thoughtful frown. Then decisively she made her way around to the other side of the desk.

"Whatever are you doing?" Monique demanded as Amaryllis began opening and closing drawers.

Amaryllis shook her head by way of reply until, pulling open the last, her search yielded what she sought. "Here we are," she announced as she pulled forth a partially full bottle.

Monique stared, open-mouthed, before allowing herself a small smile. "How daring. Do you really mean that we should drink it?"

"Of course." She liberally laced each cup of tea with the dark red liquid, then handed one to her. "Gentlemen always seem to fortify themselves in a time of crisis, so why should not we? We *are* modern women, are we not?"

Giggling, Monique sipped at the potent brew, then delicately choked. "I believe I feel quite fortified already," she declared between gasps before taking another drink.

Amaryllis grinned as she settled in the chair across from the girl. She grimaced as she took her own first hesitant swallow. Still, by the time she finished off her cup, she, too, felt fortified.

"A bit more tea?" she suggested with a hint of a grin.

Monique eagerly nodded. Amaryllis poured them both another cup, then reached again for the port bottle. She splashed an ample portion of the bloodred wine into both delicate cups before resuming her chair.

"Now that we are better able to face the situation," she said, "what would you prefer to do—talk about the murders or distract our minds with a more cheerful subject?"

"Do let's talk about something else," Monique determined from behind her raised cup. "Let me see . . . perhaps you would like to hear about how I first found Wilhelm."

"Oh, yes, your parrot. Where is he tonight?"

"He is upstairs, asleep in his cage. He needs his rest, you know, or he will be quite out of sorts come morning."

With that introduction, Monique launched into the tale of how she had been at the docks with her father. Hearing a merry whistle, her attention had been caught by a ship's boy carrying a red-and-gray bird in a tiny, open-weave basket. Her heart had gone out to the captive creature, and she had pressed her father to buy him for her. The earl, who always was wont to indulge his only daughter, promptly took her in search of Wilhelm's owner.

That man had proved to be the ship's captain, who fancied the rare bird as a mascot. The parrot had come from darkest Africa, the grizzled man had stated with a sour look, and he was not prepared to part with him for any price.

Monique's delicate brow furrowed at the memory. "But I could not bear to see poor Wilhelm stuck in that tiny cage with only that awful man to care for him," she declared, sloshing a bit of her port in her enthusiasm for her own tale.

Thus, she continued, while the two men were distracted while standing at the ship's gangway, she had unfastened the cage door. After a puzzled squawk, Wilhelm had flown free of the ship and down to the teeming dock below.

"But Wilhelm is here," Amaryllis pointed out. "I presume you managed to find him again?"

"Just wait, and I will tell you."

The girl took another long sip of her port-laced tea; then, her words a bit fuzzy now, she went on. "The captain was in a rage, to be sure, and I fear my father was not very happy, either. It cost him every cent he had upon him to appease the man, and me with nothing to show for it. But then, as we were walking back along the dock again, I heard that same whistle."

She paused and gave Amaryllis a tipsy grin. "When I looked over, there was Wilhelm perched upon a piling—free as a bird," she exclaimed with another giggle. "I called him, he flew onto my shoulder . . . and we have been fast friends ever since."

Then she sobered. "I fear that he and Victor do not get along too well, however. Indeed Wilhelm once swooped down on him and bit him on the ear. Victor was quite put out, as you might guess, especially since it was right before he was to go out that night, and he bled all over his new linen shirt."

For some reason, that last struck them both as exceedingly amusing. They gave way to gales of laughter that, when they subsided minutes later, left them weak.

This time it was Monique who refilled their cups with equal portions of both beverages. Next was Amaryllis's turn to regale Monique with a story. She thought a moment and then recounted the time when, as a child, she had played ghost in St. Pancras's cemetery and sent the bishop himself running in terror.

They passed the next hour, and the next, in a similar companionable fashion. The level of port in their pilfered bottle dropped in direct proportion to their growing hilarity. The fire had died as well, but neither of them bothered to stir it up again. By the time ten o'clock struck, Amaryllis's head was spinning. As for Monique, she lay sprawled in her brother's chair, eyes closed and mouth open in an unladylike snore.

And it was this way that Victor found the pair of them when, a few minutes later, he made his weary way into his library.

Nineteen

I vow that I am Most Confused in regard to my feelings for Victor. I must Despise Him for casting me aside as if I were of no account . . . and yet if he would only take me back, I fear that I would quickly swallow my pride and return to him.

—letter from Miss Amaryllis Meeks to
Miss Mary Godwin

Victor halted on the threshold and raked a weary hand through his disheveled dark hair, hardly countenancing the sight before him. Here he'd spent the greater portion of the day in the local magistrate's dank office, answering endless questions and denying his guilt. His sister and his erstwhile lover, meanwhile, both had spent that same time comfortably ensconced in *his* library.

Ignoring Amaryllis's cry of surprise, he stalked over to the chair where his sister sprawled, sleeping. Even before he bent over her, he was assailed by fumes of an unmistakably alcoholic origin. Frowning, he glanced at the desk to see an empty bottle of port—*his* port—abandoned alongside two dainty teacups.

The frustration of the entire day rose to a dangerous pitch within him as he abruptly rounded on Amaryllis.

"What in the bloody hell do you think you're doing here, getting my sister drunk as a lord?"

She rose from her chair, swaying slightly as she did so.

The lamps were turned down, and the fire had died to a sullen red glow of embers, lending her pale face a rosy flush against the shadows. Had he been in the mood to appreciate such images, he would have deemed the tangle of red curls that had worked loose of their pins to dance across her brow quite fetching. As it was, he merely glared as her green gaze—slightly unfocused by the port—met his.

"I am here because Monique asked me to come," she declared in the careful, dignified tones of one who has over-indulged and is trying to disguise that fact. "As for being drunk, we had a sip or two of port to fortify ourselves while we awaited your return."

"A sip or two?" he echoed in disbelief, slanting a disgusted look at the empty bottle. Then he frowned. "You are telling me that my sister asked you to come here to wait for me? What purpose did she think that would serve?"

"She was concerned for your well-being and felt in need of a friend." She paused, then added, "Especially since all but three of your staff gave their notice tonight and left her virtually alone here."

"Bloody hell," he muttered, raking his hand through his hair again. The place *had* seemed empty when he'd returned, but he had chalked that up to the late hour. He'd had no notion that, just because he'd been questioned about a few murders, everyone from footman to parlormaid would abandon the place.

He walked over to the bell pull and gave it an angry tug, then waited in silence the moment it took for Peters to appear.

"Is what Miss Meeks told me true," he demanded of the man, "that the entire staff has given notice?"

"I fear so, my lord. All the less steady of the servants— that is, the women and a number of the younger men—had strong feelings about staying in your employ, given the circumstances. I tried to dissuade them, of course, but to no avail."

"I see. Now would you be kind enough to carry Lady Monique to her room. I'm afraid she is in no condition to make it upstairs on her own."

Peters spared a disapproving glance at the snoring girl before turning a well-bred look of alarm on him. "But, my lord, her ladyship's maid and all of the other female servants have left us. What shall I . . . that is, how should I go about—"

"She can bloody well sleep in her gown, if that is your concern," Victor growled. "Now get her the hell out of here so I can finish my conversation with Miss Meeks."

He waited until Peters, puffing under his slight burden, had quit the library and closed the door after him before he rounded on Amaryllis once more.

"Very well, I can appreciate why my sister would want the company," he conceded as he took the other armchair for himself, then gestured her to sit back down again. "But why ask for you, of all people, rather than one of her usual friends?"

A flicker of what appeared to be offended anger heated her green gaze, and two spots of pink burned high on her cheeks. Still, her tone was level enough as she replied, "I believe that Monique had hoped I might speak with the magistrate in your behalf, since I am the only one who can swear that you are not the Barkshire Demon."

"Are you, now?" he softly said, some perverse inner impulse spurring him to probe this statement. "Indeed I thought you'd had some doubts on that account from the very first. Perhaps the man who attacked you was not the Demon after all . . . which still could mean I *was* the one who killed all those women."

"But you did not."

Something in her soft words acted as a balm on his angry frustration. The band of tension across his chest that had been there these past hours loosened, so that he felt able to breathe normally once more.

"No, I did not kill them."

Abruptly he stood again, needing the release of movement to keep apace of his thoughts. He spared a wistful glance at the empty port bottle. He could have used a nip right now himself, the way his entire body was screaming with a weariness he could not yet allow himself to indulge. Then, seeing his sister's cup on the desk before her was still half-full, he caught it up and took a long swallow.

He all but spewed the liquid right out again, so disgusting did it taste. With an effort, he managed to choke the mouthful down. Then, sparing a disbelieving look at what remained in the cup, he glared back at Amaryllis.

"What in the bloody hell did you do with my port . . . mix it with tea?"

She gave him a rueful smile. "As a matter of fact, yes. That is how my father takes his gin, so I thought it would work as well in this case."

"Christ," he muttered at that sacrilege and set the cup down again with a clatter. A moment of silence stretched between them, so that he wondered if she had heard or believed his declaration of innocence after all.

"It matters little that I believe you innocent, if the authorities do not," she finally said. "I presume, since you are here, that you're not formally accused of the women's deaths?"

"Not as yet. They want to be very sure of their case before they bring an earl up on charges of multiple murder."

Victor managed a humorless smile. "I imagine that by tomorrow morning, my name will be in all the scandal sheets, and the entire city will be clamoring for my head. Since the evidence is rather damning, and the magistrate anxious to solve the case before the Crown steps in, it is only a matter of time before I'm in the docks."

"And if you are found guilty, you will hang, will you not?"

"I rather suspect so."

Too bad that he had not yet finished writing his book on

roses, he thought with no little regret. If nothing else, his notoriety would doubtless guarantee impressive sales of that particular volume . . . no matter that he might not be around to enjoy his success.

He was distracted from that last thought by the look of gratifying distress that had settled over Amaryllis's pale features. It occurred to him—not for the first time this night— that perhaps he should have handled the situation between them differently than he had.

On a practical level, had he made Amaryllis his mistress at the very start, he would have been in bed with her that fateful night. Thus he'd not now be a suspect in Penelope's murder. And maybe by now he would have had the opportunity for a relationship with a woman based upon mutual care and respect, rather than the depths of his pockets.

"Would it help to talk about what happened today?" she broke in on those thoughts, her voice trembling a bit now.

He met her warm green gaze, tempted to put aside his pride and tell her everything. But what could he say? That they had dragged him into a bleak, lamplit room where he'd seen the shape of a woman's naked body beneath a soiled blanket? That they'd whipped aside that cloth to reveal Penelope Worthington's bloated body and blackened face, the angry marks of brutal fingers still on her throat?

He shook his head. Maybe he could tell her that he'd seen the angry red slash across the pallid flesh of Penelope's chest where someone had split her open, broken her breastbone, and cut out her heart. He could confess that, despite his time spent in the army, where mutilated bodies were a common sight, he'd nearly retched at the sight and smell of her.

Or he could tell her how he'd spent the next ten hours denying that he had performed this sort of barbarity upon a woman for whom he'd once held a true affection . . . and that no one had believed a bloody word of it.

"It was not pleasant," he admitted instead as he paced about the room. "I saw the murdered woman's body, and they talked at length about my possible motives for killing her." He hesitated, seeing the question in her eyes, then added, "At one time, Penelope and I knew each other . . . quite well."

"She was your mistress, was she not?"

He nodded, expecting a caustic comment or flash of anger from her. Instead true concern washed over her features as she met his gaze.

"I can imagine how difficult it must have been, seeing someone that you cared about brutalized in so horrid a fashion," she said. "Did you love her very much then?"

"We understood each other, was all . . . and in the end, I fear, we did not like one another very well. Still, I would never have wished such a fate upon her."

"But what about your watch? Monique said something about it being found alongside the murdered woman."

Victor let out a slow, considering breath. "It sounds quite ludicrous, I know, but the simple fact was that a footpad had attacked me a few nights earlier, yet all he stole was my watch. At the time, I thought it rather odd, since my driver had been lured away by a false message. It almost seemed that I had been chosen, rather than a victim picked at random."

Amaryllis straightened in her chair, any last trace of fuzziness vanishing from her gaze.

"Do you mean to say that the actual killer robbed you with the deliberate intent of leaving something of yours at the murder scene to make it look as if *you* had done the deed?"

"I think perhaps I do."

She stood, her face taking on a determined expression of defiance, like a she-wolf prepared to defend her cub. "Then we must find the man who did this and prove your innocence."

We.

He halted a few paces from her, that single word shatter-

ing the vestiges of his hard-won composure. Despite the way
he had rejected her, she was offering to throw in her lot with
him, to stand beside him, to be tarred by the same brush of
scandal as had colored him.

And, to his disgust, he was just ignoble enough to let her.

In the room's dim light, Amaryllis watched the uncertainty play across Victor's face and knew her own moment
of doubt. He had come bursting into the library but moments
before like a man trying to outpace a demon. To be sure,
she had seen him before in a similar disheveled state—without his jacket, his waistcoat unfastened and his cravat untied.
But she had never seen those lines of weariness that now
bracketed his eyes and mouth, making him look older . . .
harder.

She could only guess at how he had spent these past
hours, taken from his home and accused of brutal murder.
She was almost certain that they no longer beat accused men
to force confessions from them—at least, no men of Victor's
station. Still, the strain that was evident in his face spoke
of some other, equal unpleasantness that he had undergone
in the process.

Did he not want her help, she wondered in consternation,
or was he afraid to accept it? And did it matter to her which
of the two was the case?

It doesn't, her heart cried. She must give it to him or
always regret the lost chance. And that last, she was not
prepared to do.

Whether it was that knowledge or the port—or maybe a
bit of both—that made her bold, she did not know. All that
she did know was, a moment later, she was in his arms and
kissing him.

She sensed his final attempt at resistance before, with a
soft groan, he tightened his arms about her and kissed her
back. His mouth was hot and demanding on hers. Eagerly
she opened her lips to him, parrying every thrust of his
tongue with her own.

When he lowered his mouth to nuzzle the soft flesh of her throat, she made no protest but only sighed and held him closer. By now his hands had slid down the curve of her back to her hips, pressing her against him so that she could feel the hard heat of his arousal. The sensation sent a sudden, similar need burning through her, so that she gasped aloud.

The soft sound was enough to halt him. With a ragged curse, he broke free of their embrace and stared down at her. His dark gaze was hot with an angry sort of longing, the sight of which twisted her heart.

"I suppose I don't have much right to be doing this sort of thing, do I?" he said with a harsh, humorless laugh. "Not after what I said to you the last time we were together."

"But I am willing to forget all that."

Dropping her gaze, she ran her hand across the expanse of his chest. She could feel the warmth of his flesh and the rapid beat of his heart through the barrier that was the fine lawn of his shirt. The sensation vividly called to mind what had happened between them that afternoon in the hothouse. She might forget his harsh words . . . but she would always remember his actions, the glorious things he had done to her body.

And if he could excite such wondrous feelings in her, perhaps she could do much the same for him.

Lightly she let her hand run down the solid length of his torso. When he made no move to stop her, she moved her hand lower still, until her fingers brushed the hard ridge of his swollen shaft as it strained against the fabric of his trousers. Then his fingers closed over hers, and he guided her hand more firmly across his erection.

She could feel his shaft stir beneath her fingers, and the sensation caused an answering damp warmth between her thighs. Bolder now, she continued to stroke him. He groaned and reached out to cup her breasts in his hands.

His thumbs brushed the fabric that covered her nipples.

They tightened into twin buds of sensation, while her breasts swelled in eager response. She shut her eyes, reveling in his touch. Vaguely she realized he had tugged the bodice of her gown low enough to reveal her breasts, covered now only by a thin camisole. Then, in a quick, efficient move, he plucked at the bows tying that sheer garment closed until both pale globes bobbed softly free of that confinement.

The sensation of cool air upon her exposed breasts made her open her eyes again. Victor's heated gaze bore into hers, and she read the question in his eyes that only she could answer.

"Yes," she breathed, "oh, yes."

Barely had she spoken the words than he began to unfasten the pins and tapes of her gown. Almost before she realized it, the bottle-green fabric was pooled about her feet, so that she stood before him wearing only her untied camisole, her stockings, and her pantalets. Then, as if he feared somehow breaking her, he slid the camisole from her shoulders so that it fluttered to the floor alongside her gown.

He halted then, his dark gaze traveling with unabashed hunger over her. Though the library's dim light offered welcome shadow, she still felt embarrassingly exposed. Her first impulse was to cover her breasts with her arms, but she stayed that reaction and met his gaze.

"Remember what we talked about in the hothouse?" he asked in a husky voice. "You said that the next time, we would take off our clothes first . . . and I agreed that we would do it any way that you liked. So tell me, my sweet Amaryllis, is this how you like it?"

"I like it this way very much," came her truthful reply.

He groaned and began to shed his own clothes until, a moment later, he stood naked before her. The sight of his firm body gleaming in the dying light of the fire held her in momentary awe. Had she her pencils or paints, she would have made his portrait right then, dubbing that finished work with the name of some Greek god or another, so well-formed did her artist's eye find him. As it was, she would be content for the moment just looking at him.

Curious, she let her gaze drop below his waist. His swollen shaft jutted proudly from a thick patch of dark hair at the apex of his thighs, offering both a threat and an enticing promise. The sight sent a delicious shiver through her. The first time, she'd had but a glimpse of his maleness. Now however, she could look her fill.

He shot her a ragged grin and moved a bit closer. "Touch me," he urged her in a husky tone. "You don't know how many times I've imagined those clever artist's hands of yours on me, holding me like you would one of your brushes and doing all sorts of interesting things with me."

His frank words made her blush, even as they exerted an unexpected fascination on her. She gave in to temptation and reached out one hand to stroke the long, hard length of him. She heard his quick intake of breath as his shaft quivered against her fingers, and she hesitated, fearful she might have hurt him.

"You're doing it just right," he assured her, his words very near to a groan. Emboldened, she cupped her fingers about his length, marveling at the silken warmth of his flesh that sheathed so formidable a blade.

This time he groaned outright and clutched at her shoulders as he began moving within her grasp. Swiftly she took up that rhythm, her palms growing damp from the warm moistness that spilled from the swollen tip of his shaft. She felt herself grow warm and damp in response, while an urgent tension built low in her belly.

Then he was untying the tape that held her pantalets, so that they slid to her ankles. She needed no urging but stepped free of them so that she was wearing nothing now but a modest pair of stockings tied at her knees.

Abruptly he eased himself from her grasp and swept her up in his arms, carrying her over to the fireplace. He laid her on the rug before it, then knelt between her bent legs.

She shut her eyes, expecting the sharp surge of him entering her body. The sensation that abruptly assailed her, however, was something completely different.

"Oh, Victor."

Her eyes flew open, and she saw to her amazement that he had lowered his head between her spread thighs. His tongue was exploring every fold of her woman's flesh in a most intimate fashion, licking and probing her as if she were some rare delicacy served up on a silver platter before him. She would have protested this treatment in embarrassment, save that every flick of his tongue sent spirals of almost unbearable sensation through her, so that she was incapable of speech.

Just as she thought she must swoon from the wonder of it all, he raised up again. The blunt tip of his engorged shaft nudged momentarily at her damp, swollen cleft. Then, with a swift thrust, he entered her.

Just like the first time, she wrapped her legs about him and mindlessly matched his rhythm as he swiftly moved in and out of her. As if urged on by their passion, the fire beside summoned a final burst of sparks and flame. The blaze of their own making burned hotter still until, in a final shuddering climax of sensation, they reached release together.

All that remained of the fire was a bed of glowing embers when he took her a second time. This time, rather than the explosive flare of rushed passion, their lovemaking generated the glowing warmth of carefully banked coals urged into flames. Afterward, as they lay entwined before the hearth, the pale red glow that bathed them reminded her of rose petals.

Twenty

Amaryllis awakened from uneasy slumber hours later to find herself sprawled naked in a bed that was not her own. Indeed the massive piece of mahogany furniture with its columnlike posts, draped in yards of patterned green velvet so dark it was almost black, would have taken up the whole of her own tiny room at home. It was, however, quite the sort of furnishing one might expect to find in the bedchamber of an earl.

"At least nothing here is blue," she murmured as she clutched a tangle of fine white bedclothes to her breasts and struggled upright against a veritable cloud's worth of pillows.

That action proved more difficult than she might have imagined. Besides the lingering soreness that assailed her from last night's lovemaking, she had the remnants of a headache and an unsettled stomach. Those symptoms, she realized, were a result of the port, though she could not recall drinking quite that much of it. Or had she?

If only Talbot were there to prescribe her some nostrum, she thought with a sigh. Then again, she was glad he wasn't. Her brother had little use for those who imbibed, and he found that habit particularly abhorrent in women. Now, as bits of memory returned to her, she shamefacedly decided that he might be right.

Her last clear thoughts concerning last night were of those memorable minutes in the library. They had been, as

Monique would have put it, quite an educational experience. Beyond that, everything was fuzzy. She vaguely recalled how, afterward, a still-naked Victor had swept her up and— with her in the same state of undress—carried her up the stairs like some conquering medieval lord carting home a captured foreign princess. Her enjoyment of that deliciously high-handed treatment had been dulled, however, by the sudden queasiness that had assailed her.

She had made it just as far as the bedchamber. No amount of stern-mindedness had been able to banish the wave of outright nausea that had gripped her as soon as he had set her down just past the threshold. She had made an inelegant dash for the chamberpot and emptied her stomach of the noxious port and tea mixture.

Her cheeks flamed now at that memory. What Victor had thought of such a performance, she dared not guess, though she would not have blamed him for abandoning her in disgust. He had first tucked her into bed, for which she was grateful. Whether he had deigned to spend the rest of the night with her, she did not know. If he had, he'd long since risen . . . for she was here now alone.

Even as she registered that fact, she caught a glimpse of her reflection in the ornate pier glass in the far corner of the room and groaned. Dear Lord, no wonder Victor had abandoned her, given that she resembled a ragged tavern wench. Doubtless he had spared her but a single look this morning and then made a strategic retreat.

Feeling decidedly out of sorts now, she gathered the topmost blanket about her like a toga and climbed from the raised bed. After making use of the chamberpot, she availed herself of the washbasin to scrub her face and rinse the sharp taste of last night's port from her mouth. Then, somewhat more revived, she took a closer look at her surroundings.

Sullen gray daylight pierced the heavy drapes that someone had pulled shut against the bustling street below. The resulting light was sufficient for her to see all but the smallest details.

The room *was* Victor's, she was certain. Whose else could it be, given its dark and starkly masculine air? The only touches of softness were the two framed drawings—one a charcoal sketch, the other a watercolor—that hung in odd juxtaposition together on the wall opposite his bed.

Curious, she made her way over to them. Elegantly matted and framed as they were, and beneath a protective glass covering, it took her a moment to recognize the drawings as her own work.

Once she'd thought them little more than clever depictions drawn for her own amusement. The gnarled hand had been but a study in bone and sinew, with the withered rose an object for those twisted fingers to clutch and better display the effect of lax muscle beneath aged skin. Now however, she could see the poignancy in those lines, the depiction of irreparable longing and loss with which—consciously or not—she somehow had imbued that sketch.

As for the watercolor of the white Alba rose, it had been a means to display her skills with light and color, so that her new employer would be pleased with his decision to hire her. The spatter of blood drops that turned its fallen petals crimson, and the nightingale's feather, had been but devices to accomplish that. But viewing the painting afresh, as if it were another artist's work, she could see beyond the skill involved to the deeper meaning within those casual symbols. She had captured on paper the pain and uncertainty that was love, as well as the hope that sprang eternal from it.

And the fact that Victor thought enough of both works to keep them for his own made her heart swell with grateful pride.

The click of the door behind her shattered her reverie, and she swung about with a gasp. When the intruder proved to be Victor, it did little to lessen her nervousness, the more so as she compared her appearance to his.

Alexa Smart

He was fully dressed, down to a dove-gray morning coat and starched cravat. At first glance, he appeared none the worse for yesterday's travails as he strode into the room and shut the door behind him. As he drew closer, however, she noted the tautness of his features and the shadowed look about his dark eyes. His rest had been even less easy than hers, she judged. Even so, when he halted before her, she saw the faintest hint of a smile on his lips.

Aware of the picture she presented—naked save for a pilfered bedsheet, her hair in a gypsyish tangle down her back, and her face puffy from lack of sleep—she felt herself blush. Surely any mistress worth the name would have made her first appearance of the day carefully coiffed and wrapped in a lavish dressing gown. But, more to the point, she had not yet grown accustomed to appearing before a man in a state of partial dress.

Victor took his time surveying the woman before him in weary appreciation. Wrapped in nothing but a blanket, her red-gold hair spilling over her shoulders in a tangle, Amaryllis exuded an air of wanton innocence that sent an answering stir through his loins. The effect was all the more charming for the fact she seemed embarrassed about appearing before him in such a state—this despite the way she had been in his arms writhing in passion's throes but a few hours before.

Had they the time, he would have swept her up and carried her back to his bed, where she belonged. Other more pressing matters, however, stood in the way of satisfying that desire this particular morning.

"I'm glad to see you're awake," he told her instead. "Monique has already risen, and is waiting for us downstairs in the dining salon."

"So early? Why, it cannot be much past dawn?"

"Actually it is already nine of the clock." He paused at her sound of surprise and, raising an amused brow, added, "Perhaps your sip or two of port last night, combined with our later . . . exertions, left you more tired than you had realized."

He grinned outright as the delicate blush suffusing her cheeks deepened to crimson. For his own part, he had slept far better than might be expected of a man accused of murder. The fact that he'd made love to her twice and then dozed off with her warm, soft female form wrapped in his arms doubtless had helped.

"I—I shall need just a few moments to wash up a bit and get dressed," came her embarrassed reply. Then she paused and gazed uncertainly about her. "My clothes—"

"—are in the adjoining dressing room," he assured her, adding, "I managed to collect everything from the library early this morning, before anyone else was about."

Not that it mattered, given that none of the staff had returned this morning. The recollection deflated his optimistic mood, bringing home to him the fact that the scandal surrounding him was not going to decamp on its own—not this time.

Amaryllis, however, appeared grateful for that small consideration. "I will be down in just a few minutes. I don't suppose Monique has managed to prepare you any sort of breakfast, has she?"

Recalling his sister's pale face and the way she had inched her way down the stairs this morning, as if she feared any sudden movement might cause her to shatter, Victor almost grinned again.

"I rather suspect Monique will not care to look at food anytime soon, given the state of her health this morning. But Derek, Moresdale, Peters, and I foraged quite well on our own and even left a bit for you as well."

"Thank you," she replied with a rueful smile, adding, "still, I fear I may follow Monique's lead in the matter of breaking my fast."

"As you wish. Either way, I'll expect you downstairs in a quarter of an hour. We have some matters to discuss that concern all of us left here in the house. And Monique has laid hands on a drawing that she is quite insistent I look at . . . but she refuses to let me see it until you join us."

In his sense of urgency, the words came out more brusquely than he'd intended. To dull their effect, he crossed to her and brushed a kiss across her temple.

He'd meant it as a comforting gesture. But then she wrapped her arms around him, her body pressing to his, and his intentions shifted to something less altruistic. The faint scent of their lovemaking still clung to her, reminding him of just how enticing a female she was. Meanwhile the blanket she'd wrapped around her had slipped, exposing the curve of her back to him.

Unable to resist that sweet temptation, he let his fingers explore that warm flesh and bent to kiss her again.

Amaryllis raised her lips to meet his, her headache forgotten as a pleasurable little shiver raced through her. She'd been uncertain of her reception this morning, dreading that the light of day would dissolve the fragile bond they had built up between them the night before. His kiss, however, dispelled any such fears.

She gave herself up to the warm pressure of his mouth against hers, the taste of him bringing back memories of their lovemaking. Yet last night's heated urgency was gone, replaced now by a controlled sort of passion that was no less compelling.

It was she who finally broke their embrace and took a shaky step back. "Remember, my lord, you gave me but a quarter hour to make myself presentable," she chided him. "I fear I will never be able to do so if you persist in this way."

His dark gaze burned into hers, and he gave her a slow, dangerous smile that sent a curl of warmth spiraling within her. "Believe me, love, I find you quite presentable as you are . . . but you are right. I'll wait for you downstairs."

Once he'd closed the door behind him again, Amaryllis

dropped her makeshift robe and rushed through her ablutions. As she once more pulled on her bottle-green gown—now rather sadly crumpled—she reflected on the advantages of being a modern woman as opposed to a fine lady. The latter would have required a good hour and a lady's maid by way of assistance to dress, she knew, while the former was well able to manage on her own.

Not that it mattered, she reminded herself, since Victor had all but said he found her acceptable wrapped even in a blanket.

It was almost exactly fifteen minutes later when, having dressed and bundled her hair into a sensible knot, she made her way to the dining salon. A cheery blaze crackled in the fireplace, a toasting fork propped on the hearth. Victor had taken his place at the table's head and was spreading marmalade on an overly browned slice of bread that doubtless had been prepared before that very fire.

Monique sat opposite him, face wan and gaze shadowed as she stared down at her own untouched plate of burnt toast and sipped at a cup of tea. The ubiquitous Wilhelm perched on her shoulder, looking quite as ruffled as she. Both girl and bird glanced up at Amaryllis's approach.

"I shall never fortify myself again," she vowed in a mournful tone. Setting aside her cup, she sagged back in her seat. "To be sure, it made for an enjoyable night, but I feel quite horrible this morning."

"Quite horrible," Wilhelm echoed, fluffing his feathers.

His words and Monique's pinched features drew a wry smile from Amaryllis as she seated herself across from the girl. "I must admit I don't feel quite up to snuff, myself."

"Bloody well serves you both right," Victor remarked in a voice devoid of sympathy. "Still and all, Monique, you'd best try eating something. It will be a long journey, and you'll need to keep up your strength."

"Journey?" she and Amaryllis echoed in simultaneous confusion, both turning their attention to him.

He nodded. "After last night, I want you far from all this lunacy. You'll be leaving for the country within the hour, just as soon as you've eaten a bit and packed any essentials. I've already had Moresdale bring up a trunk for you, and Derek is readying the carriage even now."

"But I don't wish to go to the country," the girl wailed, then turned to Amaryllis for sympathy. "Our estate in Sussex is simply frightful. I dare say there's not a stick of furniture less than a century old, and every room is dark and drafty. Why, Wilhelm and I will both take the chill . . . besides which, there's not a neighbor for miles around, nor any amusement to be had besides riding about the grounds."

"No matter, you're still going . . . and you'll stay there until this business is put to rest."

He paused and gave Amaryllis a considering look. "It might be well for you to accompany her. I'm sure your father can spare you, and I'd feel easier knowing you were safely away from town."

His concern filled her with warm satisfaction; still, she shook her head.

"Have you forgotten that I am the only one who can testify that you were not the one who attacked me? I must stay here and help you find the true killer."

"As must I," Monique chimed in. "Besides which"—she paused and with more animation than she'd yet shown since waking, waved a folded sheet of paper—"*I'm* the one who has a sketch of him."

"Ah, yes, the drawing you obtained from Miss Meeks. You did say that, once she joined us, you would share it with me."

He rose, a thoughtful look on his face, and walked over to his sister's chair. Though his tone had been neutral, Amaryllis had heard a note of restrained urgency in his voice that belied his apparent calm.

She was not prepared, however, for his reaction as he unfolded the page and stared down at the portrait she'd done.

His gaze snapped up to meet hers. She watched in surprise the series of emotions—from stunned recognition to frowning disbelief to chill suspicion—that chased across his features.

And then, in a quick furious gesture, he slammed the page back onto the table.

The solid thud of flesh against wood made her jump. It all but drowned out the faint tinkle of broken china that was the shattering of Monique's teacup.

Silence hung between them for a space of a few heartbeats. Monique, after a little cry of surprise, sat motionless in her own chair, mouth agape as she stared at her brother. When he spoke again, it was in the dangerously soft tone of a man controlling his temper only by dint of extreme effort.

"I don't know what kind of perverse joke you're playing, Amaryllis, but I sure as hell don't find it amusing."

"Indeed, Victor, I don't know what you mean."

"I bloody well think you do."

The expression in his dark eyes was—dare she think it?—murderous. She shrank back in her seat as he moved around the table toward her.

By the time he halted beside her chair, he appeared to have regained some semblance of control. Still, outrage was apparent in his every move as he thrust the page beneath her nose.

"You're saying that the man in this sketch is the one who attacked you that night?"

She spared the portrait a quick look, wondering if Monique had perhaps substituted another drawing for hers. It was her work, however. She nodded. "It is . . . and a very good likeness, I might add."

"Ah, yes. It is, at that."

Coolly Victor stared down again at the drawing he held. It was a brilliant, powerful portrait—the very incarnation of a demon. How or why Amaryllis had managed to capture that particular image, he could not begin to guess. Perhaps it was somehow tied into her brother, and the actions the latter had taken the night of Jane Belfleur's murder.

All that mattered, however, was the fact that she had lied to him about her part in the Barkshire Demon murders.

He glanced over at his sister. Monique sat huddled in her chair, a look of puzzled dismay on her pale face. She'd seemed to have taken quite a liking to Amaryllis—*just as had he,* an inner voice taunted him—so that he would spare her witnessing the unpleasantness that was to come.

"You'd best go upstairs and pack," he told her in as kind a voice as he could muster. "I need to finish my discussion with Miss Meeks. Derek will be along in a few minutes to carry down your trunk."

For once, and to his immense relief, she made no demur but slid from her chair. With a final sidelong glance at them both, she and her parrot quit the room, leaving him with Amaryllis.

He stared again at the drawing. Even while he battled angry revulsion at the knowledge of Amaryllis's betrayal, one corner of his mind admired the deft way she had caught the essence of the man she'd drawn. The slack lines of its coarsely handsome face, the twist of its sensual mouth, the dull fury of its black eyes . . . all those features spoke of a certain viciousness beyond mere cruelty.

And all of those features, Victor recognized.

But as he studied that familiar face, the portrait began to bleed. *Like some ancient Papist relic,* the thought flashed through his mind. For an instant, he was swept by a wave of superstitious horror that transcended rational thought. Yet as he flung the page onto the table, he realized that the blood was his own. No miracle, it had dripped from the hand he'd cut on the broken china cup to drip onto that page.

Christ, was he some uneducated peasant gibbering in the night at the thought of creatures come back from the dead?

With a disgusted laugh at his own gullibility, he retrieved

a snowy linen napkin and used it to staunch the bleeding, then turned his attention back to Amaryllis. Her expression of astonishment appeared genuine, as did her distress as she studied his linen-wrapped hand as she jumped to her feet.

"Are you cut very badly? Perhaps I should call Talbot to take a look at your wound."

"That won't be necessary," came his grim reply. "All that concerns me now is that drawing. Tell me once more . . . *is this the man who attacked you?*"

"It is, and I cannot fathom why my saying so has put you in such a state. Why, it is almost as if you don't believe me."

She planted her hands on her hips and glared up at him, her earlier expression of tender concern replaced by a look of outraged pride. A flicker of doubt assailed him. Could he have been wrong in believing that she was attempting some deliberate campaign of subtle accusation? For surely enough time had passed for her to blackmail him, if that had been her original intent.

But what other purpose save ill could this drawing before him possibly serve?

"I *don't* believe you," he flatly stated. "Perhaps you would care to know why."

At her nod, he made a contemptuous gesture toward the picture. "Very well. The man you've drawn here just happens to be my old friend, Sir Harry Shaw . . . and unless I'm quite mistaken, he has been in St. Pancras's churchyard these past six months."

Twenty-one

We formed a most Unbelievable Theory, Victor and I, regarding the Creature. You would have deemed us both Quite Insane, had you been there . . . yet it was the only possible explanation. But more Unbelievable still is the way we went about proving the truth . . .
　　　　　　　—letter from Miss Amaryllis Meeks to
　　　　　　　　　　　　　　　Miss Mary Godwin

Before Amaryllis had time to grasp Victor's extraordinary statement, a third person interrupted.

"Beggin' yer pardon, milord," came the voice of Victor's valet from the doorway behind her, "but I'm ready. An' ye 'ad the right o' it, milord. We're much o' the same size, so erythin' fits right well."

After a cool look in her direction that warned he'd not finished with this most strange topic of conversation, Victor turned his attention to the man.

"You look quite the tulip of fashion, Moresdale," he wryly observed. "People will think that the Earl of Blackstock has at last taken an interest in the latest rages."

Her own curiosity piqued despite her distress, Amaryllis turned to see just what the pair was discussing. Her eyes widened at the sight of the manservant decked out in the most lordly of styles. From the tips of his gleaming Hessians to the clever cascade of a snowy cravat to the smart beaver perched atop his head, he looked every inch the peer.

But rather than the more monochromatic look that Victor favored, Moresdale had combined gray trousers with a dark blue coat. He'd tied those two garments together with a gaudy blue-and-gray brocaded waistcoat that Amaryllis doubted came from the earl's own wardrobe. As for his neckcloth, it was tied in a far more exaggerated style than she'd ever seen Victor wear, while the points of Moresdale's collar swooped like bird wings quite up to his cheekbones.

"What do ye think, milord?" the valet anxiously asked. "Will I pass as ye?"

"At a distance, with your hat pulled low, and so long as you don't say anything, I think you will do."

He paused to consult his pocketwatch, then went on. "I told Lady Monique to be packed and ready in a quarter hour, and her time is almost up. Lend her a hand, if you will. And pass on the word that I'll expect to see everyone gathered in the main hall by ten o'clock."

With a bow, Moresdale quit the room. Victor waited until the echo of the valet's boots had died away before again turning to her.

"Very well, you've had a few minutes' grace to think over the situation," he clipped out. "Now are you ready to tell me just what in the bloody hell you're trying to do here?"

Amaryllis picked up the drawing again and gave her head a helpless shake. "I—I don't understand. Why, I even posted a copy of this picture to the police to help them solve the murders. And now you are saying that this man is dead?"

"As the proverbial doornail. But I must confess it is beyond me to guess why you would claim Harry was the one who attacked you. It would make rather more sense if you had drawn my picture instead."

She shot him a peeved look. "But you did not attack me. *He* did!"

Victor's hand shot out and grasped her wrist, so that she stumbled against him. "Damn it all, quit playing games. I want to hear the truth for a change."

"You would not recognize the truth, my lord, if it walked up and bit you in the buttocks."

With that heated reply, she jerked herself free of his grasp and took a step back. "The man in the drawing *is* the man who attacked me. Why he happens to look like your dead friend, Sir Harry Shaw—whose name I'd never heard until afterward—I cannot explain."

Unless, of course, Sir Harry was not dead.

"Do you think that perhaps your friend is still alive?" she ventured. "Could it be that he somehow feigned his own death so that he could commit murder with impunity?"

"Not a chance," Victor answered with a decisive shake of his head. "I attended the service, and I saw him lying in the box. Hell, I don't think he'd thawed out by then."

If such were true, Amaryllis thought with a shiver, then that left but another explanation to them. It was a fantastic notion, to be sure . . . and yet, a supernatural air did cling to the Barkshire Demon murders. Had she not sensed something quite unholy about her attacker from the very start? What if the tabloids had been more accurate than they'd known in dubbing the killer the Barkshire Demon?

What if Sir Harry, through some foul means, had come back from the dead?

She abruptly plopped back into her chair as memory assailed her. The odor of decay had clung to her attacker like some foul perfume. It was a stench that, as a sexton's daughter, she knew far too well . . . the stench of a rotting corpse.

She had mentioned as much to Talbot when she had told him of the attack. He had dismissed that bit of intelligence so swiftly that she had practically forgotten it. That was, until now.

"Perhaps the truth is stranger than we might believe possible," she said in a small voice. "Perhaps your dead friend has not passed from this world but still walks among us as a reanimated corpse murdering the living."

She saw a flicker of outraged disbelief light Victor's dark

eyes. His tone, however, held only a hint of sarcasm as he asked, "Are you saying that you were half-murdered by a specter?"

"He was no specter," she protested, her cheeks flaming at his tone. "I felt his hands around my throat. He was flesh and bone, though not quite like us . . ."

At her words, Victor gave a disbelieving snort and took the chair beside her, gripped by uncertainty of his own now. He'd not wanted to believe that Amaryllis had deceived him, and her protests of innocence had an authentic ring to them. Moreover, he knew what it was like to be branded guilty of a crime one had not committed.

Still, if what she proposed was too fantastic for *him* to believe, what would the authorities make of so wild a tale? He recalled one, in particular, of the Bow Street runners who had questioned him the day before.

His name was Chapel, a carrot-haired little ferret of a man whose pale blue eyes had gleamed with uncanny intelligence. Unfortunately, unlike his compatriot and even the magistrate, himself, Chapel had not been cowed by Victor's wealth or title. Neither was he swayed by Victor's protests of innocence.

Ye've been up for this sort o' thing before, milord, 'ave ye not? came the man's blunt words as they had gathered around Penelope's mutilated body. *That actress wot was murdered a few months back, she was beaten bloody before she died. The other gent wot was wit' ye that night—Sir 'Arry Shaw, was it not?—said 'ow ye was angry she wouldn't do the sort o' things ye was wantin' 'er to do in ye bed.*

If you'll recall, Mister Chapel, I wasn't ever charged in her death, Victor had pointed out, as his stomach had lurched at the sight and smell of the corpse. *Besides which, Harry was the one who killed Miss Belfleur, not I.*

The runner had shrugged. *Witnesses at the Golden Wolf all said 'ow ye'd 'ad a few words wit' Miss Worthington the night she disappeared. Not that can I blame ye, exactly. I can see 'ow a proud gen'leman like ye wouldn't take kindly to a bit o' fluff leading ye about by the privates before a crowd. Mayhap ye're the sort o' gent who don't take it kindly when a woman o' that sort acts above 'erself.*

Their discussion had deteriorated from that point, with the runner still hot upon him up until the final moments before the magistrate had ordered Victor released for the time being.

I'll be watchin' every move ye make, Lord Blackstock, the man had muttered in a voice meant only for Victor's ears. *Sooner or later, I'll catch ye makin' some misstep . . an' I'll see to it that ye meet the hangman, right enough.*

He had no doubt that Chapel meant every word of it. He was equally certain the runner would lock him up on general principle if he tried to claim that a dead man, and not he, was the Barkshire Demon.

Weary all at once of the whole business, he got to his feet again. "We'll speak of this later. My concern now is getting Monique out of harm's way; that, and buying a bit of time for myself to do some investigating on my own. So come along now."

She made no protest as he marched her from the dining salon and out into the main hall. Derek and Peters already stood waiting, while Moresdale and Monique were making their way down the stairs. Once everyone had gathered, Victor stepped apart and eyed them like a general preparing for battle.

Which, in a sense, he was.

"Derek and Moresdale already know what this is about," he began, "but I will explain again for everyone else's benefit. Chances are quite good that I will soon be arrested for the Barkshire Demon murders, and the only way I can save myself is to discover the true killer before that happens. Unfortunately that will be a bit difficult since the authorities—and one Robin Redbreast, in particular—are keeping close tabs on me.

"Already this morning, I spotted a couple of scruffy-looking types watching the house. As long as they think I am here, I'll not be free to move about . . . so my intent is to convince them I've fled London."

He nodded in the direction of his flamboyantly garbed valet. "Moresdale will pose as me. Acting guilty as possible, he will escort Monique to the coach, and Derek will drive off with the pair of them inside."

His gaze moved to his driver. "I anticipate that our friends will follow after the carriage. When they do, Derek's job is to lose them and then leave the city in an alternate route from that which he would take traveling to Surrey. Blackstock Manor will still be his ultimate goal, as our friends will undoubtedly guess. By the time they figure that out, however, the three of you should have arrived there. Moresdale will then change back into his usual attire and assume his role as valet—"

"And what about me?" Monique interrupted in an eager voice. "I want to help as well."

Victor gave her a fond look. "Your part in all this shall be quite as important as everyone else's. When the Bow Street runners arrive at the estate, you will tell them everything that they want to hear. You will admit that I accompanied you to Surrey, that the journey was my idea, and that you suspect my desire to leave town was prompted by the fact I was questioned about the murders."

"But what happens when they ask to see you?"

"Then you will bat those long eyelashes of yours and prettily tell them that I rode off again on horseback almost as soon as we arrived at the estate. You will even allow them to search the estate, if they like, so long as they do so in an orderly fashion. My guess is that they'll take a cursory look and then spend the next few days scouring the countryside for any sign of me."

"And I, my lord?" Peters asked as Monique preened with importance. "What would you have me do?"

"You'll watch out for things here, and deal with any tabloid reporters who come snooping about."

"And what about Amaryllis?" Monique wanted to know. "What will *she* do to help?"

"I have decided that Miss Meeks might prove of more use to me here," he flatly said. Not giving anyone a chance to comment on that vague response, he went on. "Now, if everyone is satisfied as to their respective roles, I suggest that we begin."

What followed was, to Victor's mind, something akin to a Drury Lane burlesque. Derek and Peters proceeded to load Monique's trunk onto the carriage waiting just outside the front stoop. Then, while the butler took up his post at the open door, Moresdale—chin sunk well below his collar points and hat pulled down to his brow—escorted Monique and the caged Wilhelm out to that vehicle.

Once Derek had shut the carriage door after them, the curtains fell into place, blocking any view of the passengers within. With the pair thus settled, Derek climbed atop his usual perch and set off at a quick pace down the broad avenue.

From his vantage point at the parlor window, Victor noted a familiar red-haired figure promptly climb from the same nondescript hackney that had been parked at some distance from the house all morning.

"Right on schedule," he muttered, then turned to Peters. "Our friend, Mister Chapel, should be ringing the bell any moment now. When he asks, tell him that Lord Blackstock and his sister have departed the city. Your understanding is that they have gone to visit friends to the north, though his lordship refused to be specific as to their destination."

"Very good, my lord," Peters said with a firm nod, quitting the room in preparation to answering the summons.

Amaryllis at his side, Victor twitched aside the curtain again just as Chapel mounted the step and turned the bell.

The exchange between butler and Bow Street runner was brief. A moment later, the red-haired man turned on his heel and started back down the street toward the hack. Once he'd settled inside that vehicle, it started off with a clatter in the same direction as Derek had taken.

A knock at the parlor door sounded, and Peters entered. His round face shining with professional pride, he said, "I followed your instructions to the letter, my lord. The gentleman seemed quite interested in my story, thanked me, and took his leave."

"You did well, Peters. Now I would suggest that you resume as usual a routine as possible. Miss Meeks and I will remain here at the house until tonight. Then, we'll take a leaf from Mister Chapel's book and do our own investigation."

He waited until the butler, with a bow, had quit the room again before turning back to Amaryllis.

"Congratulations, my lord," she murmured. "Your plan worked quite well, it seems."

"Well enough, to this point," he absently agreed, frowning as he again scanned the street. "Tonight will tell the story, or I miss my guess."

No sign of anyone watching the house, he determined, letting the curtain fall into place once more. He'd half-expected the runner to return again, perhaps hoping to catch them by surprise. It seemed, however, that Chapel had taken his bait. He wasn't sure whether to feel relief or unease at the knowledge.

With that thought, Victor turned from the window to face Amaryllis. She had moved to one of the velvet sofas and sat stiffly on its edge, her back ramrod straight. From her shuttered expression, he guessed she had not forgiven him for doubting her wild tale about Harry.

A flicker of inner anger heated his gut. Hell, he had every

right to his suspicions, given that she had lied to him once before regarding her true identity—hardly a minor issue, to his mind. And what she was asking him to swallow now was almost beyond believing.

"All right, we're going to settle the matter now," he clipped out as he stalked over to her. "You have no doubt that the man in your sketch is the same one who attacked you."

"I thought I had already made myself quite clear on that issue," she snapped, "but, yes, I have no doubt."

He paused, taking a deep breath. What he was about to propose went beyond reason; moreover, should they be caught, they risked any manner of punishment. Still, it was the only way he knew to put the matter to rest once and for all.

He let out the breath and coolly faced her. "Very well, then, there's only one thing to be done. Come midnight tonight, we'll dig up Harry's grave to see if anyone is in it."

Velvet darkness wrapped St. Pancras's churchyard, the moon above but a sliver of silver against black crepe, doing little to pierce the shadows. Only a hint of a breeze stirred beneath the top-heavy trees, so that every breath and every footstep echoed with disconcerting loudness. Moreover, it was fast coming upon midnight, making the hour ripe for ghosts and demons and other undead creatures who roamed the night.

Indeed, one might choose no more ideal a time for digging up a grave.

Amaryllis shivered despite her snug cloak and with one hand gripped Victor's gloved fingers more tightly. His presence was a comfort, though she peevishly reminded herself that she would not be here in the first place if not for him. Why could he have not taken her at her word instead of demanding proof?

Still, had she not once proposed to him that they track down the Demon together? It seemed she had gotten her wish at last . . . and now that she had, it was the last thing that she wanted.

They had spent the greatest part of the day closeted separately—he in his library working on his manuscript, and she in the hothouse resuming her painting. Her subject had been, not the usual roses, but an unearthly landscape of dark and shadow. It was unlike any which she'd ever done, a fearful yet angry expression of looming shapes and threatening terrain that bore a distorted resemblance to the churchyard at St. Pancras. The finished work had left her physically drained but, oddly enough, spiritually revived. For she had caught the worst of her fears upon paper, the act of doing so leaving her better able to face what was to come.

Abruptly her booted foot collided with a grave marker in the shape of a weeping angel. The unexpected pain caused her to stumble, while the lantern that she held in her other hand swayed like a will-o'-the-wisp. She would have fallen had Victor not lent her swift if single-handed support—his other hand already occupied by the cloth-wrapped bundle he carried.

She nodded to indicate she was unhurt, then continued toward their destination. Only the fact that she had grown up almost within this very churchyard allowed her to move through its tangle of headstones, shrubs, and drooping trees with any measure of confidence. Victor earlier had admitted that he doubted he could find Sir Harry's resting place again, were it broad daylight. Thus it had fallen to her to take the lead based upon his vague recollections of the grave's location, aided only by the single candle of her lantern.

A night bird called, and then another, and she bit back a nervous cry. *Sternness of mind,* she told herself, though for once the bolstering motto did little to comfort her. For what they were about to do was a crime; moreover it was nothing short of sacrilege . . . at least to her mind. She could only pray that her father was safely in bed with his cup of gin-laced tea. If he decided to take a turn about the grounds, he surely could not help but notice their candle.

A few minutes later, and by dint of much stooping and squinting at lichen-scabbed inscriptions, they found Sir Harry's grave. It was situated near where Mary's mother lay at final rest, though it was a far newer plot that had not yet settled level with the surrounding earth. The stone marking it was a simple one bearing the man's name, followed by the dates that marked his birth and passing.

She was uncertain whether to be relieved or dismayed by the fact that, unlike many of the surrounding plots, no wrought-iron cage covered his grave as a deterrent to the Resurrection men.

Amaryllis set down her lantern beside that simple monument and turned to Victor. "Are you quite sure that you wish to do this?" she murmured.

Victor nodded. "Neither of us will rest easy again until we know what we're up against."

Already he had divested himself of his jacket—which he draped with casual disregard over the tombstone—and was rolling up his shirtsleeves. That accomplished, he unwrapped the length of cloth tied around one of his own garden spades. Luckily, none of the hired drivers who had carried them on their bizarre journey had either noted or else not deigned to comment upon the odd bundle. Fortunate, as well, was the fact they had not misplaced it by now.

For, at Victor's insistence, they had switched carriages twice while taking a roundabout route to the churchyard. She had questioned the need as doing it a bit brown, until he had pointed out to her an unmarked black coach following the same route as theirs . . . a coach that continued to trail them even after they exchanged their original hack for another and continued in a different direction.

She had made no further protests after that. Indeed she had gamely leaped from that second hack as they rounded a slow corner, then crouched beside Victor in a darkened alley until their pursuer rumbled past. Neither had she complained as they retraced their route on foot a few blocks before hailing yet a third hired carriage to continue their journey minus their unwelcome company.

Now freed of its cover, the shovel gleamed ominously as its metal caught the candle's faint glow. Victor's gaze met hers, and she read the grim determination in his eyes just before the shovel made its first slice into the soft dirt.

In the few minutes given over to conversation during their lengthy carriage ride to St. Pancras, she had regaled him with what she knew of Resurrection men and their techniques. Rarely did those men unearth an entire coffin; rather they dug a broad shaft in the general area where the corpse's head would lie. Reaching that spot, they would break open the wooden box and slip a rope around their victim's upper torso. All that remained was to drag the corpse up through that opening and then fill in the disturbed dirt again. Conducted by a professional grave robber, the entire process took only minutes.

Victor was following her instructions, digging at a spot just beyond where the headstone was situated. Amaryllis, meanwhile, had retrieved the lantern and held it up to guide his progress. Though he was the one doing the physical labor, she felt a trickle of perspiration slide between her breasts that was but a result of pure nerves.

The hole grew progressively deeper; still, it seemed an interminable progress. Every scrape of the shovel sounded as loud to her ears as a plank dragged across cobbles, while every creak of a tree limb or hoot of an owl made her start. As for conversation, there was none, with the only human sound a growing heaviness to Victor's breathing as he toiled on.

Once he paused to swipe at the sweat that trickled from his forehead, and she saw in some concern that his sweat-dampened shirt clung to his torso. The sooner they completed the ghastly business, she told herself, the better. If they remained in the cool night air much longer, he could well catch a chill, so that it might as well have been *his* grave he was digging.

How much time had passed before Victor stood shoulder deep within that shaft, she could not guess. The candle began to flicker, however, so that in another few minutes they would be without light. *Hurry,* she silently urged, gnawing her bottom lip in frustration.

And then she heard it . . . the distinctive thud of metal against wood.

She dropped to her knees beside the open grave, angling the lantern until she could glimpse the upper section of the coffin. The box appeared undisturbed, which eliminated the possibility that Sir Harry's body had been carried off by the Resurrection men. By now Victor had cleared away the final shovelful of dirt. He halted and gazed up at her.

Covered with fresh dirt and standing as he was in an open grave beneath the candle's sputtering light, he appeared distinctly sinister. Yet her uneasiness had nothing to do with him now, but only with what they might see next.

"Leave the light there and move back a little," he said in an undertone. "I'm going to break it open."

She nodded and set the lantern on the new mound of dirt, then scrambled back a few paces. He glanced up a final time to make certain she was safely clear. Then, gripping the shovel before him in both hands, he lifted it head-high and then, daggerlike, plunged the tool into the coffin lid.

The wood split with the sharp crack of a pistol shot. Amaryllis jumped, then gave a fearful look around them. To her mind, the sound had been loud enough to wake, if not the dead, then the living. Yet she heard no slam of the sextonage door. No one rushed from the shadows to confront them.

When she looked back in Victor's direction, he had thrust the shovel into the mound of fresh dirt beside him and was bent over the shattered planks. The muffled pops and creaks she could hear told her he was prying them apart with his

gloved hands. Doubtless the damp earth had worked upon
the wood long enough so that it had begun to decay. Sections
of board broke off readily in his hands, until he had amassed
a pile of broad splinters. Then, brushing the grave dirt from
his hands, he reached for the lantern and lowered it into the
shaft.

"Holy Christ," she heard him choke out. "I bloody well
don't believe it."

A thrill of horror swept her at the words. Steeling herself,
she eased forward to peer over his shoulder at what lay in
that open grave. It was then that the candle guttered a final
time and flickered out . . but not before she had managed
to see what Victor had seen.

The coffin where Sir Harry Shaw should have lain was
empty.

Twenty-two

Choking back a curse, Victor heaved himself out of the open grave so that he sat on its edge. His feet dangled above the shattered coffin, and he gave his head a grim shake. No need to worry about some gibbering ghoul reaching up to wrap dead fingers about his boots. The grave was long unoccupied.

He glanced over at Amaryllis, whose pale face against the shadows likely mirrored his own uncertain countenance. To be sure, she was dealing with the entire gruesome situation with more fortitude than he might have expected of a female. But then, of course, she *was* a modern woman.

"Do you believe me now?" she whispered, and he heard the mingling of terror and triumph in her voice. "Somehow your friend has come back to life and is murdering helpless women."

"There's got to be another explanation . . . a logical one," he hissed back. "I can't believe that Harry Shaw is wandering the streets of London in his grave clothes, and no one but you has noticed."

"But you said that you saw his dead body," she pointed out with incontrovertible truth, "and now the grave is empty. You were present when they buried him, were you not?"

"Actually, no."

He paused, recalling that day six months earlier. It had been a bitter cold morning, so that even within the chapel walls his breath had frozen in the air before him. Only a handful of other mourners besides Victor had gathered for the bleak occasion. His own presence had been less a tribute to his former friend's memory as it had been grim assurance that the man was indeed dead.

The ceremony had been conducted with what he recalled had been an almost unseemly haste. Given the circumstances, however, Victor had understood. Accusations of Harry being a murderer had been followed by sly whispers regarding the circumstances of his death. His own opinion was that it had been, pure and simple, an accident. He knew better than most that Harry lacked even the vestiges of a conscience. The chance that the man had felt remorse for the Belfleur woman's death and thus had taken his own life as penance was a remote likelihood at best. Still, the resulting turmoil had caused what remained of Harry's family—a mother and an aged aunt—to bury him posthaste lest the Church deem him a suicide and forbid his interment in hallowed ground.

Frozen as said ground had been, however, it was some hours after the service before the sexton and his workers had finished digging the grave. None of the mourners had witnessed the burial . . . if indeed it had been conducted at all. The fact that no lingering stench of decayed flesh wafted from the damaged coffin made him doubt that Harry's body had lain within it much longer than it had taken to complete the hurried church service.

Still, there *was* one person who could clear up that particular mystery for them.

"There is someone who will know for certain if Harry was in that box when it was buried," he declared in a low tone as he got to his feet. Offering Amaryllis his hand, he pulled her up to stand before him. "We need to speak with your father."

"My father?" Amaryllis echoed in soft despair.

She clutched at his hand, glad for the warmth of him as a slow chill filled her soul. She'd already had her suspicions as to her father's possible involvement with the Resurrection men. Always before, she had managed to dismiss the idea from her thoughts. Now, however, she could only wonder if perhaps Ezra were involved in something far more diabolical than simply turning his head while the grave robbers did their work.

Abruptly she released his hand and took a deep breath. "If I agree to this, then you must do something for me. You must tell me what happened the night Sir Harry murdered that actress."

"Christ, Amaryllis, this is hardly the place—"

He paused and glanced about the darkened cemetery, then shrugged. "Well, perhaps it is at that," he conceded. "But I warn you, it is not a pleasant tale. And I suppose I should begin by telling you that I met Harry Shaw when we were in the army together. We were not friends, merely the most casual of acquaintances . . . and even then he had a cruel streak to him.

"A few months before the murder, he and I met again at some function or another and renewed our acquaintance. As my excuse, Harry could be the most entertaining of friends when he was sober—which I soon learned was a rare state of affairs with him. He was drunk, as usual, the night that we met Jane Belfleur."

Victor's mouth thinned into a grim line. "Among Harry's flaws was the fact he derived sexual pleasure from hurting women. Still, it might surprise you to know that there are females enough who willingly seek out such abuse . . . or who are willing to endure the pain for a price. Jane fell into the latter category, which is why he brought her home with us."

He paused again, his gaze now fixed on Sir Harry's disturbed grave. "The worst of it all is that I could have saved her. I could have put her in my coach and had Derek drive her home, and that would have been an end to it. Instead I was just jaded enough to believe that what two consenting adults do behind closed doors was their own business. Thus I let Harry drag her upstairs while I took myself off to the library."

Amaryllis waited in an agony of fearful anticipation for what was to come, though she knew too well how the story would end. And Victor did not disappoint her.

"I don't know what made me change my mind and follow after them but, about a quarter of an hour later, I did. Perhaps some part of me had recognized the murder in his eyes and knew what would come of this night. At any rate, I reached the second floor in time to hear Jane screaming."

He shook his head, his features hard beneath the faint moonlight. "Sometimes I hear those screams in my dreams, and I see her the way she looked when I walked into that room, naked and covered in blood.

"There was nothing to be done for her at that point, though I checked just to make certain. As for Harry, he seemed hardly to notice I was there. He'd had the presence of mind to burn his shirt in the fireplace, and he was in the process of washing her blood from his hands."

He glanced down at his own hands then, as if the dirt that covered them was the dead actress's blood. Amaryllis felt a shiver wash over her, even as she yearned to offer a word of comfort. But she knew, too, that no pat words from her could banish the guilt he must feel. Only he could absolve himself.

"When I demanded an explanation," Victor slowly went on, "Harry said only that she had gone back on their agreement, and that he wasn't about to let her take his money without getting a bit of enjoyment out of her first. Then he passed out on the bed . . . and that is when I summoned a constable. The rest I believe you already know."

She nodded, trying to ignore the way her stomach had clenched into a cold knot at his account. "Talbot told me how the police questioned both you and Sir Harry, and that he tried to blame you for the crime. But we shan't talk of that ever again . . . that is, unless you wish it."

"Agreed. And now I think we should find your father."

"He will be home, I am certain, but I cannot guarantee he will give you an answer. He tends to be rather . . . difficult at times."

"Nonetheless, we have no other choice but to—"

" 'Ere, now," boomed out a coarse voice behind them. "Looks like we 'ave a plump pair o' pigeons nosin' in on our turf."

Amaryllis caught back a startled scream and, still clutching Victor's hand, spun about. Looming up from behind another nearby monument were two scruffy, bearded men. Both were of a height—almost as tall as Victor—though the speaker was twice as broad around as his companion. The pair were dressed in a similar fashion . . . baggy trousers, patched at the knees; thick overcoats of some dark, indistinguishable shade; ragged mufflers wrapped around their necks; and knit caps such as seafaring men favored pulled down low on their brows.

But far more unnerving than their appearance was the fact that the silent one of the pair brandished a heavy cudgel, while the other pointed a bulky pistol in their direction.

"Good evening, gentlemen," she heard Victor's cool voice beside her. "I fear there has been a misunderstanding. The lady and I were merely seeking out a bit of privacy. We have no wish to intrude on any business the two of you might be conducting."

"So ye say," the thin man spoke up with a nasal cackle, "but that don't explain wot ye're doin' diggin' up graves, when the two o' us already cut a deal wit' the sexton."

In a casual move, Victor pulled free of her frightened grip and spread his hands in a deprecating gesture. He put himself between her and the Resurrection men in the process.

"I'm sure we can sort all this out with a minimum of unpleasantness," he replied in the same even tones. "I would think it apparent that the lady and I are not in the same line of work as you gentlemen. We merely came to check on the state of a particular friend of ours. Now that we've satisfied ourselves as to his condition, we'll be on our way. And, of course, we'll have no reason to mention this encounter to anyone."

"Ye bloody well won't, at that."

The pistol-bearing man stepped out from behind the monument, waving his weapon in a threatening manner as he started toward them. He halted before Sir Harry's open grave, then peered nearsightedly into it.

" 'Tain't no bleedin' body in the 'ole," he called back to his partner, then fixed her and Victor with a vicious look. "Ye'd best tell me wot ye did wit' the bloke, an' be quick about it, or ye'll be the one needin' buryin'."

Victor shrugged. From her vantage point behind him, Amaryllis saw that he had taken another casual step—this time toward the shovel that still was planted, blade down, in the mound of dirt.

"As a matter of fact, the coffin was empty when we got here. If you take a look, you can see that I only now broke it open . . . and no bodies are lying about, that I've seen."

What happened next occurred in the space of a heartbeat. As the Resurrection man peered back down the shaft, Victor took advantage of the man's momentary distraction. He jerked the shovel free and landed it across that man's back.

The grave robber collapsed with a groan, the pistol tumbling from his lax fingers. His companion, meanwhile, gave a guttural shout of surprise. Then, brandishing his club like a member of some barbaric horde, he stumbled his way through the tangle of graves toward them.

Victor was ready for the man, parrying the first few blows of the club with his shovel. A fourth blow, however, snapped the spade in two, leaving Victor clutching a short length of oak as his only weapon.

The thin man halted and, breathing hard, gave another nasal laugh. " 'Ere, now, looks like ye're in a bit o' a fix."

Then, still tittering, he cut his pale eyes in Amaryllis's direction. "Don't ye worry none, girlie. When I'm through wit' yer gen'leman friend 'ere, I'll 'ave a li'le somethin' for ye."

With that chilling threat, he turned back toward Victor.

The latter was ready for him, however. In a single fluid move, Victor scooped up a handful of grave dirt and flung it squarely into his opponent's face.

The man howled with pained outrage, the cudgel dangling from one hand as he scrubbed at his eyes with the other. As he did so, Victor leaped upon him, tumbling them both to the ground.

Amaryllis watched for a stunned instant as they grappled over the club. Then, with a cry, she recalled the pistol that the first Resurrection man had dropped.

Avoiding the open grave, she scrambled around to the other side of Sir Harry's tombstone, where the other assailant sprawled facedown in the dirt. Frantic, she scanned the tangle of new grass for it, spotting a metallic glint just a few inches from that prone figure. She hesitated; then, as the man remained unmoving, she bent and made a quick grab for the weapon.

But as her fingers closed over the cold metal, cruel fingers clamped over her hand, so that she cried out in shock and pain.

"Not so bloody fast, girlie," the prone man hissed in her ear just before his other beefy fist collided with her temple.

The blow felled her. Still, she clung to consciousness long enough to hear her attacker man call, "Stand clear, an' I'll see to 'im," before the pistol exploded in a deafening blast.

When next she opened her eyes, she was lying facedown beside Sir Harry's grave. Excruciating pain filled her head, so that she choked back a groan. Then, raising up, she made out the figures of the two Resurrection men now standing over a still, supine form.

Victor!

The cry lodged in her throat. Swiftly she shut her eyes again and feigned unconsciousness, trying to make sense of what was happening. She recalled the sound of the pistol shot just before she had swooned. Dear God, they'd killed him.

Or had they? Perhaps he was wounded instead and incapable of movement.

Scarce daring to breathe lest she draw their attention, she opened one eye again and strained to see what was happening. Victor had not moved from his prone position, and she had no way of telling from her vantage point his condition. Then the thinner of the two men bent over him and gave him a vicious kick with one booted foot.

" 'E's still alive, but not fer much longer," that man pronounced with his nasal laugh. The casual words sliced like a knife through Amaryllis's heart even as she rejoiced that he still breathed. "Ye want 'ow I should kill 'im now, or leave 'im to suffer a bit?"

" 'Ere now, I 'ave a better notion."

His companion landed his own savage kick on Victor's unconscious form, doubtless in repayment for the latter's attack on him. Then, scratching his bearded chin, he went on. "Remember wot the sawbones said . . . the fresher, the better, is 'ow 'e wants 'em? I say we save ourselves the diggin' an' take this fine gent instead. If 'e's not dead when we get there, we can slip a rope about 'is neck an' kill 'im quick. Either way, 'e's still nice an' warm when we give 'im over."

"An' wot about 'er?" the thin man wanted to know, jerking a thumb in Amaryllis's direction. She squeezed her eyes shut again, trying to still her trembling as he continued. "Ye think 'e'd pay fer her as well?"

" 'Tain't no 'arm in askin'. C'mon, now, let's load 'em up before a Charlie comes by."

She heard a shuffling sound from where they stood. Peeking through veiled lashes, she saw them lift Victor's limp form between them. Silent now, they hurried off in the same direction from whence they'd appeared, vanishing into a tangle of shadows and vines. No doubt they had a wagon or cart of some sort waiting nearby, which they used to transport their victims.

As the sound of their footsteps faded, Amaryllis let out a shuddering breath, her thoughts flying. The men meant to kill them both, she knew. If she made her own escape now, perhaps she could summon help . . . but from where?

Her gaze flicked in the direction of the sextonage, a pinpoint of yellow light from one of its windows just visible between the drooping trees. It beckoned to her like a lighthouse to a storm-tossed sailor. Perhaps her father was yet awake. If she hurried, she could summon him before the men returned.

But what good could he possibly do?

A surge of angry dismay swept her. Had the Resurrection men not stated, after all, that they had made a deal with her father? Even supposing that Ezra had not drunk himself into a stupor by this time, he would not be inclined to confront the pair. And though paternal feeling might cause him to plead her case, he would have no reason to intervene in Victor's behalf.

Then she could search out the nightwatch, she told herself, though the prospect of help from that corner seemed just as bleak. Those men were armed with nothing more than a stick, which she had already seen was no defense against a pistol. And if she did manage to locate one of the night patrollers—let alone convince him to aid her—the Resurrection men would be long gone . . . and Victor with them.

The hasty shuffle of reapproaching footsteps decided the

question for her. All that was left for her was to let them carry her off as well. Perhaps once they were in the wagon and traveling, she might conceive of some clever plan to save both of them. At the very least, they might manage to slip from the back of the wagon while the men's attention was diverted.

Knowing what the villains had planned for her, it took more sternness of mind than she'd ever before summoned to continue to feign unconsciousness while the pair bent over her. She smelled one man's fetid breath before he wedged a booted foot beneath her stomach and rolled her over onto her back.

She let her limbs flail and her jaw hang slack, even as she strove to keep her breathing even. " 'Ere now," she heard the nasal whine of the thin man, "wot do ye say to havin' a bit o' sport wit' 'er before we're off?"

With an effort, she managed not to shudder. Dear Lord, she'd thought their plans were to sell her still-warm corpse to some unknown physician, not assault her in a churchyard! Should she try to run now or wait to see if—

"Are ye ten kinds o' fool, then?" the other man proclaimed in contempt. " 'Tain't the time nor the place, not wit' a dyin' man lyin' in a wagon but a stone's throw away from ye. Keep yer breeches up until after we pay the sawbones a visit. Then, if 'e don't want 'er, ye can do wot ye like wit' 'er."

The thin man uttered a foul rejoinder. Even as she feared he might yet ignore his partner's advice, he scooped her up and heaved her over his shoulder like she was a bag of meal. Her relief at this reprieve was short-lived, however. As they began trudging between the rows of graves, he clamped a bony hand onto her buttocks and began squeezing her as if she were a loaf in the baker's window.

Every fiber of her being recoiled at this violation. Indeed it took all her willpower to remain limp in his grasp, while she longed to land a punishing kick in his groin as repayment for that assault. Somehow, though, she managed to carry on with her act even when he dumped her in an unceremonious heap in the wagon bed.

She heard a quick snap of canvas; then the covering was pulled taut over the wagon bed, sealing her and Victor in a broad, coffinlike expanse of cloth and rough wood.

She waited until the vehicle jerked forward before she dared even open her eyes. The darkness surrounding her was total, and decidedly unnerving—the more so because the wagon's rough ride left her sliding helplessly about the bed. It was only by reaching up a cautious hand that she determined she had room enough to roll onto her side. She did just that, then groped about for Victor.

Her hand collided with his upper torso. To her immense relief, she could feel the rise and fall of his chest. Still, he did not stir at her touch, while even to her untrained senses his breathing sounded ragged and felt far too shallow.

Choking back a useless sob, she scooted closer and ran searching fingers down his body to determine where the bullet might have struck him. Along his far side, she felt the telltale stickiness of fresh blood.

With shaking fingers, she managed to unfasten his waistcoat and shirt to probe the wound with careful fingers. As best she could tell, the bleeding had slowed or even stopped. Still, how much he had already bled or how deep the wound was, she could not begin to guess. All she knew for certain was that he needed a physician and soon.

Awkwardly she managed to strip off her cloak and drape it over him as a blanket. That accomplished, she wedged her body against his to keep him from rolling about the wagon bed. From the more even motion of the wagon, she guessed they were moving along paved roads now. All she need do was spare him the worst of the jolts and jars.

But what good was protecting Victor now, she thought in despair, when the Resurrection men would kill him just as soon as they reached their destination?

Already she had abandoned her original notion of their scrambling from the wagon as it rumbled down the dark city streets. The canvas covering was tied from the outside, so that escape from the wagon bed would be nigh impossible without a knife to slice through that heavy cloth. Moreover she judged their pace far too swift for a passenger to risk leaping from the vehicle. Even if she could escape injury landing on the rough cobbles, in his current unconscious state Victor would likely be killed by such a tumble.

She wrapped her arms more tightly about him, as much to bolster her spirits as to shield him. All she could do was wait until the wagon halted and the pair loosed the cloth covering. Weaponless and outnumbered, her sole hope lay in the element of surprise. The men would expect her still to be unconscious, so that they would be taken unaware when she sprang up and attempted escape.

For that was what she must do. At the very least, the sight of a screaming woman running down the street might distract them from killing Victor. With luck her cries would bring help . . . or at least witnesses. Such a ploy could even unnerve the pair to the point that they would abandon the entire idea of selling her and Victor's bodies to an anatomist altogether.

On the other hand, the Resurrection men might simply shoot her as she fled, collect their coin from the good doctor for two fresh specimens, and then be on their way.

Determinedly she tore her mind from such a bleak scenario. She instead focused her thoughts on outwitting her captors. For, brutes that they were, they had struck her as being sly, rather than intelligent. Surely a modern woman like her possessed the wits to best such a pair!

Fright and total darkness skewed her sense of time, so that she was not sure if it was minutes or hours later that the wagon jerked to a halt. She heard one of the men curse, and the other laugh, though she had no notion as to the cause of either man's reaction. Then she felt the shifting of weight that was one or both of them climbing from their wagontop perches.

She scooted away from Victor again and rolled over so that she faced the rear end of the wagon, on her hands and knees but flattened almost double. The uncomfortable position sent her muscles protesting, but she ignored the pain. In another moment, the pair would throw back the canvas. Then she would leap up with a scream, scramble over the wagon's side, and flee in the opposite direction from them.

Even as her tensed muscles quivered in anticipation, she heard another sound, that of a heavy wooden door opening. A muffled male voice drifted to her, while the two Resurrection men broke into hasty explanation. This must be the physician with whom they were to deal, she realized, yet she would venture a guess that the man had appeared on the scene too soon . . . that was, while the ersatz corpses were still alive.

The realization stirred a bit of hope in her. Once the cover was thrown back, she could plead with the doctor, swear never to reveal his name, if only he would help. Surely a man who had sworn the Hippocratic oath would not countenance killing the pair of them outright.

" 'Ere now, doc, we'd best come back another time," she heard one of the pair say. "I don't think wot we 'ave would suit ye, at that."

Dear Lord, they were going to drive off . . . she and Victor with them! And the pair would not take another such risk, but would halt again in the nearest alley to finish their original job. If she did not chance seeking help now, she'd not get a second opportunity.

"Stop, don't let them take us," she shrieked, sitting up as best she could and clawing at the canvas. "They've already shot my friend, and they'll murder us both, if you don't help me! Please, for the love of God, don't let this happen—"

Abruptly the covering pulled away from the wagon bed, and Amaryllis found herself blinking into the bright light of a lantern. Half-sobbing, she rose up on her knees and reached a frantic, pleading hand toward the shadowed figure behind it.

"Please," she choked out, "these men will kill us. Surely a man of medicine such as yourself cannot condone outright murder."

"That quite depends upon the circumstances, my dear Amaryllis," a familiar voice replied in a cool tone.

At those words, she could only sink back onto her heels and stare in astonishment as the lantern was lowered. Now she recognized the part of the city—indeed the very building—where the Resurrection men had taken them. Moreover she could now make out the face of the man who had spoken, a face that she knew quite as well as her own.

"Take your case," Talbot went on in the same unconcerned tones, as if they met at a cotillion, rather than in the company of killers. "Sister or not, I'd cheerfully strangle you for getting yourself into such a fix, and Lord Blackstock with you."

Twenty-three

So saying, Talbot caught her by the arm and half-dragged her from the back of the wagon bed. She stumbled but quickly regained her feet, clinging to him for support when her trembling limbs seemed unable to hold her upright.

What matter if her brother were furious with her, or if he would tell their father what had happened this night? The important thing was that he had saved her from the murderous thugs, and that he might yet heal Victor of his injuries.

Rarely demonstrative, Talbot allowed her this moment of weakness. He wrapped an arm around her waist and gave a cool nod in the direction of the Resurrection men.

"You there," he demanded, "remove Lord Blackstock from the wagon and set him here on the step."

" 'Ere, now, we can't do that," the thin man protested, his features twisting into a dark scowl. "I can name ye a dozen other sawbones wot would be payin' our rate for 'im, an' glad t'do it. We'd be losin' a night's pay, we would, leavin' this bloke behind."

"You'll do as I say, or I shall see to it that the pair of you are brought up on murder charges."

"An' wot about ye?" the bulky man challenged, thrusting out his barrellike chest as he moved closer. "Ye're as guilty as the two o' us, buyin' wot we 'ave to sell."

That physical threat combined with the man's heated words sent a shiver through her. For, if Talbot had indeed been paying the pair to bring him fresh corpses, in the eyes of the law he *was* quite as guilty as they . . . the ethics of it all notwithstanding. He could be jailed, too.

That was, if the two Resurrection men did not turn their pistol on him beforehand.

If Talbot was unnerved by this show of force, he gave no sign of it but favored the pair with a humorless smile. "I think you will find that my word carries a bit more weight with the local magistrate than yours," he countered in a cool tone. "It so happens that the man is a patient of mine, and I am in the position to divulge certain medical matters that he would prefer not be made public. I rather think he would be quick to dismiss any such charges against me. On the other hand, he would have no compunction about bringing a pair of grave robbers to justice."

The bulky man bristled. "Ye bloody well think ye're above it all, don't ye? An' wot do ye think ye'd do, sawbones, wit'out me an' Jerry to supply ye with bodies to hack at?"

"I think I would be doing business with one or another of your competitors, who doubtless would be a bit more amenable to satisfying my wishes. Now will you remove the earl from the back of your wagon, or do I need to go in search of a constable?"

After exchanging uncertain glances, the men apparently decided that Talbot meant what he said. While Amaryllis watched in concern, they reached into the wagon bed and lifted Victor out to settle him none too gently on the stoop. In a deliberate parody of gallantry, the thin man plucked Amaryllis's blood-stained cloak from where it had snagged on the wagon and returned it to her. Then, muttering a steady stream of imprecations, the pair climbed back onto their wagon and whipped up the horse.

As soon as the Resurrection men were out of earshot, she turned an admiring look on her brother. "Talbot, your stern-ness of mind in this situation was splendid," she cried. "I feared those two horrid men would call your bluff and do you some harm, but you never even faltered. You . . . you delivered us, to be sure."

"Save your thanks, my dear Amaryllis," Talbot replied as he disengaged himself from her grasp. "Had their hapless victims been anyone but you and your earl, I fear I would have left them to their fate. As it was, I simply was avoiding a scandal. Just think what would happen should those fools have taken you elsewhere. Why, the esteemed Doctor McArdle might have found himself dissecting his worst enemy's sister."

Half-fearing that her brother truly meant that extraordinary sentiment, she made no reply but turned her attention to Victor. He lay sprawled against the damp wall, like a gin-sodden vagrant. She crouched beside him and pulled aside his shirt to examine his injury. By some miracle, the rough ride had not caused the wound to resume bleeding; still, he had yet to regain consciousness, and she noted in growing dismay that his pallid skin now had a clammy feel to it.

Talbot, meanwhile, had lifted the lantern again and was slanting a considering glance in Victor's direction.

"I suppose you'll be wanting me to patch up your earl, will you not? Very well, let's bring him on in. You'll see to the door, won't you?"

Not waiting for her reply, he thrust the lantern into Amaryllis's hands, then bent to hoist Victor over his shoulder. She struggled a moment with the heavy door, then pulled it open for him to enter. Once they both were inside, he paused long enough to say, "Bar it, if you would. We don't want your brutish friends changing their minds and popping back in for a visit," before starting down the hallway with his patient.

Amaryllis did as he said, dropping the broad iron bar into its catches. Then, juggling lantern and cloak, she followed after him. It took her a moment to realize that Talbot's destination was not his examining room, nor even his own per-

sonal chambers. Instead he continued down the narrow hall
to the portion of the old chapel where he conducted his
anatomy lessons.

Their footsteps echoed on the stone floor within as they
walked toward the converted sacristy. The place reminded
her of nothing so much as an empty stage rising before rows
of ghostly spectators. Within it lay the familiar table where
she had watched Talbot perform his work that night of the
anatomy lesson. She eyed both the table and the now-silent
electrical generator beside it with misgivings. Surely he did
not mean to administer to Victor here!

But even as she opened her mouth to question him, he
turned to the curtained confessional to one side of the pews.
He pulled aside the purple velvet hanging and, Victor still
balanced over his shoulder, stepped inside the narrow antechamber.

Thoroughly perplexed now, she hurried to join him. She
reached his side in time to see him twist a carved rosette
on the confessional's inner wooden wall, opposite the raised
step where countless penitents once had knelt while con-
fessing their sins. To her shock, that paneled section
promptly swung back into the very wall itself, creating a
narrow doorway that opened into yawning blackness.

"You have the lantern, my dear," Talbot remarked, as if
this revealing of a secret passage were nothing out of the
ordinary. "I suggest that you lead the way. And do be careful . . . the steps are quite steep."

She eased around him and peered into that darkness. A
cool draft ruffled her hair, which by now had all but fallen
from its pins. "But where do the steps lead?"

"Downward," he told her with incontestable logic. "Now
do be quick about it, if you want your earl to live."

Concern for Victor won out over any trepidation. Raising
the lamp to spread its yellow glow as far as possible, she
made her cautious way down the first few steps. When they
seemed safe enough, she forged on, squinting against the

shadows. All she could see was what lay directly before her, for the yellow glow of the lantern did little more than envelop the three of them in a halo of light.

The stairway, she quickly discovered, was open on one side, so that a misstep would send her plunging into unknown darkness. On the other side, the stone wall served as the only handrail, so that she clutched at the rough rock with her free hand to keep her balance. The steps themselves were hewn from the same damp limestone as made up that wall, slightly hollowed at their midpoints from what she guessed might be centuries of climbing feet. As she moved farther downward, the sensation was rather like plunging into the depths of an unexplored cave, the air around her cool yet stale.

By the time they reached level ground below, she estimated they had descended the equivalent of the broad marble staircase that rose from the entry hall in Victor's town house. Talbot was right behind her, moving with the ease of one who had traversed those stairs many times before. As she paused at the bottom step, he halted as well.

"You'll find a small niche containing a lamp at this spot in the wall," he told her. "Light it, and then move along the wall another dozen feet until you find the next one, and the next one, after it. By the time you've circled the perimeter of the room, you should have found a dozen lamps in all. Now make haste so I can attend Lord Blackstock."

She discovered the first lamp where he'd told her it would be. With shaking fingers, she set a fire to its wick, then moved on to the next niche. Though the process seemed to take an interminable time, each succeeding lamp banished an increasingly larger area of shadow. By the time she'd lit the dozenth one, her brother had deposited his unconscious patient onto one of the several wooden tables set up in the antechamber's center.

Unable to bear watching the proceedings, she focused her attention on her surroundings. As Talbot had implied, the room was an immense circle, likely half as large in diameter as the main church above it. Indeed her first impression was that of standing at the bottom of a formidable well that had long since gone dry. The chamber's perimeter was ringed by three rows of stone benches that might once have accommodated an audience . . . or a congregation. One row was built directly into the wall. The others formed successively smaller rings with gaps at quarterly intervals, allowing passage to the chamber's center.

Her next impression, oddly enough, was one of light.

For the antechamber was lit bright as day, though even a score of lanterns would not have so thoroughly illuminated an area of that size. It took her a moment to realize that it was the pale gray stone of the walls themselves that reflected back the lantern light like a hall of mirrors doubling and redoubling a single candle flame. Thus, despite the cavelike atmosphere, it was remarkably bright within . . . though even the cheery glow could not dispel the unsettling atmosphere about her.

Craning her neck, she gazed back up to the narrow door that topped the stairway. From her small knowledge of architecture, she guessed that the antechamber dated back to Roman times, though it appeared little affected by the passing of centuries. The fact of its condition was perhaps unusual, but its existence was not.

For Roman ruins abounded in London, she knew, with artifacts from the time of Julius Caesar's occupation unearthed by its current citizens with regularity. Indeed had not St. Pancras Church and its surrounding grounds once been a Roman encampment . . . and later, so it was rumored, a pagan shrine? Just had that church been built upon such a spot in hopes of diverting the shrine's followers to the Christian God, likely this place had been constructed atop a similar place of worship.

The contrast, then, with the modern surgical equipment arranged before her was striking.

The effect nearly duplicated Talbot's examining room. At the center of the antechamber lay two wheeled wooden examining tables, upon one of which lay the unconscious Victor. Another pair of tables flanked those, each with a sturdy wooden stool, taller than a regular chair, stowed beneath it. Both tables were cluttered with glass jars and racks of glass vials—most empty, others filled with liquids in a rainbow of colors. Various gleaming surgical instruments were spread in meticulous array, as if in preparation for an operation.

Frowning, Amaryllis took a few steps nearer. Beneath the very table where Victor lay, the gray stone floor was stained a rusty color. It was as if someone had spilled copious quantities of some dark liquid which had soaked into the porous rock, so that no amount of scrubbing could banish it.

Unsettled by the sight, she returned her gaze to the drama unfolding before her. Talbot had long since divested himself of his own jacket and rolled up his shirtsleeves, then stripped his patient of waistcoat and shirt, so that Victor lay barechested on the table before him. Now Talbot was probing with a pair of forceps at a spot along Victor's left side. A moment later, he held up the instrument so that she could see clamped between its narrow jaws a small, misshapen ball of lead.

"There's your culprit, my dear," he said with satisfaction as he dropped it with a dull clink into a small tray on the table beside him.

But Amaryllis's attention was held, not by the bullet he'd removed from Victor's side, but by the few drops of fresh blood that had dripped from the forceps to patter on the floor at his feet. They gleamed a moment like crimson tears atop the gray stone and then vanished into the surface of that rock, leaving behind a familiar rust-colored stain.

A prickle of horror danced along her spine as a sudden, awful possibility arose in her mind. Just as quickly, she dismissed it. For all she knew, those stains had been there for years . . . or even centuries.

Talbot, meanwhile, seemed not to notice her dismay as he busied himself with bandaging his patient. Finishing, he glanced her way and beckoned her.

"Do come take a look at your earl, my dear. I believe he shall live after all. His wound was rather serious, to be sure, but probably not fatal for a man of his constitution."

"Th-Thank you, Talbot," she replied and managed a smile despite the way her innards were quivering. "I am grateful."

She started toward them, moving across that cursed floor with the same wariness she would use to traverse an adder-infested field. Reaching Victor, however, her trepidation was replaced by a more immediate fear as she reached out a cautious hand to his cheek.

His flesh, though still pallid, now held a healthier warmth than before. He stirred at her touch, only to lapse back into his earlier unmoving state.

"He seems to be sleeping so deeply. Are you quite certain that he will be all right?" she asked, glancing at her brother.

Talbot had rinsed the blood from his hands and was drying them on a strip of clean linen. Putting basin and cloth aside, he shrugged and began rolling down his sleeves again.

"He will rouse soon enough. As to his condition, I would suggest keeping him in my care for a few days, just in case any infection sets in. But if he continues to hold his own for the next few hours, I see no reason that he cannot make a complete recovery. And now let me attend to you."

"Really, I am quite fine—"

"Nonsense. You have what appears to be the start of a nasty bruise on your temple," he curtly diagnosed and reached up to brush aside a few tangled curls. "Did those brutes assault you?"

"The big one did hit me," she admitted, wincing as his surgeon's fingers moved across her tender flesh. "I was un-

conscious for a few moments but, other than a slight headache now, I feel fine."

"Indeed. And would you care to tell me how you and
Lord Blackstock just happened to stumble across a pair of
Resurrection men . . . and why they felt compelled to sell
the two of you off as anatomy subjects?"

"We—We were in St. Pancras's churchyard, digging up
the grave of Sir Harry Shaw."

Haltingly she told her brother what had occurred over the
past two days, how Victor had been questioned in the Barkshire Demon murders because he'd been seen in the company of the latest victim just before she was murdered. She
told him, too, that Victor had recognized the sketch of her
attacker as being that of his dead friend. She then went on
to recount how Victor had deceived the police inspectors
into believing he had left the city, and how she and he had
proceeded to the cemetery just around midnight to determine whether or not Sir Harry was dead.

"But the coffin was empty, Talbot," she cried, shivering
at the memory. "Victor wanted to ask Father about it, but
then the Resurrection men came and accused us of trying
to interfere. That was when they shot Victor. They would
have killed him then, except that the one man reminded the
other that the physician who had hired them wanted the
newly dead. *The fresher, the better,* is what they said. Talbot,
that physician is you."

She halted and stared up at him, wide-eyed. "Father may
have been guilty of turning a blind eye to what they were
doing, but *you* were the one who hired them, were you not?
Surely you must have guessed that these sort of men would
not stop at robbing graves!"

"I believe we had a similar conversation not long ago,"
he countered, turning from her to pick up another cloth and
a stoppered bottle of clear liquid. "How or where these two
obtain my subjects is none of my concern. All I do is pay
them for their night's work."

"But in doing so, you are an accomplice to murder!"

"I prefer to think of it as a necessary sort of human sacrifice conducted for the betterment of mankind."

So saying, he unstoppered the bottle and poured a few drops onto the cloth, then replaced the cork and set the container aside again. A sharp, sweet odor assailed her, but she ignored it in favor of his words.

"Necessary human sacrifice?" she echoed in horror. "Surely you cannot mean what you are saying?"

"The knowledge I have gained from my experiments benefits countless others who might otherwise die. Compared to that, the loss of a few prostitutes is of no great concern."

The truth struck her at the same instant that he caught her arm and pulled her to him. Before she could free herself, he clamped the cloth over her mouth and nose.

"Ether," he explained as she choked against the sweet smell. "Don't bother struggling, my dear. It takes effect almost at once. Indeed I predict that it shall one day come into common use as a surgical anesthetic, as well as—"

What other prediction he might have had for the substance, she did not hear, for a cloud of mind-numbing blackness had enveloped her.

Twenty-four

You must promise, dear friend, that you will never speak to anyone of this fantastic tale which I have told you. Burn all my letters, once you have read this last. For all of us have sworn that we will Never Reveal what happened that night, lest people deem us all insane . . . or, worse, that they try to duplicate those foul experiments.

> —letter from Miss Amaryllis Meeks to
> Miss Mary Godwin

When Amaryllis awoke from her drugged sleep, it was to find herself strapped, wrist and ankle, to the second of the two examining tables. Head spinning, she glanced over to see that Victor still lay unconscious upon the other. He, too, had been bound by means of four leather straps, so that even should he regain consciousness, he would be powerless to assist her.

"Ah, you are awake," she heard Talbot's cool voice to one side of her. "I must apologize for stooping to such tactics, but I could not risk your trying to leave until we had settled matters between us."

"Let me go," she managed in a fuzzy voice, tugging at the leather bonds as she twisted about to catch a glimpse of him. "We can talk about this without your holding me captive."

"Perhaps . . . or perhaps not."

His tone thoughtful, Talbot moved so that he was in the range of her vision. His pale features were composed, but his gray eyes glinted with a gray light that reminded her of the stones around them. Despite herself, she shivered. Her brother was a dedicated humanitarian whom she had always admired. As for the man standing before her now, he was someone she did not recognize despite his familiar face.

"I presume you would like some sort of explanation, would you not?" he went on in the same conversational voice. "Very well, I shall tell you. You see, I discovered this antechamber quite by accident in the process of converting the chapel proper into a lecture hall. At first, I thought of it only as a curiosity, until I delved into some old texts I found boxed away in a room just off the sacristy."

He paused and gave her a small smile. "The books, of course, were written in Latin . . . in which language I happen to be quite conversant, given that I am a physician. It was only when I perused their pages that I learned just what sort of power actually lay beneath the ground here."

"This chamber—it is Roman, is it not?" she interjected, trying to keep up the pretense of normalcy.

He nodded. "It seems that certain pagan rituals once were held here, rites pertaining to life and to death. Are you familiar, perhaps, with the Welsh legend of Bran the Blessed?"

When she shook her head in confusion, he went on. "Bran was king of Britain before the time of Arthur, and quite a revered figure, from all accounts. Among the sacred objects in his possession was the so-called cauldron of rebirth. As the story goes, one merely needed to place a dead man within it to bring him back to life. An unfortunate side-effect, however, was that these Celtic Lazaruses lacked the power of speech. Still and all, being mute would seem a small price to pay for the chance to be born again."

"But what does such a legend have to do with murder?" she cried, tugging again at her straps.

Talbot quelled her struggles with a cool look. "The legend

goes on to say that the cauldron ended up in the hands of the Irish king who had married Bran's sister. Not long after, it was destroyed by Bran's brother who, during a visit, had instigated a bloody political clash between both sets of relatives."

"The brother, it would seem, felt guilty over his role in the affair. In the heat of the battle, he committed suicide by climbing inside the cauldron, whose miraculous powers apparently had a detrimental effect upon the living. He died a rather unpleasant death and shattered the cauldron in the process. But even if that original cauldron of rebirth no longer exists, another one does . . . and here, within this very chamber."

Abruptly he seized her bound hand, his fingers cold against hers. "Can you not guess what such a find means? Combining the ancient rites with modern medical knowledge can make it possible to bring back the dead, to revive the dying. To save Cordelia."

At the mention of his ill wife, his voice broke. A heartbeat later, he recovered himself and loosed his grip on her.

"My dear Amaryllis, you must have sensed the power that exists within these walls. I tell you that I have proved that it can be harnessed . . . and you, yourself, have been a witness."

"S-Surely you don't mean S-Sir Harry Shaw?"

He nodded, a small smile of triumph twisting his pale features. "I do. He seemed quite the appropriate subject for such an experiment, given the tidy way that he met his end. Between the cold and the vast amount of alcohol in his veins, he had not quite thawed out by the time I laid hands on him. It was but a simple expedient to distract Father with a pint of gin and remove Shaw's body. Afterward I brought him back here and commenced the process of bringing him back to life."

Amaryllis shut her eyes, overwhelmed by disbelief and horror. Such a thing could not be possible . . . and yet she had seen Sir Harry, had almost met her own end at his dead hands!

"This magic cauldron," she weakly said, "where is it now?"

"I shall show you."

He maneuvered the table about so that she faced the far wall. There a portion of the outermost stone bench rose higher than the rest of it, reminding her of a stone-capped altar.

"That, my dear, is the cauldron," he said with the enthusiasm of a Tower guide showing off the Crown Jewels. "In actuality, it is a spring-fed well, with its source somewhere beneath the city. The water that flows from it appears much the same as what you and I would drink—though I fear it would be fatal to do so."

He paused and held up his hand, indicating a faded red patch on his forefinger. "Indeed I gave myself a nasty little burn by merely dipping my bare hand into it. However, I managed to take a proper sample and analyze it. I discovered that the water contains minute traces of certain metallic compounds unlike any with which I am familiar . . . and which react quite differently with living tissue as compared to dead."

"Really, Talbot, this is most absurd," she protested, growing more uneasy with every moment. "Are you saying that you baptized Sir Harry in that spring, and that he miraculously returned to life?"

"I fear it was not quite that easy. Perhaps the centuries diluted the spring's powers, or maybe its keepers combined the spring with some other ritual. At any rate, I had managed at that point to revive nothing larger than a stray cat that had been hit by a passing carriage. Then, with Sir Harry, I hit upon the idea of combining the spring with my experiments in electrical stimulation.

"And I succeeded."

The cold triumph in those last words echoed against the

gray stones, reverberating in her mind for several moments. Talbot, meanwhile, had left her side and halted before the cauldron. With a grunt of effort, he slid its altarlike top into a narrow recess carved behind it, revealing a deep trough filled with crystalline waters. The foul, sweet odor of decay promptly filled the chamber.

That accomplished, Talbot returned for a trunk-sized object that she recognized as similar to the generator he had used during the anatomy lesson. He positioned the equipment a few feet from the cauldron, then busied himself with its coils.

Amaryllis, meanwhile, had raised up on her elbows to manage a look within that sepulchurian basin. She glimpsed a naked human figure floating just below the water's glittering surface.

Sir Harry!

A muffled cry of denial burst from her. Talbot seemed not to notice, however, positioning as he was the half-dozen metal rods connected to his generator by long lengths of wire. One at a time, he plunged those rods into the cauldron, then took up position beside the generator again.

"The accompanying light is rather blinding," he told her. "You might wish to look away for a moment."

But as he began turning the generator's crank, she found herself riveted by the sight of blue sparks and steam exploding from the water's surface. A deafening crackle filled the chamber, while the stench of hot metal and burning flesh assailed her nostrils. Horrified, she watched Sir Harry's body thrash as if in some grotesque struggle against an unseen attacker.

That last was too much for her. She squeezed her eyes shut . . and then silence fell.

Dreading what she might see but unable not to look, she opened her eyes again. Sir Harry—or rather, the body that had been his in life—sat up in the water-filled trough. He stared back at her with black eyes alight with the same empty fury she remembered from that night in the alley.

This time she managed to choke back the cry that rose in her throat, even as a shiver of revulsion shook her. For his part, Talbot beamed upon his creation with the proud look of a new parent.

"Ah, yes, there we are," he murmured in approval. "Now then, Harry, I want you to step out of the cauldron and sit in your usual spot."

The creature lurched to its feet, yellow light gleaming against his wet, naked form. He was fleshier than Victor, if much of a height, and Amaryllis recalled the comparison she had once made between them of a bull and a stallion. Sir Harry, as she well knew, had the former beast's strength, if not the latter's grace. Moving like an automaton, he stumbled his way over to the bench and collapsed like a sack of bricks upon it.

"I fear that my success with Harry was not all I might have wished," Talbot said with a shake of his head as he returned to her side. "It took me several attempts to revive him, and by the time I finally did so, I fear that the decaying process had already begun. As you can see, he understands but the simplest of commands and is unable to speak. To truly test my theories, I will have to try again, but this time with a healthy corpse."

Even as she marveled at the irony of those last words, she saw his gaze drift toward Victor. Before she could acknowledge a flicker of uneasiness at that look, he went on. "But the real problem with Harry is that he is not actually alive . . . and thus his body cannot repair itself like a living organism can. Indeed, given the damage to his entire structure, he can remain in an animate state for only a few hours at a time. Had he been completely intact at the moment of revival, I would venture to say that he could have continued on indefinitely, never aging beyond his years. As it is, he will not last much longer."

"Do you mean that he can die again?" she whispered, a flicker of hope rising within her. If so, perhaps Talbot would see the futility of playing God and cease his experiments.

If he sensed her question was anything more than academic, however, he gave no sign.

"He *is* dead, my dear," he explained. "As for his state, the best comparison I can make is that he is like a clock that must be rewound at intervals lest it cease running altogether. But since he is made of flesh and not metal, his resiliency is rather less than even that of a poorly crafted pocketwatch. He has, however, quite served his purpose."

The dead women, she thought with a shiver. Talbot had used Sir Harry as a general uses a soldier, sending him out with instructions to kill.

"But why did you have him murder all those poor women?" she demanded, unable to reconcile those brutal killings with the late Sir Harry's blasphemous resurrection. Then, as a more telling question remained, she softly asked, "And—And why . . . me?"

"You were in the wrong place at the wrong time. I never meant for you to be hurt," he replied, and she could hear genuine regret in his tone. "Had you remained here that night, as I had instructed, you would have been safe.

"As it was, the moment I realized you were gone, I set out to find you. Unfortunately Lord Blackstock stumbled across you first, though I will concede that his interference *did* likely save your life. As for the other women, they were chosen at random from the streets . . . except for the last one."

The stark glitter returned to his gray eyes. "I fear that your earl had become a bit of a nuisance. The only way I could think to make certain you never saw him again—and to absolve myself of any possible suspicion as well—was to have *him* convicted of the murders. And so I followed him to the Golden Wolf that night. It was a simple matter to cosh him over the head and rob him of his pocketwatch."

He paused and gave her a chill smile. "For once I did not bother with Harry but took care of matters myself. I lured the woman I'd seen with Blackstock out into the street and wrapped my hands about her throat. I must admit, it was an interesting experiment, taking a life rather than saving one. Afterward I did with her as I did with the others that Harry brought me . . . save that when I was finished, I left your earl's watch with her in that alley."

She shuddered at his words, even as a memory assailed her. That explained, then, why the Barkshire Demon had struck on a clear night. Talbot would not have needed the cover of fog to wander the streets.

"But you still have not said why you murdered them, nor why you cut out their hearts!"

"My foolish sister, that was the entire purpose of my experiments. I had to know just how long I could keep a living heart beating outside its body, and if I could make it beat again inside a new body. The cauldron would be the instrument of rebirth, but mere revival would not be enough."

Restlessly he began pacing the stone floor, then halted and faced her once more. "Don't you understand? Cordelia's heart is defective, and no nostrum or powder can repair it. And it will continue defective even should I manage to revive her after death. The only solution is to first substitute a healthy organ for her damaged one and then attempt a rebirth."

A healthy organ.

The murders had not been random killings for their own sake but—as he earlier had termed them—necessary human sacrifices in pursuit of a cure for Cordelia. Doubtless he had conducted his experiments on the same table as where she now lay, and the rust-colored stains on the floor beneath her were those women's blood.

The very notion made her own blood run like icewater in her veins, but she managed to keep her tone even. "This . . . substitution, when will you make it?"

"It must be soon. Already she is at the point of death, so that I have arranged for her to be brought here. She should arrive this very night, and then I will make my final plans."

So saying, he managed a faint smile. "Never fear, I do not mean to use you as my dear Cordelia's donor. Indeed I dare say she would never forgive me should you suffer in my pursuit of her cure. Still, I cannot risk the possibility that everything for which I have worked might fall victim to your tender conscience. That is why I must leave you and Blackstock alone here for a time, with Harry to watch over you."

"Dear Lord, no! You cannot leave me with that—that thing!"

She raised up on her elbows and shot her brother a beseeching look that held more than a modicum of fear. Talbot, however, merely gave his head a gentle shake.

"Harry will not—cannot—act on his own. All I will do is order him not to let you or your earl try to escape the chamber. If you behave, you will be quite safe in his company, and I shall return in an hour's time."

Ignoring her flood of protests, he spoke a few words in the creature's ear. Then, with a final nod, he started up the stone steps to the wooden door high above. A moment later, the door shut behind him. The distinctive click that she realized must be some sort of outer locking mechanism followed.

The resulting silence was almost overwhelming. It was as if she had fallen into some supernatural space that was neither dusk nor dawn, day nor night, so that time seemed to stand still. All she could hear now was the soft, ragged rhythm of Victor's breathing that seemed to match hers. As for Sir Harry, she could not hear whether or not his dead lungs functioned.

Morbidly curious, she shifted her position for a glimpse of him to determine that answer. The dozen lamps had begun to flicker, as if no one had refilled them in some time, and in that diminishing glow he appeared made of scabrous stone. As for the slight rise and fall of his chest that she thought she detected, that might well be but a trick of the light. But the blind rage in his dead black eyes was no illusion, so that she averted her own gaze lest a single look somehow rouse him to action.

Sternness of mind, she faintly thought, though that maxim seemed but a feeble weapon in light of her current plight. Instead she focused her attention on Victor. The way they now were situated, he lay facing the opposite direction from her, so that she could study his still features.

An almost painful shaft of tenderness tore through her as she recalled the way he had tried to defend her from the armed Resurrection man. Though his feeling for her might not have the depths of her, she had to believe that he cared for her just a little. True she had no illusions that he would actually marry her. For now the simple fact that he had put her life before his was enough.

Then concern supplanted her momentary lapse into sentimentality. Though his color was better, he appeared far paler than was healthy. She noted, too, the occasional chill that wracked him since Talbot had not bothered to cover him with any sort of blanket. As for his earlier stillness, it seemed to have given way to a more natural sleep; still, she'd feel more relieved in mind when he finally awoke.

Whether by design or not, their tables were positioned close enough together that, were her arm free, she could reach over and touch him. Indeed her fingers fairly itched with the need to run her hand along his chest, to brush aside the thick lock of black hair that had fallen across his brow. Yet she dared not even whisper his name for fear that the words might somehow trigger the foul creature imprisoned with them to rise and murder them both.

Her imagination promptly took flight as she contemplated the rituals that might have been performed there long before Talbot had first started his own string of blood sacrifices.

Corruption seemed to ooze from the stone walls themselves, so that she sensed with certainty that—Bran the Blessed or not—no benevolent god was ever worshipped here.

Neither, she guessed, was the spring an instrument of healing, but rather a tool for perpetuating evil. She could well believe that it was this long-forgotten place that turned her brother from a staunch preserver of life to conscience-less purveyor of death.

But even as such thoughts flitted through her mind, the late hour and the silence of the antechamber began to work upon her. It might have been minutes or hours later, when she roused from a state of half-dozing to hear someone softly calling her name.

For an instant, she feared she might be dreaming. Then she realized that the familiar voice was indeed the one which she longed to hear.

"Victor," she cried, choking back a sob of relief as she glanced toward him. Though he looked haggard in the dwindling lamplight, she could see that he was alive—and fighting mad.

"What in the bloody hell is going on here?" he asked in an undertone, raising up a few inches to struggle with his own bonds. "And where in the hell is *here,* anyway?"

"We're in an antechamber below the converted chapel where my brother lives," she told him. "The Resurrection men shot you and then brought us here. Talbot patched you up again."

"Christ, I remember."

He sank back upon the table, looking shaken. "I was fighting with the one grave robber, when his partner shot me. My last thought before I passed out was that I'd never forgive myself for dragging you along with me."

"But I wanted to come along," she reminded him. "Besides which, we're both still alive."

"But for how long?" he muttered. "Where *is* your brother,

anyway . . . and what in the bloody hell are the pair of us doing strapped to tables?"

She managed a tremulous smile though, in truth, she felt more like crying at that moment. "I'm afraid what I'm about to tell you is slightly unbelievable, but every word of it is true."

In a swift undertone, she recounted what had happened once the Resurrection men had carried them off in their cart, explaining how Talbot had forced the men to give up her and Victor, despite the villains' plans to kill them both. She went on to tell him about Talbot's so-called cauldron of re-birth and his experiments—including the fact he had deliberately killed Victor's former mistress to make it appear that Victor was the Barkshire Demon.

Victor interrupted her only once, and that to cast a quick, disbelieving look in Sir Harry's direction. The sight apparently left him quite as shaken as it had she. With a muttered *bloody hell, it* is *he!* he let her continue on.

Having explained how Talbot had left them alone with the creature, she paused. "But this last, Victor, I'm not quite certain how best to tell you."

For, indeed, how did a person put her deepest fears into words? *I'm afraid I shall die without having one last chance to kiss you good-bye? I fear that you shall be murdered before I can ever tell you that I love you?*

Helplessly she shook her head . . . and then opted for the most blunt truth of all.

"Talbot swore he would not harm me, but I am not so certain about you. You see, his experiment with Sir Harry was not as successful as he would have liked. I—I believe he wishes to try again but this time with you."

Twenty-five

"Not bloody likely."

Victor shook his head to clear the remaining fuzziness. It had been bad enough when people had been coshing him over the head, but being shot by some rabble was the final indignity. He could only be thankful that the rogue obviously was as poor a shot as he was a businessman.

He ran an experimental hand along his left side, then sucked in a pained breath. His flesh burned as if someone had dragged a red-hot poker along it. At the same time, a dulling weakness seemed to have seeped into his very bones, leaving him no stronger than a babe. Still, he'd be damned if he would lie back and die, leaving Amaryllis to her brother's questionable mercies.

And he bloody well wasn't going to let Meeks resurrect him as some sort of undead fiend to do his bidding!

With a muffled oath, he lunged sideways, straining against the leather straps. As he'd hoped, the motion scooted his wheeled table a fraction closer to hers, even as the effort left him shaking. A second attempt gained him another inch.

Realizing what he was about, Amaryllis swiftly followed his lead, by increments moving her own table closer. Then he changed tactics, hiking himself forward. A few moments later, both tables lay edge to edge, so that he could grip her hand.

Her fingers promptly linked through his, warm and comforting against his own chilled flesh. Victor managed a triumphant grin and tried to ignore the fact that even that small effort of maneuvering about had caused sweat to bead his forehead.

"All right then," he murmured. "Stay where you are, and I'll try to unbuckle your wrist."

"Wait," she cried, ignoring his feeble attempt at humor as she shot him an anxious look from beneath a tangle of red curls. "What about Sir Harry? What if he realizes what we're about?"

Victor flicked a distasteful glance in the direction of his former friend. "Harry never was the brightest of fellows, even when alive. You said that your brother claims he can only understand the simplest of commands, that he cannot act on his own, did you not?"

At her nod, he shrugged. "Then we'll simply take the chance that he'll interpret his instructions literally, and that he won't bother us unless we try to make it up that staircase."

So saying, he began fumbling with the heavy buckle that held her wrist strap in place. Though it should have been a simple enough task, bound as he was it proved difficult in the extreme. Still, a moment later, he had freed her hand.

When she gave a soft cry of relief and would have sat up, he caught her wrist. "Don't make any sudden moves," he cautioned. "Just slide your hand over and unfasten your other buckle."

She nodded her compliance, and a moment later turned back to him. "Both my hands are free," she murmured. "Now, what should I do?"

He glanced in Harry's direction again. So far as he could tell, the man—creature?—had not moved these past minutes.

"We'll have to risk it," he determined. "Sit up—very casually, mind you—and unfasten your ankles. Then, if Harry doesn't seem to notice anything amiss, you can free me. Agreed?"

She nodded again and raised up, slanting a look in Harry's

direction. When her action did not rouse him, she made quick work of both straps, then lay down again. "Shall I try freeing you now?" she asked in a soft, anxious tone.

"I think it's safe enough," he wryly replied. "I rather suspect we could dance a jig and not disturb him, so long as we stayed clear of the door."

This time she managed the slightest of smiles at his attempt to cheer her. Rolling onto her side, she unfastened his nearest wrist. Abruptly he reached out to cup the back of her head in his hand, tangling his fingers in her wayward red curls as he pulled her to him and kissed her.

She gave a soft moan and kissed him back, so that a shudder of pure need wracked him despite his injured state. The taste of her lips was like a potent draught, renewing his strength and his hopes. And at that moment, he realized that he could not bear to lose her . . . and that he would not, if it were in his power to keep her safe.

Reluctantly he broke their embrace, fearing if he didn't he would give way to his need and drag her atop him, then do his best to make love to her. Instead he gave her a weary grin.

"We might have quite an interesting time of it, with my being tied down and all," he told her, enjoying the blush that rose on her pale cheeks. "But under the circumstances, I think we'd best make haste."

So saying, he unfastened his other wrist; then, wincing at the pain, he sat up and unstrapped his ankles. The effort left his head spinning, so that he shut his eyes to regain his equilibrium. More difficult was ignoring the truth of his current physical condition.

He knew full well the kind of violence Harry had been capable of committing in life, and he rather suspected the man's savage tendencies would not have abated with his death. In his own current state, he'd be no match for his former friend should it come to a struggle.

And something told him that it would.

"Victor, are you all right?" he heard Amaryllis ask, concern evident in her tone. He opened his eyes again and glanced her way, then nodded.

"Just a moment of dizziness," he coolly lied. "Now I think we'd best determine how we're going to get out of here. Where does that door lead to anyhow?"

"It's a secret panel inside one of the confessionals in the chapel above us. When Talbot left through it, I heard something latch after him, so he may be able to lock the door from the outside as well as in."

"So even if we make it to the top ahead of Harry, we might not be able to get out."

Frowning, he glanced around the circular antechamber. Though no expert at Roman architecture, from his boyhood schooling he had a layman's casual knowledge of the subject. Chances were this place had once been used for some sort of pagan worship . . . likely forbidden, given the catacomblike secrecy of its construction. If so, he could not believe its builders would have equipped such a chamber with but a single entry that could be blocked off, leaving those within trapped.

"Did you have a chance to explore the place when your brother first brought you down here? Have you seen anything that might look like another way out . . . a tunnel, perhaps?" he softly demanded of her.

She shook her head. "I had no idea this chamber even existed until tonight," she replied in the same low, urgent tones. "I was the one who lit the lamps, so I walked the room's entire circumference, but everything seemed of a piece to me. The stairs and the rows of benches all seemed cut from the same rock as the walls themselves."

"What about the cauldron? Did your brother give you any clue as to the source of that spring?"

She shook her head again, then stared at him, green eyes wide with alarm. "You can't mean for us to swim down it and look for a way out? Even if it were possible, Talbot says there's something in the water—acid or some such—that makes it deadly to anything living."

"I suppose not. Unfortunately, I'm rather short of any other brilliant ideas at the moment—"

He broke off at the distinctive sound of the door above them unlatching. "Lie down," he hissed, matching his own deed to words. "I'll think of something."

Though what sort of plan he might come up with was open to debate, he grimly told himself even as his weary flesh welcomed this momentary respite. Now he could glimpse Meeks's shadowed figure at the head of the stairs. The only advantage he would have over the man would be surprise . . . or would it?

His gaze strayed to the table on the other side of his, and he allowed himself a humorless smile. Among the various vials and bottles arranged on its surface, he'd spotted several surgical knives gleaming in the lamplight. Though not a weapon of choice—he'd much prefer a sword or a pistol— one of the larger scalpels might do in a pinch.

The sound of a man's harsh sob abruptly drew his attention upward again. Now he could see Meeks descending the stone steps. But what in the bloody hell was he doing carrying a woman in his arms . . . unless perhaps she was another victim of the Barkshire Demon?

"Dear God, it's Cordelia," he heard Amaryllis's horrified whisper beside him. "But something must be wrong."

Cordelia.

That was the name of Meeks's ill wife, the young woman in whose name all those other women had been slain. Warily he watched as the physician continued down the stairs with his frail burden. At this distance, he could see little of her face, but her emaciated limbs that dangled from the folds of her frilly white dressing gown were as pale as that cloth.

The sole hint of color about her was a thick plait of blond hair. Its very weight seemed too much for her swanlike neck to support as her head lolled against Meeks's shoulder. At the sight, Victor frowned. Something about her very limpness struck him as wrong, so had he to guess, he would not have said the woman was gravely ill.

He would have said she was dead.

Another harsh sob tore from the other man's throat, all but confirming Victor's guess. Beside him, he heard a stifled moan of distress from Amaryllis, though she did not stir from the table. He reached out a cautious hand to squeeze hers. Doubtless the two women had been friends, so that she would not be unaffected by Cordelia's passing.

By now Meeks had reached the antechamber floor. Victor watched as, seeming to forget his and Amaryllis's presence, the man made his way to the inner stone bench and laid the dead woman's body atop it. Then, with another ragged sob, he sank to his knees on the stone floor beside her.

The sight of her brother's anguish was more than Amaryllis could bear. "I must go to him," she helplessly murmured as she turned to meet Victor's sympathetic gaze. Not waiting for his response, she slid from the table and hurried toward him.

Talbot did not turn at the swift brush of her slippers as she crossed the stone floor. Even when she knelt beside him, he appeared oblivious to her presence. Then, his gaze still fixed upon his wife, he spoke.

"She's . . . gone."

The two simple words held a note of angry bewilderment that tore at her heart. Choking back a sob of her own, she let her gaze rest upon her sister-in-law.

In death Cordelia's face had assumed a doll-like waxiness that smoothed the ravages of her long illness from her delicate features. She had the look of peace about her that Amaryllis had seen upon many dead faces, and despite her own pain she gave a silent prayer of thanks that Cordelia was now free of hers.

But even as she reached out to place a comforting hand on Talbot's shoulder, he abruptly seized her.

"It's not too late even now," he harshly told her, scrambling to his feet and dragging her up after him. "She died but a few minutes ago, just after I tucked her into her bed. Her flesh is still warm, the blood not yet settled in her veins. All I need is a new heart for her, and I can revive her yet!"

"Talbot, what are you saying?" she choked out in horror, trying to twist free of his grasp. "Cordelia is at peace now. You must let her be . . let her go!"

"I cannot!"

His gray eyes glinting with fevered urgency, he smiled down at her. "Just think, my dear sister, I can have you both. It will be Cordelia's body, but alive with your heart. I promise you, you won't feel any pain when I cut into you. None of the others did. You'll die quickly, peacefully . . . and Cordelia shall live. Now, do not deny me this!"

"Talbot, no—"

Her frantic cry of horror was cut off as her brother's fingers closed about her throat. This time, however, she fought back, clawing at his hands in a frenzied attempt to save herself.

Her strength was no match for his, however. It was as if a burning band of steel somehow had wrapped about her neck and was tightening with her every frantic breath. An explosion of red light burst before her eyes as she flailed at his arms one last time. Red turned to black, and she felt herself sinking . . .

Abruptly the cruel band about her throat loosened. She dropped to her knees, unable to do more than gasp for breath. Then the sounds of a struggle drifted to her, and she dragged her gaze upward.

Before her, Victor and Talbot struggled in a deadly embrace, both men's hands locked around the other's throat. They appeared matched for the space of a heartbeat. Then Victor broke her brother's grip and sent him flying against one of the tables.

The impact sent once-sterile surgical instruments clattering against the stone floor in a symphony of disarray. Vials and bottles crashed to the ground, so that the foul stench of sulfur and the deadly hiss of acid filled the air around them. The heavy table itself remained standing, however, and Talbot pulled himself upright against its edge.

Victor was on him again before Talbot gained his balance. While Amaryllis watched in horror, the pair exchanged vicious blows. Though Victor had the advantage in size, she knew that his wound had weakened him more than he had let on. As for Talbot, madness and grief had given him more than his usual strength. He returned Victor's punches, blow for blow, despite the blood that now spilled from his torn mouth.

"Stop it!" she choked out, unable to bear the sight of the two men she loved best trying to kill each other. But even if they had heard her ragged protest, neither man yielded . . . that was, until another well-placed blow sent Talbot sprawling a second time.

Victor, gasping and clutching his wounded side, halted before him. "It's over," he decreed. "I'm taking your sister out of here, and we're bringing back the magistrate to sort things through. So I suggest that you make yourself comfortable while we—"

"You're not going anywhere . . . not while I'm still alive."

With that ragged pronouncement, Talbot dragged himself to his knees and gave Victor a twisted parody of a smile. "I still hold the advantage here, or had you forgotten?"

Then, sinking back onto his heels, he harshly cried, "Kill him, Harry. Kill Blackstock!"

A guttural sound from the far side of the antechamber drew all their attention. Sir Harry Shaw lumbered up from where he'd hunkered like an automaton since right after Talbot had revived him. His beefy, naked form gleamed in the yellow lamplight, while his black eyes glowed with a hellish sort of enjoyment. The sharp sweet stench of decay that clung to him grew more pronounced with his every move as, with lurching steps, he started toward Victor.

The sound of his bare feet dragging against the stone reminded Amaryllis of that night in the fog, when she had listened in horror as some unseen man stalked her. Now, however, her terror was for Victor. Already he was weakened by the bullet wound and his struggle with Talbot. How could he hope to defeat an undead creature with the strength of two men?

Clutching the burning wound in his side and struggling to remain upright, Victor could only watch in disbelief as the scabrous corpse of his former friend staggered toward him. True, he'd seen the man sitting on the bench like some macabre figure from the waxworks and conceded that something unnatural was afoot. It was only now, however, that he actually believed Harry Shaw had come back from the dead.

Snatching up a fallen scalpel from the cold stone floor, he dodged to one side just before the creature swung a hammerlike fist toward him. Had it connected, the impact doubtless would have knocked him senseless. As it was, his head was already spinning as he raised up again and slashed the scalpel across Harry's bare chest.

It was like slicing through a thick pudding. The torn flesh gaped, but no blood poured from it. Neither did the wound seem to cause Harry any pain, for he did not halt but merely lunged again at him.

This time Victor's reflexes were slower. The beefy fist glanced off his temple, so that he dropped the scalpel and stumbled backward into one of the tables.

Fire tore through his wounded side, and he clenched his teeth against the reflexive cry of pain that threatened to escape him. His vision cleared in time for him to see Harry coming after him again. The creature's movements were slower this time, as if every step took more of an effort than before. Still, with the table at his back, Victor had no means of escape.

Instinctively he dropped to the stone floor. Heedless of broken glass and spilled chemicals, he proceeded to roll beneath the table and out the other side. When he managed to stagger to his feet again, the table formed a solid barrier between him and his attacker.

"The acid!" he heard Amaryllis's choked cry. "Throw it at him!"

He glanced down at the table to see that a few full vials of liquid remained intact upon it. Not stopping to guess which might be the potion in question, he grabbed up an entire rack of various colored liquids and flung the lot in Harry's face.

The dozen different chemicals splashed together and promptly erupted in a foul-smelling chain reaction of tiny explosions that had Victor diving to one side and shielding his own face against the burning spatter. Choking against the fumes, he raised up to see that Harry's face and much of his upper chest now hung in blackened tatters.

The sight sent a rush of primitive triumph through him . . . until he realized that Harry was still moving.

Bloody hell, the grim thought flitted through his mind, *what does it take to kill a dead man?*

He snatched up one of the wooden stools that had tumbled to the ground and, half-staggering around the table, swung the sturdy chair like a club. It connected with Harry's naked back with a dull thud that reverberated through the chamber. For a moment, he merely stood there; then, like a felled oak, he came crashing to the stone floor.

Victor waited for the space of several heartbeats before he slowly lowered the stool and, clutching his side, took a step forward. Harry had not moved, nor did he even when Victor cautiously nudged him with a booted foot. The eyes in that ravaged face stared sightlessly back at him, the unearthly fury that had burned there snuffed like a candle abruptly blown out.

For a second time in but a few months, Sir Harry Shaw was dead . . . though whether or not the man's soul was finally at peace, Victor dared not venture a guess.

He raised his weary gaze from Harry's ravaged corpse to find Amaryllis's frantic gaze upon him. Though he could feel his face swelling from a dozen new bruises, he managed a slow smile and started toward her.

It was as if she had become one with the stone floor. Unable to believe it finally was over, Amaryllis merely stood unmoving as Victor looked up from Sir Harry's ravaged corpse to meet her gaze. Then he smiled . . . a ragged, sexy smile filled with triumph and promise that wrenched at her heart even as he started toward her.

With a soft cry, she broke free of the spell that held her and rushed to meet him. His arms wrapped around her in a fiercely protective gesture. Heedless of the dirt, blood, and sweat that streaked his bare chest like some primitive warpaint, she clung to him. But the sob that lodged in her throat was one of pure happiness as she raised her lips to his.

Theirs was but a brief kiss, however. He brushed his mouth to hers and then gently released her. Then, arm still wrapped about her waist, he turned to face Talbot.

Her brother had long since risen from where he had fallen. Now he sat on the stone bench beside the dead Cordelia, her limp hand clutched in his as he dully stared into the distance.

A wave of tender pity swept her as she watched her brother. No matter what he had done—no matter that she had almost died at his hands—she could not find it in her heart to hate him. For he had sacrificed his ethics, his physician's sacred oath, his very humanity . . . all that in the vain hope of saving his dying wife.

And in the end, he had lost everything.

It was Victor who broke the silence. "Very well, Meeks,"

she heard his weary voice, "let's try this once again. I'm taking Amaryllis out of here, and, this time you're bloody well not going to stop me."

"I won't stop you," Talbot agreed in the rusty tones of a defeated man. "All I ask is that you first vow your intentions toward my sister are noble . . . and that you will do everything in your power to keep her happy."

"I do vow it, and I will make her happy."

The simple words were directed, not at Talbot, but at her. She raised her gaze to meet his, joyful pride filling her like a rose bursting into bloom as she linked her fingers with the hand he'd placed on her waist.

If Talbot was equally touched by that declaration, he gave no sign. Instead he turned his bleak gaze upon them and nodded. "Then go with my blessing . . . and do lock the door after you, will you not?"

Victor squeezed her hand. "I think we should hurry, before he changes his mind," he murmured and urged her forward.

She took but a few steps, however, before she halted. "How can I just leave him here? We must do something for him."

"This is what your brother wants," Victor said with a stern shake of his head, though she glimpsed a flash of momentary pity in his eyes to match her own. "We'll leave him here to finish off matters in his own way."

Obediently she let him lead her to the steps, even as her heart cried a protest at abandoning her own flesh and blood this way. But what *was* left for him after all? He would stand trial for the murders and be executed. Perhaps it was best if he sought his own punishment.

Then her thoughts were only for Victor as she lent him her shoulder for support. But barely had they mounted the first step, when the paneled door high above them creaked open, and a shadowed figure appeared upon the narrow landing.

Twenty-six

"An interestin' setup ye 'ave 'ere," observed an unfamiliar voice. Then the speaker started down the steps, and Amaryllis gasped as she recognized the red-haired Bow Street runner who had called at Victor's door the afternoon before.

"Mister Chapel," came the latter's dry greeting as the man joined them below.

Casually Victor straightened so that he no longer leaned upon her shoulder. From the sweat that beaded his brow and the chills that almost imperceptively shook him, however, Amaryllis knew how much the effort cost him. Still, his tone was even as he went on. "I must confess you are the last person I expected to see here tonight."

"Then ye underestimated me, yer lordship," the runner returned in the same matter-of-fact tones.

His pale gaze flicked over Victor's battered state and the fresh pistol wound that gouged his side. All he said, however, was, "Surely ye didn't think I'd be taken in by yer little game o' dressin' up yer valet to look like ye. I sent the other two lads off to yer country estate for a peek, just in case, but I 'ad a feelin' ye'd be somewhere about the city."

Then he addressed Amaryllis. "Good evenin' to ye, Miss Meeks," he added with a respectful nod.

As with Victor, his keen gaze seemed to take in every detail of her appearance, from the fresh bruises she knew must show on her throat to the grave dirt that stained her clothes. Then he squinted past them to where Talbot sat beside the dead Cordelia, with Sir Harry's corpse sprawled some distance away.

The runner's pockmarked features hardened. He crossed the chamber to check both bodies for any sign of life before returning to confront Victor. "It looks like ye've had an interestin' night, milord. Perhaps ye'd care to give me an account o' it?"

"As you wish," Victor answered with a humorless smile, wincing as he settled on the lower step and leaned against the cold stone wall. "I hope you don't mind if I take a seat. This might take me a while to tell . . . though I rather suspect you won't believe me this time, either."

"I'll listen, milord, right eno'. That's all I'll promise ye fer now."

At that slim assurance, Victor grimly launched into his story. To Amaryllis's relief, he avoided any reference to their tumultuous private relationship, explaining only that he had hired her to illustrate his book on rose cultivation. Chapel listened, as promised, his keen gaze never wavering. Only when Victor fell silent did he finally speak.

"Ye must admit, milord, 'tis a fantastic eno' story. Yer only savin' grace is that I've been keepin' an eye on Miss Meeks's brother for a bit now, so I can corroborate some o' wot ye say."

He paused and shook his head. "Seems a fellow by the name o' McArdle 'ad an ax to grind wit' the doctor an' was watchin' 'im, 'isself. 'E reported 'ow as the gentleman was doin' business wit' the Resurrection men. That, an' 'e saw the doctor makin' off wit' a woman one foggy night, just before we found another o' the Demon's victims."

Victor's dark eyes narrowed. "Do you mean to say that you had another suspect at the same time you were accusing me of being the Barkshire Demon?"

"Ye were a likely eno' suspect yerself, milord," the runner replied. "But that's not why I'm 'ere."

The runner recounted how he had been the one who had

followed their hired hack from the town house, keeping on their heels even after they had switched vehicles the first time. "But ye gave me the slip that second time, milord," he conceded with a nod of admiration.

After following the now-empty hack for the better part of an hour, only to learn he had been duped, Chapel had tried a different tack. He made his way halfway back across the city to St. Pancras Church, planning to question Ezra Meeks regarding the recent activities of his son and daughter.

"But 'twasn't much to be got from 'im."

For it had been well after midnight, and Ezra had long since imbibed his ration of gin. What he did get from the man was the admission he had heard a pistol shot from the direction of the churchyard an hour earlier.

Wondering if that had some connection to the Resurrection men who supposedly were in Talbot's pay, Chapel had then made a search of the darkened cemetery looking for clues. Almost an hour later, he had practically stumbled into Sir Harry's open grave. A quick look about him had revealed signs of a recent struggle, along with a discarded coat—too finely tailored to belong to the average grave robber—lying atop the headstone. A search of that garment's pockets had revealed a dozen calling cards belonging to the Earl of Blackstock.

"So I made my way 'ere. 'Twas no sign of anyone about, but I 'ad a feelin' something were amiss. It took me a bit, but I managed to get inside the place an' search it from top to bottom. 'Tweren't much of use to be found . . . until I 'eard somethin' in the chapel an' I found the 'idden door."

He broke off at the sound of Amaryllis's gasp. She had glanced toward her brother to see what effect the runner's words might have on him. To her horror, she saw that he had risen from the stone bench and was making his determined way to the opposite side of the antechamber.

"The cauldron," she choked out as she saw him draw near

it. "He told me that the spring waters it holds are dangerous
to the living. If he climbs inside, he might die."

But her cry came too late. Barely had she spoken the
words than, with a final look at his dead Cordelia, Talbot
flung himself into the stone trough. She heard his single
anguished scream before the waters erupted around him in
a boiling geyser and hid him from sight. A heartbeat later,
the spring subsided back into its trough . . . but of Talbot,
there now was no sign.

"Dear God, no!" came Amaryllis's answering shriek.

Yet even when she would have run to his aid, Victor
leaped to his feet and seized her arm, pulling her to his
chest.

"It's over. There's nothing you can do for him now," he
insisted, holding her as a sob wracked her. His words were
all but drowned out, however, by the rumble that filled the
chamber as the floor beneath them started to shake.

Fear supplanted grief, and Amaryllis clung to Victor lest
she lose her footing. "What is happening?" she cried, meeting his grim gaze with a look of fright.

He shook his head. "I don't know . . . but I bloody well
don't like it."

And then the cauldron itself began to crack. Tainted water
began pouring from its sides from a myriad of tiny fissures,
spilling like blood even as the ground continued to tremble.
Finally, with a thunderous boom, the entire trough shattered.

Blocks of gray stone shot heavenward, while water continued to boil out with the devil's own fury from the gaping
hole that remained. A veritable tide washed over Sir Harry's
body and began tumbling inexorably toward the stairway.

For an instant, Amaryllis merely stood transfixed by the
sight. Then Victor gave her a shake.

"Christ, let's get the bloody hell out of here," he shouted
over the sound of rushing water as he turned toward the
stairs, half-dragging her after him.

She needed no further urging but hurried to follow, the

Bow Street runner close on her heels. Before they were halfway up the staircase, the gleaming waters were lapping at
the bottom step. By the time all three of them reached the
paneled door above, the water had risen to the tops of the
stone benches.

Glancing below her, Amaryllis choked back a cry. Amid
the floating vials and wooden tables, Cordelia's frail body
bobbed upon the water's sparkling surface, her sodden blond
hair streaming about her. Sir Harry's naked corpse also
drifted about, graceful in death as he was not in life.

Yet even as she gazed in horror upon that disturbing
scene, the waters abruptly stilled. Then, with an obscene
sucking sound, the spring began to reverse its flow.

She heard Victor's muffled oath that was echoed by
Chapel. As for herself, she merely clung to Victor's hand
and willed herself to sternness of mind.

For the sight below was indeed the stuff of ancient legend.
Like some invisible sea monster, the spring greedily swallowed back its waters, consuming in the process every trace
of Talbot's equipment. Cordelia's body, and then Sir Harry's,
followed into that gaping maw.

The last to be dragged down were the heavy blocks of
gray stone that had formed the cauldron. With eerie sym-
metry, those rough-hewn bricks tumbled into the broad gash
in the floor and began settling side by side. As the final
trickle of deadly water drained away, the last stone fell neatly
into place, so that no one would ever guess the floor had
been disturbed.

As for the cauldron, the only reminder that it had ever
existed was a broad gap in the outermost stone bench.

It was some moments later when the three of them silently
filed out the wooden door, stepping out from the confessional into the lecture hall. Clutching his side and looking
pale, Victor slumped into the nearest pew and shook his
head.

"Bloody Christ," he muttered, "I wouldn't have believed it if I hadn't seen it with my own eyes."

"Nor I," Amaryllis replied as she settled beside him and brushed away the tears she'd only now noticed had spilled down her cheeks.

Then the sound of the runner clearing his throat drew both their attention. Beneath the lecture hall's dim light, his pockmarked face had taken on a greenish hue. Still, his tone was remarkably unruffled as he said, " 'Ere now, milord, 'twasn't much that 'appened tonight, save that we learned who the Barkshire Demon truly was."

Shrewdly he shook his head. " 'Twas a sad thing, 'ow the good doctor gave way to grief over 'is poor wife an' committed such 'orrid crimes. 'E confessed it all to me, when I came 'ere to his doorstep. 'E said in particular 'ow 'is sister was innocent a victim as any wot he murdered, an' he prayed no scandal would fall on 'er for 'is actions."

"But what about the bodies?" Victor demanded. "How do we explain away their disappearance?"

" 'Tis no mystery, milord," the runner replied. "After 'e confessed, the doctor asked to say good-bye to 'is wife. Bein' 'e was a gentleman, I took 'im at 'is word. 'E got clean away, an' the lady wit' him. All 'e left behind was a note wot told me to search for their bodies in the Thames . . . tho' all manner o' people vanish into the river wit'out a trace. As fer the magistrate, 'e'll fall in wit' my account, never fear."

"It might work, at that," Victor conceded, "and there are sure to be any number of new scandals to satisfy London's craving. But if we do agree to all this, Mister Chapel, I trust you'll also see to it that the scandal sheets print a full retraction concerning my own guilt."

"Indeed, milord, I shall . . . but for now, wot shall we do about wot lies below this place?"

"Board it up," Amaryllis said with a gesture toward the

confessional, "or better yet, build a wall across it so no one will ever guess there's a hidden passageway behind."

Chapel nodded. "I know a couple o' fellows wot could do the job, an' no questions asked."

"Send them out straightaway," Victor told him. "I'll see to the bill."

"Very good, milord. An' now, I'll see about findin' a coach to take the two o' ye 'ome again. 'Tis dawn, ye know."

Amaryllis glanced up in surprise at the circular stained-glass window above them. That mosaic of colored glass *had* begun to brighten with the sun's first rays, softly glowing now against the shadowed ceiling like a jeweled crown. The sight brought a prickle of tears to her eyes. Indeed, in the past few hours, she had almost come to believe that dawn might never arrive again.

She waited until the runner had made his way from the hall, snuggled closer to Victor, and gave a soft sigh. "Home," she breathed, leaning against his bare chest so that she could hear the faint rhythm of his heartbeat. "I vow, I've never heard a better offer than that."

"As so it happens," Victor casually murmured, "I had hoped you would say the very same thing about the offer I was about to make you."

At his words, Amaryllis straightened in his embrace and shifted about so that she could meet his gaze. Her heart, meanwhile, began a wild thrumming in her breast, even as she willed herself to sternness of mind.

"Indeed, my lord," she replied, "I suppose that will depend upon the offer."

A spark of amusement lit his dark gaze as he lifted a wry brow. "What if I offer to make you Lady Blackstock?"

"But that would mean I would be consigned to the Blue Room, would it not?" she asked, wrinkling her nose in mock dismay, even as her heart gave a joyful leap. "I don't think I could spend every night there. Moreover I am not so certain that a modern woman such as myself would make a very successful countess."

Victor slanted her a meaningful look. "Believe me, I had no intention of letting you spend your nights in the Blue Room. And as for your being a modern woman, I suspect the peerage will survive it . . . besides which, I wouldn't allow any other sort of woman to raise my children."

Children.

The notion of bearing Victor's sons and daughters sent a sudden possessive warmth through her. She smiled as she envisioned herself standing before an easel, painting a trio of chubby-cheeked toddlers, crowns of red rosebuds askew in their dark hair. But even as she longed to seize that dream, practicality stood in the way.

"But what about my painting?" she ventured, almost afraid to ask the question. "I fear I could never give it up, not even for a dozen titles."

"Nor would I expect you to do so . . . at least, not before you finish the plates for my book on rose cultivation. And if that text proves popular, I had been toying with the idea of a second volume focusing on the more recent hybrids. Certainly such a project would call for a new set of plates."

"Yes, I am certain that it would. And that, my lord, is your offer?"

"It is."

She fell silent then, content for the moment simply to study the face of the man that she loved. Then, reaching her decision, she softly replied, "After much consideration, my lord, I've determined that going home is still the best offer I have ever heard . . . so long as that particular home happens to be the one I will share with you and our children."

And as Victor drew her into his embrace for the first of a lifetime's worth of passionate kisses, the rising sun spilled through the stained-glass window above and enveloped them in a rose-colored glow.

Epilogue

The following evening, every tabloid and scandal sheet in London had printed the lurid final chapter to the Barkshire Demon murders. The killer had been revealed to be the respected physician, Talbot Meeks, whose influential patients included an earl and the local magistrate.

> *Grief Over His Dying Wife Led Him to Madness!*
> *Unspeakable Experiments Rumored!*
> *Murderous Physician Believed to Have Taken*
>   *Own Life.*

In paragraph after sensational paragraph, the public was treated to the most intimate details of both the killer and his victims' lives. A search promptly was made of the banks along the Thames, but neither Meeks's body nor that of his young wife washed ashore. Calvin Chapel, of Bow Street, was credited with solving the case, though he modestly proclaimed that luck had played a major role in his connecting Meeks to the murders.

No mention was made of undead creatures stalking the London streets. And as for the notorious Earl of Blackstock, his name was conspicuously absent from those accounts . . . save for a mention that he was no longer considered a suspect in the brutal killings.

And a week later, when the naked corpses of a minor baronet and the young wife of an aged earl were found together in the same bed, the reading public promptly forgot about the tragic doctor and his string of victims.

That summer the horticultural world experienced a small stir of its own when Victor Saville, Earl of Blackstock, was discovered to have written a new tome on the history and care of roses. The volume became an immediate success . . . due in no small part, it was alleged, to the glorious illustrations by a young female artist who just happened to be the earl's new bride.

As for the artist's father, he made a bit of coin himself over the affair, selling a handful of Lady Blackstock's old sketches to the *ton* . . . and earning quite enough to keep him in gin for some time.

With his literary success, the unsavory rumors regarding Lord Blackstock faded from the *ton's* fickle memory. That change in the social winds also boded well for his young sister, Lady Monique, who made her belated debut the following Season and was promptly dubbed an Original . . . setting the rage for gray-and-red parrots and rose petal baths.

And the following summer, when the Earl of Blackstock's wife presented him with their first child, a baby girl, the proud parents christened her with the only name possible . . . Rose.

I was Quite Thrilled, dear friend, to hear of your nuptials. I am certain that your Lord Blackstock is quite as wonderful as you claim. I only wish Shelley and I had been there to witness your joy. As you may have heard, he and I have finally managed to wed—so that I, too, have never been happier in my life . . .

As for your letters of last Spring, I have long since burned them all, as you asked. I must confess, however, that your fantastic tale has had an influence upon me. Soon after I read your last account, the four of us— Shelley, Lord Byron, Doctor Polidori, and I—con-

ceived the notion that we should each write a ghost story.

The gentlemen all began scribbling with Great Zeal at their tales but, alas, no idea came to me those first few days. And then, one night, I had a Waking Dream in which I saw a pale student of Unhallowed Arts kneeling before the thing he had put together. It was a Reanimated Corpse, such as that horror that haunted your life those weeks. When I awoke, I knew that I had my ghost story—and thus, I set to work writing.

And now, my dear friend, it is I whom your creature now haunts. Indeed, Shelley has encouraged me to continue working on my tale, which I have boldly titled Frankenstein; or The Modern Prometheus. *Percy tells me this is my finest work yet . . . and I confess I have hopes that my little story might one day be published.*

—letter from Mary Wollstonecraft Shelley,
nee Godwin, to Amaryllis Saville,
Lady Blackstock

SPINE TINGLING ROMANCE
FROM STELLA CAMERON!

PURE DELIGHTS   (0-8217-4798-3, $5.99)

SHEER PLEASURES   (0-8217-5093-3, $5.99)

TRUE BLISS   (0-8217-5369-X, $5.99)

ROMANCE FROM HANNAH HOWELL

MY VALIANT KNIGHT   (0-8217-5186-7, $5.50)

ONLY FOR YOU   (0-8217-4993-5, $4.99)

UNCONQUERED   (0-8217-5417-3, $5.99)

WILD ROSES   (0-8217-5677-X, $5.99)

PASSIONATE ROMANCE
FROM BETINA KRAHN!

HIDDEN FIRES   (0-8217-4953-6, $4.99)

LOVE'S BRAZEN FIRE   (0-8217-5691-5, $5.99)

MIDNIGHT MAGIC   (0-8217-4994-3, $4.99)

PASSION'S RANSOM   (0-8217-5130-1, $5.99)

REBEL PASSION   (0-8217-5526-9, $5.99)